Also by Frank Becker

You Can Triumph Over Terror
   (Emergency Preparedness)

The Depression Proof Church
   (Preparing for Persecution)

The Chronicles of CC
   Book 1, *War's Desolation*
   Book 2, *The Heav'n Rescued Land*
   Book 3, *Freemen Shall Stand*
   Book 4, *Our Cause It Is Just*
   Book 5, *Conquer We Must*

Conquer We Must

Frank Beecher

Dear Carol,

With deep gratitude for your book and for nearly 50 years of friendship with John & you.

Frank

Greenbush Press

Conquer We Must!

Published simultaneously worldwide.

Becker, Frank
Series: "The Chronicles of CC"

Book Five
Conquer We Must / Frank Becker

Paper – ISBN: 0-9766720-6-5; ISBN13: 978-0-9766720-6-7

E-Book – ISBN: 0-9766720-2-2; ISBN13: 978-0-9766720-2-9

Library of Congress PCN, 2015917424

Greenbush Press, Houston, TX

Printed in the United States of America

For Joy, the love of my life

– prayerful, loving, caring, and encouraging –

a true *Proverbs 31* wife.

The Star Spangled Banner
Francis Scott Key, 1814

Oh, say can you see by the dawn's early light
What so proudly we hailed at the twilight's last gleaming?
Whose broad stripes and bright stars thru the perilous fight,
O'er the ramparts we watched were so gallantly streaming?
And the rocket's red glare, the bombs bursting in air,
Gave proof through the night that our flag was still there.
Oh, say does that star-spangled banner yet wave
O'er the land of the free and the home of the brave

On the shore, dimly seen through the mists of the deep,
Where the foe's haughty host in dread silence reposes,
What is that which the breeze, o'er the towering steep,
As it fitfully blows, half conceals, half discloses?
Now it catches the gleam of the morning's first beam,
In full glory reflected now shines in the stream:
'Tis the star-spangled banner! Oh long may it wave
O'er the land of the free and the home of the brave!

And where is that band who so vauntingly swore
That the havoc of war and the battle's confusion,
A home and a country should leave us no more!
Their blood has washed out their foul footsteps' pollution.
No refuge could save the hireling and slave
From the terror of flight, or the gloom of the grave:
And the star-spangled banner in triumph doth wave
O'er the land of the free and the home of the brave!

*Oh! thus be it ever, when **freemen shall stand***
*Between their loved home and the **war's desolation!***
*Blest with victory and peace, may **the heav'n rescued land***
Praise the Power that hath made and preserved us a nation.
*Then, **conquer we must**, when **our cause it is just**,*
And this be our motto: "In God is our trust."
And the star-spangled banner in triumph shall wave
O'er the land of the free and the home of the brave.

Part One:
The First Winter

To the Woodshed

Butter Creek Inn
Butter Creek, Vermont
Christmas Eve

As his captors manhandled him out the front door of the
Butter Creek Inn, CC wondered why they considered him wor-
thy of such special attention.

He knew that the occupying army had declared all unreg-
istered Americans subject to arrest, but he did not understand
why they felt it necessary to seize an unimportant individual
like himself at gunpoint.

Just a few minutes earlier he had been sitting in a dimly-lit
corner of the dining room, sipping a bitter coffee substitute
brewed from ground acorns and minding his own business.
He'd been staring off into space when he suddenly became
conscious of the unusual attention being paid him by the bartender. The man was alternately peering at him, then turning
his attention to a poster on the far wall.

Surprised at his interest, CC turned to examine the few other patrons. He noticed that their clothing was worn and patched, and he suddenly realized that the locals had to be wondering how he had come by his new clothing. Virtually everything of value in America — clothing, food, medical supplies, fuel, flashlight batteries, and firearms — had been seized by the Chinese or the American turncoats who served them. Since this bartender was still allowed to operate this country inn, it was obvious that he had pledged his loyalty to the invaders. So naturally he would wonder how CC had come by his obviously new and high-quality clothes. Following that line of reasoning, it didn't take much imagination for CC to conclude that he had made a serious and perhaps fatal mistake in coming to this little village on Christmas Eve.

It's my own fault, he had realized. *I stupidly imagined that I might find someone here with whom I could share a little pleasant conversation. Instead, everyone appears afraid to open his mouth, and I'm being studied as though I'm a freak of nature...or an enemy of the state.*

CC was sitting too far away to make out the words on the poster, but after the innkeeper stared at him for a long moment, then stepped into a back room, his concern grew. And when the serving girl walked past CC's table and hissed a warning to him to run for his life, he'd been too slow to react. By the time he reached the outside door, the innkeeper was waiting for him, and when CC tried to bluff his way past, the man pulled a revolver. It couldn't have been a minute later that several armed men came through the front door and put an end to his plans to flee.

It was obvious from their behavior that his captors believed they knew his identity, and he devoutly wished that they would share that information with him. He'd very much like to know his name as well. The few flashbacks he'd experienced since awakening in the hospital in Black River Junction nearly a year earlier comprised his entire knowledge of himself and of his history. Being an amnesiac was terribly unnerving, and the infrequent recurrences — those rare moments in which he recalled a little of his past — produced great emotional pain and remained indelibly imprinted on his soul.

As his captors shouldered him through the front door, he was momentarily dazzled by the headlights of a black SUV parked in the deep snow out front.

Once clear of the door, the men took hold of his upper arms and pushed him through a snow drift toward the back of the inn. The vehicle's headlights were reflected off the snow, illuminating the area, and as CC was hustled along the side of the vehicle he noticed a woman's face framed in the open window. Her expression was frozen, a combination of amazement and shocked recognition.

CC wasn't sure whether his heart stopped, or he'd tripped on something that lay beneath the snow, but he suddenly found himself staggering. The shock of seeing a familiar face among these repro- bates took his breath away. He tried to tell himself that his mind was playing tricks on him, that the ghostly apparition that had appeared for an instant in the darkened window was merely a figment of his imagination, a manifestation of his feverish and troubled mind. To make matters worse, he thought for an instant that he'd seen the fa- miliar face of a little boy appear beside her.

And with that *hallucination*, the amnesia that had served as a wall between his present existence and his former life was chipped away just a little bit more, allowing a shade more light. He wondered whether he was close to remembering everything, or in even greater danger of succumbing to the madness that sometimes seemed so near. He was frequently terrified of facing his past, of learning who he might have been, and what he might have done. Up until now, he consciously attempted to bury many of the hints of the past that came to him. Since there was nothing he could do to change the horrors he'd experienced since awakening, a practice of denial seemed more comfortable. Now, however, he was faced with having to deal with what looked like two faces out of the past, faces of the dead.

That couldn't be my wife and son, he thought. *I'd like to be- lieve that they are alive, but I watched with my own eyes as the EMS people slid their charred remains into body bags and loaded them on gurneys before rolling them away from our ruined home.*

Just as quickly, he tried to bury the memory. *It has to be a figment of my imagination,* he thought, *brought on by the trauma of my being arrested.* He was confused and frightened. *What am I thinking? What wife and son? What fire? I have to get a grip!*

In spite of this resolution, he was suddenly lost in what he recognized as a recurring nightmare. He could almost see the smoldering flames and breathe the acrid smoke. His chest tightened and heaved with the horror of it, and tears ran unbidden down his cheeks. It didn't occur to him to wonder why the vision of the three body bags on those gurneys seemed more real to him than the spectral faces he'd just seen in the window of that SUV.

The hands on his arms had tightened, helping him to get his feet under him, and someone was pressing something hard into the small of his back, presumably a gun.

CC was trying to recover his balance, both physically and emotionally, when an angry voice near the SUV captured his attention.

"Hey, kid. Get your head back inside the car," and CC turned just in time to see the top of a child's head disappearing as the tinted window, like an inverted guillotine, swept upward.

One of his guards, oblivious to the cause of CC's stumbling, shouted at him. "Keep moving, bud!" and pushed him through the snowdrift toward a small outbuilding located some distance behind the inn.

When CC hesitated in front of the unlighted building, someone pushed him from behind, and he windmilled through the doorway and across the small room where he slammed into the far wall. The noise of his impact was met with a laugh from his captors. Then the door slammed solidly, and he heard someone fumbling to secure the latch.

He stood there for a moment before he realized that he had lost his gloves. He began rubbing his freezing hands together, and his fingertips found his gold wedding band, causing his mind to race back to the day the war began, the day he awakened on a hospital X-ray table, struggling with pain and confusion.

He remembered becoming angry because no one on the hospital staff came to check on him. Then, through nausea and pain, he had begun his struggle for survival. When he realized that he'd lost his memory, he searched in vain for any clues to his identity. The chart hanging from the X-ray table had identified him as "John Doe." His wallet was missing, and all he could find was a wedding band on a small table. The ring had the initials C.C. and D.R. engraved inside, and he arbitrarily decided to call himself CC.

As he'd wandered around the basement of the hospital, he discovered the cafeteria. The food in the steam table was still fresh and hot, but there was not a soul on the floor. He spooned up a plate of roast chicken and dumplings, poured himself a cup of strong coffee, and sat down at a table to eat. He realized that he was famished, and while he shoveled down the food, he directed his attention to a radio that someone had left playing on a counter nearby. His hand froze halfway between plate and mouth when he heard someone announce that America was under nuclear attack. Then the radio went dead. *That explains the loud rumbling I heard,* he concluded, too traumatized to grasp the implications.

He had stayed in his lead-lined X-Ray room for two weeks while the radiation levels declined. He learned later that the staff, and all the ambulatory patients, had deserted the hospital. When he finally ventured out, he was appalled to discover that virtually everyone had either left the town or had perished from the radiation.

He located a tractor-trailer, and drove from place to place, loading anything and everything that he thought might contribute to his survival. Then he drove into the mountains, and ultimately discovered a cavern where he survived for the next eight months. During that time, he gained no clues as to his identity, but he became the accidental foster parent to a little girl and a teenage boy.

And on Christmas Eve, of all times, his hunger for news and for the fellowship of other adults had driven him out of his cavern to this rundown historic inn in a remote mountain hamlet. He should have realized that the invading army that occupied this part of Vermont would be on alert for strangers roaming about. The fact that his photograph had evidently been posted on the wall of the inn's dining room was a shock to him. He had no idea that his existence might be of interest to anyone, much less that America's invaders would offer a substantial reward for him.

Now, locked in a woodshed and shaking with cold, CC understood that by succumbing to his loneliness he had betrayed the children's trust. They had looked to him as a father, and he had deserted them in spite of their pleadings. Without him they would ultimately perish from hunger or disease, and because he had been arrested in this remote location, it was likely that they would never even learn what happened to him, let alone see him again. *It's ironic* he thought, *that the Lord has allowed me to be taken to a literal woodshed for my sins.*

The Wheeler-Dealer

Butter Creek Inn
Butter Creek, Vermont
Christmas Eve

McCord's lips twisted upward in the rictus of a smile as he watched CC's captors drag him out the front door of the inn.

What a reversal of fortune! he exulted. *I've got people in high places searching for me because I failed to finish him off, and now he turns up here in time to pull my chestnuts out of the fire.*

Just hours earlier, McCord and Elizabeth Ross had slipped out of the dismal little cave they used as a shelter, and hiked down the mountain in light snowfall hoping to find something to eat. They'd made their way to this tavern, and he'd left her in a wagon shed behind the inn while he slipped through an outside door to find himself in a poorly lit kitchen. Something simmering on the stove drew him, and he was dishing stew into a bowl when the innkeeper suddenly appeared, pistol in hand.

McCord's initial impression was of a porcine and slovenly man who would always place his own interests first, and he wondered whether he might turn this to his advantage. The innkeeper's impression of McCord was that he was a good looking but dissipated man of about thirty who was down on his luck, and the shrewd look in his eyes and the strange pout to his lips indicated that he was both untrustworthy and greedy.

The innkeeper broke the silence. "Well, what have we here?" Then he proceeded to answer his own question. "We have a man who needs a shave, who is dirty and ragged, and obviously hungry enough to steal food from honest people."

McCord returned a smile that could only be interpreted as ironic, but failed to reply.

"And since you are stealing from me," the innkeeper pressed on, "it seems obvious that you are not registered with the local authorities and that you are probably an indigent refugee. And that makes you an outlaw!"

"Well, look now," McCord responded, "let's not jump to conclusions. And please be careful with that gun."

"Be careful with the gun, is it? I don't think I'll take your advice on how to handle my gun. Step out here by the bar and let me get a look at you in the lantern light."

He pressed the muzzle of his revolver against McCord's spine and they moved into the barroom. While the innkeeper studied his face, McCord looked around the room, hoping to find some inspiration that might help him talk his way out of his predicament.

Will miracles never cease? he wondered in amazement, as his eyes fell upon a man sitting in the shadows near the fireplace. *It can't be,* he thought, and blinked his eyes.

The innkeeper saw a look of amazement and what might pass for happiness on his prisoner's face. Keeping his gun on McCord, he turned his head to look for the object of his attention. While looking about the room, he didn't notice McCord's studying a wanted poster on the wall.

What incredible luck! he thought. The notice bore the man's picture and posted a substantial reward for his capture.

"You know that man?" the innkeeper whispered, tipping his head toward the dining room.

"Maybe," McCord answered, a sly smile on his lips. "Why don't we step back into the kitchen before he notices me?"

The innkeeper scratched his chin with the muzzle of the gun, pursed his lips, and said, "Sure, why don't we do that?" Once again out of sight, he braced McCord.

"Okay, who is he?"

"Wait a minute," McCord answered. "What's it worth to you to catch a really big fish?"

"For all I know, you're a really big fish."

"Compared to him, I'm a small fry," he lied.

"Yeah. Well, why don't I just keep both of you?"

"Why don't you play it smart? You give me some food, and I'll tell you who he is. You let me go, and you collect the entire reward."

"Why should I let you go?"

"I told you. I'm a small fry. If you keep me, how do you know I won't get half the reward. Maybe all of it."

The innkeeper gave him a foxy look. "Maybe there's a reward for you, too."

"Not today."

"So, why should I let you go?"

"Because catching him will be a feather in your cap. And if I'm here, I'll claim half the reward. And one more thing. If you let me go, I'll return here from time to time with other useful and profitable information."

The innkeeper held out his hand. "Give me your backpack."

McCord slipped the empty nylon pack off his shoulders and handed it to the innkeeper. The man took it and crossed the room in what McCord thought of as a waddle, swinging his weight from hip to hip as he walked to a pantry. He took a dozen cans from a shelf and dropped them into the bag, then placed two loaves of fresh-baked bread on top. Turning to stare at McCord, he held the pack up with one hand, his eyebrows raised.

"Okay," he told McCord. "Tell me about the man."

His eyes followed as McCord pointed through the archway toward a poster on the opposite wall.

"Go out to the bar," McCord told him, and compare the photo of the man on the poster to the man sitting in your dining room."

The innkeeper swore in surprise. "You wouldn't kid me, would you?" he asked. He tossed the backpack to McCord as he headed for the dining room. McCord caught the pack before it dropped to the floor, slipped his arms through the straps and quickly exited the back door.

Within minutes, he and Ross were on the way out of the hamlet and on their way back up the mountain, moving through an increasingly heavy snowfall. Once they were sure that they were free of pursuit, they stopped in a copse of evergreens where they each opened a can, and began wolfing down the contents.

Kim Ling
Headquarters, Chinese People's Liberation Army
Burlington, Vermont
Christmas Eve

The office into which Kim Ling had been ushered was plain in the extreme, except for the desk behind which the Chinese general lounged. It was exquisite. The front and side panels of the massive desk were in bas relief, rich with fine detail. It was a hand-carved masterpiece of intertwined dragons, cherry blossoms, bamboo and fir trees. Even the diamond shaped scales on the backs of the writhing serpents were given dimension and depth by the use of woods of different colors and shades. But Kim's aesthetic reflections were short-lived.

He jumped in surprise when the door was slammed by the officer who had ushered him into the room. He was now alone with the commander in chief of all Chinese special forces in America. For several minutes Kim Ling stood there at something resembling attention, while the general ignored him. The general didn't say a word, but his appearance spoke for him. His face was flushed, his eyes bleary, and his uniform rumpled.

This increased Ling's anxiety because the general was ordinarily a spit and polish officer. As Kim Ling studied the general from beneath hooded brows, everything about the man seemed out of character. And when the general lifted a pistol from the desktop and offhandedly used it to point him to a chair, Kim wondered whether he would live out the next hour.

The general's real name was Ng, but since it was not pronounceable in English, he allowed what he called the American barbarians to call him Eng. The general's subordinates resented Kim Ling because of his rare ability as an American to properly pronounce the general's name in Chinese and they considered his favorable treatment as unwarranted.

Now, however, Ling was justifiably apprehensive, and his mental state wasn't helped by the fact that he had to take shallow breaths to avoid choking on the thick cloud of cigarette smoke that filled the room.

As Kim sat down, the phone rang, but the general ignored it. When it began ringing a second time, he picked it up, cursed at the caller, and told him that he was not to be disturbed. Then he threw the phone down, scattering the jade chess pieces that had been set in neat rows on the board before him. This violent gesture reminded

Kim that he was little more than a pawn in the game the general played.

The Chinese who had invaded the United States distrusted all expatriates, and Kim Ling was a fourth-generation American. Worse, Kim had refused to volunteer to join their cause and was now being forced to serve as a civilian conscript. Although Kim tried to avoid the general as much as possible, it had been difficult because he was one of just two surviving helicopter pilots.

The general sat staring at Kim Ling for a long moment, then abruptly swiveled his chair so that he was facing the side wall. He leaned back, eyes half-closed, cigarette dangling from yellowed finger tips, and stared vacantly up at the ceiling.

Kim remained rigidly still. *I don't want to trigger the wrong response,* he thought. He gritted his teeth. *"Trigger the wrong response? I don't want him to trigger that gun!"*

The general's appearance and demeanor were far out of character, and Kim grew even more concerned because the man was not his usual sarcastic self. He was becoming, in fact, almost affable. This odd change in temperament frightened Ling even more because he'd once overheard several officers who served under the general joking about him.

One had quipped, "When the general treats you nice, it's far too late to hide your rice." After the laughter had subsided, another had warned in an exaggerated whisper, "Eng wants both your hide and your rice."

Kim Ling's musings were interrupted when the general began speaking in a monotone, almost as though he were talking to himself.

Has he forgotten I'm here? It sounds like a soliloquy from "Hamlet."

As the general spoke in a dull voice, he wandered from subject to subject, drifting without any seeming logic from year to year and place to place, as though he was thinking aloud. He went down memory lane, speaking of experiences he'd had, places he'd visited, even women he'd known, and then he turned to his military experiences, actually weeping a little for a friend whom he said he'd tortured and executed.

Kim knew that Eng spoke excellent English and had heard that he had graduated with honors from one of America's Ivy League colleges. Ling had also learned that the general controlled vast industrial holdings in China, and that he was ruthless in his dealings.

The general swiveled around and slammed his chair forward into an upright position, impaling Kim with a glare. "How long have you been here?" he demanded.

"Just a few minutes," Kim replied. "Your adjutant brought me in."

"No. I meant, how long have you been serving us," the general replied, almost absent-mindedly, but it was obvious that he did not expect an answer because he turned back toward the wall, ignoring Kim and resuming his ramblings in a lifeless voice.

A few minutes later, again shocking Kim, the general spun his chair to face him, all signs of inebriation gone.

"Did I mention that we are in grave trouble here? Are you aware of that?"

Kim waited, hoping not to have to answer.

"I said, do you know that?"

Kim decided to follow the old axiom, *When all else fails, tell the truth.*

"I've heard rumors that there were problems, but not that they were serious."

"Well, there are problems, and they are serious," the general snapped. He belched, then picked up an open bottle of beer and took a swallow. He tipped his head at an angle, and stared over his nose at Kim. "Do you want one of these?"

"No, thank you."

Disobedient Foster Children

The Motorhome
Hidden Valley, Vermont
Christmas Eve

Sarah giggled as she picked up one of her checkers and jumped Jonathan's only king.

"What's so funny," he asked, clearly annoyed.

"Oh, nothing," she replied archly.

"Nothing?"

"Well, it seems to me that a boy who is sixteen...."

"I'm almost seventeen, and I'm not a boy. I'm a teenager!"

"Boy, teenager, what's the difference? Anyway, a boy who is almost seventeen should be able to beat a seven-year old at checkers."

"You're nearly eight," he corrected without thinking, and she laughed again. "Besides," he added, "CC said that you are seven going on seventy, so that makes you a lot older than me."

She giggled again. Then her face suddenly grew serious, and she shivered.

"What's the matter? Are you cold? You're not getting sick, are you?"

They were sitting at the dinette table in the motor home that CC had driven into the cavern months before. Jonathan had the portable electric heater. The source of that electric power was a fascinating story in itself. It was generated by an old water wheel in the cavern below their feet. The heater was so efficient that Jonathan had to open a window to cool the place down, and he couldn't understand any reason for Sarah being cold.

She stared unseeingly at him for a moment, then he saw her eyes focus on him.

When she spoke, her voice was almost shaking with fear. "Jonathan?"

"What's the matter?"

"CC needs help!"

"How could you know that?"

"I just know. Sometimes I have these feelings, and I'm always right."

His face grew serious, but he didn't argue with her. On several occasions, CC had remarked that this child seemed to have a special conduit from the Lord, and more than once, her premonitions had saved them much grief.

His pique at losing the checker game gave way to a far more serious tone.

"Okay, Sarah, what now? What do you think is wrong?"

She looked as though she were going to cry.

"I don't know what's wrong. But it's something really bad."

"Sarah...."

"Jonathan, you have to go help him."

"Half-pint?" His words were almost a plea.

"No, Jonathan! You need to go, and you need to go right now."

"But Sarah, CC told me that I'm not to leave you. There's a blizzard out there, and if anything happens to me, and CC doesn't come back, you'll be all alone."

"I was all alone in the cave when the war started, with just my grandma, and she was dying from the bomb's rays."

"Yes, but this is different. CC showed up in time to help you."

She smiled. "Yes, I was down to my last can of soup, and he got there just before my Mimi went to be with Jesus."

"That's right," he countered. "I don't want to scare you, but there might not be another CC to rescue you this time."

"The Lord is my Shepherd, Jonathan, and he will take care of me."

How can you argue with a kid when she says things like that? he wondered. *For that matter, why would you? I can't crush her faith.* He laughed. *On second thought, I'm not sure that anything could crush her faith.*

He stood to his feet, and began striding back and forth in the small living area.

"Suppose I can't find him, Pot Roast?"

"Don't call me Pot Roast! You know I hate it when you call me that." Then she looked up with the adoration she had for this young man whom she'd adopted as her big brother.

"Sorry, Peach Pit."

This time, she ignored him.

"We'll pray, Jonathan, and the Lord will help you."

"Oh, I don't know, Sarah. If I get there, and there is nothing wrong, CC will skin me."

"Oh, he will not!" She smiled her impish grin. "He might say some nasty things, but he wouldn't spank you. Besides," she added, "if he's okay, you can try and sneak back here without him knowing you left."

Then her face took on the gravity of a troubled adult. "Besides, there is something wrong."

And Jonathan somehow knew she was right, but he still balked.

"Sarah, there's a bad storm out there. I'd have to find my way out of this valley, down the mountain, and then into Butter Creek."

"Take the toboggan. Then you can slide all the way down the mountain road and not get tired. It's over a mile. Maybe I'll come along. It will be fun."

"You're not going with me," he declared flatly, and even as he said it, he realized that she hadn't merely defeated him at checkers.

It wasn't lost on her, either, that he'd committed himself to making the journey. He'd gone from speaking about what might happen to what would happen, and had accepted her seemingly groundless arguments.

"How will I see in the dark and snow?"

"Oh, Jonathan, you're just making excuses!"

She's right, he thought, *and to tell the truth, I've been worried about CC since he left.*

But he found that he was still unable to stop arguing, and this surprised him because he generally tended to act impulsively.

"Take the big flashlight."

"Huh?"

"You asked how you'd see in the dark. I said, take the big flashlight."

"Oh, sure." Then he asked, "Suppose someone sees it?"

"Who's going to see it? Who, beside you and CC, are dumb enough to go out in a blizzard on Christmas Eve?"

He laughed. "You've got me there." Then he added, "You know, it will be a miracle if we can get back."

"Well, then, I'll pray for a miracle."

"Thanks a lot."

"Are you scared?"

"No, of course not," he lied.

"Then don't you think you'd better get started?"

A half-hour later, Jonathan was dragging CC's six-foot toboggan across the snow-filled swale that marked the east end of Hidden Valley. He stumbled forward and stopped in what he imagined was the center of Vermont Route 19. As he turned the toboggan so that it pointed down the mountain highway, it started to slide away, and he gripped the steering rope tightly to keep from losing it. When he seated himself on the wooden floor of the toboggan, he kept his feet anchored in the snow alongside.

He'd brought along a backpack that contained a thermos filled with hot coffee, along with a change of clothes for himself and CC. He'd taped the barrel of the flashlight to the straps of the backpack and positioned it at the front of the sled so that the light pointed more-or-less straight ahead down the road. Reaching out to each side, he grasped the ropes that ran along both edges of the toboggan, lifted his feet onto the deck, and began coasting down the mountain road.

I've got to remember that to steer left, I press my right foot forward and lean toward the left, and to steer right, I do the opposite. Suddenly he was aware of the icy wind blowing in his face. *Man-O-man, am I really going as fast as I think I am?*

It was good that the road down the mountain did not twist and turn because, even though the flashlight barely penetrated the blowing snow, the reflected glare nearly blinded him. He'd been confident that he would remain safely on the road because the mountain rose on his left, and the stonewall on his right should protect him from sliding over the cliff. His confidence was shaken when he realized that the snow was so deep that it was drifting over the top of that stone guard wall in places, and he realized that he might find himself flying out over the top of a hundred-foot-high cliff.

He hammered his right foot forward and leaned hard toward the mountainside on his left, almost overturning the toboggan as it turned toward relative safety. Just in time, too, for he had been about to shoot out over the edge of the cliff. Now, however, he found himself careening across the road toward the dark mass of the mountain that rose sheer on his left. Before reaching the rock wall, however, he crossed a narrow berm and crashed into the base of an evergreen.

His backpack, with flashlight attached, flipped over the curved front of the toboggan and wound up buried in a snowbank, while he landed uninjured, head and shoulders buried in a drift. The wind was shrill, the snow blowing, and his surroundings were in pitch darkness.

As he wiped the clotted snow from his freezing cheeks with snow-covered mittens, he found himself addressing God. *It's a little late, Lord, to ask for help, but I sure want to thank you for being there before I called.*

It was then that Jonathan noticed the glow from his flashlight buried under a thin layer of snow, and was able to claw out his pack. Digging the toboggan out of a drift, he checked it for damage, propped his pack back in place, and started back down the road. This time, he periodically dipped his heels into the snow to slow his speed, and finally made it safely to the bottom. As he was maneuvering his way down the mountain highway, his thoughts turned to CC.

I was the third person that he met after he woke up in that hospital on the day the war began. He later told me later that he didn't meet a single living soul the entire time he was in Black River Junction, and he avoided the pillagers he heard firing their weapons and driving trucks around town.

And it was a few weeks later, on his return trip to the hospital, that I met him. I was hungry, and he gave me food. Then I led him to an electrical generator that he could tow with his pickup truck. I wanted him to take me wherever he was going, but he seemed so stern that I was afraid to ask, so when he went back into the hospital to look for more stuff, I just hid under the canvas that he used to cover the pickup bed. That old truck was pretty near breathing its last. CC had to stop several times to add water to the radiator, and once to change a tire.

One thing I'll never forget, and I think it is the thing that convinced CC to let me stay with him. He was taking a shortcut along an old dirt road in the mountains when we were strafed by a small plane. CC slid to the side of the road, parked under the trees, got down behind some rocks, and emptied his pistol at the plane. He still wouldn't have known I was in his truck if I hadn't cut my way out from under the canvas. Then, when those guys were trying to land their plane to finish him off, God helped me shoot down their plane with my .22 rifle. CC might have had mixed feelings about my showing up in the midst of a crisis, but he wasn't about to abandon me, so he made me climb in the truck before heading out.

That old wreck wheezed and rattled while we got off that dirt road and back onto the main highway. He drove maybe another mile or so. Then he made me cover my eyes with a knit cap so that I couldn't see where we were going. I think he coasted down the mountain highway a little further, then turned onto some very rough ground.

When I finally got to take off that mask, I was looking out across a pretty little lake in the most beautiful valley anyone could imagine. And that's when CC told me that I could stay with him. He didn't care that I was just a kid, or came from a Jewish family, or anything. He just cared about me. I have no doubt that he saved my life.

And that's when I met Sarah. CC had discovered her a while earlier in a cavern at the far end of the valley. She was actually the first person he had met after leaving the hospital. She led him to her dying grandmother. CC thought that Sarah's grandmother recognized him, and seemed to consider him to be someone special, but she passed away before telling him who she thought he was. So there was Sarah, then her grandmother, and I was number three. Funny thing is, CC always makes me feel like number one.

His mind raced over the memories, and he marveled that it had taken him so long to follow Sarah's suggestion and come looking for CC.

And now, maybe he's met number four and five. And suddenly Jonathan understood CC's need to get out and meet some adults. In all the months that had passed, the only people CC had talked to had been a little girl and a teenage boy.

No wonder he felt he had to get away. But where would he have gone? Then it came to him. *There aren't many places where a stranger could go on Christmas Eve. He'd have to have something to eat, so the thing for me to do is look for a place where they serve food!*

When Jonathan realized that he had almost reached the bottom of the mountain, he let the toboggan run free, hoping it would carry him up the hill ahead. When it finally came to a standstill, he climbed off and dragged it into the woods and leaned it against a tree.

When he reached the edge of the village, Jonathan was careful to avoid houses where the light from unshaded windows reflected off the snow. He made his way to the hamlet's only inn and began looking through windows, trying to spot CC. By now he was shaking with cold, so he made his way around to the back of the building. Cracking a door, he peaked in and discovered that he had happened on the kitchen. It was poorly lit by a gas lantern that shined through an archway from an adjacent room.

Jonathan slipped quietly in and immediately moved to the big wood-burning cooking range to get warm. After the bitter cold, the heat seemed almost suffocating. Then he noticed a pot on the stove, and whatever was in it smelled wonderful. He found a large ladle laying on the stove next to it, dipped it in, and began gingerly tasting its contents. It was venison stew.

Oh, Lord, that tastes good, he thought. *Thank you!* He wondered what people would think about his eating directly from the pot, then realized that no one would ever know, and he didn't care anyway.

He heard voices just outside the kitchen, and sidled over by the open door to try to eavesdrop. Peeking around the edge of a serving window, he saw a pretty young woman, probably in her early twenties, in serious discussion with two men. As he listened, he realized that they were talking about someone who had been arrested, and the men were encouraging this woman to help the captive. Jonathan realized that they were probably talking about CC.

When he heard one of the men tell the maid that he needed a bottle of whiskey in order to get the guards drunk, he saw her hesitate, then turn toward the back bar. Frightened that she might see him through the arch, Jonathan made his way as quietly as possible out the back door, hoping that in the darkness, she wouldn't notice his wet footprints on the floor. After the heat of the kitchen, the outside air seemed even icier, the night darker, and he could feel the snow flakes fluttering down against his face. Feeling his way through the darkness, he turned a corner. He heard someone cough, and immediately halted in the shadow of the building.

He could see a man making his way down a path by the light cast from the inn's windows. The man stopped, and his face was suddenly illuminated when he struck a match. The man's hand was shaking, and after a moment Jonathan stifled a laugh when the man yelped and dropped the burned-down match.

The teen's eyes narrowed thoughtfully when he saw the man fumble in his pockets for something, then raise a bottle to his lips. Then, staggering slightly, he moved on down the dark path toward a small building.

As drunk as he is, Jonathan reasoned, *he must have a very special reason for making that walk on a miserable night like this.* As the man faded in the darkness, Jonathan followed him.

The Reluctant Conscript

Headquarters, People's Liberation Army
Burlington, Vermont
Christmas Eve

The general blathered on while Kim Ling stared unseeing at the face of the cheap wristwatch that one of his Chinese captors had "traded" him when he had stolen Kim's smart watch months before.

It's ten minutes after eight, and our esteemed general sounds as though he's just getting started. I wonder if he's just using me as a sounding board.

Kim looked again at the inexpensive watch the thief had pressed on him in exchange for his new smart watch. *It's ironic,* he thought. *The smart watch that was stolen won't be very smart without access to cell towers and the Internet, but this inexpensive watch that the thief forced on me will serve me well. I wonder whether he realizes that he didn't really make a very smart trade.* Kim smiled. *From my point of view, it's just another proof that "All things work together for good to those who love God, to those who are the called according to his purpose."*

Kim struggled to return his attention to the general's words. It appeared that he planned to go on talking all night. Kim had trouble believing that he was spending all this time with him. Just being around this egomaniac at any time would be a trial, but tonight of all nights, when Kim was reminded of the past Christmases that he had spent with his family, it had become nearly unbearable.

I have to focus, he told himself. He began to review what he'd learned about this enemy whom he'd been forced to serve.

When General Eng's troops had exited their secret underground shelter near Lake Champlain just two weeks after the war began, they had with them a carefully prepared list of Americans whom they planned to put to work — willingly or unwillingly — to aid in their conquest of America.

One of the people they had targeted was KimLing, a fourth generation Chinese-American. By profession, he was a TV news analyst and commentator, but he was also a licensed helicopter and light aircraft pilot, holding both instrument and commercial ratings. Having those certifications had given Kim the advantage he'd needed to secure his job as a TV newsman in a New England state where the total ethnic population, including blacks and Hispanics, was less than five percent. That was a striking statistic because, when the war began, whites represented less than half the total U.S. population.

Unlike other TV newsmen, Kim didn't require a pilot. He could fly himself and his cameraman to remote locations, thus saving the station the extra cost of a dedicated pilot. In addition to saving a pilot's salary, the station could get by with a smaller two-seat helicopter, rather than a more expensive three or four place machine. As a result, the station management had been thrilled to get Ling's combined skill sets for one modest paycheck. Money was always tight, and Burlington, with a pre-war population of just over 40,000, had not been a major TV media market. The network stations in Houston, Texas, for example, enjoyed a viewer base nearly 150 times that number, with commensurate revenue.

In view of the substantial savings that Kim Ling's employment would mean to the station, any concern over his ethnicity evaporated. In fact, the station's owners immediately began to think of additional advantages, such as satisfying equal-opportunity laws and gaining an aura of political correctness. So when Ling had insisted he should receive an increase in salary because he was performing two jobs for the price of one, the management shed a few tears, but soon forked over a little extra cash.

During his years with the station, Kim had led a life of contentment, marrying and starting a family. He spent most weekdays, and an occasional evening or Saturday, chasing stories for the network, a few of which ran nationwide. On Sunday mornings, however, he invariably took his family to a local Pentecostal church where he served as a deacon, and his spare time was divided between his family and quietly preparing for what he, with the eye of a newsman, considered the inevitable collapse of the United States.

That crash occurred far sooner than Kim Ling had anticipated. The economy and all civil order collapsed with nuclear attacks on several U.S. cities. America's aggressors did not want to destroy its infrastructure, just cripple it, for they coveted it for their own people. But, as Robbie Burns wrote, "The best laid plans of mice and men gang aft agley." And with those relatively limited attacks, the national power grid went down, and everything that required electricity to operate ceased to function.

The broadcast industry was among the first to die. Its cessation required no human decision-making. The loss of electrical power meant that only radio and TV stations with their own generating capabilities could remain on the air, and lack of fuel was sufficient reason why virtually every broadcaster was off the air within days.

As it turned out, the Chinese invaders had no interest in restoring power, much less putting the stations back on the air. They had no intention of giving potential enemies a voice, let alone providing broadcasters with the opportunity to pass clandestine messages to fledgling resistance movements.

As it turned out, the Chinese were delighted that there weren't any working TV sets, movie theaters, or other forms of entertainment in New England. It made it easier for them to enforce their curfews, knowing that most surviving Vermonters went to bed hungry when the sun went down. The fact that there were no refrigerators to preserve foods or store medicines meant nothing to the invaders. As far as they were concerned, they had a war to win and a country to pacify. If more Americans perished, it simply made their jobs easier.

Nor were they concerned with political correctness. The invaders considered such a concept absurd. As far as they were concerned, their brand of communism was the only form of politics allowed, and those who opposed them would forfeit their lives.

The Chinese, however, were also interested in Kim Ling's ethnicity because they hoped that he might have a shred of loyalty left in him for his Chinese heritage. They weren't at all interested in his experience as a newscaster, but they sorely needed his skills as a pilot. They wanted him to voluntarily and even enthusiastically sign on to fly one of the two helicopters that they had confiscated from the TV network affiliates in Burlington.

Kim had heard a rumor that these two helicopters had become vitally important to the Chinese invaders because the cargo ship that was to bring them dozens of copters had been sunk, and was now blocking a lock at the Pacific end of the newly enlarged Panama Canal. As a result of the sinking, they had also lost scores of armored personnel carriers, light tanks, and their Mengshi military vehicles — a knock-off that was arguably superior to America's Humvee. Now, instead of being able to shock any American adversaries by moving entire battalions of troops around the Northeast in mere hours, the Chinese would have to try to adapt far slower and more vulnerable civilian automobiles and trucks for their use. As a result of these unexpected losses, the two helicopters had become vital for surveillance and rapid travel.

Kim had grown up in Burlington. His parents had scrimped in order to send him to a classical school, one of those elite private schools where — apart from English, history, math and science — they taught Latin and Greek, required students to study logic and ethics, and to become effective debaters. It was a Christian environment, and Kim was one of it's most enthusiastic students.

No one considered him a nerd because he was the star of the school's soccer team, and he was modest and close-mouthed about his achievements. In fact, if it were not for the scholastic demands placed on him by his school, he would have spent a lot more time exploring the city with his more "normal" neighborhood chums. When he reached his teen years, he found numerous occasions to slip away with his friends.

One summer, while his parents were overseas, the group spent a lot of time exploring the crumbling ruins of a huge swimming pool in the Fairview neighborhood. It was part of a long-abandoned amusement park. The concrete was cracked, rusting rebar protruded through wide cracks in the walls, and there were trees growing out of the broken floor of the pool. It was considered a dangerous place for kids to gather, but the entire area was overgrown with trees and brush, and anyone passing more than a hundred feet away had no idea of its existence.

Some kids in his neighborhood spent their time building tree houses in the nearby woods, but Kim and his friends spent their time in the labyrinth of underground tunnels that ran around the perimeter of the pool. The teens had been able to reach these tunnels through manholes that had discovered buried beneath fallen leaves. The tunnels had been constructed of reinforced concrete, were several feet wide, and over six feet high, so the teens were able to race through them carrying flashlights. Large iron pipes, heavy with rust and scale, ran along the walls. The tunnels connected with underground rooms where chemicals had been stored and filter tanks had purified the pool water. The teens made one of these rooms their headquarters.

Early on they'd used the crumbling facilities to play hide-and-go seek and capture the flag. As the years passed, some of his former friends found other uses for the remote passages and darkened rooms, so Kim ceased visiting the place.

Kim had never forgotten this abandoned facility, however, and when war was imminent he had rushed his family there with enough food, water, blankets and emergency supplies to survive for several weeks. And while millions across America perished, his family survived. But when they finally returned home to gather possessions and look for a safe place to live, they were unpleasantly surprised to discover several Chinese soldiers awaiting them.

The Lings were treated politely, but they were ordered to pack one suitcase per family member, and the family was immediately broken up, with Ling taken to the Chinese military headquarters in Burlington, while his wife and children were supposedly driven to an intern center.

Kim Ling was immediately taken to meet General Eng where he insisted they speak in Mandarin. It was obvious that the general concluded that Kim was fluent in the dialect, and expressed pleasure that Kim's parents had taught him the language and familiarized him with the ancient Chinese traditions. The general was even more pleased to learn that Kim had spent two years in China between high school and college. He mistakenly assumed it was because Kim's family loyalties lay with China.

Not only did Kim speak two dialects fluently, but he knew how to write many of the ideograms. This held special value for the Chinese invaders. Since both the Chinese and Americans lacked a reliable electrical supply to operate computers, they were unable to operate sophisticated encryption systems. As a result, they were unable to encode messages that couldn't be broken by the Americans. With enough people like Kim available, however, the Chinese would be able to rely on Chinese pictograms to securely communicate, and the Americans would be unable to read them.

When the general told Ling what a wonderful opportunity he was being offered as a civilian member of the new order, he watched Kim's face carefully for any reaction. Kim was somehow able to hide his consternation, and the general went on blithely telling him what an unusual honor it was to be attached to his command as an interpreter and helicopter pilot.

Instead of responding positively to what amounted to a command performance, Kim asked about his family. The general was stumbled for a moment by his audacity, but sought to reassure him, "We will be taking good care of your wife and children."

Kim felt there was a sinister undertone to the general's words, and he was terrified by the implications of his ambivalent response. So while trying to sound neither obsequious nor demanding, he pursued the issue. "When will I be able to see them?"

"You should have the opportunity to visit with your family from time to time," was the general's cryptic reply. When Kim persisted, and asked whether the general knew when that first opportunity might arise, the man grew testy, repeating himself and flipping his hand through the air as though brushing away a fly.

"End of conversation," were the blunt words he used, but a moment later he added, as though in conciliation, "Let's see how you work out for a few months and then we will speak of this again."

"A few months?" Kim gasped in disbelief.

But the general ignored his response, and instead allowed a moment for his implied threat to sink in.

Kim needed no additional time to interpret the innuendo. *A few months? They are holding my family hostage!* It was ominous, and he realized that the general meant it to be so.

The general understood Ling's frustration only too well. He'd used this method of blackmail to secure cooperation countless times, and fully expected Kim's reaction. In fact, he'd counted on it. He was confident that he could control Kim Ling, but if he turned out to be wrong, he would simply have him eliminated. He had already arranged to have Kim Ling's wife placed in a comfort station where she would entertain his troops, while his children had been assigned to a loyal farmer who would put them to work. The children would be expected to earn their room and board and the general had no doubt, would work many hours every day for the scraps they would receive. The general was indifferent to their ultimate fate.

During the weeks that followed, Kim Ling had ample to reflect on his situation, and he realized how desperate it really was. He was under continual surveillance and never allowed the opportunity to escape. And even had he been able to get away, he had no idea where to look for his family. But he realized that these measures were unnecessary.

In not so many words he had been made to understand that if he in any way failed the Chinese, the lives of his family would be forfeit. So he decided to make of himself a model prisoner, becoming whatever he was required to be, always on time, properly attired and equipped. Whether that meant coveralls and a tool chest for repairing a copter, or flight suit and map case for flying duties, he was always prepared and punctual.

Whenever he could manage a little privacy, he took his needs to the Lord in prayer, but he often felt as though the heavens were brass and God was no longer listening. Then an opportunity arose, and he was able to slip off to that abandoned swimming pool where he began stockpiling items that might prove useful in an escape. If his wife were able to get away, he believed that she would try to reach their former hiding place at the abandoned swimming pool.

Kim Ling had a stubborn streak and decided that he would actually accomplish only as much work as was absolutely necessary to avoid the general's wrath. At the same time, he worked hard to impress his captors with his seeming faithfulness.

He was growing more and more frustrated with his situation, and continually envisioned himself escaping, locating his family, then finding a place to hide from the Chinese. He embraced that fantasy until the day he accidentally overheard a conversation between the general and one of his subordinates. That was the day that his dreams turned to dust.

The Rescuers

The Butter Creek Inn
Butter Creek, Vermont
Christmas Eve

An hour had passed since CC had been locked in the old shed, and his body, already numbed by the piercing cold, was surrendering to the euphoria that precedes death. Near unconsciousness, he was unaware that anyone else had entered the woodshed and was indifferent to the presence of the woman who knelt by his side. He actually felt annoyed when she began wheedling him to sip the hot coffee she'd brought him.

For her part, she was terrified, wondering whether she was leaping out of the frying pan into the fire, exchanging one evil master for another.

One of the two farmers who had been sitting at the bar had told her that she should run for her life. Ironically, his were the same words she had used just an hour earlier to warn the man in the dining room that he was in danger. The second of the farmers suggested that her best chance for survival lay with helping the man that had just been captured to escape. As she considered their warnings, she realized that helping the captive might actually represent not only her best chance, but only chance to survive the night. She had to find a place with shelter and food where she couldn't be tracked by these lackeys who served the Chinese. *Christmas Eve,* she thought, *and I might not live through Christmas Day!*

The farmers had been particularly concerned because she had just left the lecherous innkeeper lying unconscious on the floor of the inn's only guest room, his scalp opened by the bed post with which she'd struck him when he assaulted her.

Her arm had grown tired from supporting the man in a sitting position while he drank his coffee, and her thoughts returned to the present. The coffee was evidently breaking the hold that the cold had on him. She started helping him to his feet, thinking they might actually make good their escape, when the drunken guard appeared. Her hopes faded for a moment, but then the alcohol that he had consumed over the course of the evening took its toll, and he collapsed to the dirt floor.

Again thinking they were free, the young woman helped a stumbling CC move toward the door of the woodshed, only to have a second guard appear, this one armed with a pistol. He was relatively sober and determined to march them both back to the inn.

As the escaping maid and a benumbed CC preceded the guard up the dark, snow-covered path, she thought she heard a dull thunk, following which the pressure of the weapon in the small of her back disappeared. She turned her head slowly, and saw their captor collapse into a snow bank. Another figure stood over him, a length of firewood in his hands. Then there was a hoarse whisper.

"CC, is that you?"

In amazement, CC turned to discover that Jonathan had somehow traveled miles through the blizzard, and had in fact come to his rescue. *Correction,* he thought. *He's come to our rescue,* and he peered at the woman, finally realizing that she must be the young serving girl from the inn.

The three of them dragged the unconscious guard back into the woodshed and laid him next to the drunk. When the woman secured the door so that they couldn't escape, CC started to object.

"They left you there to freeze to death," she argued. "And if they get out of there too soon, we won't be able to get away."

"Yes, I guess you're right," he told her, and turned to follow Jonathan.

They fought their way through the deepening snow for twenty minutes before they reached the Green Mountain Feed and Grain Store. In danger of freezing and famished from the unaccustomed exertion, they entered the building through the cellar door. Discovering cases of food stacked all over the cellar, they opened several cartons, selected a variety of cans, and made their way up the stairs to the snack bar on the main floor.

Rachel immediately revealed her determination to be useful. "If you don't mind, I'll take charge of the cooking." Firing up the gas range, she heated several cans of beef stew, then kept pace with CC and Jonathan as they wolfed their portions down, finishing with fruit cocktail for dessert. They ate quickly, knowing that they dared not tarry long in this place with their enemies undoubtedly searching for them.

They could sense that CC was becoming concerned. "We've been here too long," he warned, "and we have to move on while there's still enough snow falling to cover our tracks."

"What about that stuff stacked in the cellar?" Jonathan asked. "It looks as though the Chinese have confiscated all sorts of things that might be valuable to us."

CC looked at the teen and after a moment, nodded in grudging agreement. He glanced at his watch and came to a decision. "We need to get out of here, but I agree with Jonathan. We can't afford to walk away from here without checking through those cartons they've hidden in the basement."

The truth was that none of them was in a hurry to leave the relative shelter of the unheated building, so they made their way to the cellar and began rooting through various cartons. As they began setting aside items they felt would be of value, Jonathan noticed several packframes in a corner. It took them about fifteen minutes to select the useful items they planned to take with them, and to load them. They buttoned up their coats, helped one another to strap on their backpacks, pulled on the dry gloves and scarves they found in the cartons, and made their way outside.

CC was thinking of the many people who were suffering from cold and hunger across America because these invaders had initiated war, and were now seizing and stockpiling the very food and clothing the Americans needed to survive.

There is no time to grieve over something we can't presently control, he realized. *The time will come for retaliation, but not tonight.*

As they were making last minute adjustments on the straps that balanced their loads, he led the way out of the cellar and across the snow-covered parking lot toward the mountain road.

The snow was again coming down with a vengeance, and while CC was encouraged that it would cover their tracks, he almost despaired of their finding their way back to their cave through the blizzard. To make matters worse, there was ice beneath the snow, and each of them fell several times because of the treacherous footing. Rachel discovered that it was easier to keep from falling by walking in the deeper snow along the side of the road, though it was much harder to push through.

At one point the blowing snow became so thick that they almost passed by the entrance to CC's valley. The storm had become a real Northeaster, but the wind dropped away when they reached the shelter of the trees in the valley's narrow entrance.

As much as they'd like to remain there, CC knew that they didn't dare linger in the gulch, exposed as they were to both the elements and the possibility of pursuit. He wanted to get as far away from the highway as possible, particularly so that he could count on the drifting snow to fill the deep footprints they were leaving behind them.

He took several candy bars from an inner pocket and passed them around. The three of them had to gnaw hard to break off pieces of the near-frozen chocolate, then wait for it to melt in their mouths, but the rare treat provided the much-needed energy they required to begin the hike up the length of the valley to CC's cavern.

Adam Salay
> Sennett Mountain
> Central Vermont
> Christmas Eve, 6:30 p.m.

Adam Salay leaned back in the primitive room's single chair and considered the comforts, or lack thereof, that surrounded him. He sat in near darkness, and tried to imagine that the red, green and yellow lights emitted by the LEDs on the various electronic components in the room were actually Christmas decorations. The lights really did look cheerful, and gave the otherwise dismal and utilitarian room a festive glow.

The room was unfinished, and had been erected inside a cave. The two-by-four studs were exposed on the inside, and had been sheathed with plywood, as had the floor and the roof. He was facing a crude workbench that ran the length of the room. The workbench, along with the shelves above and below it, was crowded with electrical components. Behind him, in one corner, was a double bunk. Next to it was a plywood wardrobe and a beat up chest of drawers. In the other corner was what might be charitably called a bathroom. The corner of the room had been squared off with more plywood, leaving a narrow opening for access. There was no door, not even a curtain, but since he was the only one in residence, it hardly mattered. The bathroom contained a small prefab steel shower with its molded concrete floor, as well as a toilet and a pedestal sink.

Next door was a small room that served as a kitchen and dining area. It had several working appliances, all electric, including refrigerator, stove, and even a microwave. Dishes had to be washed by hand, but Adam had been using disposable products for his meals. He'd been so busy that he rarely did more than open cans, heat the contents, choke them down, and get on with his work. Oddly, he did not look the worse for wear, and it might be attributed to both his youth and his excitement over his work.

He'd been very busy for the past few months, and his intense labors had kept him occupied and able to avoid feeling too lonely, too often. He probably wouldn't have even noticed it was Christmas Eve if he hadn't happened to turn on an old a.m. radio, hoping to pick up some outlaw broadcaster and maybe learn something about what was happening. What he got was some carefree soul, acting in

defiance of Chinese law, wishing him a merry Christmas and playing
the same Christmas album over and over.

Salay was not critical of his seemingly primitive surroundings.
They were far better and more secure than those of most who had
survived the violence of the war to this point. Thanks to his friend,
Joe Sennett, he had a secret and secure shelter with its own electrical
supply and many of the comforts of the pre-war world. He had an
abundance of food, a remarkable assortment of medical supplies –
not just band aids and aspirin – and things to keep him busy. *Oh
boy, do I have things to keep me busy!* he thought.

Adam Salay had found his way to Joe Sennett's cave in the Vermont mountains just as hostilities began. He had made his way
through the forest toward a man-made lake that was impounded behind a very old and not very secure looking dam. Adam had faced a
lot of problems reaching this remote area, but his most frightening
moment came when a forest ranger had stepped out from behind a
tree and threatened to arrest him for hunting without a license.

When Adam started to argue with him, the ranger demanded to
know why he was carrying a rifle when it wasn't hunting season.
Adam tried to explain that he was only here to camp, and was carrying the rifle in case he was attacked. The ranger was going to arrest
him and take him in, but after he examined Adam's driver's license
and business card, he decided to let him go. He instead, however,
that Adam give him the rifle, and told him he could pick it up at
ranger headquarters when he was ready to leave the area. In the
meantime, the ranger was satisfied that there was no way he would be
able to poach on these lands.

Adam was tempted to argue that these lands belonged to Joe
Sennett, not to the government, but decided that he didn't want to
risk making the ranger angrier than he was, so he went on his way.
Turning as he walked around a tree, Adam looked back to see that
the ranger was watching him. Adam immediately began moving in
circles, determined to make it as difficult as possible for anyone to
follow him.

He walked down the west side of the lake, as Joe had instructed him, and then down the steep hillside that bordered the dam on the south end of the lake. About a quarter mile beyond the dam he'd spotted a wall of rock that formed the west side of the valley, and made his way toward it. Night was falling when he finally located what he thought must be the mouth of Sennett's cave. He was relieved to locate the entrance because he didn't want to be forced to sleep in the open again, particularly since he no longer had a weapon. America had become increasingly lawless over the past year, and he didn't want to run into any outlaws.

The cave's entrance faced east and was cloaked in gloom as the sky darkened. Adam's eyes were probing the dark entrance when it was suddenly illuminated from behind him. He wheeled in surprise, then stood transfixed as he watched a mushroom cloud rising far away in the east.

In spite of the fact that he had anticipated the outbreak of war, he had calculated that its beginning was still several days away, and it took him a moment to grasp the enormity of the catastrophe. It was impossible to calculate the horror that was descending on the human race, but he could not allow himself to dwell on those matters. Although he had periods of deep emotional sensitivity, and a true concern for others, he was constitutionally unable to dwell on subjects that were, for him, of secondary importance. He had no control over the forces that were impacting millions of people, and he therefore immediately put them from his mind.

He was a rationalist by nature and not by choice, and his mind immediately took control. Like one of his highly sophisticated computer programs, he began sifting data, dispensing with anything that was not essential to him, and prioritizing that which was. Whether a gift or a curse, Adam had what others considered a cold-blooded ability to logically isolate priorities and spew out best-case solutions to the challenges he faced.

He had seen the mushroom cloud and he had allowed himself just thirty seconds to appraise the overall situation. He would, if opportunity permitted, consider other less essential matters later. Staring for just an instant at the radiant and deadly cloud of radioactive gas that was rising high into the heavens over what he was sure was Boston, he drew a couple of conclusions.

It must have been a big warhead, maybe two megatons. I'm well over a hundred miles away, and the flash from the detonation lit up the woods around me. He pulled his sunglasses from his vest pocket and put them on.

That cloud is miles high! His mind was racing. *It's obvious that they detonated the weapon on or near the ground, or there wouldn't be that enormous mushroom cloud. And since it was near the ground, it scooped up thousands of tons of earth and is turning it into radioactive fallout.*

His eyes seemed to look beyond America's shores, out across the Atlantic toward Europe. *That dust will get into the atmosphere and float around the world, falling out a little at a time, contaminating crops that will be ingested by farm animals, and ultimately poisoning the food chain for tens of millions of helpless people.* His mind clicked along. *The cloud at Hiroshima rose to about 45,000 feet, and it was caused by only a 1.5-kiloton bomb. This one must have been at least one-and-a-half megatons, something on the order of ten to twenty times the size.*

Adam turned away, removed the sunglasses, and twisted his way through the narrow opening to the cave, staggering a little under the weight of his backpack. Using a flashlight he looked for the second tunnel on the right, as instructed. It was even a tighter fit, not so attractive as the two other tunnels he'd passed on either side as he made his way in.

He walked down the tunnel about ten yards before he came to the stout plank door that Joe Sennett had told him about. He shrugged out of his backpack, and let it slip to the cave floor. Then he rummaged through his pockets for the key ring that Sennett had given him. He tried several keys, and finally unlocked the two deadbolts in the face of the heavy door. Then he caught hold of the flimsy little handle, and pulled the door open. Joe had told him that he had made the handle fragile so that, if anyone tried to force the door, the handle would break loose. They would be left with a flat surface and nothing to tug on. "Unless they have some pretty sophisticated tools with them," he had told Adam, "there's no way they'll get through that door."

"Unless they set fire to it," Adam has laughed. They'd have to wait until the smoke cleared, but they'd get in."

"No, it's a fake," his friend had answered. I wanted the door to look stout, but not impassable. I don't want anyone to think that whatever is behind the door is worth the trouble of breaking it down. If the door is too impressive, they will conclude that no effort will be too great to get in."

"I can understand that," Adam agreed, "but what's to keep them from breaking through the wooden door?"

"The wood is just a veneer."

"Veneer?"

"Yes. Beneath the plank surface is a half-inch thick steel door. Anyone who tries to get through that will need more than a sledge hammer or a hot fire."

Adam laughed appreciatively. He realized he should have known that Joe would be thorough about protecting his secret lair.

"One last question, Joe."

"Yeah?"

"How did you get all that stuff together, and through the forest to the cavern?"

"I bought an old farm tractor and a hay trailer, and I took a load in every time I went to the cavern."

"But how did you manage all the heavy stuff?"

"There are a couple of trustworthy friends, big guys, who helped me. And I had hydraulic jacks, come-a-longs, and hoists to help me."

"So it took you a long time...?"

"Years," he said, dismissing it with a wave of his hand.

That conversation had occurred months before, and Adam had come to the cave just in time, and he was still there, working alone, wondering whether Joe Sennett was dead or alive. Then his thoughts returned to the nature of his own loneliness, and he thought sadly that he was a lot like his namesake.

God considered the plight of the first Adam, he thought, *and observed, "It is not good that man should dwell alone." And it's not good that this Adam should be dwelling alone, either.*

But the girl I wanted to wed and bring here to save her, the girl I thought I loved, and I thought loved me, decided at the last minute to stay in Boston, instead of following what she called my hair-brained scheme to come here in anticipation of a war that simply wouldn't happen.

She loved the bright lights and the fast pace of the big city, and I loved the rhythm of small town and rural life. He bit his lip. *We were evidence that opposites attract, but we found out just in time that the ideas we valued and the things we loved were very different. So here I am. And,* he thought sadly, *she may well be dead right now. I can only guess.*

That last meeting had not been happy.

"You're a flaming conspiracy nut," she had finally told him, "and I just can't stand the way your negativism brings me down. I'll admit that some of the things you've predicted have come true, but nothing earth shaking." Then she said something that he had never realized, something that clearly separated them.

"You would fight to the death for free speech or the right to own a gun, but I just want to get along. If it were the 1960s, I'd be part of the crowd that shouted, *Better Red than dead.*"

He remembered standing there, shocked by her admission, and realizing that their relationship was over. No. He had to admit to himself that it had never really begun.

As he stood there, too stunned to respond, she put the lid on the coffin of their relationship.

"You say that there is going to be a war, right?"

"Yes," he choked, finally recovering his voice.

"And you say that millions are going to die, and it will be the end of life as we know it, right?"

He nodded.

"Well, I don't want to live in that kind of world," she said emphatically. "I'd rather be dead."

He shook his head in disappointment. "You may change your mind when and if you face that possibility," he said, "but by then your choice will be made for you."

He thought back to the journey that had brought him here. His decision to leave Saugerties several days earlier than planned turned out to be providential. He would otherwise have waited too long. The conclusions he'd drawn from his research had been inaccurate. He had calculated that he had nearly a week before he would have to leave the Hudson Valley and travel to Sennett's cave in the mountains of central Vermont. Under normal circumstances, a day would have been enough. These, however, were not normal circumstances and, as it turned out, he had barely two days.

He had locked himself in his little shop in Saugerties. It was a run down little place where the locals thought he repaired computers and sold software. All they saw was the rundown store out front, not his incredibly elegant office in the rear, or the store room full of sophisticated electronic gear. No one had any clue that he had once been a prime software contractor to the NSA, CIA, and FBI. He'd walked away from them when he saw these organizations working against America's best interests. He was not as his girlfriend thought, a conspiracy theorist. He was a conspiracy realist.

It was only after he had ceased doing business with them that they realized the extent of his knowledge, and the danger he represented. It was very likely that he could bring their infrastructure down. Worse, he could embarrass certain officials, and bring them down. He knew the truth, and because of that, and because he no longer worked for them, they now considered him dangerous. As a result, there were several agents in the little town of Saugerties watching his every move, and he had little doubt that a termination notice would go out at any moment.

He'd returned from his ill-fated trip to Boston only to realize that he was under observation. Although he knew that others of his friends had suddenly disappeared without explanation, he didn't take the threat seriously until whoever was watching him had become either so clumsy in their efforts or indifferent to their exposure that he couldn't miss seeing them.

It was his belief that his life was suddenly at risk that caused him to act earlier than he thought necessary. A teenager, Jonathan Whitkowski, who lived a few miles south, had walked through the front door of his computer shop. His unwelcome visit precipitated Adams' decision to leave.

Over the preceding month he had focused on tracking events around the world. He'd sent some of the results to a few trusted acquaintances, including a former CIA staffer named McCord and a preacher in central Vermont. He'd begun hacking government and military websites around the world, exactly what he had told the Whitkowski boy he must not do.

And there were few people better at it than Adam Salay. He graduated from MIT at fifteen, and became a lecturer. Then he offered a powerful software program to the FBI. That opened the door to further opportunities, and became a source of significant income. When he quit serving government agencies, he rented the old store front in Saugerties under an assumed name. He realized it wouldn't remain secret for long, and he was right.

The morning that Jonathan showed up unexpectedly, he learned that the boy had been trying to track the activities of potential enemies. He knew that the boy was in danger simply because he had exposed himself to sniffers that he had created for the agencies. When he tried to break into their networks, they would have identified him within seconds. The only reason they wouldn't have already arrested him was because they had too many bigger fish to fry.

With the teen walking into his store, however, the people who were busy betraying America would believe they were somehow involved together, and that could well mean a death warrant for both of them. They certainly were not going to take a chance on a teenager hindering them from reaching their imminent goals. If it did not inconvenience them, they would simply eliminate him and his family.

Adam had tried to impress on the teen how dangerous it was to be hacking government websites, and then he had found it impossible not to warn the boy of the impending attacks. The kid had already made a pretty good guess at what was happening, and it would have been unconscionable to withhold information that might save his life.

No sooner had the boy left his shop than he hung up a sign that read, "Closed, Out of Business," and left the shop by going down into the cellar and sneaking out through a coal chute that had been used for this and the neighboring store prior to World War II.

Upon his arrival at the cave, he began on the project that Joe had planned for them to undertake together. He unpacked a couple of 3-D printers, set them up, and began turning out the two odd pieces required to convert AR-15 rifles from semi-automatic to the military equivalent of the old military M-16. There were over two hundred of these weapons in moisture- proof wrappings at the back of one of the tunnels, plus large quantities of ammunition.

Adam was shocked. He had asked his friend, "Where in the world did you get the money to pay for two-hundred rifles, let alone get your hands on them?"

Joe Sennett had laughed. You remember when the President issued his infamous Executive Order to shut down all civilian arms manufacturers?"

"Sure."

"Well, between the time he issued that order, and the time one of his minions realized that they might need to set guards over any undelivered weapons that might remain at the factories, I received a call from an old friend who had worked at a plant in Massachusetts."

"And?"

"He told me that he and a few friends had gone to the plant after dark one night and used a forklift to move several hundred weapons out behind the plant to the waste disposal and recycling area." Joe laughed. "They carefully stacked the weapons in some scrap metal recycling bins, and locked the gate. When the federal officials arrived to look for any guns, they found a few cases in the building and took them away."

"Weren't they suspicious that there might have been more?" Adam asked.

"Not really. My friend made certain that the computer records were altered to indicate that they had all of the finished arms."

"But how did you get your hands on them, Joe?"

"After the feds left, my friends loaded the guns and about 100,000 rounds of ammunition on an old truck and drove the load to a little village in southern Vermont where we swapped vehicles. They took the car I was driving back to Massachusetts, and I drove the truck within five miles of here."

"And you moved all the weapons here by yourself?"

"It took me a some time, and a lot of sweat, but, yes! I made several trips with my faithful old hay wagon and carried them in here."

"Didn't you leave tracks?"

"I went in on the back side of the mountain. There's a huge old quarry, and I drove the tractor for nearly a mile over rock before reaching the cave. One good rainstorm and all signs of my passing were washed away. Then I moved them through the tunnels using a small farm tractor and cart."

"That's an amazing story, Joe."

"Yeah, isn't it? And that's how I got everything else here. There are no neighbors within two miles because the land is either privately owned or part of a state park. And since there's a little farm between here and the highway, anyone who might have seen me would just assume that I was working my farm."

Adam had wondered aloud about the risks Joe had taken. Sennett believed that the prize was worth the risk. If America were invaded, the guns would be priceless to those who wanted to resist. Adam remembered one of Joe's quips. "The media always liked to call them *assault weapons*, but the are really self-defense weapons."

Adam was now the protector of those *self-defense weapons*. He had no idea where Joe was, but he was determined to convert the weapons and maintain the facilities in the caverns. It was lonely, but it was a better life than most people had.

If Joe doesn't show up here before I'm finished converting these things, he decided, *I'll go out and look for people who can and will put them to good use in defense of our country.*

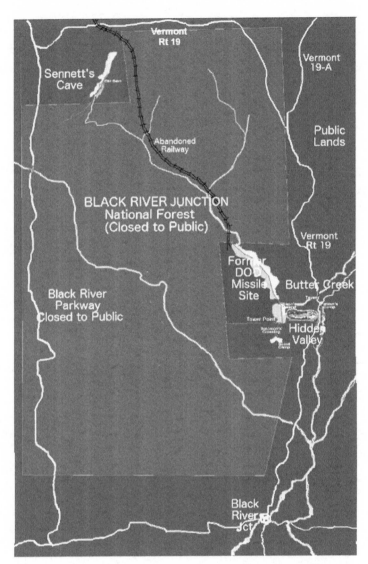

Vermont's Central Mountains

Kim Ling's Deception

Headquarters, People's Liberation Army
Burlington, Vermont
Christmas Eve

As the general droned on, Kim continued to meditate over the events that had occurred since his initial conversation with Eng months before and why the general continually made excuses as to why Kim could not see his family.

"They are many miles to the north where they will be safe," the general had assured Kim on one occasion.

Safe from whom? Kim wondered.

On another day, the general remarked, "They are living in a pleasant little village in the mountains near the Canadian border." And when Kim joked that "The moss only grows on the south sides of the trees that far north," and "There are no pleasant little villages near the Canadian border," the general frowned. But when Kim had persisted by asking for the name of the village, Eng had grown testy, and dismissed him.

The last time they had spoken, the general added a new twist: "Your wife has many important responsibilities now and is busy traveling from place to place." When Kim had asked him what those important responsibilities consisted of, and when he might expect her to appear in Burlington in connection with those responsibilities, the general exploded.

"As I have told you, your wife has very important responsibilities." Then, as though to pacify Kim, "I am certain that you will run into her one of these days." But by then, Kim knew he was being lied to.

Kim's crisis had come just a few days before. He had been rummaging in the back of a dark storeroom, searching for anything that might aid in his escape, when he heard the door rattle. He managed to shut off his flashlight and slip behind a row of shelves just as the general and his other helicopter pilot entered. The two were talking and laughing, and Kim obeyed an impulse to remain out of sight.

As he eavesdropped on their conversation, he realized that they were sharing stories about the American women that had been forced to serve at what they called their *comfort stations*. Kim Ling already despised these men for both their immorality and their physical and verbal abuse of women, and he had only been able to restrain his growing hatred because of what his actions might ultimately cost his own family. But when he heard their next words, he went cold.

The pilot asked the general, "What do you think the American would do if he discovered that his wife had succumbed while performing her duties?"

What American? Ling wondered. *I'm the only American here.* The general's cryptic response answered Kim's unspoken question.

"You are not to give Kim Ling even a hint of such a possibility," the general snarled, his voice icy.

"No, of course not," the man stuttered, genuine fear in his voice.

Kim felt his stomach turn over and he squeezed his the barrel of his flashlight so tightly that the plastic tube collapsed against the batteries inside.

"Well, I can't say I'm sorry," the pilot went on. "Nobody trusts Ling, and it's just as well that his wife is gone."

"Not just his wife," the general said.

There was a hint of disbelief when the pilot asked, "You don't mean his children too?" His surprise was undisguised. Even the most unfeeling Chinese often expressed deep affection for children, especially for boys, and as crass as this pilot had shown himself to be, he appeared to be no exception. "Did you send Ling's children to a labor camp?"

"Of course," the general said scornfully. "They were only half-breed Americans, hardly more than barbarians." Kim's eyes filled with tears as in the light from the hallway he saw the general shrug it off. "The work was too hard for them," he explained. "They didn't last long."

Kim knelt there, his fist in his mouth, choking back sobs while trying to process this unspeakable news. His sorrow suddenly turned to rage, and he had an intense desire to rush out and attack them with his bare hands. Then his wrath inexplicably went from white hot to ice cold. He realized that it would be futile to attack these two well-armed men. In fact, they would probably welcome his attempt and would not hesitate to shoot him down. And while they carried pistols, Ling was permitted no weapons, though he had begun to carry a dagger taped to his left forearm beneath his shirt sleeve. So far no one had noticed that he had the knife, but he didn't think he could keep it hidden much longer.

Time seemed to drag, but when the general and his pilot failed to find what they were looking for, they left the building. Now that he was free to weep, Kim could not make the tears come. His grief was like a stone, and he knew he must resist the hatred that was beginning to well up within him. To hate was to surrender to the dark lord of hate, the one he knew to be a liar from the beginning.

Kim did not know how long he knelt there, trying not to think, trying not to speak, trying not to let the Lord speak to him. He wanted to yield to the hatred, but somehow felt himself constrained, as thought their was a faithful friend within the room constraining him. Finally he reasoned, *Whatever action that I take must be with the motive of resisting this evil. I must not act out of hatred or I will become no better than these men.*

He rose to his feet. He was praying, but he knew that his words were hollow, insincere, meaningless.

If you want me to feel as you feel toward them, then you will have to overcome the hatred I feel for them. Right now it is irrelevant to me that they need Christ, but you'll have to find someone else who is ready, willing and able to give them your words. As far as I'm concerned, they are hardened in si, and will not listen to reason. To speak peace to them would be tantamount to committing suicide, and

I intend to live to exact revenge. I do not intend to die and let them repeat these evils.

His tried to see things from God's point of view, and came to one conclusion. *Whatever is done to these people must be done in deepest secrecy, with the motive of ending their evil works, and if that means killing them, then so be it!*

Kim Ling laughed bitterly. *That's pretty high-sounding.* He realized that he was at war with himself. *The truth is that I want to kill them all, and I want to die when I've finished it.*

Over the next few days, Kim understood that although his family was gone from him, they were in a far better place. And he came to realize that he might still be able to help many other women and children who were still suffering under the heel of the invaders. *It is sufficient justification for my fighting on,* he resolved.

He often lay awake at night, tossing and turning, his eyes filled with tears. *I have nothing to live for,* he thought. *I just want to join my wife and children in heaven.* But then he would call himself double-minded, a quitter and a coward, and imagine how his wife might exhort him to fight on. Then he would be both ashamed of his thoughts and proud to have been chosen by her to be her husband.

Finally he would remind himself that he was already inside the enemy's camp, and that perhaps there was something significant that he could do from here to stop the horror.

His thoughts returned to the present, and he found himself still sitting in the smoke-filled room before the general's desk, as the man continued speaking aloud. For the moment, it took all of the self-control Kim could muster to keep himself from drawing his hidden knife and diving across that ornate desk.

Chris Escapes

Butter Creek Inn
Butter Creek, Vermont
Christmas Eve

A little more than an hour had passed since the two farmers had helped the serving girl leave the inn with the intention of helping the prisoner in the woodshed escape. Since neither she nor the two guards who had followed in that direction had returned, the farmers were hopeful that the two of them had made good their escape. But in order to assist them, they had been providing the two remaining constables inside the inn with all the free alcohol they desired, which was substantial.

One of these was the driver who'd brought Chris and her children to Butter Creek. He felt comfortable in imbibing freely, confident that he had satisfied his responsibility for his passengers by making certain they'd had something to eat and been settled on the floor of the dining room for the night. No one was going anywhere in this blizzard, he was assured, and there was now no question about his being fit to drive his vehicle if the snow were to stop any time soon.

The other man was a local constable who'd been appointed by the Chinese invaders to promote their interests. His limited thought processes were already pretty clouded when it occurred to him to ask one of their benefactors about his two absent associates. Receiving the farmer's assurance that his two missing compatriots were probably interrogating the man in the shed out back, he was content to remain inside and accept the drinks proffered him.

The only thing that the farmers knew for certain about those two men was that they had not returned from the shed. Their success in helping the serving girl and the other prisoner escape, and the absence of any adversaries, had emboldened them and resulted in their sudden decision to come to the aid of the woman and her two children. As soon as the two remaining turncoats drank themselves into a stupor, the farmers helped the woman and her two children to escape.

When they asked, she told them that her name was Chris. She didn't offer her last name and they didn't ask. Nor did she ask for theirs. It seemed the prudent thing. Whatever their motives, she realized that their clever exploitation of the rapidly changing circumstances was providential. One of the men found a stash of winter clothing hidden in a closet, and bundled the three of them up. The other man went outside, and when he returned, he told them he had a snowmobile out front which they could use to make their escape. They only had time to provide her with the most rudimentary instructions on how to drive the unfamiliar machine, and that's why she now found herself into pitch darkness in the middle of a violent blizzard.

One of the farmers, a man named Kenzy, had given her the barest directions to reach his farm. She was to stop there to warm up and gather food and other items they would need to survive.

The snowmobile's dashboard was dimly lit, and the built-in compass indicated that she was heading due east. Whether she was still on the road that led from Butter Creek to the Kenzy farm was an entirely different matter. With the snow around her in the darkness and deep drifts covering the fences that bordered the road, it was impossible to tell whether she had lost her way and might actually be driving across some farmer's field miles from her goal.

It would be easy enough, she thought, *to pass within a hundred yards of the farmhouse and not even see it.*

She squinted into the bright tunnel that her headlights bored through the blowing snow, and struggled to keep her bloodshot eyes from closing in the intense glare. She was not a tall woman, and the necessity of leaning forward to grasp the grips on the handlebars was resulting in back pain.

It was bitterly cold, and Chris was grateful that the men who had helped her and the children had made certain that they were all warmly dressed. Her inexperience with snowmobiles caused her to drive very slowly. Even barely above walking speed, however, she knew that she would already be severely frost-bitten were it not for the scarf they'd wrapped around her face and the goggles that the men had somehow provided. Even so, the scarf was damp with ice crystals as a result of the moist air she had exhaled.

Chris had been without sleep for nearly twenty-four hours, and the glare of the headlights reflecting off the blowing snow, along with the steady hum of the engine, were almost stupefying. She found herself staring at the compass to avoid looking directly forward into the glare, and frequently checking the rear-view mirror in fear of pursuit, but all was dark. Instead of providing her with a sense of relief, however, a mindless fear that she was being followed gnawed at her. *It's just paranoia brought on by cold and stress,* she tried to tell herself. *And I have plenty to worry about without that unlikely threat.*

Her burning eyes had begun involuntarily closing, and she had actually awakened once just in time to avoid crashing into a tree. She knew that she had to find shelter soon, before the cold or her pursuers overtook them. If she couldn't find the farm to which she'd been directed, she and her children would very likely freeze to death.

The kids had long since stopped asking, "Are we almost there yet?" and had sunk into some sort of uneasy slumber.

Visibility was now limited to little more than a half-dozen yards through the snow, and it was all she could do to stay between between the tops of the fence posts that ran alone either side of the road. At least, she hoped that she was still driving between the fences that bordered the narrow farm lane.

Her thoughts had melded into a strange, almost feverish litany consisting of fragments of Bible verses intermixed with the briefest of prayers. She tried repeatedly to recite the Lord's prayer, but found herself drifting off, and after a while, she would begin all over again. When she became aware that she was repeating certain phrases over and over, like "the valley of the shadow" and "Give us this day," she wondered how her words could mean anything to the Lord, but she consoled herself that he would be pleased simply because she was trying to keep him in her thoughts.

Every so often her eyes would fool her, and she would imagine that some cloud of snow, like the icy counterpart of a dust devil, was actually a person standing in the middle of the road. With her heart in her mouth, she'd jerk the handlebars one way or the other to avoid hitting it, then find herself panicking again because she might have steered away from the relative safety of the road. She became terrified that she would find herself and the children out of gas and hopelessly lost in some field or forest, without shelter, heat, or food. She was so tired that she was even afraid to blink her eyes because they might stubbornly refuse to open again.

The lane suddenly curved to the right, and strange shadows loomed on both sides of the road. Chris wondered if they were optical illusions, like the mirages people see in the desert, but as she drew nearer, they seemed to take on substance. She breathed a sigh of relief when an old barn appeared on her left. It had probably been built more than a hundred years before and lay just a few yard from the road, undoubtedly in anticipation of a night just like this, when deep snow would become a severe obstacle to the nineteenth century farmer fighting his way from house to barn.

Her headlights picked out a sign hanging from a post, and though it was partially obscured by a thin layer of snow, she could make out the name, "Kenzy," and the image of a milk cow. This was the place the farmers had told her she might be able to find help. The sign confirmed her estimate that she'd traveled the four miles from Butter Creek.

She stopped the snowmobile in the middle of the lane to offer thanks for bringing them safely there, then she looked around. On her right, on a slope opposite the barn, and just far enough from the road to provide for a front lawn, was a large two-story farmhouse.

She turned the snowmobile's handlebars in order to flood the building with light. It had a covered porch that wrapped around the front and one side of the first floor. Its roof was now heavy with snow, and enormous icicles hanging from the eves refracted her lights in a spectacular display of nordic beauty. She was disappointed when she realized that there were no lights showing in the windows. In fact, many of the panes were broken, and the front door seemed to hang at a crazy angle. Her heart sank. The place appeared to be a derelict, and there was no indication that anyone lived there.

Why would they mislead me like this? she wondered.

As Chris puttered toward the house, she noticed several more outbuildings. One was reasonably large, and sat just behind the deserted house. It appeared to be a carriage house. Judging from the size of the house and barn, she realized that this had once been a very prosperous farm.

Without conscious thought, she yanked the handlebars around to the right and headed for the big doors of the carriage house. She stopped a few feet away and found herself so stiff from the cold that she almost fell when she dismounted.

Although her benefactors had found ski suits for them in at the tavern, the front of hers was now coated with a layer of ice and snow, and her hips and knees ached from the cold. She stood in the blowing snow for a moment, holding onto the handlebars. When she got her shaking knees under control, she pushed her way through a snowdrift to the carriage house doors.

She was glad to see that they did not swing out on hinges, for she knew that she wouldn't have been able to drag them open against the deep snow. Standing in the path of her own headlights, she was pleased to see that there was no padlock securing the doors. She reached up, opened the hasp, slipped her gloved fingers into the crack between the two big rolling doors and put all her weight into trying to slide one of the doors to the side. It scarcely budged. She looked up. The tops of the doors hung from rollers suspended on a long railing. The bottoms of the doors, she realized, were probably designed to slide through a narrow trench, and were obviously gripped by snow and ice.

Chris was so weary that she felt like crying, but she was, when it really mattered, a very tough lady. She smiled to herself as happier days were brought to memory. Her Uncle John used to laughingly tell others, "She's as good as any two men." Remembering those words brought heart to her, and she began pushing and pulling on the bottom of the big door until she had it swinging back and forth an inch or two, first toward the barn, then away.

She could hear ice cracking, so she began jerking the door back and forth from right to left, until it finally rolled open a couple of feet. Moving into the narrow gap between the two doors, she pressed her back against the edge of one, put her feet against the bottom of the other, and used her legs to push them apart. There was the loud shriek of metal on metal as the door she'd been wiggling broke free and rolled a couple more feet. Then she again leaned her upper back against the unopened door, put her feet against the bottom of the other door, and pushed with all her strength. The hardware chirped and the door opened another foot, causing her to lose her footing and wind up sitting on the snow in the open doorway.

She was gasping now from her labors, her heaving lungs painfully struggling to heat the freezing air, and her heart was racing to move the blood to oxygen-starved muscles. The snowmobile's headlamps cast a narrow beam into the building, and she moved cautiously through the opening.

The headlights of the snowmobile now reached the dark interior of the barn, and as her eyes adjusted, she saw an antique car setting up on blocks off to one side. Then she was struck dumb by the sight of a beautiful old horse-drawn sleigh parked in the center of the floor. It was painted a glossy white, and its trim was picked out in red and gold. As she studied it, she realized that the area behind the driver's seat was stacked with duffle bags. She laughed aloud, wondering if Santa might be about to make an appearance.

After her eyes adjusted to the half-light, she noticed a black snowmobile sitting in a stall beneath a hay loft on her left. She looked up at the loft and saw that it was stacked with hay.

That's odd, she thought. *Where are the people who put up that hay, and what did they use for equipment?*

As she moved toward the snowmobile, she was startled to hear the heavy tread of an animal, and jumped when a cow suddenly mooed. Its lowing was answered by the nicker of a horse, and he was in turn answered with the whinny of another. Obviously this place was not deserted. Cows have to be milked morning and evening, and horses have to be fed, so there had to be someone nearby. She felt a twinge of fear, knowing that many of the survivors in this area had surrendered their loyalties to the Chinese. She and her two children might only be mere seconds from recapture.

Chris walked to the black snowmobile, removed her glove, and put her hand on the hood. It was warm, which meant that someone had parked it there in the past few minutes. She moved back to the doors and turned to stare out toward her own snowmobile. It was only a few yards away, but even with its lights on, it was almost invisible through the growing storm. She had no choice. She had to get her children in out of the cold, even if it meant risking capture.

Chris pushed through the growing drift to reach her machine. She was sobered by the fact that the snow already seemed deeper than when she'd pulled up to the doors just moments before. She looked at her sleeping children and noted that the snow on the hoods of their parkas was nearly an inch deep. *It's really coming down,* she realized. *I need to hurry.*

She drove the snowmobile into the carriage house and parked it next to the Santa Claus sleigh, leaving the motor running and the lights on. She took one more look around the barn and took note of the fact that there was an identical set of large rolling doors centered in the rear wall of the building. As she dismounted, she noticed a number of garden tools hanging on one wall. Grabbing a shovel, she went back outside and began chipping away the snow and ice from the base of the door she'd opened. She planned to close it before heading for the house, and she could only hope that it would open again if she had to leave in a hurry.

One at a time, she rolled the big doors closed. Then she opened a smaller passage door next to the barn doors. Returning to her snowmobile, she awakened Michael and helped him off the rear seat, then gently lifted her sleeping daughter into her arms. She held Mary in one arm, her head resting against her shoulder, then took her son's hand, and they went out through the passage door and started through the darkness toward the house. She breathed a prayer that she would be able to find the structure in the blowing snow and wouldn't miss her goal. She'd read stories of people who'd gotten lost in blizzards, and were later found frozen to death just a few feet from their front doors.

Chris was peering into the darkness when all of a sudden she found herself bathed in an intense light. A man's shout was heard above the roar of the wind.

"All right. Walk slowly toward me and don't make any sudden moves. I'm holding a shotgun, and I won't miss."

In her fatigue, Chris was shocked to find herself giggling. It all seemed so surreal.

The wind must have been favorable to carry the sound of her giggling to the man, because the light was quickly turned aside. He must have been satisfied that a woman with two small children didn't pose any particular danger. His light now illuminated a strange door, its surface identical to that of the siding on the house, and she realized that it had been built to be nearly indiscernible once it was closed.

When he told her to follow him through in, she recognized his voice. It was the older of the two farmers who had helped her escape from the inn.

What was his name? Kennedy? Kenzy? Yes, that was it! Pastor Jack Kenzy, she remembered. *He must have beaten us here by racing cross country,* she thought. *On the other hand, I drove so slowly that an amateur would have outdistanced me. One thing's certain; he didn't follow the same route, or I'd have seen his lights when he passed me.*

He led them into some sort of a mud room, and Chris became busy brushing the snow off her daughter's snowsuit. When he turned to her, she told him that she wished he had been guiding her through the storm.

"I would have, but I didn't want the Chinese to suspect that I was involved in your escape, and I needed to make a stop along the way." He didn't explain the purpose of that stop, but she suspected it wasn't to pick up a loaf of bread and a dozen eggs.

While she was taking off the children's boots, he took a moment to explain how they had disguised their home. He told her that he'd actually trashed this farmhouse in order to fool the Chinese and their sympathizers into thinking it was vacant. He explained that there was little danger of anyone else occupying the house. Countless structures were vacant as a result of the war.

As she'd already seen, he had left the front door wide open, hanging crookedly from just one hinge. He told her that he'd also broken many of the window panes out of the frames, removed or destroyed furniture, and generally created the look of a house that had been pillaged. It was his hope to give it the appearance of an abandoned and worthless derelict. He even kept all but one of the inside doors ajar to promote the illusion that the house held nothing of value.

The one exception was an interior door that connected the old kitchen with this wing of the house. He had hidden that passage door by securely fastening a large old cupboard over the front of it. Now this small wing served as their home, and it had just this one well-disguised outside door.

As Jack Kenzy showed her around, she thought, *This is a very clever man.* Then she had a second thought. Perhaps that's why he is still alive and not slaving away in a Chinese labor camp.

Kim Ling's Politics

Headquarters, People's Liberation Army
Burlington, Vermont
Christmas Eve

In Kim Ling's mind, the general's monologue somehow took on the steady cadence of a drummer tapping out time to the shrieks and groans of the storm that raged outside.

He looked from the general's eyes to the frost-rimed window behind him, and was unable to penetrate the dark violence hidden behind either of them, neither the storm within nor the storm without.

With every word the general spoke, Kim was increasingly amazed at how obtuse and even stupid the Chinese military planners had shown themselves to be.

No! he thought. *Perhaps not stupid, but all too human. Human and sunk in depravity and sin. Human — but without hope or solace because they rejected the Truth.*

Just in time, he caught himself starting to shake his head in denial as the general ranted against all those that he claimed opposed him. Then the general began boasting that he possessed a better understanding of Americans because he had attended college in the United States. Kim nodded in indifference, and the general smiled. The general liked people who agreed with him.

He went on to mock the Chinese war planners in Beijing who had spent only a month or two in the United States as tourists, but somehow had come to believe that they were experts on the American culture. Eng laughed, and Kim found himself joining him.

The general was just warming up. "Attending state dinners and rock concerts, visiting theme parks, and pirating ideas from manufacturing plants or military installations does not mean that a person understands a country," he argued.

"As a matter of fact," the general continued, "it was almost impossible to leap the culture gap that existed between a faltering

America and our enlightened and disciplined China. America had lost whatever it might have called its moral compass, while China had a vision to become the most productive and powerful nation on earth. America boasted of its cultural diversity, while China sought racial purity. Even in their race for electoral votes, many American politicians exploited the races by setting them against one another, while China tolerated no activities which might undermine her strength."

"Right," Kim said. "If any of your college students, factory workers, or religious groups sought more freedom, you simply imprisoned and tortured their leaders or staged a Tiananmen Square massacre."

The general's smile abruptly vanished.

"Those students brought that on themselves," he retorted, glaring at him, and Kim wouldn't have been surprised if he suddenly picked up his pistol and shot him. But he felt emboldened, and nevertheless persisted.

"That's what I said," he laughed. Then he went off on a tangent.

"Many nations had ambitions to seize the United States," the general began, "but we and the Russians actually planned to invade. It turned out that we were fools, confused and blinded by events that seemed to be controlled by a mind far more clever than those of any of our leaders."

He had his attention now. Kim wouldn't ordinarily have any interest in the general's opinion of the causes of the war. They were, after all, long since caught up in the consequences, and they had to make the best of it, but it was the general's remark about a mind far more clever that caught his attention.

"We were all thinking of military and economic power," he mused, "but somehow the execution of our plans meant very little in the grand scheme of things." Then he was silent, the smoke drifting around him in a cloud, nearly as nebulous and impenetrable as whatever he was suggesting.

"It was the Islamic radicals that shifted the balance of power," he suddenly suggested. "And we didn't even realize it was happening." Another puff on the cigarette and another hiatus in the conversation.

"Maybe they didn't." He tipped his head to the side to see whether Kim was listening, then went on. "That's why, if I believed in the possibility of an all-knowing, all-seeing, all-powerful deity, I would attribute what was happening to him."

"Whether they knew it or not," the general went on, "the Muslims turned the concept of modern warfare on its head. In every major war in history, it was a matter of going head to head, bringing to bear the most expeditious mix of men and materiel, the best tactical and strategic approaches. In most cases, the goal was to control land masses and populations, regardless of their beliefs. But things changed."

After a long silence, Kim said, "I don't understand."

The general ignored his comment.

"It was the Muslims," he finally said. "They had the brilliant idea." They didn't infiltrate; they emigrated, and undermined from within!"

Kim shook his head slightly, not understanding, but the general didn't notice.

"In retrospect, it's laughable," the general said.

"I don't understand," Kim repeated.

They played upon the generosity and so-called openminded nature of their hosts.

The Russians were fighting Muslim majorities in former subject states along their own borders, while attempting to bargain with Muslim states in the Mideast. They thought they could somehow deal with these people on a political, military, and economic level."

"And?"

The general's laugh was almost a bark. "The Muslim idealists had a religious objective, and everything they did, either individually or collectively, was intended to secure that objective."

"I see that," Kim said.

"Their agenda is to convert everyone in the world to their religion," the general said. "You Americans have a quaint old word for dying. What is it? Ah, yes. *Croak.*

Kim looked at him quizzically.

"The Muslim message to the infidels in the world was, *Convert or Croak.*"

Kim thought that the laugh that followed was disturbing – bordering on insanity.

"I don't get your point."

"Be patient," the general snapped.

He puffed on his cigarette, and held the smoke in as though drawing inspiration from the toxins.

Canada

Russians

New Brunswick

Quebec

Maine

Vermont

New Hampshire

Atlantic Ocean

New York

Massachusetts

Boston

RI

Connecticutt

New York City

Chinese

Radical Islam

New England Invasion Routes

"We Chinese, along with the Russians, had our own game plans. We made alliances and created treaties with various nations — including one another — with the intention of breaking each and every one as conditions dictated. When war started, you Americans didn't even realize that we had a nuclear arsenal, much less the capacity to delivery the payloads. We were nonetheless able to target missiles all over the world, including many to Europe and the United States. But we knew that the Russians were massing most of their troops on their eastern border with China as well as along the narrow border that lies between Kazakhstan and Mongolia. So we had nearly a million men massed along those same borders to repel the Soviets and to counter-attack."

Kim Ling listened with growing interest.

"The Russians, of course, had many armored divisions ready to sweep across Eastern Europe, with the plan that they would ultimately take France and Germany. That left them with very few troops to enter the United States. We too only had a few thousand troops ready to enter New England, but we thought it might be enough. The Russians planned to have their troops wait in Canada while our attack was hopefully blunted by the remains of the America military."

The general laughed.

"And this is when things began to go awry, and you, Kim Ling, almost caused me to believe in your God."

Again he tilted his head to stare at Kim.

"No comment? All right. While the major powers had been planning their little war games, those eternal enemies, your God and your devil may have had their own battle going on, and they were working through the Muslims and Jews who had their own problems. The Israelis were basically in a defensive mode, particularly after the US began to turn away from them and coddle their Middle Eastern enemies, especially Iran. But when Iran finally sent two nuclear warheads at Israel, the Jews still had a few tricks up their sleeves and somehow diverted and destroyed them."

Kim knew nothing of this, and remained silent in the hope of learning more.

"But by then," the general continued, "millions of refugees from the Middle eastern states had already "emigrated" to Europe, particularly Germany, France, Austria, and even Turkey. They already had a large presence in these countries."

"Are you saying that this was intentional?" Kim asked.

"For the most part, these were young men, and they weren't immigrants; they were invaders."

Kim was stunned.

"I don't know why you Westerners didn't see this coming," Eng told him. "It should have been obvious. What was ironic was that the European nations and the United States contributed billions of dollars to help these people settle in their countries. Couldn't they see that many of these people were trained terrorists, equipped, and waiting for the signal to attack? And attack they did. Their goal was to terrorize the public in numerous countries, and they did so by burning cars in the streets, murdering religious leaders, and attempting to take over the military bases. And it might have worked, leaving them in control of most of Western and Central Europe. But, again ironically, most of these holy warriors died from the nuclear fallout, leaving the West in complete disorder and confusion, and everybody the loser."

"And that's pretty much what happened here, isn't it?" Kim said, but it was an observation, not a question.

"And that's pretty much what happened here," Eng agreed.

"But I don't understand why you joked about almost believing," Kim said.

"That's easy enough to explain. When I was in college, I took the prescribed comparative religion course. It's clear now that the syllabus was prepared by atheists with an agenda, and very effectively guided us students through a slanted program to make us sneer at religion. Since it was pretty much what I'd heard all my life in China, it was easy enough to accept. But now...."

"But now, what?"

The general was silent for a moment.

"But now, when I see how matters appear to have fallen out, how I see the malice of the Muslims toward the Jews, how some of the Jews have been amazingly preserved, I am tempted to look at this as a war between light and darkness, good and evil, and I cannot find any other rationale for explaining the way things are going."

"So?"

"So." He seemed to be thinking it through. "So I am a Chinese general, and what I see now is world-wide confusion and suffering."

"And you plan to do something about it?"

"I have concluded that someone will arise, a powerful leader, who will take control."

"And?"

"And I want him to be Chinese."

"So you don't think it's a battle between good and evil?"

"Actually, I doubt it. But I will remain where my loyalties lie, and that is where I shall center my efforts."

"Not on the side of what you called the *light* and the *good*?"

The general looked befuddled for a moment, then took Kim's meaning, but instead of pointing his gun at him, he began to roll with laughter. He tried to point a finger at Kim, but he was shaking with mirth.

"Those are empty concepts, passing fancies."

Kim looked sad, but didn't respond.

"And the innocent people in America, and around the world?"

Kim looked sad, but didn't respond.

"And the innocent people in America and around the world?"

"There are no innocents. Everyone had done evil. Everyone deserves death!"

Now it was time for Kim to laugh, but he held back. *Eng just paraphrased Paul's words in Romans 3:23,* he thought.

Kim had long since concluded that Americans had been compounding their collective sins for so long that it was inevitable that a righteous God must sooner or later have to judge the nation. *Love and long suffering are one thing,* he thought, *but righteous God must balance his love with justice.*

Those who had built the country, who had fought her wars, built her economy, practiced their religion, and sought to improve her character, were in the minority, and those were in power had suddenly been overwhelmed by a flood of immigrants who brought far different political and religious philosophies to America's shores.

There were too many of them, and they insisted that their own beliefs and traditions should not only be respected, but should be held superior. Instead of being assimilated into society, they became the tail that wagged the dog. They became huge voting blocks who were exploited by those politicians who held their own selfish short term interests, and not those of historic America.

As a result, Kim had concluded that the nation was divided between materialists who were focused on their own pleasures, and numerous groups with diverse agendas, including those who wanted to overturn the government and make everyone submit to whatever religion or philosophy they practiced.

But things are different now, Kim believed. *Many of these people are dead. And the horrors of this war have brought home to the survivors the preciousness of the liberties that they had surrendered. And even those Americans who once rejected Christianity or questioned the value of the U.S. Constitution, have begun searching for the God who they now realize is the fountainhead of freedom.*

The bottom line is that the Chinese and Russian leaders have no understanding or appreciation of any political-economic-religious system apart from their own. And in spite of the fact that many of them have visited the United States, they remain blind to reality. All the time that they lived in America, they continued to think as though they could impose their despotic system of government on this society and achieve the same economic results.

Kim turned to the general. "With all due respect, general, you live in a philosophical box. You are incapable of entertaining any ideas but your own because you've been brainwashed since childhood. You believe that the harsh and narrow strictures under which you live are the proper norm for the entire world, even though you know that those limits are unfair, inequitable, and often infuriating. You have the audacity to insist that a loss of personal freedom is necessary to the achievement of your so-called ideal society, but like every would-be dictator you want that loss of freedom to be restricted to others than yourself. You would be very unhappy if it affected you. That's your problem," he continued. "Yours is the argument that the individual must be sacrificed for the good of the masses, while, in contrast, Americans once embraced the concept that the rights of the individual must be protected."

The general laughed. "I like you, Ling. You've got guts! None of my men would dare challenge me like that. And to show you that I mean it, I'm not going to kill you."

Kim laughed too. He was almost, but not quite, indifferent to the threat. "I'll tell you something else, general. You're going to lose this war because your men don't dare challenge your authority, and you wouldn't listen if they did."

"We've as good as won already," the general retorted. "The Americans are broken!"

"Oh, really?" Kim said. "Well, I've been shot at many times while flying your helicopters."

"So, Kim Ling, you think there is still fight left in the Americans?"

"General, I think there is victory in the Americans."

"And where do you stand, Kim Ling?"

Kim stood to his feet, a broad smile on his face. "Why, general, I stand right here."

The ambiguity of his reply delighted the general. He hadn't enjoyed a conversation so much in years. Lighting yet another ciga-

rette, he stared at the window behind his desk. Each man was en-
grossed in his own thoughts, and after a moment Kim sat back down.

The truth is, Kim thought, *that the Chinese are unable to comprehend what freedom is, let alone why anyone who has tasted the
heady wine of independence is unwilling to surrender it in exchange
for any brand of totalitarian slavery. The reason I grudgingly began
working for Eng was because he was blackmailing me. He doesn't
know that he's lost that leverage or that I'm continuing to work for
him for far different reasons.*

*Initially, Eng had no doubt that I would work for them, evi-
dently because their records indicated that my family was of noble
Chinese ancestry. Fortunately, any reference to the fact that my ancestors actually resisted communism in China during the 1930s and
40s has somehow been lost. Otherwise I'd probably be dead.*

Kim's grandfather had served as an interpreter for General
Claire Chennault, leader of the AVG, the famed *Flying Tigers,* who
fought against the Japanese just prior to America's entry into World
War II. Toward the end of that war, he was sent to China to work
with an old friend and dedicated Baptist missionary named Birch.
The missionary spoke fluent Chinese and had been recruited by
Chennault as a lieutenant in the U.S. Fourteenth Air Force, but was
later seconded as a spy to the super-secret Office of Strategic Services, forerunner of the CIA. Birch insisted that, as a matter of faith,
he would continue his service as a missionary while spying for the
OSS.

When Birch and Kim Ling's grandfather were on a mission to
free captives from a Japanese prison camp near Xi'an, members of
the communist Chinese People's Liberation Army murdered the
lieutenant. John Birch was shot to death ten days after the Japanese
surrender in August, 1945, making him arguably the first martyr of
communism at the close of World War II. He was awarded the Dis-
tinguished Service Medal.

Fortunately, America's Chinese invaders knew nothing of the anti-communist activities of Ling's ancestors, and Kim, who was proud of his Christian heritage, wasn't about to tell them. The communists, on the other hand, weren't so naive as to rely on the loyalty of those they conscripted. In order to be assured that every recruit would loyally serve them, they had, wherever possible, imprisoned wives and children, using them as hostages.

Kim Ling hid his feelings well as he went about his duties. The Chinese around him knew that he was a married man and might well be a loyal American, so they felt uncomfortable around him, having to guard their tongues at every moment. None of them regretted the fact that he absented himself from their gatherings.

Ling went quietly about his own work, making the occasional flight when ordered, but continually aware that he was being shadowed. He'd been given an "assistant," but he held no illusions about the role this man really played. He was a brute, and it was obvious to Kim that he was there to keep an eye on Kim and even terminate his life if he considered it necessary.

Kim had longed for the moment when the general might call upon him to fly him somewhere — anywhere! He imagined himself crashing his helicopter in some remote area, sacrificing his own life in order to put an end to the life of the general. And though that seemed a paltry trade off for the loss of his family, he reasoned that the general's death would at least demoralize and cripple the effectiveness of the invaders. If he could cut off the serpent's head, perhaps the dragon would die.

In his planning, Kim Ling had scoured topographical maps of the area and had marked out heavily forested places at all four points of the compass, places where it would be difficult for searchers to find his copter if he dumped it. He was never, however, to fulfill his wish. Shortly after Kim had learned of his wife's fate, the general had changed his policy, only allowing his Chinese pilot to fly him places. It seemed clear to Kim that the general was taking no chances and had pre-empted any possible act of revenge.

Kim had been assigned the use of the older of the two helicopters in what he privately thought of as *The Chinese Communist
Air Force*. Two other copters had been shot down by unknown
marksmen who freely roamed the forests to the east of Lake Champlain. The general was enraged that his own men could not capture
or kill these civilians. In fact, he was now forced to keep his troops
out of the mountains because they had proven to be easy prey for the
American sharp shooters.

The copter that Ling flew was an ancient Enstrom F28A. Kim
found it to be a real workhorse in spite of its age. Powered by a Ly-
coming 205-horsepower piston engine, it cruised at nearly a hundred miles an hour. It seated Ling and one passenger, generally his
personal shadow.

Ling realized that any further opportunities to fly alone were
unlikely. He nevertheless prepared for such an occasion. Someone
had inexplicably mounted a life-preserver in a plastic bag beneath
the pilot's seat in his copter. Kim removed the life-preserver from its
canvas bag and replaced it with items he'd filched from the Chinese,
items that might prove useful if he survived an opportunity to escape. These included a couple of freeze-dried meals, three plastic
bottles of drinking water, a mylar space blanket, a box of matches, a
first-aid kit, and an LED flashlight. His greatest find was a 45 caliber
ACP pistol with two clips and eighteen rounds of ammunition that
he found in a dusty shoe box in a storeroom. He now carried this
with him.

When his burly shadow left the hangar to visit the outhouse,
Ling thought he might have just enough time to stuff his improvised
survival pack back under the pilot's seat, and had just begun to stuff
the unwanted life-preserver in a trash can when he heard someone
rolling back the door of the barn that served as their hangar. Kim
Ling had just enough time to turn to a workbench and pick up a tool
before the other pilot, Feng Jiang, saw him. The first words out of
his mouth indicated the contempt he felt for Ling.

"Ah, I see you are trying to keep this ancient piece of junk in the air."

Ling knew that he should not let this man bait him, and had told himself that he should avoid any arguments, but he got under his skin, and he was unable to let this slight go unanswered.

"This copter may be older than you are," he said with a smile, "but it was so popular that Enstrom was still building a similar model right up until the day the war began."

Feng Jiang smirked, but Ling persisted.

"It has an impressive cruising speed and gets about nine miles per gallon," he said evenly.

"Humph," was the only reply, so Ling went on. He knew that he had to be careful of this man, and he didn't want this to turn into an ugly confrontation, but he wanted to rub in one more thought. "Once I set the trim, it will remain stable even if I remove my hands and feet from the controls."

The response he got was wholly unexpected, and made Kim Ling realize that he might have overplayed his hand.

"Ah, then perhaps I should request this machine for my own use."

Ling thought quickly, realizing that Feng Jiang could undoubtedly get the general to assign him this aircraft.

"Yes, I'm sure you can, and I wouldn't mind at all," Ling lied. "On the other hand, the general prefers the more comfortable seats in your craft, and since it's faster, quieter, and has a greater weight-carrying capacity, I suspect he'll continue to use it for his personal flights."

"Ah, there is that," the other pilot responded, realizing that he might gain a copter and lose his status as the general's personal pilot. "Well," he replied imperiously, "I shall give it some thought."

"You do that," Ling smiled agreeably. "I'll be ready to swap on an instant's notice."

"Yes," the other man rejoined. "But I'll want to give this a thorough going-over before I take it up. To make certain it is reliable."

"An excellent idea," replied Ling, "as I will certainly wish to do with the aircraft you've been flying."

The other man glared at him.

"One of these days, Ling, you will overstep yourself. I am watching you, and when the right time comes, I will act." Then he spun around and left the barn.

Chris Meets the Kenzys

The Kenzy Farm
East of Butter Creek, Vermont
Christmas Eve

The Kenzys had shown Chris and the children great kindness during their stopover at their farm. From the moment the Kenzys had welcomed them into their secret hideaway, they had rushed about trying to make them comfortable. Their brief visit, however, provided little more than enough time to have something to eat, thaw out their frozen fingers, and regain a little of their waning strength before heading back out into the blizzard.

Now that Chris was again coasting along on the snowmobile through wind-whipped snow, it seemed almost like a dream, and she found herself reliving the precious moments with the Kenzys as a means of staying awake. It seemed strange to her that she felt more exhausted now than before their visit. The fact that she was once again bouncing along through the blizzard on the snowmobile was not improving her state of mind either. *It's the fatigue,* she thought. *That and the stress.*

But thinking about their brief visit seemed to reduce her stress, and she found herself smiling at the memories. The Kenzys' cozy little makeshift home had a strange charm. Her senses had been nearly overwhelmed. The rustic ceiling, with the flickering candles dimly illuminating the 19th Century hand-hewn beams, had captivated her and the children. But the combined odors of evergreen boughs, the damp clothing drying by the fire, and the baking bread, somehow transported her back to happier times.

After Abigail Kenzy had helped her strip off the children's snowsuits, she had hung the wet garments up to dry. And while her husband wrapped each of the children in a warm blanket and sat them down in front of the open door of the wood stove, she began dishing up something hot for them to eat. Within minutes they were spooning down corn chowder and crusty homemade bread slathered with real butter. The chowder even contained pieces of chicken, something they hadn't tasted in a year. While they began to wolf down that simple but delicious meal, Mrs. Kenzy insisted, "Please call me Abigail!"

Perhaps because she considered it important, or perhaps just to make conversation, she informed them that her husband Jack had not only been a successful farmer, but was also the local pastor. And while she filled the conversational void, Chris experienced a little shame because the three of them were wolfing down the Kenzys' precious food. In this post-war world they were enjoying what was a rare feast by any measure. Yet, ashamed or not, she found it impossible to restrain herself. At that moment, she was convinced that she'd never tasted anything more delicious. Even her daughter, always a picky eater, was devouring the meal.

When Chris realized that she was wiping the bottom of her bowl with the last piece of bread, she looked up in embarrassment, only to discover her hostess smiling at her in understanding. Then, suddenly, Chris felt tears well up in her eyes. It had been so long since anyone had shown them any kindness.

Abigail put her arm around her shoulder and whispered, "It's okay, honey. We understand." And, for the moment, Chris believed that they really did.

Then Chris discovered that she was having a difficult time keeping her eyes open. Perhaps it was the warmth after the cold, the food after the hunger, or the love after the loneliness, but she realized that a strange lassitude was overtaking her and she had to struggle to keep her eyes open. So many wonderful things had happened in the past few hours, especially the unbelievable sighting of her husband. True, he had been a captive, but she now knew that he'd survived an entire year. He was still alive!

The last time Chris had seen her husband was prior to the outbreak of war, when he was leaving home for Chicago on a business trip. Now, after months of uncertainty, she had actually seen him, and even though he had been held captive, she had been thrilled beyond words. She realized that if she hadn't been preoccupied with keeping the children quiet, she might have leapt from the car and given their relationship away.

In spite of the fact that he hadn't seen either her or the children in the dark interior of the SUV, her joy was little diminished. Even after he'd disappeared from sight, she had to struggle to keep herself and the children from giving their relationship away.

Then, just a short time later, she learned that her husband had somehow escaped from those same captors, and she was almost giddy with relief. Finally, when this man and his friend helped her and the children escape, it seemed by far the best Christmas Eve she'd ever experienced.

Considering her fatigue and the stresses she was bearing, however, her euphoria could only carry her so far. By the time she had reached the Kenzy farm, she was nearly at the end of herself.

She owed a lot to Pastor Kenzy and the other man who had assisted them in their escape, but by the time she and the children had finished eating, she wanted nothing more than to lie down and sleep. At the same time, an anxious voice within her seemed to be warning that neither she nor her husband were yet safe, and this sense of disquiet kept her on edge.

To make things worse, Pastor Kenzy had begun hinting that she and her children would be unable to remain with them very long, and he had outright warned that their enemies were probably already on her trail.

And sure enough, here she was, back in the darkness and the blowing snow, with her two kids nestled precariously on the back of the snowmobile. Her daydreaming was interrupted when the machine slid up over some unseen obstruction beneath the snow, and she had to wrench the handlebars to keep it from flipping over. Regaining control, she wanted to shed her fears, so she returned her thoughts to the pleasant warmth of the Kenzys' kitchen.

She remembered noticing a spruce tree standing in the corner. It was strung with popcorn, and the light from a gas lantern had been reflected back in a dazzling array of colors by the glass ornaments. Following her gaze, Abigail Kenzy had smiled.

"It's not the sort of Christmas Eve that we're used to, is it?"

The children had turned to see what had attracted the adults' attention, and with yelps of delight they discarded their empty bowls and covered the distance to the dark corner of the room in a matter of seconds. Then they were standing beneath the tree's boughs, staring rapturously up at the pinnacle where a golden angel, trump in hand, seemed to be looking down protectively on them from its place of primacy.

Chris broke the silence. "With the Chinese forcing us to work seven days a week, and with no means to keep track of time, I'd forgotten that it's Christmas Eve." They could hear the sadness enter her voice. "There wasn't a single Christmas decoration at that tavern."

"It's an abomination that all Christian holidays have been outlawed," the pastor said, making no effort to hide his bitterness. "We have been invaded by three nations – the communists from China and Russia, plus the self-described defenders of the *One True Faith*. They're competing with one another to rule America, and the only policy that they have in common is that there is to be no reminder of the existence of Judaism or Christianity — not anywhere, not any time."

Chris didn't seem to hear him, but instead remarked wistfully, "The children will miss it."

Her son had turned and smiled at her. "It's okay, Mom."

She smiled at him and, for just an instant, her eyes sparkled. "I'm so proud of you, Michael."

"Are you proud of me too, Mommy?"

"Of course I am, Mary. I'm proud of both of you."

Pastor Kenzy crossed the room, knelt down, and put out his hand.

"Your name is Michael?"

"Yes, sir."

"How old are you, Mike?"

"It's Michael," he corrected him, "and I'm eleven."

"Oh, excuse me," the pastor replied, suppressing his smile. "Okay, Michael it is!"

The boy had turned to face his sister. "And this is my little sister Mary. She's only eight," he added, a touch of disdain in his voice."

"Well, Michael, eight-year old girls like your sister Mary have a way of growing up very quickly." The pastor grimaced. It occurred to him that such an observation might have been appropriate a year or two earlier, but not any more. Countless boys and girls would never grow up at all because they had already perished, and many more were likely to, including perhaps this beautiful child. He said nothing more, but the other adults understood only too well what was going through his mind.

Although only eleven, Michael surprised them by seeming to read their thoughts. He hugged Mary to him. "I'm going to take care of my sister so that she can grow up just the way she should," he said. Then he added, "And I'm going to make sure we have a Christmas tree at our house every year."

The two seemingly disparate declarations brought a chuckle of appreciation from the adults.

"Well, we have to celebrate Christmas in a different way this year," Chris had said, "but we already have the most important thing."

"What's that, Mom?"

"Just as the birth of Jesus brought hope into a world full of hatred and suffering, we can take even greater comfort from the fact that the grown-up and resurrected Jesus continues to offer help for today and hope for tomorrow."

"And to everyone who believes on his name, right Mom?" Michael asked, "just like it says in John 3:16."

The pastor laughed. "That's right, Michael," he agreed. It had been a long time since he'd heard a youngster say something like that!

Abigail laughed. "I thought my husband was the speaker here, but that's pretty good preaching!

Chris, warmed by both the fire and their kindness, relaxed. She stared off into infinity. "How does that old song go?" she whispered, then answered her own question: *"Help for today and bright hope for tomorrow...."*

She hummed a bar or two, then in a sweet soprano voice she sang, *Great is thy faithfulness, Lord unto me."*

They were all silent for a moment.

"Those words are wonderfully appropriate on a cold Christmas Eve," the pastor's wife observed.

"Great is His faithfulness!" agreed the pastor in a somber voice. And then he dropped the other shoe. "...but the old saying is still true — *God helps those who help themselves.*"

"But?" Chris asked. Her anticipation of bad news was obvious in that single word that seemed infused with fear.

"The Lord is requiring us to do things differently until we get rid of these invaders," he replied sadly. His words set her teeth on edge.

"Differently?" she asked.

"Such as," he said, "we shouldn't have this wood stove going. Perhaps no one can see the smoke in this blizzard, but they might smell it."

"Well, I guess we'll have to put it out for a few hours," Chris suggested.

"I'm afraid things are a lot worse than that," he said. "In your case," he continued remorselessly, "I think that an old-fashioned nighttime sleigh ride on a super-modern snowmobile is just the thing for this particular Christmas Eve."

She looked at him with something like dread in her eyes, but he didn't relent.

She didn't like his speaking about a midnight sleigh ride in the midst of a blizzard. She was tired, and the kids were worn out from long months of hunger and hard work. Her mind raced back over the past year. She and the children had left their modest but comfortable home in Black River Junction, and arrived at her father's farm just in time to learn that the United States was under attack. They'd spent the next two weeks in the root cellar that had been carved into the hill behind their farmhouse, surviving on canned fruits and vegetables, and paying the price with unpleasant digestive problems.

Somehow Chris had gotten through the next few months, though she never learned until that night that her husband had survived. When the Chinese had arrived at her own Dad's farm to conduct a census. She and the children had been taken into custody, while her folks had been left alone to grow food for the invaders. Her own interrogation had been perfunctory, and she had rehearsed the children so that they were able to hide their true identities from their inquisitor. As a result, they had been sent together to a large communal farm to work in the fields, cultivating and harvesting crops. Chris never understood why they weren't left with her parents to help them.

And in spite of the fact that the harvest was a good one, the laborers suffered continual hunger, and the specter of starvation hung over them. Their captors had begun bribing the workers with promises of additional rations in exchange for information about their fellow internees. Just a few days before Christmas, someone had reported that Chris might be important. She and her two children were immediately locked up, and two days later they were loaded into an SUV and driven north through Vermont toward Burlington.

Their driver had been a bit puffed up with the importance of his mission, and she was able to get him to tell her where they were going. She was shocked and frightened to learn that they were being taken to see the commanding general. It implied that the Chinese really did know who her husband was and probably thought she could be forced to divulge his location. She and the children were scheduled to reach Burlington at 2400 hours on the evening of 25 December, but the unplowed roads became impassable, and their driver had just managed to get them as far as Butter Creek Tavern.

They had been parked in front of the tavern in the dark — the SUV's motor running and its headlights on — while their guard went inside to seek accommodations. Chris had been adjusting her daughter's coat when her son, standing in the open window, elbowed her excitedly. She didn't rebuke him because she didn't want to attract anyone's attention, but her eyes followed his pointing finger. She moved to the window just in time to see a group of men dragging someone out the front door of the tavern and past their window. She saw the man's face in the reflection of their headlights, and her heart seemed to stop. It looked like her husband, and she had to shush Michael so that he didn't give away their secret.

Conflicting thoughts and confused emotions had swept over her like waves crashing on a beach. She was thrilled to see her husband, but broken-hearted that she could neither let him know that they were alive, nor offer him assistance.

And now she knew that they had all escaped their captors. True, they had gone in different directions. True, he wasn't aware that they were alive. But they were all alive! At least for the time being.

We've been through more than enough, she thought. *We've been deprived of sufficient sleep and food for months. We're mentally and physically exhausted, and our clothes and our bodies are filthy.*

Chris wanted nothing more in the world than a bath and a bed. She didn't want to face the stress of further snowmobiling. Yet, she couldn't deny the pastor's words.

"The Lord is requiring us to do things differently until we get rid of these invaders."

There was nothing in his words that was unkind or spiteful. He was just stating the facts. And she really did appreciate his offhand remark about getting rid of the invaders. It was the first time she had heard anyone express the thought that they might ultimately drive these vermin from their land. And while she considered that possibility remote, it still brought a hint of a smile to her lips.

CC's Dismal Christmas

Hidden Valley, Vermont
Christmas Morning, 2:30 a.m.

When CC finally pushed his way through the last drift and stumbled onto the dry floor of the cavern, his flashlight batteries were almost drained. Rachel and Jonathan were close behind him, their clothing and hair matted with snow, their faces beginning to suffer the effects of frostbite. Hoping for something hot to drink and for his own warm bed, CC was totally unprepared for what met his gaze.

The contrast was startling. They'd stepped out of the roaring wind and blowing snow into the shelter of the cave's entrance. His eyes were inflamed by the glare of the flashlight reflecting off the blowing snow, so he thought at first that it was snow blindness that made the beam from his flashlight appear to be swallowed up in the darkness. But then they all began to choke on something acrid. It took just seconds for them to realize that the cave was filled with thick, evil smelling smoke that threatened to suffocate them.

CC found himself on his knees, fighting for air, he was coughing so violently that he was seeing stars. The events of the past twenty-four hours swept unbidden across CC's thoughts like some weird painting. There were slashes of flake white alternating with serpentine stripes of cobalt black, moments of glaring self-awareness and eye-popping truth, interspersed with near-terminal periods of impenetrable terror.

He thought of the ups and downs of the past day. Jonathan and Sarah had wanted him to remain here and celebrate Christmas with them, but he had left them in tears because he preferred to seek out some adult conversation and maybe a good meal in a friendly environment. But these hoped-for pleasures had turned to ashes. Unexpected enemies had literally locked him away in frigid darkness. That was followed by a miraculous escape — the result of these two companions putting their lives on the line for him. Now they were trusting him with their lives, and were in danger of perishing because of his failure. They'd reached the hoped-for safety of his cave. And now this!

He could almost see the painter's brush sweeping across the canvas. Black stripe, white stripe, black stripe!

His eyes were burning from the smoke, but he was able to see that all three of them were bent over, choking from the fumes that filled the cave, trying to clear their lungs. He swung his free hand to the side, striking Jonathan.

"C'mon," he choked, and began crawling backward toward the cave entrance. The woman had already turned toward the opening, and the three of them made their way back out into the bitter cold.

As they knelt together, trying to expel the poisons from their lungs, he was trying to clear his mind. Unable to deal with what he faced right now, he was thinking back to his arrest at the inn.

What was that all about? Why would the Chinese be after me? As far as I know, I've done them no harm, and they should have no special reason to hunt me down.

He remembered his captor's excitement as they examined that wanted poster.

Maybe they believe that they do have reason to pursue me, but I don't know why. Maybe I shouldn't be surprised. I can only remember back just one year. It's funny, he thought. *I thought I was starting over. I thought the past didn't matter anymore. Well, if the Chinese are my enemies, I guess I couldn't have been all bad.*

He looked at the other two to see how they were doing. Their coughing was not so violent now.

We sure didn't improve our relationship with the Chinese, he thought. *The fact is that we left two of their men lying unconscious in the snow, and they can't be happy with that. And that woman I saw? It appears that they don't like her much either.*

Jonathan shouted to gain his attention, and CC turned to see him pointing toward the far end of the cave. The smoke didn't seem as thick now, and CC realized that the high winds were helping to dissipate it.

He blinked to clear the tears from his eyes and squinted toward the back wall. The remains of a wood fire smoldered against the artificial wall he'd built to close off this outer cave and to camouflage the cavern beyond. It was the choking odor of burnt paint and charred fiberglass that made the traumatic difference between the cave and the crisp winter air outside.

Jonathan wrapped a scarf around his nose and mouth to serve as a filter, and walked to the back of the cave where he shined his flashlight on the camouflaged wall. A hole had been melted through part of the fake partition. Worse, the hidden door was sprung open and twisted out of shape.

It was a disaster. Strangers had obviously stumbled onto their cave by accident, and moved inside to escape the storm. In an effort to keep warm, the interlopers had built a fire against the fake wall, then discovered the hidden entrance and made their way inside.

Little Sarah is in there, CC thought. *Oh, Lord, let her be okay.*

Jonathan was choking again when he returned from the cave. As the two of them observed CC's stricken face, Jonathan had a far better understanding than Rachel of the despair he was feeling. Sarah's life might be in danger, their secret hideaway was no longer secret, and their lives were at risk.

The Caverns

Hidden Valley, Vermont
Christmas Morning, 2:30 a.m.

When CC finally pushed his way through the last drift and stumbled onto the dry floor of the cavern, his flashlight batteries were almost drained. Rachel and Jonathan were close behind him, their clothing and hair matted with snow, their faces beginning to suffer the effects of frostbite. Hoping for something hot to drink and for his own warm bed, CC was totally unprepared for what met his gaze.

The contrast was startling. They'd stepped out of the roaring wind and blowing snow into the shelter of the cave's entrance. His eyes were inflamed by the glare of the flashlight reflecting off the blowing snow, so he thought at first that it was snow blindness that made the beam from his flashlight appear to be swallowed up in the darkness. But then they all began to choke on something acrid. It took just seconds for them to realize that the cave was filled with thick, evil smelling smoke that threatened to suffocate them.

CC found himself on his knees, fighting for air, he was coughing so violently that he was seeing stars. The events of the past twenty-four hours swept unbidden across CC's thoughts like some weird painting. There were slashes of flake white alternating with

serpentine stripes of cobalt black, moments of glaring self-awareness and eye-popping truth, interspersed with near-terminal periods
of impenetrable terror.

He thought of the ups and downs of the past day. Jonathan and
Sarah had wanted him to remain here and celebrate Christmas with
them, but he had left them in tears because he preferred to seek out
some adult conversation and maybe a good meal in a friendly environment. But these hoped-for pleasures had turned to ashes. Unexpected enemies had literally locked him away in frigid darkness. That
was followed by a miraculous escape — the result of these two companions putting their lives on the line for him. Now they were trusting him with their lives, and were in danger of perishing because of
his failure. They'd reached the hoped-for safety of his cave. And now
this!

He could almost see the painter's brush sweeping across the
canvas. Black stripe, white stripe, black stripe!

His eyes were burning from the smoke, but he was able to see
that all three of them were bent over, choking from the fumes that
filled the cave, trying to clear their lungs. He swung his free hand to
the side, striking Jonathan.

"C'mon," he choked, and began crawling backward toward the
cave entrance. The woman had already turned toward the opening,
and the three of them made their way back out into the bitter cold.

As they knelt together, trying to expel the poisons from their
lungs, he was trying to clear his mind. Unable to deal with what he
faced right now, he was thinking back to his arrest at the inn.

*What was that all about? Why would the Chinese be after me?
As far as I know, I've done them no harm, and they should have no
special reason to hunt me down.*

He remembered his captor's excitement as they examined that
wanted poster.

*Maybe they believe that they do have reason to pursue me, but
I don't know why. Maybe I shouldn't be surprised. I can only remember back just one year. It's funny,* he thought. *I thought I was*

starting over. I thought the past didn't matter anymore. Well, if the Chinese are my enemies, I guess I couldn't have been all bad.

He looked at the other two to see how they were doing. Their coughing was not so violent now.

We sure didn't improve our relationship with the Chinese, he thought. *The fact is that we left two of their men lying unconscious in the snow, and they can't be happy with that. And that woman I saw? It appears that they don't like her much either.*

Jonathan shouted to gain his attention, and CC turned to see him pointing toward the far end of the cave. The smoke didn't seem as thick now, and CC realized that the high winds were helping to dissipate it.

He blinked to clear the tears from his eyes and squinted toward the back wall. The remains of a wood fire smoldered against the artificial wall he'd built to close off this outer cave and to camouflage the cavern beyond. It was the choking odor of burnt paint and charred fiberglass that made the traumatic difference between the cave and the crisp winter air outside.

Jonathan wrapped a scarf around his nose and mouth to serve as a filter, and walked to the back of the cave where he shined his flashlight on the camouflaged wall. A hole had been melted through part of the fake partition. Worse, the hidden door was sprung open and twisted out of shape.

It was a disaster. Strangers had obviously stumbled onto their cave by accident, and moved inside to escape the storm. In an effort to keep warm, the interlopers had built a fire against the fake wall, then discovered the hidden entrance and made their way inside.

Little Sarah is in there, CC thought. *Oh, Lord, let her be okay.*

Jonathan was choking again when he returned from the cave. As the two of them observed CC's stricken face, Jonathan had a far better understanding than Rachel of the despair he was feeling. Sarah's life might be in danger, their secret hideaway was no longer secret, and their lives were at risk.

A Hurried Visit

The Kenzy Farm
East of Butter Creek, Vermont
Late Christmas Eve

Chris had been sitting there staring hypnotically at the glowing coals, when Abigail Kenzy held out a cup of real coffee.

Coffee was a very rare and precious commodity in war-torn America, and it was therefore incredibly generous of her. Then Abigail set a dish of maple sugar before her. "It's from our own trees!" she said proudly. She followed that with a pitcher containing fresh, thick cream that she proudly announced had come from their one remaining cow.

Chris stirred the mixture carefully, so that she wouldn't spill a single drop, then waited until no one was looking, and licked the spoon. Holding the cup beneath her chin, she let the fragrant steam rise around her. She breathed deeply, inhaling the aroma. Finally she began to sip it, taking time to savor every drop, trying to make it last.

How long has it been since I last had a cup of real coffee?" she wondered. *Not since that last morning at Dad's farm. The five of us were sitting at the wrought-iron table on their back porch, eating mom's homemade raisin toast, sipping the last of their coffee and watching the sun rise.* She remembered holding the porcelain cup in her hands while she tried to encourage her mother with a smile. *"It tastes wonderful,"* she remembered telling her, but even then she was wondering, *How long until any of us tastes real coffee again? Maybe never...."*

She found herself inexplicably giggling.

Abigail looked at her strangely, her eyebrows raised in question, and Chris couldn't help but quip, "And the condemned woman ate a hearty meal."

Abigail smiled in sympathy. "I suppose it is funny, in a macabre sort of way." Then she began coughing, and when perspiration appeared on her brow, the pastor put his arm around her, waiting for her to recover, his deep concern obvious.

When Abigail recovered, he helped seat her across the table from Chris, and the conversation became even more grave. The first words out of his mouth crushed her hopes for any opportunity to clean up a bit, let alone enjoy a warm place to spend the night.

"I am really sorry that you can't spend any time here," he told her.

"Oh, Jack," his wife interrupted in a husky whisper, her breath coming in gasps, "can't they at least stay the night?"

"I wish they could, honey, but this is not just their problem."

Their eyes met, and she nodded, acknowledging that matters must have become far more serious than she realized. Her husband was silent for a moment, evidently trying to find some easy way to break the news.

When he spoke, it was in a gentle voice, and he was looking into his wife's eyes.

"It's not just Chris and her children. You and I have to leave too, and we have get out of here as soon as possible."

"But, why?" Abigail asked, clearly shaken.

"Because," he answered, "the Chinese military leaders will be enraged when they discover that their quisling supporters in Butter Creek have allowed this woman and her two children to escape, let alone the fact that two other people also got away."

"But won't they consider those other two more important?" she persisted.

"It doesn't matter," he replied, resignation in his voice. "The dragnet they are about to spread may focus on that man, but it will just as likely snare all of us."

Abigail shook her head. "Jack, I just don't understand."

"In order to appease their Chinese masters, those American renegades will send out every turncoat they can muster to search for all of the escapees." He looked across at Chris.

"And that includes me and the children."

He nodded, and turned back to his wife, his expression unreadable. "And you and I will also be swept up in the search."

"I'm so sorry," Chris said quickly. "It never occurred to me that my escape would put you at risk."

"It doesn't matter," he replied. "We are to bear one another's burdens. Sometimes we are unable to anticipate the costs involved, and therefore we cannot weigh them. But even if we could, we would not back off from our godly obligations."

He cleared his throat. "When we help others, we are in a very real sense giving our time, our resources, maybe even our lives. Yet the Bible teaches that he that lends to the poor, gives to the Lord, and the Lord will somehow repay." And he looked meaningly at his wife, a sad smile of resignation on his face. "This may prove to be our last opportunity to lend to someone who is in need."

Chris stared at them, and realized that these were the kind of people that she and her husband would have valued as the greatest of human beings, and treasured as real friends.

"But we're not poor," Chris replied. She paused, and there was resignation in her voice. "I'm wrong. I guess we are poor, aren't we?"

"Oh, not in the sense that we usually think of poverty, as a matter of financial resources. That's relative. But at the moment you are impoverished in terms of safety, of shelter and the protection of the law."

"I see," she said, and started to ask another question, but the pastor wasn't about to take any more time for discussion.

"The bad guys are probably out searching right now. If not, they certainly will be by daybreak."

Chris smiled at his use of the phrase, "bad guys." If he'd used a more heavily-loaded idiom — such as enemy invaders, hired mercenaries or paid killers — it would tend to sap her waning courage. On the other hand, "bad guys," was certainly less frightening to the children; and, if she were completely honest with herself, it was easier for her to handle as well. She had been drifting again, and her mind had to race to catch up with his words.

"They will be searching for your snowmobile tracks, and unless enough snow has fallen to cover them, they will arrive here sooner rather than later."

With no bitterness in her voice, Chris suggested, "Maybe the kids and I should head back toward town. It might be better for us to be captured rather than running off somewhere in the blizzard, and then the *bad guys* wouldn't follow us here."

Kenzy stared at his wife. It was more like an examination. He was deeply concerned with her failure to recover from the flu, and was tempted to embrace the suggestion, but Abigail soon made it clear that she would have no part of it.

"There is no way in the world that we are going to let you willingly expose yourself to those vermin," she declared, and if Chris didn't understand her determination, her husband most certainly did. His immediate reply, though perhaps tinged with regret, was, "Yes, dear; you are absolutely right!"

"It was just a thought," Chris commented.

"But not well thought-out," Abigail insisted. "Would you willingly put your children back in their hands?"

Chris looked pensive, then told them a story. "There were two little Chinese-American children on the big farm where we were working. I think their last name was Ling. I tried to look after them, but I had my hands full just trying to get enough food for my two."

"That's not true, Mommy," her son Michael interrupted. "You always made sure they got as much food as us."

"I tried, honey, but it wasn't always possible."

"And they...?" Abigail asked.

"They didn't make it," Chris replied, a catch in her voice. And they weren't the only ones."

But Michael didn't hesitate to pronounce their fate.

"They went to be with the Lord, didn't they Mommy?"

"Yes, they did go to be with the Lord, honey," and she hugged him to her. She looked at Pastor Kenzy, and said, "I know that the Lord isn't going to let two innocent children, who have not reached the age of accountability, be left behind."

He smiled and nodded in enthusiastic agreement.

Abigail turned to her husband. "This all sounds so melodramatic. Would other Americans really hurt us if they discovered we had helped Chris and the children when they happened to stop here?"

Yes, they would certainly hurt us in an attempt to learn where Chris had gone. Then they would burn the house and maybe the barns. And that's why we all must leave here as soon as possible."

Chris blurted, "Oh no. You're really in danger because of us!"

"First," the pastor responded, "apart from helping you a little, we are in danger because of other actions we have taken, things I have done that have antagonized those people. Second, you can't be blamed for escaping. In fact," he smiled, "I can only blame our troubles on myself because, if you'll recall, I helped you escape."

"But if you hadn't, you wouldn't be in this fix."

"Never mind that," Abigail said. "We wouldn't have it any other way."

"It wouldn't matter," the pastor replied. "Even if you had not escaped, the Chinese would still be all over the countryside looking for those other two — the innkeeper's slave girl and the man she helped escape — and I had a part in that escape too." He leaned forward and spoke earnestly. "Listen," he insisted, "we all did the right things. We must never stop resisting evil."

Chris was about to agree, then shook her head in confusion. "But look at the result!" she cried.

"I have to admit that it was a bit like knocking down a hornets' nest," he agreed. "Anyone in the vicinity is apt to be stung."

"Oh, I understand," Chris said, but it was clear to him that she still didn't want to be the cause of anyone else's pain.

"Hey, I helped you, right?" he demanded.

"Well, of course," she replied.

"And we're patriots," his wife added. "We're all in this together."

"That's right," her husband quickly agreed.

"But, my husband wouldn't want this," Chris said.

The pastor looked at her in confusion.

"Your husband?" he asked, confused by her outburst.

"He's the man who escaped from the inn."

"You mean that he went off and left the three of you captives?"

"Oh, no! He didn't even know we were there."

The Kenzys shared a look of bewilderment.

"Let me start from the beginning," Chris said. "When the war started my husband was out of town on business, and we didn't even know whether he was still alive until earlier this evening."

"You know for a fact that he's alive?"

"Yes, we all saw him." And her face seemed alight for just a moment as she put an arm around each of her smiling children and drew them to her. "They saw their daddy for the first time in nearly a year."

"Do you think he'll be all right, Mommy?" Michael interrupted.

"I don't know why I feel this way, honey, but, yes, I think your daddy is going to be just fine." She laughed. "In fact, I'm beginning to think that the Lord allows him to walk between the raindrops."

The pastor laughed, but the laugh seemed a little hollow. *If he was arrested,* he thought, *he must be considered important. And if he has escaped, the Chinese will be after him hammer and tong.* But he didn't share that disturbing conclusion with the others. Instead, he said, "I'm pleased to learn that," but his words held little conviction. He hesitated for a moment, then remarked quietly, "You haven't told us your last name, Chris."

She searched his face. "Do you think that's a good idea? No insult intended, but the reason we've survived this long is because we've learned to avoid sharing our true identities with others."

"On the other hand," Abigail gently suggested, "the people who arrested your husband must have had a pretty good idea of who he is."

Chris frowned. "That's possibly true, but it appears that our captors hadn't yet made the connection between his name and that of mine and our children. And," she added, "I hope they never do."

"Well, we'll leave it to you," the pastor said. "It's just that if we hear something, we won't know who to try to pass it on to."

"That's true," Chris agreed, with just the slightest suspicion, "but for the time being, I think we should stick to first names."

"That's the safest approach," the pastor conceded, "although you already know our last name."

His immediate agreement caused the exhausted woman to relax a bit, but that last statement could certainly be considered argumentative. His next statement, however, helped put her at ease.

"One thing is sure," he said to console her. "If we don't know your name, then no one can force it out of us." He smiled ruefully. "I can't believe that I just said that. It sounded so melodramatic, like something out of a second-rate espionage movie."

"But," Chris said in agreement, "we really have learned the hard way that our enemies will stop at nothing to gather information that is of even the most limited value, anything they believe might help them gain their objectives."

He nodded.

Then he started down a different avenue. "Let me ask you a different question, because maybe there is something we can do to help your husband without learning his name."

"I don't understand."

"Well, for example, maybe some associates of mine could try to set up a diversion in some other part of Vermont that would draw resources from where he might be traveling."

"I suppose," she said, "if you had some means of communicating with them," and she looked at him doubtfully, "but that assumes that I have some idea where he might be going, and I really don't know any more about that than you do."

I wonder if she really means that, he thought. *She's obviously a very transparent individual and not at all an experienced liar. It's equally obvious that she's a really decent human being, and I'll bet that she hasn't been faced with many situations in which she's felt the need to hone such unholy skills.*

He decided not to challenge her veracity. Instead he asked, "Do you have any idea why they were dragging him out of the tavern? Is your husband anyone of note?"

Her son jumped up. "Sure," he said, "Dad was..." but before Michael could finish his sentence, his mother gently clamped her hand over his mouth.

"Children!" she said, as though exasperated, "should be seen and not heard. They are always interrupting." She tried to cover her words with a stiff smile, and it was clear to all of them that her verbal response was an instant too late. "Like any child," she went on lamely, "Michael is proud of his father's accomplishments, but I don't think that being leader of his scout troop or the coach of his soccer team qualifies him as a threat to the invaders, do you?"

"Dad never coached my soccer team, mom! He was hardly ever home."

The pastor smiled, and it was obvious to everyone that she was withholding something. He was surprised when, after a moment of silence, she seemed to relent.

"When they dragged my husband away from the tavern, I thought for a moment that he looked a little like, oh, what's his name? Yes, David Rhodes." She scarcely had the words out of her mouth before she wanted to bite her tongue. *Of all people, why would I name him?*

"But Mom, we all saw him in the headlights...."

"For the last time, Michael, be quiet and go to sleep!"

Now Kenzy spoke in a very soft voice. "You realize that it's difficult to assist one another if there is any question of mutual trust."

"Yes," she replied. "And I also realize that it's very difficult to develop real trust in a few minutes of time."

He nodded. "Yes, you're right. On the other hand, we did help you escape."

"And, arguably, that could have been a ruse to elicit my trust," she replied, again surprised at herself, realizing that her fatigue was overcoming both her good manners and her judgment, and that she had just insulted her hosts.

"Jack!" Abigail said. "You are not a CIA interrogator, and this woman is not a Chinese spy. Now, stop this hurtful discussion right now!"

He nodded sheepishly to his wife, then turned to Chris. "Abigail's right," he told her. "I'm suspicious of everyone nowadays, and I apologize. I was wrong to push you."

And I too am suspicious of everyone, Chris thought ruefully.

The Kenzy Farm
East of Butter Creek, Vermont
Late Christmas Eve

Chris had been sitting there, staring almost hypnotically at the glowing coals, when Abigail Kenzy held out a cup of real coffee.

Coffee was a very rare and precious commodity in war-torn America, and it was therefore incredibly generous of her. Then Abigail set a dish of maple sugar before her. "It's from our own trees!" she said proudly. She followed that with a pitcher containing fresh, thick cream that she proudly announced had come from their one remaining cow.

Chris stirred the mixture carefully, so that she wouldn't spill a single drop, then waited until no one was looking, and licked the spoon. Holding the cup beneath her chin, she let the fragrant steam rise around her. She breathed deeply, inhaling the aroma. Finally she began to sip it, taking time to savor every drop, trying to make it last.

How long has it been since I last had a cup of real coffee?" she wondered. *Not since that last morning at Dad's farm. The five of us were sitting at the wrought-iron table on their back porch, eating mom's homemade raisin toast, sipping the last of their coffee and watching the sun rise.* She remembered holding the porcelain cup in her hands while she tried to encourage her mother with a smile. *"It tastes wonderful,"* she remembered telling her, but even then she was wondering, *How long until any of us tastes real coffee again? Maybe never...."*

She found herself inexplicably giggling.

Abigail looked at her strangely, her eyebrows raised in question, and Chris couldn't help but quip, "And the condemned woman ate a hearty meal."

Abigail smiled in sympathy. "I suppose it is funny, in a macabre sort of way." Then she began coughing, and when perspiration appeared on her brow, the pastor put his arm around her, waiting for her to recover, his deep concern obvious.

When Abigail recovered, he helped seat her across the table from Chris, and the conversation became even more grave. The first words out of his mouth crushed her hopes for any opportunity to clean up a bit, let alone enjoy a warm place to spend the night.

"I am really sorry that you can't spend any time here," he told her.

"Oh, Jack," his wife interrupted in a husky whisper, her breath coming in gasps, "can't they at least stay the night?"

"I wish they could, honey, but this is not just their problem."

Their eyes met, and she nodded, acknowledging that matters must have become far more serious than she realized. Her husband was silent for a moment, evidently trying to find some easy way to break the news.

When he spoke, it was in a gentle voice, and he was looking into his wife's eyes.

"It's not just Chris and her children. You and I have to leave too, and we have get out of here as soon as possible."

"But, why?" Abigail asked, clearly shaken.

"Because," he answered, "the Chinese military leaders will be enraged when they discover that their quisling supporters in Butter Creek have allowed this woman and her two children to escape, let alone the fact that two other people also got away."

"But won't they consider those other two more important?" she persisted.

"It doesn't matter," he replied, resignation in his voice. "The dragnet they are about to spread may focus on that man, but it will just as likely snare all of us."

Abigail shook her head. "Jack, I just don't understand."

"In order to appease their Chinese masters, those American renegades will send out every turncoat they can muster to search for all of the escapees." He looked across at Chris.

"And that includes me and the children."

He nodded, and turned back to his wife, his expression unreadable. "And you and I will also be swept up in the search."

"I'm so sorry," Chris said quickly. "It never occurred to me that my escape would put you at risk."

"It doesn't matter," he replied. "We are to bear one another's burdens. Sometimes we are unable to anticipate the costs involved, and therefore we cannot weigh them. But even if we could, we would not back off from our godly obligations."

He cleared his throat. "When we help others, we are in a very real sense giving our time, our resources, maybe even our lives. Yet the Bible teaches that he that lends to the poor, gives to the Lord, and the Lord will somehow repay." And he looked meaningly at his wife, a sad smile of resignation on his face. "This may prove to be our last opportunity to lend to someone who is in need."

Chris stared at them, and realized that these were the kind of people that she and her husband would have valued as the greatest of human beings, and treasured as real friends.

"But we're not poor," Chris replied. She paused, and there was resignation in her voice. "I'm wrong. I guess we are poor, aren't we?"

"Oh, not in the sense that we usually think of poverty, as a matter of financial resources. That's relative. But at the moment you are impoverished in terms of safety, of shelter and the protection of the law."

"I see," she said, and started to ask another question, but the pastor wasn't about to take any more time for discussion.

"The bad guys are probably out searching right now. If not, they certainly will be by daybreak."

Chris smiled at his use of the phrase, "bad guys." If he'd used a more heavily-loaded idiom — such as enemy invaders, hired mercenaries or paid killers — it would tend to sap her waning courage. On the other hand, "bad guys," was certainly less frightening to the children; and, if she were completely honest with herself, it was easier for her to handle as well. She had been drifting again, and her mind had to race to catch up with his words.

"They will be searching for your snowmobile tracks, and unless enough snow has fallen to cover them, they will arrive here sooner rather than later."

With no bitterness in her voice, Chris suggested, "Maybe the kids and I should head back toward town. It might be better for us to be captured rather than running off somewhere in the blizzard, and then the *bad guys* wouldn't follow us here."

Kenzy stared at his wife. It was more like an examination. He was deeply concerned with her failure to recover from the flu, and was tempted to embrace the suggestion, but Abigail soon made it clear that she would have no part of it.

"There is no way in the world that we are going to let you willingly expose yourself to those vermin," she declared, and if Chris didn't understand her determination, her husband most certainly did. His immediate reply, though perhaps tinged with regret, was, "Yes, dear; you are absolutely right!"

"It was just a thought," Chris commented.

"But not well thought-out," Abigail insisted. "Would you willingly put your children back in their hands?"

Chris looked pensive, then told them a story. "There were two little Chinese-American children on the big farm where we were working. I think their last name was Ling. I tried to look after them, but I had my hands full just trying to get enough food for my two."

"That's not true, Mommy," her son Michael interrupted. "You always made sure they got as much food as us."

"I tried, honey, but it wasn't always possible."

"And they...?" Abigail asked.

"They didn't make it," Chris replied, a catch in her voice. And they weren't the only ones."

But Michael didn't hesitate to pronounce their fate.

"They went to be with the Lord, didn't they Mommy?"

"Yes, they did go to be with the Lord, honey," and she hugged him to her. She looked at Pastor Kenzy, and said, "I know that the Lord isn't going to let two innocent children, who have not reached the age of accountability, be left behind."

He smiled and nodded in enthusiastic agreement.

Abigail turned to her husband. "This all sounds so melodramatic. Would other Americans really hurt us if they discovered we had helped Chris and the children when they happened to stop here?"

Yes, they would certainly hurt us in an attempt to learn where Chris had gone. Then they would burn the house and maybe the barns. And that's why we all must leave here as soon as possible."

Chris blurted, "Oh no. You're really in danger because of us!"

"First," the pastor responded, "apart from helping you a little, we are in danger because of other actions we have taken, things I have done that have antagonized those people. Second, you can't be blamed for escaping. In fact," he smiled, "I can only blame our troubles on myself because, if you'll recall, I helped you escape."

"But if you hadn't, you wouldn't be in this fix."

"Never mind that," Abigail said. "We wouldn't have it any other way."

"It wouldn't matter," the pastor replied. "Even if you had not escaped, the Chinese would still be all over the countryside looking for those other two – the innkeeper's slave girl and the man she helped escape – and I had a part in that escape too." He leaned forward and spoke earnestly. "Listen," he insisted, "we all did the right things. We must never stop resisting evil."

Chris was about to agree, then shook her head in confusion. "But look at the result!" she cried.

"I have to admit that it was a bit like knocking down a hornets' nest," he agreed. "Anyone in the vicinity is apt to be stung."

"Oh, I understand," Chris said, but it was clear to him that she still didn't want to be the cause of anyone else's pain.

"Hey, I helped you, right?" he demanded.

"Well, of course," she replied.

"And we're patriots," his wife added. "We're all in this together."

"That's right," her husband quickly agreed.

"But, my husband wouldn't want this," Chris said.

The pastor looked at her in confusion.

"Your husband?" he asked, confused by her outburst.

"He's the man who escaped from the inn."

"You mean that he went off and left the three of you captives?"

"Oh, no! He didn't even know we were there."

The Kenzys shared a look of bewilderment.

"Let me start from the beginning," Chris said. "When the war started my husband was out of town on business, and we didn't even know whether he was still alive until earlier this evening."

"You know for a fact that he's alive?"

"Yes, we all saw him." And her face seemed alight for just a moment as she put an arm around each of her smiling children and drew them to her. "They saw their daddy for the first time in nearly a year."

"Do you think he'll be all right, Mommy?" Michael interrupted.

"I don't know why I feel this way, honey, but, yes, I think your daddy is going to be just fine." She laughed. "In fact, I'm beginning to think that the Lord allows him to walk between the raindrops."

The pastor laughed, but the laugh seemed a little hollow. *If he was arrested,* he thought, *he must be considered important. And if he has escaped, the Chinese will be after him hammer and tong.* But he didn't share that disturbing conclusion with the others. Instead, he said, "I'm pleased to learn that," but his words held little conviction. He hesitated for a moment, then remarked quietly, "You haven't told us your last name, Chris."

She searched his face. "Do you think that's a good idea? No insult intended, but the reason we've survived this long is because we've learned to avoid sharing our true identities with others."

"On the other hand," Abigail gently suggested, "the people who arrested your husband must have had a pretty good idea of who he is."

Chris frowned. "That's possibly true, but it appears that our captors hadn't yet made the connection between his name and that of mine and our children. And," she added, "I hope they never do."

"Well, we'll leave it to you," the pastor said. "It's just that if we hear something, we won't know who to try to pass it on to."

"That's true," Chris agreed, with just the slightest suspicion, "but for the time being, I think we should stick to first names."

"That's the safest approach," the pastor conceded, "although you already know our last name."

His immediate agreement caused the exhausted woman to relax a bit, but that last statement could certainly be considered argumentative. His next statement, however, helped put her at ease.

"One thing is sure," he said to console her. "If we don't know your name, then no one can force it out of us." He smiled ruefully. "I can't believe that I just said that. It sounded so melodramatic, like something out of a second-rate espionage movie."

"But," Chris said in agreement, "we really have learned the hard way that our enemies will stop at nothing to gather information that is of even the most limited value, anything they believe might help them gain their objectives."

He nodded.

Then he started down a different avenue. "Let me ask you a different question, because maybe there is something we can do to help your husband without learning his name."

"I don't understand."

"Well, for example, maybe some associates of mine could try to set up a diversion in some other part of Vermont that would draw resources from where he might be traveling."

"I suppose," she said, "if you had some means of communicating with them," and she looked at him doubtfully, "but that assumes that I have some idea where he might be going, and I really don't know any more about that than you do."

I wonder if she really means that, he thought. *She's obviously a very transparent individual and not at all an experienced liar. It's equally obvious that she's a really decent human being, and I'll bet that she hasn't been faced with many situations in which she's felt the need to hone such unholy skills.*

He decided not to challenge her veracity. Instead he asked, "Do you have any idea why they were dragging him out of the tavern? Is your husband anyone of note?"

Her son jumped up. "Sure," he said, "Dad was..." but before Michael could finish his sentence, his mother gently clamped her hand over his mouth.

"Children!" she said, as though exasperated, "should be seen and not heard. They are always interrupting." She tried to cover her words with a stiff smile, and it was clear to all of them that her verbal response was an instant too late. "Like any child," she went on lamely, "Michael is proud of his father's accomplishments, but I don't think that being leader of his scout troop or the coach of his soccer team qualifies him as a threat to the invaders, do you?"

"Dad never coached my soccer team, mom! He was hardly ever home."

The pastor smiled, and it was obvious to everyone that she was withholding something. He was surprised when, after a moment of silence, she seemed to relent.

"When they dragged my husband away from the tavern, I thought for a moment that he looked a little like, oh, what's his name? Yes, David Rhodes." She scarcely had the words out of her mouth before she wanted to bite her tongue. *Of all people, why would I name him?*

"But Mom, we all saw him in the headlights...."

"For the last time, Michael, be quiet and go to sleep!"

Now Kenzy spoke in a very soft voice. "You realize that it's difficult to assist one another if there is any question of mutual trust."

"Yes," she replied. "And I also realize that it's very difficult to develop real trust in a few minutes of time."

He nodded. "Yes, you're right. On the other hand, we did help you escape."

"And, arguably, that could have been a ruse to elicit my trust," she replied, again surprised at herself, realizing that her fatigue was overcoming both her good manners and her judgment, and that she had just insulted her hosts.

"Jack!" Abigail said. "You are not a CIA interrogator, and this woman is not a Chinese spy. Now, stop this hurtful discussion right now!"

He nodded sheepishly to his wife, then turned to Chris. "Abigail's right," he told her. "I'm suspicious of everyone nowadays, and I apologize. I was wrong to push you."

And I too am suspicious of everyone, Chris thought ruefully.

Kim Ling's Opportunity

Headquarters, People's Liberation Army
Burlington, Vermont
Christmas Eve

General Eng turned to Kim Ling,. "Our first major problem lies in the fact that we have no contact with our command centers in China."

"None?" Kim asked in disbelief.

"Weren't you listening?" the general demanded. "Do I have to repeat everything I say to you?"

"No, sir. No excuse, sir."

"Listen up!"

"Yes, sir.'

"To make matters worse, we have little or no hope of reinforcement."

"But you are well-armed, well-organized, and well-trained. I don't understand why you can't overwhelm any remaining resistance."

"You've put your finger on the problem. It's what I call the *ten to one rule*."

"The what?"

"Do you know much about America's involvement in the Vietnam War, Ling?"

What does a war we fought and 50 years ago have to do with this, Kim wondered, but decided to humor the general.

"No, sir. Only the little I read in school history books and saw on TV."

The general stared at him for a moment. "Why do you call me "Sir?"

"It's a term of respect, sir."

The general pretended indifference, but clearly liked the answer.

If it will keep you from shooting me, Kim thought, *I intend to keep calling you 'sir' until the day I can escape from here and begin fighting back.*

The general blew a smoke ring, and settled back to lecture Kim.

"The war in Southeast Asia actually ran from the 1940s until 1973, but America's peak involvement was in 1969 when they had over half a million military involved. Did you know that over 3-million people died in that war, including 58,000 Americans?"

"I had no idea."

"America stupidly became bogged down in a ground war in Asia where the indigenous population was largely opposed to them."

"I don't understand."

"Close your mouth, and I will explain."

"Yes, sir."

Eng glared at him, trying to decide whether or not he was being mocked.

"During the early years of the war, the Americans fought against irregular troops — guerrillas. Those men were dressed like any other civilian, and they lived off the land. They were fed and hidden by the villagers."

"And these guerrillas were able to compete with the Americans?"

"That's where my *ten to one rule* comes in?"

"Sir?"

"It requires as many as ten conventional soldiers to contain one guerrilla. For example, one man, wandering through the countryside with a rifle, can snipe at a squad of troops a few hundred yards away. Even if he doesn't hit one of them, they will be forced to take cover, and then send a patrol out to try to find and neutralize their attacker. And they rarely can."

"Kill him?"

"Find him. By the time they decide where the shot might have come from, and send troops after him, he will be long gone. And," the general swept his hand over his desktop and knocked a couple of chess pieces to the floor, "his pursuers will not be too eager to get within range of their unseen enemy. He might be leading them into a trap. There might be a lot more of them. He most certainly has diverted them from their initial purpose.

And the problems he causes are significant. If he has killed someone, they will have to bury him, and they will be be down one man. If the guerrilla wounded someone, it could take two to four men to carry that casualty to a place where he could be evacuated."

He went on. "The Vietcong irregulars would infiltrate American positions at night and raise havoc. The American troops became terrified. And while the Americans were accused by their own media of atrocities, sometimes justifiably, the Vietcong did not hesitate to commit all sorts of barbarous acts against them. The Americans were forced to build base camps, strongholds where their men could be gathered. Then the Vietcong became proficient with mortars. They'd attack in the middle of the night, and bring incredibly accurate fire down on these base camps, first taking out the communications, then the strong points, and finally opening the way for their men to dash in and kill the survivors. Even with all their helicopter gun ships, tanks and artillery, the Americans could not defeat their growing numbers."

Kim nodded his head, beginning to appreciate the scope of the general's problem. *There has to be hundreds of Americans doing just that...sniping at the Chinese. And Eng only has a little over two-hundred men.* It didn't take a mathematician to compute the general's problem. According to his *ten to one rule,* "two hundred Americans could tie down two thousand Chinese troops, and Eng only had two hundred.

It was as though the general was reading his mind.

"So, you see, Kim Ling, it would take just twenty Americans to nearly neutralize my two-hundred troops."

No wonder he's doubtful about the outcome of this war. Suddenly Kim felt so unbearably light, that he was unable to keep a straight face. *I like his 10 to 1 rule!*

The general's lips twisted in a parody of a smile. "I see you understand the implications of my rule, Ling." It was immediately clear that the general also understood Kim's response to that information.

That was stupid of me, Kim realized.

The general changed course, again confusing Kim.

"Do you play poker?"

"I have?" *Does he want to play poker now?*

"Well, I thought we had what you Americans call an ace in the hole."

Ah, he's not talking about us playing poker. From the beginning, this has all been a game to him.

The general frowned. "But we didn't have an ace in the hole. In fact, things haven't worked out well at all."

Well that certainly doesn't make me unhappy. And I can't believe the things he's already told me. If Americans were to learn this, their resistance leaders would soon be swamped with recruits.

"A couple of weeks after the outbreak of hostilities, we landed several thousand troops in Providence, Rhode Island. They were to wait there for a cargo ship that was to bring us tanks, rocket launchers, armored personnel carriers, trucks and supplies, and then they were to march north to rendezvous with us in Black River Junction."

That must be the ship that's rumored to have been sunk in Panama.

"Well, aren't you going to ask what happened?"

"I don't want to presume on the general's confidence."

"You are a glib one, aren't you?"

Again Kim kept his silence.

"And maybe not so stupid either."

He crushed the remains of his cigarette in an ashtray already overflowing with the remains of dozens of others.

"Well," he went on, his voice slurring, "the cargo ship never arrived. It was sunk in the Panama Canal," the general continued, confirming the rumor Kim had overheard.

"The general officer in charge of this substantial force decided to lead his troops through Boston." As he spoke, the general seemed to be studying Kim Ling, looking for some reaction, and he wasn't to be disappointed.

Kim face was a study in shocked disbelief.

"I heard that Boston was hit with a nuclear missile."

"It was," the general confirmed. He opened another bottle, took a deep swallow, belched, then went on. "By the time he had marched his entire regiment around ground zero, most of the men, including the officers, were suffering from radiation poisoning."

Ling's concern for all human life exploded from his lips. "Why Boston? Why didn't they just go north out of Providence toward Auburn? They could have picked up the Mass Pike west, and then gotten on I-91 north and driven right up the Vermont/New Hampshire border? There'd have been no opposition.

The general took another swallow, set the empty bottle down, watched as it tipped over, rolled off the desk, and broke on the floor. An instant later, the office door burst open, and two men ran in, their weapons leveled.

"It's all right," the general shouted, holding his hands out as though to restrain them.

"General, we thought we heard a shot."

"Just a beer bottle falling on the floor," he told them, pointing at the broken glass.

"Are you sure everything is all right, General?"

"Yes, everything is fine. You may withdraw."

The two men stared fixedly at Kim Ling for a moment, noted that his hands were empty and firmly gripped the arms of his chair, and after one more look at the general to confirm his well-being, the started to back out the door.

"We'll be right outside the door, sir, if you need us for anything," and the guard closed the door.

The general lit another cigarette, and inhaled deeply. As he exhaled, he peered through half-closed eyes at Kim Ling. His next words served as a warning that a person would risk much to underrate this coarse and drunken man, for in a very precise voice, he quoted:

> *"Not tho' the soldier knew*
> *Someone had blunder'd:*
> *Theirs not to make reply,*
> *Theirs not to reason why,*
> *Theirs but to do and die:*
> *Into the valley of Death*
> *Rode the six hundred."*

"The Charge of the Light Brigade," Kim Ling said.

"Very good," the general replied, waving his finger in Ling's direction. "Everyone loves that *do or die* line. More to the point, however, *Someone had blunder'd.*"

"Tennyson's words," Ling said.

"No! They are my words," the general shouted. When he heard rustling outside the door, he lowered his voice.

"Our planners blunder'd." He sat there a moment, and Kim decided that, just as discretion would have been the better part of valor for the six hundred, so it would be for him. He remained silent while Eng resumed his tale of woe.

"Because the general exposed his troops to near lethal doses of radiation, he was forced to leave many of his men behind to fend for themselves. Many of his men, including himself, so there is a mere understrength battalion left to straggle toward Black River Junction on foot."

"On foot?"

"The counted on getting gasoline for their vehicles from the tank farm at the port in Providence, but your countrymen decided to burn the fuel supply rather than let it fall into our hands.

Kim was stunned. "But how could you learn all this?" he stumbled. "I mean, if your communications were down."

"How do you know our communications were down?" the general asked, suspicion in his voice.

"I understood you to say that you are having communication problems."

"Oh, yes. I did say that, didn't I? I should be more careful."

Kim wasn't about to commiserate with the general, but he had begun to wonder how far this conversation was going. It was as though the general needed to share his thoughts with someone, and he didn't care who.

But the general does care, Kim realized. *So why is he telling me things that he has very clearly not shared with his own subordinates? He has a reason. He already told me that he has no contact with China. The regiment that he was to join in Black River has been winnowed down to less than a quarter of its original strength, and they don't have the high-ranking officer or the armored vehicles they were promised. And Eng is not anticipating any additional reinforcements from China. So why isn't he sharing this with his troops?* Kim's mind raced, and his eyes opened wide with understanding. *He doesn't dare tell them because the desertions that are rumored would multiply. It appears that his army is evaporating.*

Kim wanted to get up and shout praises to the Lord, but instead fought to keep his expression neutral. *This would be wonderful news for America if I could get it to someone in a position of leadership who might be able to act upon it.* Then Kim wondered again, *So why is the general telling me this?*

Obviously the general knew that a secret is no longer a secret once two people share it, Kim's anecdote about the ill-fated rabbit returned to haunt his thoughts. And his next question left Kim numb. He spoke so softly that Ling almost didn't make out the words. It didn't matter. The general didn't expect an answer.

"Ling," he asked, "What am I going to do about you?"

Not "What am I going to do **with** *you?" as he asked me earlier tonight, but "What am I going to do* **about** *you." He's not talking about further involvement with me. He's talking about taking action either for or against me.*

Kim was struggling to assess the significance of this peculiar change in wording when the general said something else that refocused his attention. Kim caught himself backtracking, trying to recall the general's earlier words and wondering whether they might explain what the general was going to do "about him." One way or the other, they could represent a reversal of fortunes, possibly a violent reversal. Then Kim recalled the important words.

He had said, "You will be accompanying a small contingent to Butter Creek."

Kim tried to grasp the implications. It would be dangerous traveling to Butter Creek, but getting out into the mountains with just a couple of Chinese officers represented a far greater opportunity for escape than remaining here surrounded by a couple of hundred crack Chinese troops.

No matter what the general really has in mind, it represents a chance for escape, albeit a small one.

"I've already alluded to the mission of the group to whom you are assigned," the general repeated. "You are to pick up a captive who might be a stumbling block to our pacification of Zone One."

Kim Ling knew the area the general was referring to. He had seen a map of North America on which the invaders had drawn lines indicating their plans for conquest. "Zone One" was comprised of New England and New York.

"You will be traveling to Butter Creek to pick up this potential suspected guerrilla leader," the general continued. "And as I already mentioned, you will act as interpreter during his interrogation."

"Will we leave the man there?"

"No. His fate is a foregone conclusion. If you can secure useful information about operatives in that area, Captain Wei will act on them while you are there. Whether or not you can get anything out of him, you will ultimately bring him back here where he will be more thoroughly interrogated, and then disposed of."

Not if I can help it, Kim thought. *It's a long shot, but maybe I can get some help when we reach Butter Creek, and free this guy.*

Kim Ling had heard it whispered among the Chinese that many Americans, operating independently or in small groups, had become a real threat to China's timetable for conquering the United States. Open discussion of this threat among the Chinese and the American turncoats who supported them was discouraged. In fact, any expression of defeatism might find the offender facing a firing squad made up of his peers.

The more Kim thought about this journey, the greater his doubts. He would have been suspicious of the general's motives in sending him anywhere, let alone into an area disputed by American patriots. Kim's suspicions had been heightened when the general informed him that he was to go along as an interpreter. Recalling the limerick, he was now reluctant to go, but he knew he had no choice.

What does the general have up his sleeve? Is it already too late to protect my hide? If I had the power to bargain with him, this is one time that I would definitely look a gift horse in the mouth. Then he reconsidered. *No, this is my chance, and I will trust God to help me take advantage of it.*

Although Kim was supposed to be ignorant of the strategic situation across New England, he was continually processing information from conversations he happened to overhear. He didn't need anyone to tell him how dangerous a journey into those mountains might prove. And if he were riding with Chinese troops, they were dangerous to him as well.

The limited presence that the Chinese had been able to establish in the central mountains had already been whittled away by small groups of Americans making piecemeal attacks on Chinese supply lines. A number of Vermont natives were beginning to call themselves the "Green Mountain Boys" after their ancestors who had fought in the American Revolution. They had redirected their skills as hunters of wildlife to hunters of the invaders.

The only thing more dangerous than being a Chinese soldier was to be identified as an American turncoat. The Americans regularly attacked Chinese supply convoys by cutting down trees to block the roads as the trucks were approaching, then assaulting the drivers and guards, and either destroying the vehicles or used them to carry away their increasingly rare and precious cargoes.

While the number of these attacks had increased, the number of China's American supporters had declined. Some of the traitors had been discovered hanging from tree limbs. These attacks had become so numerous, in fact, that the turncoats living in the sparsely populated areas were afraid to venture out of the few remaining Chinese strongholds.

Now Kim understood that this was General Eng's *Ten-to-One Rule* at work.

When the general told Kim Ling that he would be accompanying two Chinese officers to Butter Creek, he fortunately misinterpreted Kim's look of surprise.

"You wonder why I am sending two of our dwindling cadre of junior officers into that rugged terrain in the midst of a blizzard, merely to secure a prisoner?"

"Yes, sir." Ling started to say something more, and the general beckoned for him to continue. "Well, general," he went on, "I've heard rumors that some of the Americans have been sniping at your patrols."

If the general noticed that Ling had referred to them as "your patrols," and not "our patrols," he didn't comment. He instead con-descended to reply, and Ling found the general's unusual patience with him disconcerting.

"We have already lost too many English-speaking officers to these cursed New England marksmen, and sending these two men is a means of conserving assets."

Kim Ling's eyes widened at this crass confession.

"I am not willing to risk any of our few remaining bi-lingual of-ficers by sending them into those mountains to be targeted by filthy American snipers. If these two are captured, they cannot speak English, so the Americans will not be able to learn anything from them."

A chill went down Kim Ling's spine at this cold-blooded expla-nation.

No, he realized. *That's not all of it, general. True, you're not sending your precious English-speaking officers, but you are sending a Chinese-speaking American. Me! Is that what suddenly makes you so friendly? For that matter, I've yet to meet a single one of your peo-ple who cannot speak English. What have you got up your sleeve, you double-dealing demon? You know as well as I do that the Amer-icans could make me interpret for their interrogators, and the truth is, I'd be eager to do so.*

And with that thought, another chill swept over him. The gen-eral was watching him closely, and Kim put on what he hoped was a look of indifference while he tried to reason out the general's ac-tions.

You plan to win a little of my loyalty by pretending an interest in my welfare, but your concern for me will quickly end if your men are captured. And though I'm merely a pawn in your little game, I may be a key piece in what you call your "conservation of assets."

The general was lighting yet another cigarette, and it provided Kim time to think.

What you really mean is that it will be no great sacrifice to you if something happens to me. On the other hand, you can't afford to have me survive if your subordinates are captured because I might wind up serving as an interpreter for my countrymen.

Kim's eyes widened in understanding. *That's it! You are testing me. If your officers actually speak English, they will know if I don't accurately interpret your prisoner's words. Therefore, you have ordered them to silence me if I fail to do so correctly, or they find themselves in any danger of capture. In fact, you may have ordered them to terminate me anyway, but to keep me off guard, you are acting in this unusually friendly fashion.*

Kim wanted to get out of that office, and in his unconscious desire to stand, he shifted his hips back against the rungs of the chair. The momentary discomfort he experienced as a result of shifting his weight brought him back to reality, and his momentary fears were more than compensated for by the reminder that he had a handgun tucked in the small of his back beneath his belt.

The general, secure in his own sense of power and self-importance, was oblivious to all of this. What came next really surprised Kim Ling.

"You have been most cooperative," the general commented, "especially considering the fact that when you drive into the mountains, you will be at risk along with my officers. So I will elaborate." He waved his hand in the air, the smoke from his cigarette drifting toward Kim who tried unsuccessfully to suppress a cough.

"The man you will bring back here is considered a great threat to our efforts to pacify the northeast United States."

"I don't understand."

The general gave a tight smile. He didn't like to be interrupted.

"I will explain." He took another drag on his cigarette. "If our people at Butter Creek have accurately identified him, then he is truly a great catch. Before the war, he was a well-known Christian radio talk-show host." Eng pronounced the word *Christian* with obvious distaste, as though he'd tasted spoiled fish. He met Kim Ling's gaze. "He's also considered to be a staunch anti-revolutionary."

Kim shrugged his shoulders as though to ask, "So what?"

"The fact that he was a respected public figure is sufficient reason to silence him. Far more important is the fact that he is a potential lightning rod. His magnetic personality might attract those individuals who have been fighting singly and in pairs to resist us. If a large number of these radicals were to turn to his leadership, well..." His voice trailed off. "You can understand our concern. We cannot allow such a possibility."

Kim Ling nodded gravely *Perhaps*, he thought, *I can have some small part in helping to provide this "lightning rod" with an opportunity to exert his magnetic personality.*

Kenzy Questions Chris Rhodes

The Kenzy Farm
East of Butter Creek, Vermont
Christmas Eve

Kenzy's wife piped up with a question, perhaps to break the glacial atmosphere that had chilled the room.

"Did you really believe, even for one minute, that you saw the *Colossus of Rhodes*?" she asked.

"The Colossus of Rhodes?" Chris asked, looking bewildered.

"Well, that's what Jack and I used to call him, we and a few of our close friends; actually, quite a few of our friends."

"I don't understand," Chris replied.

"You told us that when you saw the turncoats bringing your husband out of the tavern, that for a moment, you thought it was David Rhodes. Obviously he must be similar in appearance, or you wouldn't have made that mistake."

"Oh, yes, sure!" Chris answered. "It was dark."

Michael was wiggling in her arms, and she shook him to make him subside.

"The pastor suddenly laughed aloud. "I met him once."

"Who?"

"David Rhodes!" he said, smiling proudly.

"Oh, no!" his wife said, laughing gaily. "Now you've done it, Chris! We'll be here all night."

"I wouldn't mind that," she answered, and the room seemed warm once more.

The pastor went on as though he hadn't heard his wife, a thoughtful look on his face.

"I was really proud," he said, looking over at Chris. "Since you thought at first that it might have been Rhodes at the tavern, it seems obvious that you've seen his photo." He pointed across the room, a big smile splitting his face. In a frame on the wall hung an autographed photograph of David Rhodes.

Chris was watching Michael, and when he she sensed that he was going to say something, she pinched his arm. "I suspect that most Americans would recognize him," she replied in an effort to re-direct the conversation. "After all, he was continually attacked by the media, and they used the most unfavorable photos of him that they could find."

"Pictures of your husband, you mean?"

Chris opened her mouth, caught herself in time, and simply smiled at him.

He smiled back, and she felt a little like a mouse being toyed with by a cat.

"Well," he went on, "if you are like most Americans who may have been brain-washed by the leftist press, you may not agree with us, but Abigail and I considered Rhodes to be one of America's last great heroes of the faith. We called him...

...The Colossus of Rhodes," Abigail finished for him, a smile splitting her face, "because he was one of the few men of God who stood so boldly for Biblical values."

"Really?" Chris replied.

"I remember some liberal preacher condemning Rhodes for being unloving," the pastor said, "but we found him to be just the opposite."

"How so?"

"He rightly expected and demanded more character from those who claimed that the Lord had called them to Christian service, especially those that the Lord blessed with numerous gifts."

Chris raise her eyebrows.

"You know, they were born with good looks, good speaking voices, and better than average intelligence. They might possibly boast of how they developed those gifts, but at their core, they were gifts from God, not the result of the recipient's efforts, and certainly nothing that a Christian leader had the right to boast of."

"Yes, I agree with that."

"Well, David was always ready to forgive any preacher for falling into sin if he would not only confess, but repent and turn. A period of rehabilitation might be required, but unless he'd brought great shame to the kingdom — so much so as to stumble believers or disqualify himself in the eyes of non-believers — then David would one day welcome them back to some level of service. On the other hand, he would not forgive and forget when a so-called man of God flagrantly continued in a practice of a sin."

"And we agreed with Rhodes," Abigail said. "Our Lord and his apostles were outspoken against those who walked in sin or exploited their ministries for personal gain, whether Jewish priests or Gentile preachers. Rhodes frequently quoted the Lord's words, *For unto whomsoever much is given, of him shall be much required.* And David was no hypocrite," she added. "He was willing to have his own life and ministry judged by the same criteria."

"Well," Chris observed, "from what I saw, Rhodes infuriated most preachers and politicians alike, especially when he exposed their waste, dishonesty and failures."

"True," the pastor agreed. "I was initially surprised at how many popular church leaders failed to support Rhodes — and even despised him — until I remembered how Jesus was treated after accusing the hypocritical Jewish leaders of rejecting the words of the prophets and of even killing those men of God. Rhodes was like a modern-day Jeremiah, unpopular because he was warning of the impending judgment that would result from our national sin."

"I suppose," Abigail added, "that there are multitudes in every age who are more concerned with their own worldly success than in being faithful to the Lord. Worse for America, many church leaders compromised their beliefs and even sided with avowed enemies of Christianity!"

"How so?" Chris asked, as though she weren't familiar with the facts.

"The religious leaders of Jesus' time sold him out to retain their wealth, power and influence," Kenzy replied. "Likewise, many of America's recognized religious leaders surrendered their Constitutional rights of free speech and religious freedom — the freedoms that millions had fought and died to secure — and even began denying the Bible so that they could hang on to their own positions as long as possible."

"It's ironic!" Chris agreed. "Their cooperation with their real enemies got them nothing in the long run. They lost their churches and seminaries, and even their lives."

"I suppose," Abigail suggested, "that the Lord's words to the church of the Laodiceans could apply here."

"I beg your pardon?" Chris replied.

"*So then because thou art lukewarm, and neither cold nor hot, I will spew thee out of my mouth.*"

"Oh, right," the pastor agreed. "Revelation 3:16. Strong words.

"Ironic!" Chris said.

"Why?"

"Because in spite of the fact that, "...God so loved the world, that he gave his only begotten Son, that whosoever believeth in him should not perish, but have everlasting life," he has to turn around in Revelation 3:16, to say that God will vomit an entire lukewarm church out of his mouth."

"And those hypocrites and unbelievers might have found forgiveness from the Lord," Jack agreed, "but now it's too late. And since everything rose and fell with their spiritual leadership – or lack of it – America, and the world, is paying the price for their failures. They gave America a confused picture of what the Church was to be, and of what salvation means and how we are to attain it."

"Most of those men knew they were wrong," Abigail said, "but they would nevertheless do just about anything to keep from surrendering their own wealth and influence."

"Even going so far as to fail the people they were supposed to be saving," Chris agreed.

"Even going so far as to destroy people like David Rhodes," he answered. "To many modern churchmen, the members of their congregations were merely a means to an end, not the purpose for their ministries."

"And because the true representatives of God were systematically silenced – men like Rhodes – the entire nation is now suffering," the pastor finished. We chose to cease being *one nation under God.*"

"So we have our own evidence that the rain of judgment often falls on both the just and the unjust," Chris concluded.

"So, at least we are in agreement on that," the pastor said soberly. And his words reminded them of the wall of distrust that seemed to have been erected between them.

For a moment the room was silent. Then Kenzy threw a couple of chunks of firewood into the wood stove, and the clanging of the cast iron door was a signal that that philosophical conversation was ended, and they must return to the issues of the moment.

"I thought you were going to let the fire go out," Chris observed.

"By the time those two small logs burn down, we had better be long gone," he replied. Then his face took on a pensive cast.

"Turning the subject of David Rhodes in a different direction, I want to mention this. Before the war I was a member of a small network of people who were concerned about America's future. We gathered any information that might have a bearing on the future, but unfortunately we had no mechanism for using the information we gathered to save our country.

"Our group wasn't militant," he continued, "but we did have some people in high places who provided us with a good deal of frightening intelligence. Much of it dealt with crimes — both financial and treasonous — being committed by high elected officials and their appointees. But by that stage in the nation's decline, it had become dangerous to be a whistleblower, and we risked our lives simply by possessing such information."

"In most cases, we quietly passed this information on to one another." He laughed. "About the only time we seemed to make a difference was when we passed it on to David Rhodes, and he used a lot of it on his broadcasts.

He glanced at Chris, and realized that she didn't seem in the least surprised by hearing this, and he went quickly on.

"I guess it doesn't matter that I'm sharing this now. Most of the people in our little group are gone."

"I assume that your use of the word *gone* is a euphemism for *dead,*" Chris said. It was a question.

He nodded. "The secretary of our loosely organized group was a guy named McCord — James McCord. I never wholly trusted him, but I figured he couldn't do us much harm. Turns out that I was wrong."

She seemed to remember that name from somewhere, and her thoughts drifted. It was a moment later that she realized that the pastor was asking her a question. She tried to play back the conversation, but couldn't for the life of her remember what he'd been talking about.

"I'm sorry," she said. "I was wool-gathering."

Abigail Kenzy was setting cups of fresh coffee before them and smiled at her. "I guess a little wool-gathering can be understood."

"Understood, but not accepted," her husband said. "This is serious business and times a wasting."

"Jack!" his wife said. "That was rude, and these folks are exhausted."

"That may be," but they don't want to be dead."

"Jack!"

"Abby, this is no game. We're at war, and whether these three know it or not, they are running for their lives, so please let us get on with it."

She stared at him for a moment, finally nodded her head, and turned away. *He's not always right,* she thought, *but he is this time.*

"A week or so before war broke out, we heard a rumor that someone was being paid to destroy David Rhodes. It was rumored that the perpetrator was spending a lot of money hiring people to assassinate his character, steal his identity, tamper with his financial records, clean out his bank accounts and even empty his IRA. We later learned that he even managed to get David's nationwide radio broadcasts canceled. That perp turned out to be none other than our own Jim McCord."

Chris gasped. He had her attention now. *This certainly explains my inability to use our credit cards to buy gas and food!*

"Whoever was paying McCord," he went on, "evidently feared Rhodes because he was so influential. They felt that he needed to be silenced prior to the initial conflagration because he might still wake people up in time to act; and if not, he might still become a powerful resistance leader. Rhodes' enemies obviously had plenty of money, and as it turns out, David was only one of hundreds of people they attacked. But they were particularly vicious to him."

"How so?" Chris asked, trying to hide her growing excitement.

"Recently we received a report that the night before the war started, David's home was burned to the ground. It seems that someone murdered his entire family."

Kenzy saw the tears well up in Chris's eyes, and stopped speaking. *It doesn't make sense,* he thought. *She has to be weeping because I told her that David's family was murdered. And if David's wife is dead, then this woman cannot be his wife. So why is she crying?*

Chris got hold of herself, inhaled deeply, and then spoke slowly, articulating every syllable carefully. "How could you know this?"

The pastor looked at her, curiosity and confusion warring with one another. It took him a moment to conclude that she was exhibiting a tearful concern for a very special, albeit unfortunate family, and her tears were probably the result of her fatigue and stress. In spite of time constraints, he decided to answer her question.

"Both the local fire chief and the county sheriff were at the scene of the fire, and both happened to be part of our little nationwide information-gathering group. I happened to meet them about a month ago, and during our discussion they mentioned that the fire was set by an arsonist."

"You said they found bodies?"

"A woman and two children," he replied, taking the three of them in with his glance. "They were pretty badly burned, and there was probably never any formal identification made because the war started just a few hours after the fire was extinguished." Kenzy hesitated.

"The sheriff told me that he was sure it was David's family. Who else would be in their house? And it all fits. One adult, presumably his wife, and their two children." He frowned. "The sad part was that Rhodes returned home from his flagship station in Chicago just after they put the fire out. He saw the bodies and was beside himself with grief. Then," he continued, "according to the sheriff, something odd happened. While he was standing near the remains of the house questioning Rhodes, the new mayor of Black River Junction, a Muslim extremist by the way, called the sheriff on his cell phone, and insisted that the sheriff arrest Rhodes on a charge of terrorism. And although the mayor had no authority over the county sheriff, he threatened to have the sheriff fired if he failed to arrest Rhodes.

"To charge David Rhodes with terrorism was obviously ridiculous, and the sheriff knew it. He became so angry that he finally hung up on the mayor. He later told me that he wondered how the mayor knew that Rhodes had arrived at his home. It was at that point that he put his phone on mute and told Rhodes to run for his life."

"Then, a few minutes later, just as the sheriff was climbing back into his patrol car, Rhodes was also pulling away from the curb in his vehicle. The sheriff saw someone running toward Rhodes' car, knife in hand, and he turned on his siren in an attempt to scare the guy off. It worked. The perp ran into the neighboring woods and escaped. The sheriff figured that he was the arsonist and had returned to make certain that Rhodes himself was dead." He shrugged his shoulders. "And, that's the last anyone has heard of the missing David Rhodes."

Until now! Chris thought. Then her heart became heavy. *What a mess! When David raced away, he must have been convinced that it was his own family that had died in the fire. He couldn't know that it was his sister-in-law and her two children in the ashes.* Her thoughts wandered. *Oh, poor Michelle! She should have gone with us to visit Dad and Mom instead of spending the night at the house.*

Chris shook her head as though to clear her thoughts, but she couldn't escape the sorrow. *So many people gone....* She had her arms around her children, and her son had been listening carefully to every word. At one point, his eyes had opened wide in understanding, but when he started to comment, she had hugged him to herself and he subsided.

The pastor missed that exchange because he was staring sightless at the fire, lost in his own thoughts. "It's too bad," he mumbled, as though to himself. "We could really use his wisdom and influence right now."

"What's too bad? "Chris asked him.

"Why," he replied, "that they got Rhodes."

"What makes you so certain that they got him?" she asked.

"Well, he hasn't been seen...."

"I'm sure I saw him last night," she replied.

"I thought you said that you originally thought it was him, but then realized it was your husband."

She bit her lip and remained silent.

"Well, which of them was it?"

After a moment, she replied, "It was my husband."

"Well, like I said," the pastor repeated, "It's too bad they got Rhodes."

"No!" the little boy said. "I saw him too."

"Shush," his mother warned.

"I'm just a bit confused now," Kenzy said, speaking to the boy. "Was it your daddy you saw or was it David Rhodes?"

Out of sight of the pastor, his mother was squeezing his elbow. "I'm confused too," the little boy said quietly. "I guess I'm too tired to talk."

"He is exhausted," the pastor's wife said.

"And how would you know David Rhodes anyway?" the pastor persisted, trying to be kindly, but at the same time, inexplicably excited.

But again Chris restrained her son, and again he obediently held his tongue.

The pastor sat there for a moment, chewing his lip and peering suspiciously at her, as though trying to grasp an illusive idea.

"What did you say your husband's name is?"

"I didn't."

"Oh, right. You didn't."

"But I can assure you of one thing," she said.

"What's that?"

"You shouldn't speak of David Rhodes in the past tense. You need to exercise more faith."

The preacher's eyes widened.

"David Rhodes may have enemies in high places," she said, "but he also has a friend who sticks closer than a brother."

"You seem pretty sure of yourself," he responded, the hint of a smile turning up the corner of his lips.

She simply shrugged, but couldn't prevent herself from smiling in return. "I'm sure of God," was her simple reply.

"Well, praise the Lord," the pastor's wife whispered, as though she'd just had an epiphany.

"What's that?" he asked her.

"Oh, nothing," she said, laughter in her voice. "I just felt like praising the Lord."

Abigail's words had brought them all back to the moment, and to the reality of their predicament. She again broke the silence and turned the conversation in another direction.

"You were saying, Jack, that you and I must also leave?"

The pastor didn't answer for a moment. He was very concerned because his wife because she was just recovering from a bronchial infection. He didn't want to take her out in the cold. He had no medicines to help her. The Chinese had seized all available medical supplies and wouldn't even share them with the Americans who were supporting them. So the pastor didn't want to take his wife on a long, cold sleigh ride that might ultimately prove fatal. On the other hand, the presence of this woman and her children left him no choice. Remaining here would almost certainly prove fatal. He turned to Abigail with a frown.

"Yes. We'll leave as soon as we get these three back on their snowmobile and on their way."

"Well, then, we have a lot to do and not much time in which to do it," she said, all business. "I'll pack up some food for them, along with some other items they'll need to set up camp somewhere."

"Well, you can't pack up much," he replied, "because these three can't carry much on that machine."

"What, then?"

"What you said. About all they'll be able to take with them is a good, high-carb meal."

"Coffee?"

"I think a thermos of hot tea would be better for the children."

"Okay. I'll have it ready in ten minutes."

"And I'll check the level in their gas tank and get their snow-mobile running so that it will be warmed up for them."

"But the first thing I want you to do," he said, turning back to his wife, "is to start heating a dozen bricks on the top of the wood stove." He pointed to a pile of red building bricks stacked beside the firewood.

"I'll take care of that," Chris laughed, "but whatever for?"

"Don't you remember your Laura Ingalls Wilder? We will wrap those hot bricks in blankets, and use them to keep Abigail's feet warm during our drive up into the mountains."

Then he was out the door on his errands. When he returned, shaking the snow off his coat, he told them that he wouldn't have made it through the blowing snow to the carriage house if he hadn't held onto the clothesline that he'd hung between the door and the carriage house.

Abigail interrupted to ask him what else she needed to do to prepare for their trip, and he told her to gather their warmest clothes. "I've loaded the last of the gear on our sled and already hitched up the horses." Then he frowned. "I tied Bessie on a long rope to the side of the sleigh, and I fastened a warm blanket over her, but I don't see how she'll endure the trip."

"On the side of the sleigh?"

"By the driver's seat, so that if it becomes necessary, I can untie the knot and let her go."

"We can't leave her here?"

"If we do, she'll either starve to death or someone will butcher her for meat. I want to try to save her, and not just for sentimental reasons. Her milk is precious."

He turned to Chris. "I moved your snowmobile so that it's parked facing the back doors of the carriage house. All I have to do is roll the doors open and you'll be able to head out the rear of the building.

The Unlucky Corporal

Butter Creek Tavern
Butter Creek, Vermont
Christmas Eve

The Chinese corporal who made the detour to Butter Creek with Chris and her children was looking back on his decision with regret. As a result of her disappearance, he realized that he could only look to his future with fear.

It wasn't my fault, he told himself. *I arrived at the inn with three captives. Why did these barbarian Americans have to arrest that man? Including the woman and her two children, the number of prisoners now totaled four. Four! Four is very bad luck. I will not even say it aloud. It sounds like death. Very bad.*

His mind raced on. *Eight would have been good. Eight is very lucky. That's why we started the Beijing Olympics on August 8, 2008 at 8:00 p.m. That's the eighth day of the eight month at 8 o'clock in the year 2008. That's a very lucky combination. We Chinese are a very wise people. Very lucky! But four is not lucky. Four is terribly bad.*

To make things worse, that man who escaped was dressed in black. More bad luck.

Why me? I was simply doing my job by calling headquarters to share the good news. Instead they send Captain Tao Li Wei, of all people! And he shows up after the prisoners escape. All four of them. Bad luck! How could I know that the drunken barbarian fools at the inn would allow their prisoner to escape? And why should I be blamed because some strangers helped the four prisoners to escape? Bad luck!

He lifted his eyes to stare at the back of the head of the man who held his life in his hands. Captain Tao Li Wei was sitting in the front seat, oversteering the snow cat, causing it to jink back and forth as they roared cross country through the blowing snow in what the corporal considered a hopeless pursuit of the fourth escapee.

Four captives. Four escapes. Worse luck! And very bad luck for me because the Captain told me, "There's no such thing as good or bad luck, only destiny." Well, since he's blaming it on me, my destiny looks like bad luck.

The captain was now zig-zagging back and forth among the trees, the lights mounted on its roof radiating back from the snowdrifts brighter than daylight. In the blowing snow, they did not so much as spot a single animal. As he drew his seat belt tighter to keep from sliding around on the rear seat, he continued staring with hatred at the back of Captain Wei's head and doubted whether he'd let him survive the night. His thoughts ran back over the events of the past few hours.

The snow had continued to accumulate in front of his SUV as he'd driven the captives — a woman and her two children — north on Vermont 19 toward Burlington. He'd soon realized that, even with four-wheel drive, he wouldn't be able to make it much further without being trapped in a snowdrift, so he'd checked his map and decided to try to reach Butter Creek. Someone had told him that there was a tavern in the village where he could expect to receive a hot meal from their barbarian allies.

He had arrived at the inn just as a far more important prisoner fell into the hands of the renegades who ran the place. As he approached the front door, the Americans were dragging the man toward a woodshed behind the inn. It was at that moment that he made his great error.

This was very good luck, and it had occurred to him that he might exploit the situation by taking credit for some part in this man's capture. So while the others were busy locking the prisoner in the woodshed, he contacted the Burlington HQ using the inn's ancient phone service. He was certain that his perennial bad luck was changing when he was able to get through immediately, and he was gratified to learn that news of this man's capture was especially welcome. He relished the praise, and somehow overlooked giving any of the credit for his capture to those who had actually identified and arrested the suspect.

Even now he was unwilling to admit, even to himself, that if he had given the others their deserved credit, he would not be in this fix.

During the course of his phone call, he was informed that Captain Tao Li Wei and Lieutenant Meng Peng Zhao were being dispatched immediately by snow cat to take charge of the prisoners.

"You'd better have something good for them to eat and drink when they arrive, Corporal, for they are being rousted out of their warm beds."

This news did not please him, but far worse was to follow. Shortly after hanging up the phone, he was joined by the others in the bar area for celebratory drinks. One drink quickly became several, and he suddenly found himself embroiled in a crisis.

The innkeeper's wife arrived and had discovered her husband — the man who had actually captured the suspect — lying unconscious in a pool of blood in a second floor bedroom. Then, to make matters worse, the man who was in charge of security for the entire village was discovered lying unconscious in a snowbank near the woodshed. And the prisoner, whose capture the driver had just taken credit for, had escaped.

The woman was shouting hysterically at the two remaining guards, and both of them, obviously drunk, were shouting back. The only thing that the driver could ascertain was that the serving girl was also missing, and it had to be assumed that she was involved in the man's escape. That, combined with the news that Captain Wei was en route to the inn, caused his stomach to turn over.

Captain Wei's reputation for brutality was legendary, and the corporal was justifiably terrified. He immediately set out to redeem himself by pursuing the escapees, desperate to recapture them before the captain arrived. His efforts were in vain. Although he was accompanied by one of the two inebriated American turncoats who had not been injured during the escape, they had no chance of success. The visibility was poor, and the blizzard had covered any tracks. He was shaking from the cold when he returned to the inn, but his discomfort would not placate Captain Wei any more than his personal opinion that the escapees would freeze to death in the blizzard. Besides, his superiors didn't want this prisoner dead. They wanted to interrogate him.

The loss of this prisoner, however, was only the beginning of his problems. Earlier, when he left the inn to pursue the escapees, he assumed that the woman he'd been transporting would be preoccupied with her sleeping children and would pose no problem. That assumption also proved faulty. During the confusion surrounding the man's escape — and with no one remaining at the inn to guard her — someone evidently assisted her in her escape.

And while he hoped to blame these additional escapes on the inept Americans, he doubted he would succeed because now the woman and her two children were his direct responsibility.

If I had minded my own business, he realized, *I'd be sitting on top of those three right now, and these other fools would receive the just blame for the man's escape. But I made an innocent phone call,*

just to get some much-deserved recognition, and now I'm the goat!
More bad luck!

Upon his return from the fruitless search, he sent the two now-sober men out into the cold to canvas the village, looking for volunteers loyal to the Chinese to help search for the escaped Americans. They didn't find a single American in the village. In violation of martial law, they had all deserted their homes and fled to the hinterlands. Apart from two old women, there was not a person left in the village.

Kenzy Outfits Chris Rhodes

The Kenzy Farm
East of Butter Creek, Vermont
Christmas Eve

The pastor turned to his wife. "What are you doing now?" he demanded, his impatience obvious.

"Why I'm washing the dishes and cleaning up the kitchen. What does it look like I'm doing?"

"Abigail," he said, unable to hide the frustration in his voice. "We're leaving here, and we're probably never coming back, but if we do, this house will probably just be a heap of ashes."

"Now, Jack, what happens to the house after we leave is out of my control, but I'm not leaving a messy kitchen!"

He shrugged his shoulders and turned away in defeat. Forty years of marriage had taught him to identify the occasions on which to make strategic withdrawals. His eyes met Michael's, and he shrugged his shoulders in resignation. The boy smiled in understanding.

Then he turned to Chris and whispered, "She was the same way the morning our first son was born; wouldn't get in the car to go to the hospital until she'd finished straightening up the place. Her labor pains were seven minutes apart, and the hospital was in Black River Junction, nearly forty miles away."

Chris laughed. "I hope you were wearing shoe laces and carrying a newspaper."

He laughed, the strain of their earlier contention evidently forgotten.

"You two make all the jokes you want," Abigail interjected, but Jack ought to remember that the dishes I washed that morning were the last clean dishes in this house until I got back from that hospital."

"Oops," Chris laughed.

"That woman can hear a pin drop across the room," he said in mock surrender, then counter-attacked.

"You'd better hurry, or they may be the last dishes you ever get to wash."

And with that, she threw her dish cloth down and left the wet glasses to dry on the drainboard while she turned to gathering a few last minute items for their journey.

While she continued working, Kenzy went to a cabinet by the door, removed something that looked like a motorcycle helmet and carefully handed it to Chris.

"What's this?" she asked.

"This is a very special snowmobile helmet," he told her. "In fact, before the war started, it was the latest thing in what well-dressed motorcyclists wore." He turned it around so that it shined in the glow of the gas lantern. "What's more, with a little judicious retrofitting, it has worked out just great for snowmobiling."

"I don't understand."

"It has a visor-mounted heads-up display unit, and it's driven by a compact GPS transceiver."

"I'm sorry. I don't speak technology."

"Okay, I'll simplify. He pointed at the clear plastic shield on the front of the helmet. "This helmet has a built-in global positioning system."

"A GPS? I thought that all our satellites were destroyed at the start of the war."

"Ah, so you do speak a little technology. And, no, all our satellites were not destroyed. I guess that the belligerents were unable to shoot all the satellites down, though it's more likely that they felt they might need them to provide navigation for their own combat forces. Whatever the reasoning of the various aggressors, it will work to our advantage tonight."

He pointed to the top of the clear plastic face plate. "While you're driving along, you'll see a real-time display of data projected onto this surface. Without moving your head you'll be able to read your speed, the distance remaining to your destination and you'll see your actual location on the map."

"Actual location?"

"Yes. It will know where you are within three feet of your exact location on the ground."

"That's incredible."

"It's handy," he agreed. "Do you remember how your GPS would indicate the number of feet to the intersection?"

"Sure."

Suddenly their conversation was interrupted by a loud beeping noise, and Jack and Abigail exchanged glances.

"Go ahead and answer it," he told her. "These are good folks, and even if they weren't, we'll be out of here in a few hours."

Abigail Kenzy reached inside a kitchen cabinet, and lifted out what looked like a walkie-talkie. She pressed a button, and spoke just one word. "Yes?"

Whoever was calling spoke for less than ten seconds, but the change in Abigail's face brought the pastor to her side. Apart from saying "Yes," the only other words she spoke were, "Good bye and God bless." Then she pressed the button to terminate the call and put the device in her coat pocket.

Jack was waiting, and there was nothing frivolous about her now. She seemed intensely focused, even frightened.

"Two snowmobiles, each carrying two armed men and traveling east, just left the Butter Creek Inn. At the rate they are moving in this blizzard, it will probably take them about thirty minutes to reach us."

Jack nodded, accepting what he'd considered the inevitable.

"God willing, if we can get out of here soon enough, they are not going to reach us at all," he told her. Then, speaking to the room, he said, "Okay, let's get cracking!"

He turned to Chris. "With the firm conviction that two heads are better than one, I want Michael in on this too."

His mother turned to him, but he was already at her side, his eyes shining with the importance that little boys feel when adults treat them as equals.

"Let me pick up where I left off a moment ago. This is pretty much like the GPS units that people were using in their cars before the war, but it's mounted inside this helmet.

He turned back to Chris, and set the helmet on the table.

"Believe it or not, this still works. I put fresh batteries in it and tried it out.

"I don't understand. How can it be to our advantage? And what's this window in the back for?" she asked, a gleam in her eye. "Is that so someone can examine my brain?"

Her question broke the tension for a moment. Abigail laughed with her, and before anyone could stop him, Michael lifted the helmet off the table, pulling it over his head. Then he took a couple of deep rasping breaths and whispered loudly, "Luke, I am your father."

The pastor's face seemed to stiffen, then relaxed. *We really don't have time to play,* he thought, *but if it helps, so be it. Besides, it was sort of funny.*

He forced a laugh. "No, it's not to examine your brain, Chris." Then he turned to the boy and said, "Be careful with that helmet, young man." Then he tried to lighten his rebuke by adding, "After all, you are much too young to be Luke's father."

The boy laughed, but his mother told him to put the helmet back on the table.

"So, what's it for?" she asked, returning to the subject of the helmet.

"This is just clever optics," he told her. "No camera, no batteries. You'll be able to see anyone following you. The image is somehow displayed on the reflective surface above the GPS, sort of like a rear-view mirror." He laughed, "It might come in handy in the unlikely event that you ever find someone chasing you."

"What about that head display thing you were talking about?" Michael asked.

"Shush," his mother said, shaking him gently. "Sit still and listen."

"Yes, Mom," he replied, with an exaggerated tolerance.

"I'll leave out the technical stuff," Kenzy continued, "and just explain what is different between this and the conventional auto GPS units."

"Non-technical is right down my alley," Chris agreed.

"Here, put it on," he said, handing it to her. He showed her where the on/off button was located, then she pulled it over her head.

After a moment, she told him, "It's asking, *Are you indoors?*"

"That's because it's not picking up the satellite signal because the roof is blocking it. You can see the display though, can't you?"

"Yes."

"Good. You said that you're familiar with the GPS units that were installed in cars before the war?"

"Sure."

"Well, this has one significant difference.

"How so?" Chris asked, now keenly interested.

"Well, as with the automobile flavor of GPS, it gets its feed from satellites, so you will still see side roads and bodies of water as you approach them...."

"Okay. It's a GPS," Michael commented. Big deal!"

"Michael, that was rude!"

"Sorry."

"...but there's also a topographic feature..."

"A *top-of-what* feature?"

"Michael, for the last time, be quiet." She turned to the pastor. "I'm sorry. I don't think any of us have had enough sleep."

"Understood," he said. Barely able to hide his own annoyance, he pointed to the helmet. "What makes it different is that the map will have squiggly lines all over it, representing changes in elevation."

"Oh," the boy interrupted again. "Just like the hand-held GPS that dad carried when we went hiking."

"You're familiar with those?" the pastor asked.

"Sure." We used it to check our elevation, and we were able to stay away from steep climbs and the edges of cliffs."

"Exactly."

"Oh, I remember," Chris said. "Every squiggly line on the map represents a change of about fifty feet in elevation, so if there are a bunch of them close together, then we'd know that it was very steep.

"Right," he continued. "What's important is that I've loaded maps for most of New England, so as you ride along, the GPS will integrate the satellite images with those maps."

"I don't understand," Chris yawned. "What's the advantage?"

Kenzy decided that she wasn't dense, only exhausted.

Her head began to nod, and he raised his voice to capture her attention.

"Chris, I'm almost finished."

"Huh?" she mumbled. Then her head snapped up. "Oh, sorry!"

"Please listen to me. We don't have much time. He turned to his wife. "Abigail, is there any more coffee? We need to wake this gal up."

"I didn't empty the pot, so it's coming right up," she replied. "But it's pretty strong."

"I think that strong is just what she needs."

"And, Jack?"

"Yes?"

She handed Chris the coffee, then turned to her husband. "I've been watching the clock. They could be here in less than 25 minutes."

"Yes, I know! We've got to hurry."

Chris took a sip of the bitter coffee and nodded, trying to force her eyes open.

"Somewhere along the route that I'm recommending, you'll pass through a very dangerous area. Since there is snow falling, you'll have no starlight to help you recognize it."

"Dangerous?"

He had her full attention now.

"Yes. The road has been abandoned for years and has had no upkeep. At one point, it's been undercut by the creek that will be flowing far below you on your left. The road surface tips steeply to that side, and since there will be ice beneath the snow, you'll probably find yourself sliding toward the left edge of the road."

"So?"

At that point, you'll be on the lip of a deep and narrow ravine. Butter Creek flows through that ravine. The stream itself won't be ice-covered at that point because there are rapids. To give you an idea of how treacherous it is, people used to go there in the summer to do white water rafting. At one point along the creek, the ravine walls are very steep, narrow and close together."

"How steep and narrow?" Michael asked.

"It's very narrow, perhaps thirty feet from edge to edge. The far bank is topped by a razorback ridge. The top of that ridge is probably ten or fifteen feet lower than the road you'll be following. As kids, we used to walk along the ridge on the far side of the stream, but it was like walking a knife edge, and very dangerous. If we were to slide off, it would have been at least a twenty-foot fall to the rocky stream bed below. If we were to have fallen the other way, we'd have found ourselves sliding down a steep incline for several hundred feet."

Now what's the point of my telling them that? he wondered. *It's irrelevant. Maybe I'm as tired as they are.*

He tried to focus. "As I was saying, the road you'll be taking tilts toward the ravine. If your snowmobile slides off the road, there is no chance of survival."

He caught her eye to see whether she understood what he was suggesting. She looked at him vacantly.

"If you keep one eye on the GPS, you'll know when you are getting close to that cliff. When you see it coming up, get to the right side of the road and try to keep your speed steady, at maybe fifteen or twenty miles per hour."

"Oh, I'd be frightened to go that fast."

"If you don't, you will probably lose control and slide across the road and into the ravine.

That sobered her. They were both again listening carefully, any flippancy gone.

"Here's the other bad news," the pastor continued. "The drop off will be on your left, but a steep rocky slope rises on your right and extends far up the mountainside. There are no trees or brush on its surface."

Chris shrugged. "I don't understand."

"We used to have government agencies and ski patrols to warn us," he said, "but they no longer exist." His voice trailed off.

Chris was confused and waited for him to elaborate.

He looked over at her, perhaps a bit embarrassed for the lapse. "Sometimes I just want things to be the way they were before, and I find myself drifting away."

"I think we all do that," she said, regret in her voice.

"Anyway," he went on, "nearly every year, when there's an accumulation of snow like tonight, there are avalanches all around these mountains, and particularly on the trail you'll be taking."

"Cool!" Michael blurted.

"No, not cool!" the pastor told him. "A couple of years ago, three teenagers were swept off that trail by the snow and buried in the bottom of the ravine. We found the remains of two of them when the snow melted the following July. The third was evidently swept far downstream during the spring floods."

"And this helmet can somehow help?"

"Absolutely! Remember what I said. When the lines start moving closer together, move to your right and speed up."

"That doesn't sound so bad."

"No, but if you discover that there is ice under the snow, and you start sliding toward the precipice, you'll be tempted to gun the engine to try to work back uphill to the right side of the road."

"So what? We've gotta keep from falling over that cliff, right?" Michael demanded.

"Yes, but if you gun the engine, there's a chance that the racket will start an avalanche, and that would definitely sweep you off the road and down into the valley below. With the population of Vermont at an estimated twenty-five percent of the pre-war numbers, and with no one hiking for recreation, it's unlikely that your bodies would ever be found."

"Oh," Chris said in a small voice. "Nice!"

"Now do you see how that helmet could be important, Michael?"

"Yes sir."

"Well, it sounds absolutely wonderful," Chris said, shaking her head to stay awake, "but can you really spare it? And how do you know it will work with that snowmobile?"

"It works independently of the snowmobile, unless you want to plug it in to keep the battery charge up. But as far as our knowing about your snowmobile, it was once ours. The Chinese confiscated it, and somehow the owners of the tavern finagled it from them. Those traitors have a lot to answer for when this is over. In the meantime, you can make excellent use of the helmet. It might well save your lives."

"But don't you need the snowmobile?"

He laughed. "No. As I mentioned, we are traveling low-tech. We have two horses and a good old-fashioned sled with runners. I've already loaded a lot more stuff on that sleigh than we could get on the snowmobile; and although it's slower, I think it will be warmer for Abigail, and we should make it safely to our hideaway." He smiled. "So don't be concerned about us. In fact, I consider it providential and a delightful irony that you are using it to make good your escape."

She yawned. "Well, we really don't know how to thank you."

"Just stay awake and stay alive so that you can get back to your husband. And when you see him, tell him that we are all praying for him. Oh, yes," he added a twinkle in his eye. "Tell him we're praying for David Rhodes too."

Suddenly they were conscious of a keening sound outside. "The wind is rising," he warned, "and I'm certain we'll have more heavy snow before morning. That's both good and bad news."

"If it snows, it will be harder for them to follow us, right?" Michael suggested.

"Right, but a blizzard may prove far more dangerous to all of us than our pursuers."

Chris nodded in understanding.

The pastor spoke more rapidly now, his words more precise and almost stern, as though he'd ceased being the friendly local pastor and had put on a military uniform.

"And now," he said, "it is time for you and me to bundle up and go out to the carriage house so that we can check everything out."

Chris' face showed her consternation, but it was Abigail Kenzy who objected.

"Really, Jack," she said, "must you take her out in this bitter cold right now?"

He didn't argue with her, but instead drew her gently to his side.

"I'm sorry, love of my life, but we must all prepare to move on."

"Right now?"

"What does the clock tell you?"

She looked at the old wind-up clock. "Twenty one minutes...."

Chris surprised them with her next words.

"Well, if I'm going out there, the children are going with me."

"Why would you expose them to the cold before you have to?" Abigail asked.

"I have vowed not to be separated from my children. Too much in this world is uncertain." She turned her ear toward the door, and they all heard the keening of the wind outside. "That carriage house could suddenly seem a lifetime away from this house," she said, "and where I go, they go."

"It's just as well," the pastor agreed. "Time is running out, and you've already been here nearly an hour. It's better that we all leave sooner rather than later."

"How long do you think we have?" Chris asked, her anxiety obvious.

"Not more than fifteen minutes," he answered, his somber reply leaving no room for argument. "We can't be pulling away while they are pulling in."

"All right," his wife agreed sadly. I have their little lunch made up and wrapped in an insulated bag. They can put it in one of the saddlebags."

"Right," he said, suddenly all business. "Get the children dressed, and wrap them in blankets. We'll all go up together."

He walked across the room. Leaning against the wall next to the door was an old wooden toboggan. He set it down on the floor so that it was pointing toward the door. After arranging a blanket over its surface, he went to the wood stove, picked up a pair of tongs and began stacking the hot bricks on the front of the sled.

He frowned. "I wish I had a gun to offer you," he said.

"I do know how to shoot," she said. "My husband had weapons at home, but we kept them secret from the authorities."

"Unfortunately," he responded, "the state did everything possible to limit ownership. Then, after the invasion, the Chinese opened the record books, confiscated what few weapons remained, and imprisoned the owners. The irony is that most of the anti-gun and anti-war folks lost their lives, either due to their lack of preparedness, or their inability to fight off the predators who seemed to come out of the woodwork with the outbreak of war."

"We know," Chris replied. "Hitler and Stalin didn't allow citizens to own weapons either."

Her daughter Mary was awake now, and Chris helped her to her feet. Then she stood and hugged Mrs. Kenzy and the pastor. Mrs. Kenzy got down on her knees, drew the children to her, said a brief prayer, gave them each a hug, and handed them each a Christmas cookie.

Neither of the children had seen such treats since the war had started. Mary was speechless, but Michael stated emphatically, "This is the best Christmas ever!"

It took the Kenzys a moment to conclude that he wasn't just referring to the cookie, but to the fact that they had, for the moment, escaped from the Chinese. Chris thought that it was more than that. It was because they'd discovered that their daddy was still alive.

Michael took a small bite out of the cookie and began chewing it slowly, savoring the flavor, and they all laughed at the beatific expression on his face. Finally, the pastor and his wife put their arms around the three of them and he prayed aloud for their deliverance.

Holding his hands up in benediction, he said, "And now, Lord Jesus, we commend all of our lives to your care. Help us all to remember that we are never alone. Amen."

He took his wife's elbow and steadied her as she rose to her feet.

When he was finished, he turned and beckoned Chris to bring the children, but Abigail was already depositing little Mary just behind the stack of hot bricks. And without the need for instructions, Michael anticipated his mother and sat down behind his sister, wrapping his legs and arms around her. She leaned her head back so that she could see her brother's face, and her weary mouth curved into a brief smile.

Quickly, so that the children wouldn't become overheated, the adults pulled on their own outerwear.

Then the pastor indicated that he wanted his wife to sit behind the children on the toboggan.

"Oh, no," she remonstrated. "I can make it on my own."

"Humor me," he insisted. "You're just recovering from the flu, and we have a long way to go tonight."

"Oh, Jack!"

"Please, Mrs. Kenzy. Do sit on the sled," Chris said. "And wrap your scarf around your nose and mouth so that you won't be breathing in that cold air."

"Oh, all right," she said, obviously with a sense of relief, but not wanting to admit her weakness. "I can't argue with both of you."

"Now," he told them, "I have my light strapped to my forehead so that hopefully I can find my way. I'll use the clothesline as a guide and drag the toboggan. Chris can help me pull it.

He handed Chris the helmet.

Finally they were out the door, pulling the toboggan up the slope toward the carriage house with wind and snow whipping around them.

The pastor expected it to be a very difficult and dangerous journey across that twenty yards of snow, but the wind suddenly abated, the snow ceased blowing, and he could see the doors clearly in the light of his headlamp.

"Inside, quick!" he hollered, as he pulled the toboggan onto the floor of the carriage house.

He hurried back toward the door, but Chris already had it closed by the time he reached her side.

She's some woman, he thought!

As they turned back toward the toboggan, the wind shrieked and the building shook as the storm resumed its fury. In the feeble light of his headlamp, they saw wisps of hay and straw floating down from the loft above.

I don't have any idea where I'm going, she thought, *but he seems to know what he's doing, and I really don't have any choice but to follow his instructions.*

In spite of the stress they all shared, the preacher seemed to maintain an air of confidence.

"There are a couple of space blankets on the seat of my sleigh," he told her. "Unwrap one and spread it out across the seat and hang it up over the back. Then lay the wool blanket you'll find there over it." As soon as she finished spreading the blankets over the seat, he shouted, "Help Abigail get up from the toboggan and into the sled, will you please? I'll load your kids onto the snowmobile."

"I'm right here, Jack," his wife said, her annoyance breaking through. "I am not an invalid, and I assure you that I can look after myself."

"Yes, dear," he replied quietly, his voice filled with a kindly tolerance that was obviously born of long experience."

Chris could not contain herself and burst out in laughter when she heard him begin to quote Frost.

The woods are lovely, dark and deep,
But I have promises to keep,
And miles to go before I sleep,
And miles to go before I sleep.

"Oh, dear," Abigail's voice came back. "I'll try to be a good little girl." And, in spite of the stress communicated to them by the adults, even the children laughed at her riposte.

Then the pastor went off on a new tack.

"Chris, if you are done tucking Abigail in, please start carrying the hot bricks from the toboggan to the sleigh, and put them on the floor under her feet. You should be able to carry them with your gloved hands."

"And please set a few aside to put under *el Supremo's* feet too," Abigail added.

Chris grinned. *This woman is not about to be one-upped.*

Now the pastor was nesting the sleeping Mary in front of Michael on the rear seat of the snowmobile.

"You'll have to keep your arms wrapped around her to keep her from falling off, Michael. Do you think you can handle that?"

"Yes, sir."

"Chris," the pastor called, "as soon as you have Abigail bundled up, come over here and I'll tell you what I think you need to do."

A gust of wind again shook the building, and they could see the snow sifting in through the cracks. The temperature seemed to be dropping, and Chris cringed at the thought of going out into the dark unknown.

Chinese Arrive at Butter Creek
Butter Creek Inn
Butter Creek, Vermont
Early Christmas Morning

The big snow cat swept into the village at high speed, its two wide tracks carrying it easily over the drifts, its cabin keeping its occupants dry and warm. There was no risk of the driver running down a child at play in the snow. Children who were forced to subsist on starvation diets had no surplus energy to waste in play.

The driver who had brought Chris and the children to the inn watched its approach through one of the inn's windows. " *Why*," he wondered, *why couldn't Wei have been attacked en route and killed by the counter-revolutionaries? Worse luck for me!*

The three men riding in the snow cat had looked forward to a brief interrogation of the prisoner, followed by a few hot drinks and then warm beds. Instead, and unfortunately for the corporal who awaited them, Captain Wei and Lieutenant Zhao arrived at Butter Creek Tavern a little over two hours after the escapes had been discovered.

Wei and Zhao were accompanied by Kim Ling. Ling was surprised that the general had been serious about his making the trip, and, as it turned out, he had been ordered both to drive the big snow cat and to serve as interpreter. While many Chinese spoke English fluently, Kim Ling had been surprised when the general had told him that these two officers were unable to speak the language. He was to soon learn that the general had lied to him, again.

Their superiors were, to say the least, very angry when they learned of the dual escapes. Using Kim as their interpreter, they began organizing those present into two separate groups of pursuers.

When the captain learned that the entire force at his disposal consisted of just himself and Lieutenant Zhao, plus two half-drunk Americans, an old woman and Kim Ling, he was beside himself with fury.

"What about transportation?" he demanded. Kim translated, and the corporal, who had already revealed that he was a proponent of the "take the credit, shift the blame" school, said the first thing that came to his mind.

"I've located two operable snowmobiles in the village," he answered proudly in his native Chinese.

"It's about time that you did something right," the captain snapped. Kim had translated the corporal's words into English, and the innkeeper's wife responded in anger.

"I got those two snowmobiles for you," she shouted in a loud voice. "And I filled their gas tanks and checked the oil myself." When Kim translated her words, she received a venomous look from the corporal. Before anyone else had an opportunity to speak, she spat, "As far as I can see, this *chauffeur* of yours has done nothing for you except lose his passengers.

The captain looked with contempt at the corporal, but it was to the woman that he directed his venom.

"Be quiet, old crow," he shouted in Chinese. "You will not judge my subordinates."

She did not need Kim's translation to know that she shouldn't have opened her mouth, and as the captain rebuked her, she seemed to sag. This brought a sly smile to the face of the corporal who believed his luck had already turned so terribly bad.

Kim, who didn't bother interpreting the captain's words, thought that she looked like one of the witches described in *Grimm's Fairy Tales.* He'd have been shocked to learn that the crone was actually only in her late forties.

Captain Wei turned to her. "Your name?"

"Benton, your excellency," the old harridan replied, staring boldly at the captain. "I'm the innkeeper."

"I thought the innkeeper was a man?"

"My husband and I operate this inn as equals."

"For the time being," was the captain's cryptic reply.

His eyes remained fixed on her, and she didn't have the sense to lower her own in deference until Kim hissed a warning at her and she tipped her head down in feigned respect. In her arrogance, she might have been slower to respond, but she and her husband had concluded that, having sold their souls to the Chinese, they had better make the most of a bad bet. If the Chinese were to ultimately lose this war, and the Americans somehow took their country back, they would have to run for their lives.

"All right," Kim told the woman, interpreting the captain's words "You'll go with me on the snowmobile that I'll be driving."

"Why would I want to do that?" she asked, her anger obvious. "My husband is injured. I must stay with him."

Kim interpreted her words to the captain.

The captain had grown impatient with her. "You will go with my interpreter because I said you will go with him," he replied in English, forgoing Kim's services as his interpreter and surprising everyone, including Kim, with the fact that he was fully capable of understanding and speaking English. He spoke very precisely and very quietly, and in consequence, his words were somehow all the more more menacing.

Mrs. Benton was not nearly as intelligent as she believed, but she was shrewd and didn't require any additional warnings to let her know what might happen to her if she objected further. She immediately nodded her head in acquiescence.

As the captain continued speaking, Kim Ling had all he could do to hide his delight at being told he'd be driving one of the snowmobiles. Even better, his passenger would not be one of the armed Chinese officers, but would instead be this frail and contemptible woman. *Evidently General Eng did not discuss my own uncertain status as a conscript with the captain. But why*, Ling wondered, *had the general told him that these Chinese officers couldn't speak English?*

The captain went on in a peremptory voice.

"Lieutenant Meng Peng Zhao, whose name incidentally means *fierce*, will drive the other machine. He will be in charge of your group."

He pointed at one of the two drunks. "You will be the fourth member of this little group. You will carry a weapon and ride on Lieutenant Zhao's machine."

"Ys zur," he replied, "but I'd rather be the driver."

"You're so drunk that you'll be lucky to hold on," Wei snarled.

The man looked as though he wanted to challenge the charge, but wound up burping in reply.

The captain turned to the innkeeper's wife. "You will show Lieutenant Zhao where you believe the missing woman and her two children might be found. Can you do that?"

"I think so."

"Don't fail me."

He turned to Zhao.

"I'll take this other drunken son of perdition with me in the snow cat," he said, pointing to the corporal, "and we will search for the escapee and the woman who assisted him."

He walked over to the innkeeper's wife. "If you'd been here at the inn, doing your job, your maid wouldn't have injured your husband, and she would not have escaped, much less helped this man." He waited a full moment for the implied threat to take hold. "If you'd been doing what you were supposed to be doing, it would not be necessary for all of us to be chasing around the countryside looking for all these people!"

She was so terrified that she dared not try to answer that unfair charge.

Then the captain turned to Lieutenant Zhao. If you should overtake the woman and her two children, leave the brats where you find them, but bring the woman back here for interrogation."

"You mean, just leave the children out in the blizzard?" the lieutenant asked?

"You heard me!" he shouted.

The lieutenant replied quietly, "Yes, sir."

He turned to Kim Ling. "You keep an eye on the woman." Then he turned to the lieutenant, and nodded toward Kim Ling. "And you'll keep an eye on our faithful interpreter."

"Yes, sir!"

"And when you've recaptured the woman and her two brats, bring them back here. Alive."

The lieutenant stood to attention. "Yes, sir!"

Captain Tao Li Wei turned toward the door, and the others followed. As he led the unlucky corporal through the front door, he hissed, "I can't believe that you let that heathen woman and her spawn escape!"

Chris Says Goodbye
The Kenzy Farm
East of Butter Creek
Christmas Eve

Kenzy unfolded a map and lay it over the hood of her snowmobile. "Okay," he said, "let me show you where you're going." When his light flooded the surface, Chris realized that it was a geodetic survey map. Her husband had collected a large number of those maps for the family's summer cross-country hikes.

"I've been thinking about your situation, Chris, and this is my recommendation."

Michael said, "I can't see."

"Move on in here, Michael," the pastor said, and he lifted the boy from behind his sister and set him on his feet next to his mother.

Mother and son leaned over to peer at the map. Fear was an effective stimulant, and she was now wide awake, listening carefully as he laid out his plan.

"You need to get away from here while the snow is still blowing wildly. They might even be ransacking our house and we wouldn't hear them, but for the same reason, I don't think they will hear your engine above the storm." He pointed to the doors at the back of the carriage house, directly in front of her snowmobile.

"Go straight out those doors, up over the knoll, and down across the field. The rear of this building can't be seen from the house and, if you don't rev your engine, the storm will cover up any sound. You'll be crossing a large corn field, and there are no obstructions until you reach the far edge, so leave your headlights turned off until you get over the crest of the hill. That's a few hundred yards south."

"When our pursuers finish searching the house, they'll hopefully check the barn on the opposite side of the street before they come here, and when they see no sign of recent occupancy in the house or in the barn, we can hope that they will assume that you continued following the paved road east without stopping here."

"But that's not likely, is it?"

"No. I'm afraid it's not." He looked in the direction of the house, as though trying to see through the carriage house wall and grasp the enemy's progress and intentions. "It's doubtful that they'll find the door into our room at the back of the house because it's so well camouflaged."

"Oh, no!"

"What?"

"We were in such a hurry that I didn't close that door tightly."

Well, that's done it, he thought. *Once they find the hot stove, they'll know we can't be far away. It's unlikely that Chris can outrun their snowmobiles, and I certainly can't get away with a horse-drawn sled.*

He shook his head slowly from side to side, and the light strapped to his forehead waved back and forth across the surface of the map. He wasn't aware that his despair showed until she said, "I'm so sorry."

"It's okay," he said, trying to reassure her.

And maybe it is, he thought.

"Look, if they find our hidden apartment, they'll start looking through all the buildings, including this one. It's almost certain that the tracks we made coming here from the house have already been swept away by the wind. Nonetheless, they will be coming, and we have to get out of here soon."

He punched the tip of his finger down on the map to return their attention to the matter at hand, and began speaking very rapidly.

"No change in plans. You go straight through this door, over the knoll, and across the field. Keep your lights turned off because they will probably reflect off the falling snow." He frowned. "You probably won't be able to see twenty feet in front of you through the driving snow, so trust your instruments and trust the Lord! At all times, keep one eye on the heads-up display. Stay focused on that map. Keep the compass on due south."

It was clear to him that her fatigue had brought her to the point of hysteria, and when she giggled, he became deeply concerned. But then she said, "Trust the instruments, huh? So we'll be walking by faith and not by sight?"

"No, Mom," her son corrected. "We'll be riding by faith."

Although the pastor was glad that the boy and his mother could still laugh at the situation, he was fighting to hide his own impatience and growing fear.

"Quiet," he snapped. He'd forgotten that Abigail could overhear them, and was startled when he heard her voice.

"Oh, for Pete's sake, Jack! Lighten up! That was funny, if not truly profound, and we don't have a lot to laugh about right now."

Afraid that she'd burst out coughing again, he replied, "Sorry, dear," and then he tried to take the sting out of his rebuke. "You're right, Michael. To paraphrase the Apostle Paul, you must snowmobile by faith and not by sight." Their answering laughs sounded wooden and dutiful.

Yet it occurred to him that he was wrong about Chris being near hysteria. She had a tight grip on herself, and her half-serious jest once again indicated that she also had a deep underlying faith. Not only that, but her words amounted to a divine reminder to both of them that the Spirit of God was always near.

This is no time for theological meditation, he thought.

He ran his index finger across the map, from what she assumed was the barn they were standing in to a stream that must border the far side of the corn field.

"If you keep your eye on that helmet display as you cross the field," he told her, "you'll see yourself approaching this brook on the far edge of the field. Turn right before you get to that brook, and try to run parallel to it toward the west." He slid his finger over the map to indicate the path of the stream. "You should be able to follow alongside it without using your headlights, but you'll need to turn them on before you get to the place where the stream abruptly turns south."

"You'll come to one of the farm's wood roads. It begin at the southwest corner of the field and zigzags south through the woods. Apart from the fact that you should be able to follow the narrow snow-covered stretch between the trees, you won't be able to identify it with your heads-up display."

"You mean it won't show there?"

"No. It's was never a road; just a logging trail. Trust the display. Just keep moving south with the stream somewhere on your left, and try to avoid rocks and trees."

"It sounds scary."

He smiled to reassure her, but didn't bother responding. *It is scary. On the other hand, if the enemy catches you, I don't want to think of what they will almost certainly do to you and your children.*

"Even if you find that you're not on the wood road," he continued, "just keep going south. When your heads-up display indicates that you've reached Old Butter Creek Road, turn right and follow it."

"Aren't I apt to run into more of the bad guys there?"

"Bad guys?"

"Sure. What should I call them? Chinese communists? Henchmen? Turncoats? They're our enemies! They're evil. They're the spawn of the devil. But I don't want to terrify myself or the kids, so I call them the bad guys."

"They don't wear white hats," Michael said, and the pastor understood her decision to use that phrase. It was non-specific, and it wasn't so scary to her children.

"Sorry. That makes a lot of sense." *And maybe I'm the one bordering on hysteria.*

"But in answer to your question: No, you're not apt to run into any *bad guys* there because it's an old east-west country lane. Nobody uses it anymore because the bridge is out where it used to cross

Butter Creek. That road will take you well to the south of the village."

Suddenly the sound of a snowmobile engine rose above the scream of the wind. They turned in the direction of the house, and through the cracks in the wall of the carriage house, they could see the glow from its headlamps as it raced along the back of the house and disappeared around the far corner.

Time had run out.

"Again," Kenzy repeated, "east-west road will show up on your GPS. Portions of it are washed out, and it's basically a hiking trail now, but with the heavy snow, you shouldn't have any trouble until you reach the base of the mountain."

"What mountain?"

"That's the place I warned you about. When you look at your heads-up display, you'll see those elevation lines drawing closer together on both sides of the road. On your right, the mountain. On your left, the ravine.

"But let me warn you about this first. Shortly after you come to the end of our wood road, and you turn right on the old Butter Creek Road, you'll come to a stream. It crosses the old road you you'll be following and runs south a few hundred yards before flowing into Butter Creek. The bridge over that stream has been washed out. The creek will probably be frozen over, but the banks are steep where the bridge used to cross. You should stop when you reach the stream, and look for the best place to cross. Get off the machine and test the ice before you try to drive the snowmobile across.

He anticipated her question.

"It's okay. It's a slow moving stream, and I'm reasonably certain it will be safe to cross the ice." His voice became grim. "The bad spot on the old road is between this stream and Route 19."

"That's the stretch where the road tilts?"

"Right. You'll be in an avalanche area. The snow could slide down the mountainside on your right, and there will be that fatal drop on your left. It's always icy there, so you'll need to be watching the display in order to know when to move to the right so that you can make it safely through."

Chris nodded in understanding, then asked, "Won't someone hear the snowmobile when we pass near the town?"

"I don't think so. Unless you're revving the engine, the sound won't travel far. The snow should soak up most of the noise." He tapped his homemade map with the point of his pencil. "Any questions?"

She was thinking, *I really like this confident, no-nonsense preacher,* but when she didn't speak for a moment, he met her eyes.

He repeated himself. "Any questions?"

"No, no questions." She tried to smile, but it was more of a grimace. "Thank you both, for everything."

They heard another snowmobile race toward the back corner of the house, and Kenzy wrapped his gloved hand over the lens of his headlamp, taking no chance that the dim light from the weakened batteries might be seen.

Inside the carriage house it was momentarily dark. They listened as the snowmobile swept around the corner, its headlights sweeping across the outer wall of the carriage house, penetrating the narrow cracks between the boards, creating vertical slashes of light that moved in parallel lines across their faces and along the back wall. The driver took the turn wide, slowing as his headlights swept across the carriage house. Evidently satisfied that the snow there was undisturbed, he accelerated again as headed toward the far corner of the house. Kenzy was beginning to sigh his relief when the machine abruptly stopped.

They all realized that the driver had probably noticed the door that had been left ajar and he would be going to check.

The pastor was again all business and began speaking rapidly.

"When you reach Route 19, which is a north-south highway, turn left and go south. Since there are no longer any snow plows in use anywhere in Vermont, I doubt that anyone will be on that road at midnight on Christmas Eve. Continue south about a half mile. The

GPS should alert you, but if not, you'll see the small sign for *Liberty Christian Camp* hanging from a tree on your right.

Turn there and follow the narrow, winding drive for about a mile. When you reach the camp, you'll find that it's pretty primitive. There are a bunch of open-sided cabins, little more than lean-tos, and some fireplaces and picnic tables. Drive slowly, and be careful because some of the fireplaces are no doubt buried in the snow. You don't want to break a ski running into one."

Chris was wondering how they could survive in an open-sided cabin with no food or camping supplies, and evidently her face showed her dismay. Before she could raise a question, however, he sought to put her mind at ease.

"There's a small cabin that the camp directors lived in during the summer. It's insulated and winterized. There's a quantity of freeze-dried foods under one of the bunks. And there's plenty of firewood, plus an indoor hand pump for water."

"Can't we just stay there for a while?"

What can I tell her? That she might be able to get a few hours sleep at most? That she must cross the lake before the snow stops, so that she can't be followed? That we have a better chance of making it to our destination than she does hers, and of surviving after we get there?

"I don't think that our cabin will be safe for anyone after to-morrow morning," was all he replied.

He turned to look at his wife, and when his light struck her face, both he and Chris could see the tears that glistened in Abigail's eyes.

"How do you know about the food in the cabin?" Chris asked.

He smiled, trying to infuse confidence where there was little possible justification for such confidence. *I can't let her go like this,* he thought. *I need to take time to tell her more, even though we ran out of time a half-hour ago.*

"I know about the cabin because Abigail and I were the camp directors." Then he warned, "You must not stay there long. There are blankets and other necessities, but I'm reasonably certain that the enemy will be visiting the camp before the end of the day."

"Have you any suggestions as to where we can go from there?"

"Yes. I've programmed both the Christian camp and your final destination into the GPS. If you follow the map, you should do fine, but...."

She looked at him expectantly.

"It seems like there's always a *but*, doesn't it?" he asked.

She frowned, waiting for the other shoe to drop.

"The reason I'm giving you these verbal instructions is in case the GPS fails."

They heard another snowmobile come around the back of the house, and Chris ran to the door to look through a crack. "We're okay for a moment," she said. "The drivers are both in your house."

"Liberty Christian lies on the east shore of Allison Lake," he told her. "There should be more than a foot of ice on the lake by now."

She looked at him quizzically, as though asking, *So what?*

He quickly folded the map and handed it to her. Then he again spoke rapidly as he backed away from her toward the horses that were hitched to his sled. He removed the feeding bags from their noses and tossed them in the back of the sled.

As he made his way toward the big rear doors, he shouted, "Mount up and get ready to go!" Then, one at a time, he rolled the big doors to the sides.

"A foot of ice will easily bear your snowmobile," he shouted in explanation. "When you're ready to leave the camp, look across the lake toward the southwest. You'll see a tall rock pinnacle soaring into the sky. It's called Tower Point. Pick a spot about a thousand feet north of that rock and head toward it. Stay away from Tower Point itself because a creek enters the lake at that point, and the ice might be too thin to hold you."

She nodded, helmet in hand.

"When you reach the west shore of the lake, continue into the woods about two hundred yards. You'll find a cabin. It's owned by a couple named Tower. Tell Don Tower that I sent you. He and his wife will do all in their power to help you, especially if you tell them your last name."

Chris nodded. She was beginning to understand the sacrifice that the Kenzys had made for them, and the risk they had taken by remaining here this long.

"I don't know how to thank you."

"Don't try. Just keep fighting the good fight. Oh, one last thought."

"Yes?"

"After this, I think my wife and I are going to become a bit more militant than merely disseminating information and praying." He gazed off into space. "Taking *Hamlet* out of context, I think that it is time that we *take Arms against a Sea of troubles, And by opposing, end them.*"

"But you're a preacher!"

"I have come to understand from God's Word that we are not to submit ourselves to those who would indiscriminately take our lives or seize our property. We are to actively and aggressively combat them because they will otherwise crush the liberty of others and prevent them from pursuing life, liberty and happiness. And if we allow our lives to be gratuitously snuffed out, then we are neither helping others nor glorifying God. Even if our deaths are inevitable, we must continue to fight back, and we must somehow make a statement of God's judgment to those who slay us."

Chris nodded. *This man sounds like my husband. And why not? He said he was one of his admirers.*

She turned to the Kenzys and said her quick farewells. Then she seated Michael behind Mary on the back seat and climbed on to the snowmobile. For a minute or two, the wind had diminished, and they heard their pursuers swearing as they came back out of the Kenzys' farmhouse.

Someone in authority shouted, "We'll go around the house and search that big barn across the street!"

Someone shouted back, "What about the other buildings?"

"We'll start at the barn and search them one at a time."

Then the wind rose to a shriek, furiously whipping the snow, and nothing else was heard.

When Chris was certain that the storm would cover the sound, she started the engine. She gave it just a moment to warm up, using the time to turn her head to make certain her children were okay. Mary was obviously exhausted. She'd been locked in a cell for two days, then driven over rough mountain roads for hours, had become terribly excited by seeing her father alive, slept only fitfully on the cold floor of the tavern, then had been dragged cross country on the back of a snowmobile to the Kenzy farm. Now she was again seated in front of her brother on the snowmobile and, in spite of everything, had fallen fast asleep.

Michael, on the other hand, had his eyes fixed on those of his mother.

"Chris," Jack Kenzy shouted, "be careful of the wind. You'll tend to overcompensate by driving toward it. Trust the GPS."

She heard him say something about being careful and waved to the him as she gunned the engine.

Then he raised his hands above his head and shouted, "The Lord of glory keep you safe until we meet again."

Michael's "Amen" was lost beneath the sound of the snowmobile's engine as Chris accelerated slowly forward through the double doors, her lights off. In a few seconds she had passed beyond the range of Jack's feeble headlamp and was lost to their view in the snow.

The Kenzys Flee
The Kenzy Farm
Christmas Morning
12:15 a.m.

Jack Kenzy stood in the rear doorway of the carriage house, staring out into the darkness, indifferent to the snow blowing around him, wondering whether he and his wife would ever see Chris and her two children again.

Then he moved back into the darkness of the carriage house and made his way by memory to the stall in the corner. Turning on his flashlight for a few seconds, he located a pitchfork, then climbed the ladder that led to the loft above and began forking down hay into the stall below.

With that task completed, he climbed back down to the main floor and crossed to his big sleigh. Climbing up, he smiled at his wife, and she smiled wanly back at him. He took her mittened hand in his and said a quick prayer. Then he clucked to the horses. They set their shoulders and jerked the old Hudson Valley sleigh loose so that it slid over the rough plank flooring and out through the big rear doors into the blizzard. As they left the barn, Kenzy turned on his LED headlamp for an instant, so that he could check the compass he'd cemented to the top of what he called the sled's dashboard.

When the horses shied in the teeth of the icy wind, he slapped the reins, and they moved out quickly. He'd lived here all his life, and knew the lands well. In the nearly stygian darkness, he turned the sled toward the east side of the snow-covered field, away from the direction that Chris had taken with the snowmobile. When he reached the brooding shadow of the pine forest, he turned right and drove south along the edge of the field until he found another old wood road through the pines that would take him northeast into the mountains.

The Pursuit

South of the Kenzy Farm
Christmas Morning, about 1 a.m.

The lieutenant stopped his snowmobile in front of the carriage house doors. Both he and the driver of the snowmobile following him left their headlights on so that when Kim Ling and the corporal rolled back the doors, the lights would flood the interior and hopefully blind any defenders. But when the lieutenant stormed into the building, weapon raised, he found no one.

Aiming a flashlight into the stalls, he looked for any evidence of recent occupation and was rewarded by signs that the building had recently been used to house farm animals. The headlights of the two snowmobiles lit the inside back wall where the rear doors stood wide open, the snow already drifting into the building.

He ran to the doorway and peered out into the heavy snowfall, looking for any evidence of someone's passing. Disappointed, he shouted for Kim Ling.

Although a conscripted civilian, Kim wisely ran to his side and assumed a position that was something akin to attention.

"You will remain here with that harridan," the lieutenant ordered," pointing at the Benton woman. "The corporal and I will search for the escaped woman and her children."

"Yes, sir. And if I see anyone else?"

"If you see anyone else," the lieutenant said, sarcastically, "hold them for our return."

Kim held his open hands out, drawing attention to the fact that he was unarmed.

The lieutenant smiled sardonically. "I'm sure you can find some means of subduing whoever might happen on you," he said, and turned away. He crossed to Kim's snowmobile, removed the key from the ignition, slipped it into his pocket and turned back to Kim. "Just in case you had any ideas about leaving here, I'll take the key along with me."

"I don't get it," Kim replied. "First I was told that you didn't speak English and needed an interpreter, and now you're leaving me here."

The lieutenant laughed. "That should give you something to think about until we return."

If you return, Kim thought.

"But what about me?" the woman shouted. "It's twenty below zero in this barn!"

"What about you?"

"You've set the house on fire," she said, pointing out the door.

"What is your point?"

"We'll have no way to keep warm."

"If you're cold," the lieutenant laughed, "you can always throw yourself on that fire." Then, with the woman cursing at his turned back, he gunned the engine and drove his snowmobile out of the barn.

The Confrontation

The Motor Home in the Caverns
Hidden Valley, Vermont
Christmas Morning, about 2 a.m.

It was after two in the morning when CC and Jonathan, followed by Rachel, entered the cavern where the motorhome sat dark and silent. Signaling her to wait near the entrance, Jonathan silently cracked open the back door of the RV, and discovered two intruders asleep in their beds. CC beckoned Jonathan back to the entrance so that they could consider their limited options.

A myriad of questions flooded CC's thoughts. *What will we do if the intruders prove belligerent? Yes, we could try to imprison them, but that would prove an impossible hardship on everyone concerned. And we'd run out of food much sooner. Or we could kill them,* he thought, but he blanched at the thought. *Murder or execution, is a totally unacceptable alternative, and an act for which I am neither emotionally nor spiritually equipped. Yet, if our unwanted guests don't prove enthusiastically cooperative, we will be faced with an insurmountable problem.*

CC slipped into the front door of the motorhome, and tiptoed back through its compact bathroom, where he quietly rolled aside the passage door that separated the compact bath from the rear bedroom. He needn't have worried. Their unwanted visitors were sleeping soundly.

CC slipped into the bedroom of the motorhome just as Jonathan stepped up through the rear door, weapon in hand. There was just adequate light coming through the hall from the RV's kitchen to keep them from stumbling around. The twin beds, with a narrow aisle between them, ran along the side walls at the back of the motorhome. Both beds were occupied. Jonathan had already taken a position at the foot of the bed by the door, and CC saw that it was to their advantage that the intruders had both pulled the blankets over their heads to keep warm.

CC decided to use the same shock technique that Jonathan had used to introduce himself to him. He'd been standing on the sidewalk outside the hospital in Black River Junction when Jonathan had slipped up behind him and pressed the muzzle of his rifle against the back of CC's head. He planned to do the same thing, hoping to terrify the intruder and stifle any response. Then he realized that he was no action-adventure hero. Someone might be seriously injured if the sleeping man reacted violently.

Our lives are at stake here, and this is not make-believe.

Instead, he moved to the foot of the bed, just across from Jonathan, and wondered, *If this turns violent, do I have the nerve to pull the trigger?*

Jonathan stood, feet slightly apart, his arms extended in what he must have imagined was the prescribed firing position, only the rigid line of his lips revealing his stress. One of the teen's legs was actually pressed against the bed, perhaps in an unconscious effort to brace himself. His handgun was pointed down toward the person beneath the blankets, the silhouette clearly revealing that it was a woman. Jonathan turned to CC and nodded his readiness. In response, CC wagged his finger back and forth in a "no-no" gesture, intending to forestall any rash action.

The boy had to remove one hand from his pistol in order to take the flashlight that CC held out to him. He turned it on and pointed it toward the head of the bed. At the same time, CC gripped the blankets that covered the man and jerked them toward him, pulling the covers down to the man's waist.

The man's reaction was so violent that CC almost pulled the trigger. In an instant, the guy was sitting up and sliding his hands around under the bedding searching for something. And that something, CC realized, had to be a gun. Then he saw it, just out of the man's reach. It was laying on the sheet behind him, protruding from under the edge of his pillow.

"Don't move!" CC barked, realizing at once how trite the words sounded, yet unable to think of anything more appropriate. When the man saw the two of them with guns pointed at him, he immediately ceased his furious movements, but the way his eyes moved about, cooly assessing the situation, made it clear to CC that he and Jonathan would have to be very careful.

"Hands behind your head!" CC ordered.

The man hesitated, then slowly complied.

"Now, move to the other bed and lie down next to your friend."

With all the racket, the woman had awakened and pulled the blanket down under her chin so that she could see what was happening. "There's no way he's lying down with me." The sentence was spoken without inflection—flat, nerveless, defiant.

CC didn't question her preference. He said to the man, "Okay, on the floor." Then, after a moment's thought, "On your stomach, and get your hands behind your head." As the man knelt to comply, CC saw his eyes flicker toward the gun he'd left laying by his pillow.

"Don't even think about it," he warned, and the man lay still.

While he was lowering himself to the floor, the woman raised herself abruptly into a sitting position. The blankets fell away from her shoulders, but she caught them before her upper body was exposed. Her lips curled slightly as Jonathan began to look away in embarrassment, before he realized that she was fully dressed. Then her little grin blossomed into a smile. She had decided that she liked the unusual innocence of this teenager.

Having assessed the teenager's personality, she now moved her attention from the boy to the man. She was not surprised that his eyes appeared to be riveted on her upper body. She'd met far too many men whose immediate response to her was something less than intellectual, and she simply assumed from his stare that he was like all the others.

But she paled when she realized that he wasn't examining her body. Surprising herself, she was at first disappointed, then frightened. *He's staring at the necklace,* she realized. *And I know what he's thinking. He's thinking, "I can't believe the size of those jewels!" And he's right!*

CC didn't know a thing about jewelry, but that clunky thing was definitely inappropriate for sleepwear. His look was accusative, and she was momentarily caught speechless.

It may be inappropriate, he thought, *but if that necklace is genuine, no woman in her right mind would ever dare remove it. Keeping it next to her skin, and well-hidden by her clothing, is probably the best place to safeguard such a magnificent treasure.*

His thoughts raced. *Those jewels have got to be artificial. If they were real, they'd be priceless. On the other hand, she might have looted them from a jewel box in some vacant mansion.*

He had never been interested in jewelry, but this necklace was, in its own way, as beautiful as the woman. It looked worth a king's ransom. The chain appeared to be white gold and was hung end-to-end with at least a dozen diamonds, each larger than any he had ever seen before. Hanging from its center was a huge, brooding, dark blue stone. It was fully an inch across, and it became a sullen throbbing eye when the beam of his flashlight fell upon it. The enormous stone was surrounded by smaller stones, but small only in their relationship to the larger one.

Even the smallest of them, he calculated, *must be at least several carats in size.*

The woman saw the incredulity on his face and immediately reached up to enclose the dark stone in the palm of her hand, an unconscious and futile attempt to conceal it from his stare. It was so large that she was unable to enclose the entire setting in one hand. After a moment, finally realizing that an explanation was necessary, and with what seemed a forced ingenuousness, she almost stuttered.

"This is just an old piece of costume jewelry my father bought for me when I was a child. I wear it for sentimental reasons."

Though he considered her unsolicited explanation to be out of character with the combative personality she had displayed a moment before, CC said nothing. He decided that, for the moment at least, the source of the jewels and their genuineness were of secondary importance, and he resumed dividing his attention between the two intruders,

"Can I get up yet," the guy on the floor whined. "It's cold and dirty down here."

"In a minute," CC snarled. "Keep still!"

The woman spoke up. "My name is Elizabeth Ross," she told them. "My companion," and she nodded her head toward the man lying prone on the floor, "says that he is Jim McCord." She introduced herself as though there was nothing odd about being discovered in someone else's bed in the middle of the night with a fortune in jewels hanging about her neck.

Chris Lights the Enemies Way

Early Christmas Morning
Kenzy's Snow-Covered Field.

Chris held the handlebars in a death grip as she steered the snowmobile across the corn field. She was moving very slowly, relying on her compass to guide her in the darkness. It was a rough ride because the wind had scoured the snow from the frozen ground, and the machine bumped up and down over the frozen rows left by the plow. She turned her head to check the children huddled behind her, and was happy to see that they seemed okay.

Then she examined the map on the heads-up display and noticed the silhouette of the stream directly ahead. Frightened that she might not judge the distance properly and might even drive over the bank and plunge into the freezing water, she yanked the handlebars to the right and headed west across the field. Shaken by what she thought had been a near disaster, she accelerated too much, and then almost lost control of the machine on the bumpy ground.

Questioning her own judgment and imagining that she might crash into some obstruction in the darkness, she reacted in fear. Without thinking out the consequences, she reached down and flicked the headlight switch. Things seemed to go from bad to worse. Now the intense glare produced by the light reflecting off a million snowflakes left her blinded. She fumbled around on the dashboard, found the switch and shut the lights back off. Now she was dazzled, seeing bright lights where there was only darkness. Feeling the wind striking her left side, she panicked and steered in that direction to compensate.

"Mommy, stop!" Michael screamed.

She hesitated, then brought the snowmobile to a halt. "What's the matter?" she demanded. "Did Mary fall off?"

"I think we might be going into the stream."

"How could you know that?"

"I was looking that way when you turned the lights on and I thought I saw water and ice. It's just over there a little way," he said, pointing to the left.

She blinked her eyes, but saw only stars. *I'd better sit here for a moment until my vision adjusts,* she thought. Then she changed her mind and turned the lights back on. Michael was right. The rushing stream was just a dozen yards ahead, and if he hadn't stopped her, she would have driven the snowmobile into the icy water. Leaving the lights on, she turned so that she was again traveling west, paralleling the stream on her left.

"Mommy," Michael called again, leaning his head out to the side so that he could shout over his little sister's shoulder.

"What now, Michael?"

"Didn't Pastor Kenzy say to leave the lights off until we turned onto the wood road that goes south?"

"Michael," she shouted in exasperation. "I'm doing my best!"

"Well, the stream is turning away from us right here, so maybe the road is just ahead."

And it was.

"Now can I leave the lights on, Michael."

"No, Mom!"

"Of course I can," she shouted back in exasperation.

"Remember, we weren't supposed to turn them on until we get on the old road to Butter Creek."

"Well, we will be on it in a moment, and we're doing fine."

"I don't think so, Mom."

"Why not?" she demanded, unable to hide her annoyance.

"Because I see lights up on the hill behind us."

When the lieutenant examined the floor around the open rear doors of the carriage house, he discovered two narrow strips of ice that ran toward the back doors. It had taken him a moment to conclude that snow must have collected on her snowmobile skis, melted from the heat of her engine, then refrozen. Then, as the snowmobile exited the building, she'd left additional tracks in the snow just outside the doors. He stepped out into the raging storm and immediately realized that they had almost no hope of finding her because the snow had already drifted over her trail. But he knew that they must try. If they returned to General Eng empty-handed, the price they would have to pay would be grievous.

The lieutenant returned to the carriage house, remounted his machine and drove out the back doors and up onto the field. He began driving in a curve to the right, hoping that by maneuvering in a wide circle they might spot some sign of her passing. He had all but given up hope and was about to return to the farm, when the corporal sitting behind him shouted that he thought he had seen a light.

The lieutenant was dubious, but his rapidly sobering rider insisted that he'd seen a glow in the sky.

"It was just above the horizon to the south," he shouted, pointing toward the crest of the hill.

The lieutenant jerked the handlebars to the left, turning toward the spot his rider had indicated, but he didn't see any light. He was hoping that what the corporal had seen was not merely an alcohol-induced figment of his imagination, but possibly the woman's headlights reflected off the gusting snow.

He went on for another minute, but realized he might be heading in the wrong direction. He was about to give up when the corporal shouted again, and he turned in time to see a light off to his right. He had a good fix on her location now and checked the reading on his compass. Turning his machine, he picked up speed, confident that he would ultimately catch her. Unlike Chris, the lieutenant was an experienced snowmobiler. Not only that, but his machine had a set of fog lights mounted well down on the hood, so in spite of the blowing snow, he was able to maintain a moderate speed and yet see well enough to continue his pursuit.

A Chinese Sherlock Holmes

The Kenzy Farm
East of Butter Creek
Christmas Morning, about 2 a.m.

Kim Ling stood in the doorway of the carriage house, watching the lights on the lieutenant's snowmobile fade in the enveloping snow. He continued staring into the darkness until the shrill voice of the Benton woman became so persistent that he could no longer ignore her.

"How long are you going to keep us out here freezing, you ninny?"

He turned slowly and stared impassively at a face long misshapen by bitterness and pride. Her lips were her signature feature, twisted into the perpetual sneer of someone who might have been sucking on a particularly bitter lemon. If one were to move his attention beyond that repulsive feature, he'd find himself transfixed by a nose that featured a Grimm's fairy-tale wart, complete with bristly hair. And above that, two sunken eyes, not shining with intelligence, but possessed with a spark of evil shrewdness. Her indescribable ugliness was, to most people, intimidating, and most would turn away rather than contend with her.

Not Kim Ling. He seemed to stare through her, his face a stolid mask.

"Wait over there," he told her, pointing his flashlight at the horse stall in the corner.

"I will not! I demand that you start that snowmobile and drive me back to town this minute!"

"I don't have the keys."

"Well, hot-wire it, or whatever you call it."

"I don't call it anything," he replied. "I don't have any tools, and I can't get behind the dashboard to reach the wires. And if I could, I wouldn't go back to Butter Creek. Now why don't you be a nice old lady and go stay warm in that hay pile?"

"I'm not old, and I have no intention of getting hayseeds all over me."

Nor are you nice, and you certainly aren't a lady, he thought, but instead said, "Suit yourself, but you would be warmer in that hay stack."

"I demand that you take me back to the inn."

"You heard the captain. He told you to feel free to walk to town. As for me, I have no intention of walking four miles through a raging blizzard at midnight."

"But we might freeze..." she began, and there was the suggestion of fear in her voice.

The lieutenant had made no secret of what he thought of her. He suggested that she had not exhibited any idealism by joining the Chinese cause. "You and your disgusting husband are merely opportunists," he had told her, "and we would be better off without you." Then he'd said that, as far as he was concerned, she'd done her job by guiding him to the Kenzy farm, and she was welcome to walk back to town through the blizzard. Finally he'd shouted that she should warm herself in the Kenzy house before starting her four-mile walk back to the inn, then he turned to watch as the remains of the house collapsed in flames.

Sharing some of the lieutenant's loathing for this woman, Kim Ling ignored her as he began examining the floor around the rear doors. The ski marks from the woman's snowmobile were already covered by the drifting snow.

Kim looked around and noticed a broom leaning against the wall by the woman. When he asked her to hand it to him, she began to harangue him and call him vile names.

"Perhaps I should have suggested that you use it to fly back to town," he told her, "but I can put it to better use," and was immediately ashamed of his outburst. He stepped around her, lifted it down, and began carefully sweeping away the snow that had accumulated on the wide plank door sill.

Moving from right to left, he quickly found the place where the lieutenant had spotted the wide curved impression of a snowmobile ski. It had left its distinctive trough as it passed over the shallow snow in the doorway. The compacted snow beneath it had frozen, then been covered over by additional light drifting snow.

While the woman continued to scream invectives at him, Kim ignored her and kept on sweeping. After another moment, the briefest of smiles curled his lips, and a whispered *Eureka* escaped his lips. The harridan, whose ears must have been as sharp as her tongue, overheard him.

"Eh? What did you find? Money?"

He ignored her, and focused his flashlight to get a better look.

There was another mark here that the lieutenant, keen on following the snowmobile, had failed to notice. This track was much narrower than that of the snowmobile and had pressed deeper into the underlying snow. The woman was now crowding him, and he shook the broom at her when she grasped his arm. Then he resumed his search. After a moment, he found the other snowmobile track, and beyond that, another narrow groove in the snow.

Whatever made those two narrow parallel grooves is wider than a snowmobile, he realized. He had little doubt that it was an old-fashioned sleigh, and his guess seemed to be corroborated when he uncovered the icy impressions made by the shoes of the two horses that had pulled it through the doors.

Kim Ling knew that he couldn't follow on foot, so he resigned himself to waiting for the lieutenant to return. He pulled his scarf tight and buttoned the flaps of his hat under his chin. When he turned to the woman, she was still standing stubbornly in the middle

of the floor, so he made his way toward the horse stall with the intention of following his own advice.

He pushed his way into the mound of hay only to bark his shin
against something hard. Reaching down through the hay, he touched
what felt like a snowmobile ski. Holding his flashlight between his
teeth, he leaned forward and scooped up an armful of the hay. Tossing it to the side, his face burst into a smile. In a moment he had the
machine uncovered.

He climbed aboard and reached around until he discovered the
key in the ignition. The engine roared to life, and after a moment, he
ran it out onto the center of the carriage house floor and shut it
down.

"Get on the back," he told the woman.

"Are you taking me back to the inn?"

"No, I'm going to follow those sled tracks. Now, get on!"

"I will not," she shrieked. "I'm not going anywhere else with
you in this blizzard."

"All right," Kim replied. "Your choice," and he swung his leg
over the seat and restarted the engine.

"Wait!" she shouted, a hint of fear in her voice. "You can't
leave me here to freeze."

As the snowmobile began slowly moving through the doorway,
he shouted, "If you're here when the lieutenant returns, tell him I'm
chasing someone else for him." Then he gunned the engine and shot
out across the snow-covered field, his lights pointing the way.

Kim Ling Pursues Jack Kenzy

The Kenzy Farm
East of Butter Creek, Vermont
Early Christmas Morning

The snowmobile that Kim Ling had found buried in the hay in the horse stall performed far better than he might have hoped. It was fast and it maneuvered beautifully as he raced along the edge of the forest bordering the east edge of the Kenzys' corn field. When he passed what appeared to be an opening between the trees on his left, he ran the sled in a circle and turned onto a farm track that cut through the woods. There was little wind here because the tall evergreens slowed it, and he picked up the tracks of Kenzys' horses and sleigh almost immediately.

Not only was he finally free from the Chinese, but he was intrigued with the prospect of meeting Pastor Kenzy again. Now that he knew his own family was in heaven, he felt as though he could throw himself into any sort of endeavor and take any kind of risk. Kenzy was just the man to help him identify his mission, and just maybe he'd be able to do something for the pastor in return.

He remembered the day he'd met Kenzy, back during the late summer. He'd been in the small clearing outside the barn that the Chinese used as a hangar. Kim had just finished changing the oil on the Enstrom that he piloted for the Chinese and was trying to figure out what to do with the waste oil. With no OSHA breathing down his neck, and with no means of recycling the oil, he was momentarily at an impasse.

As Kim Ling stood there, he was able for just a moment to put his sorrow aside as he listened to the song of a hermit thrush. The bird was perched on a limb on the edge of the copter's landing pad, and the beauty of his trilling revealed why his was called "the finest sound in nature." He was lost in the beauty of God's creation when his reverie was intruded on by someone whispering his name.

"Ling!"

Kim was leaning into the engine access opening, and since he didn't want to draw anyone's attention, he slowly turned his head from side-to-side until he saw a hand waving at him from the deep brush that bordered the clearing.

He stepped down from the copter and, pretending to concentrate on the task at hand, picked up the pan containing the dirty oil. He then walked toward the edge of the clearing, looking about as though trying to decide where to dispose of the oil. He moved toward a large tree, then seemed to change his mind.

"Wouldn't do to toss this on the roots of that beautiful old tree," he said aloud as though talking to himself, and turned to make his way toward the place from which he'd thought he'd been quietly hailed. Reaching the verge, he again looked about as though searching for the most suitable place to dump the oil. He moved back into the brush until he was standing near a man kneeling beside a bush. Kim Ling kept his back to the man as he tipped the pan, slowly pouring the thin stream of used oil into a rut in the ground.

"Ling," the man whispered. "My name is Jack Kenzy."

Ling didn't respond, but continued to pour out the oil.

"I understand that the Chinese have an outpost set up at the Green Mountain Feed and Grain Store in Butter Creek," the man whispered.

Ling barely nodded his head. "That's no secret."

"And I also understand that you have been flying General Eng over there from time to time."

"You seem to know a lot about my activities," he whispered

"I work with the resistance."

Ling gave no indication that he had heard, but instead kept his eyes on the oil pan as the stream of viscous fluid dripped to the ground.

Kenzy persisted. "I have a message that I need carried to the store manager."

"Not a chance," Ling whispered, concerned that this was probably a set-up by the Chinese to test his loyalty.

Kenzy's next remark made it clear that he understood his fears. "Check out the wanted posters on the bulletin board outside your HQ," he countered. "You'll find my picture there."

"It doesn't matter. It's too dangerous," Ling replied. "They are watching me every minute." He hesitated, then revealed his true concern. "And they have my family."

Kenzy remained silent for so long that Kim wondered whether he might have crept away, but when he turned his head slightly, he saw that the man was still kneeling in the same place, and there was a frown on his face, a look of infinite sadness.

"What?" Kim demanded, sensing bad news.

Kenzy chewed his lip for a moment.

"What do you know? Kim persisted.

"We know about your family. They've been splitting all the families up."

"I don't even know where they are," Kim replied, his voice tight with tension.

Kenzy sighed, and Kim turned enough so that he could search his face.

"You know where the are?" Kim asked, eagerly, almost accusatively.

A few more seconds passed before Kenzy grudgingly nodded.

"Well?"

He frowned, resigned to answering Kim's demand.

"Your wife was sent up north, and your children are at a work camp."

Kim Ling said, "I don't understand."

But Kenzy could see from the expression of horror on Kim's face that he understood all too well.

"She's been sent to one of those places?" he guessed. He choked, then got himself under control. "She's at one of their so-called comfort stations."

The other man's look of sorrow spoke volumes.

"And my children?"

"They are working on a farm."

"Slave labor, you mean." And that was not a question.

Again Kenzy remained silent.

"And, my wife...." He left the question hanging.

"I can't make it easy for you. You know that the women they send to these places generally suffer severe abuse and neglect."

Kim threw the oil pan against a tree, hitting it so hard that it dented the bottom, the sound reverberating across the clearing. "Yes, I know," he replied, his voice bleak. After a moment, he bent over and picked up the dented drain pan. He stood there for a moment, afraid to utter the next question. "Is there anything else?"

"Our last report stated that your wife was quite ill."

Kim stood looking off through the trees, his sorrow almost choking him. "Are you sure of this information?"

"My source is reliable," Kenzy replied. Then he added, "You can't know how sorry I am."

"Yeah, sure." A tear rolled down his cheek, and he looked back at Kenzy.

"Our people tried to get the women out."

"And?"

"We lost two of our men in the attempt."

"I'm sorry. I had no right to imply anything. I know you meant well."

"These are terrible times for all of us," Kenzy said, knowing that no amount of collective suffering could assuage this man's personal grief. Then he decided to be brutally frank. Anything less would be a disservice to this man.

"Perhaps knowing the truth will help you with your planning."

Kim shuddered. His thoughts raced back to the day when the general had told him that his family was being taken away, and he remembered that even then he'd had a premonition of disaster.

Maybe if I'd had more faith, he thought, *she'd not be in this predicament.* Then his mind was aflame with guilt and sorrow. *I'm jumping to conclusions here. And it's not this man's fault.* He found himself quoting Job aloud, "For the thing which I greatly feared is come upon me."

Kenzy sighed. "No, my friend. You are not guilty of unbelief. "It's not your lack of faith that's at fault. It's the evil that is visiting America because of our countless national sins. It would take great faith or gross stupidity to imagine that everything is serendipity.

Kim mulled over that for a moment. Kenzy sensed that he'd forgotten the danger they were in, and was about to respond aloud in a normal voice, so he hissed at him, a warning to keep his voice down.

Then Kim Ling asked with a tinge of sarcasm in his voice, "Are you an expert on spiritual matters?"

"For whatever it's worth, I'm a preacher."

Kim mulled that over for an instant. "Then I apologize," he said quietly. "I have the greatest respect for God's special messengers. It can be assumed" he added, "that you are at least something of an expert, and I'm happy to meet you.

"I used to pastor the Butter Creek Evangelical Church."

"Used to?" Kim had heard of that church, that the folks there were, for the most part, the real deal, people of faith, and Kim's face lost something of its hardness.

"All churches have been shut down," Kenzy clarified. "We meet secretly in homes now."

"I wish I were close enough to visit one."

"Maybe someday soon," Kenzy encouraged him.

It was obvious that Kenzy was having trouble choosing his words. It was equally obvious that he desperately wanted to help Ling, but both knew from long experience that only God who could help him. Kim's trials set him apart — lonely, heart-broken, almost unreachable — and there were few words that might console him. Kenzy nevertheless tried.

"The only way I know to help your wife, and to maybe shorten your trial, is for you to fight back."

"And that could cost her her life."

"Yes, it could. And yours as well." Then he added, "Of course, she may not survive anyway."

Both men's heads turned as they heard someone pushing his way through the branches that overhung the path to the clearing. Kenzy dropped flat on the ground, then reached out with a tightly folded piece of paper and began pressing it down between the leather of Kim's shoe and his instep. Kim Ling was so intent on the approaching individual that he did not at first realize what Kenzy was trying to do, but finally he arched his foot to widen the gap between the shoe and his foot. When the paper was deep enough within the shoe to escape detection, Kim rocked his foot from heel to toe to make certain that it would remain hidden.

He turned to whisper a final question, but Kenzy was already crawling away, taking care not to move the branches and cause the leaves to tremble.

Then Kim turned, and carrying the pan, still slick with the residue of the dirty oil, he walked back into the clearing.

The general had never come to the maintenance area before, and so Kim had to assume bad news, but he no longer cared. Somehow he realized that everything was already settled. There had been no voice from heaven, no epiphany...just the realization that things had forever changed. He had wanted to kill the general, and he hadn't cared whether he might die in the attempt. But now he was biding his time for he knew not what. This meeting with Kenzy might represent the start of something. Maybe not. It might also be a trap which the general was about to spring. Again, maybe not. One thing was certain: Given the opportunity, that folded piece of paper in his shoe would find its way to the owner of the Green Mountain Feed and Grain store.

He forced himself to focus on the general's appearance. It wouldn't do to ignore the danger to which he was exposed, nor to waste any opportunity his captivity might offer.

Maybe Feng Jiang has already gone to the general with his suspicions," he thought. Then Kim realized that he might only have a matter of minutes to live, and, amazingly, he found himself smiling in anticipation. The general mistook that smile as a spontaneous expression of welcome, and he was surprised, for this represented an extraordinary change in Kim Ling's usual demeanor.

Perhaps, the general thought, *Ling's loyalties are changing and I may put him to more important tasks.* He bit his lip in thought. *This is most propitious.*

Kim was unaware that he had a smile on his face, but when the general returned it with what for him passed as a smile, Kim was brought back to reality. *It would appear that I am in no immediate danger. Perhaps I can yet strike a blow. I must keep reminding myself, "Revenge is a dish best served cold."*

That meeting with Kenzy had occurred months before, before he'd overheard the conversation between the general and his subordinate in which he had learned that his family had passed on. And now he was following the tracks of Kenzy's sleigh over snow-covered slopes. *Hopefully,* he thought, *I'll catch up with him soon.*

The Old Butter Creek Road
South of Butter Creek, Vermont
Early Christmas Morning

Chris estimated that it had been over a half-hour since she and the children had left the Kenzy carriage house. The snowmobile puttered along, and she was again struggling to keep her eyes open as she fought to steer the big machine down the center of the narrow, snow-covered log road.

She had dozed off twice, and awakened in terror, once to find the snowmobile veering toward a tree on the side of the road, the second time when the front of the machine dropped sickeningly, then plowed into a tangle of shrubs and rocks that bordered the little tributary that flowed into Butter Creek. In both cases, no serious damage was done, and she was able to back up and resume her journey, but she was nevertheless badly frightened.

As Michael was helping her guide the machine out of the bushes the second time, he pointed behind her and shouted a warning. No additional explanation was necessary. With no leaves on the trees, she could see the glow of the oncoming lights far behind them.

Now she was in a panic. It wasn't simply necessary to stay ahead of their pursuers. She had to get out of their sight. Sooner or later she would have to stop, and unless she could get a significant lead, they would find her.

She attempted to drive faster, but even with this threat, she still caught herself falling asleep. Or worse, she'd find herself waking up, with no idea how long she'd been asleep. Michael's face was a mask of fear, for he watched helplessly as she would speed up, then come almost to a stop, then accelerate again. When he noticed the snowmobile heading for the side of the road, he would yell at his mother in an attempt to awaken her. And then he'd turn his head to see whether those lights were drawing closer. It was providential that, at one point, the wind rose to a crescendo and blew down the center of the roadway.

The powdery snow covered their tracks and blinded the men following them so that they drove into a tree, slightly bending one of their skis. And the time that it took them to find their way back to the road proved a godsend to Chris.

But Michael, too, was exhausted, so when the snowmobile reached the site where the bridge had once crossed Butter Creek, they had both fallen asleep. And when the front end suddenly dropped over the edge of the embankment, and the skis slammed onto the ice, little Mary was thrown off the seat into the snow and Michael crashed up against the back of the driver's seat, cutting his lip.

Now Chris was almost beside herself with terror. It took her a moment to orient herself. She quickly examined both kids, but there was nothing she could do at the moment about Michael's lip except to give him a handful of snow to hold against it to stop the bleeding. He discarded that icy blob a few minutes later, now stained with his blood. Chris was blessed because Mary never even woke up, probably because she was bundled up so well and was relaxed in sleep.

In her own case, she was convinced that it was the Kevlar helmet that had saved her from a fractured skull when her head struck the dash. She had a headache, but that was probably as much from the glare of the lights off the snow as from the blow to her head. At least she hoped so.

She breathed a prayer of thanks, then surveyed the accident scene. She realized that the snowmobile might have plowed right down through the surface of the ice, drowning them all. What amazed her was that her GPS heads-up display still seemed to be working.

Chris examined the undercarriage in the reflected glare of the headlamps, and everything seemed intact. Leaving the snowmobile running, with the headlights flooding the creek before her, she walked slowly across, checking for thin ice. As she neared the far bank, Michael cried out, and she knew she didn't need to turn to see what was wrong. But turn she did, and as she ran back across the creek to her machine, she saw the glow of their pursuers' headlights.

Well, she told herself, *I'd planned to drive slowly across the creek and up the far bank, but the 'best laid plans,' etc, etc.* She twisted the accelerator and the machine lurched forward. As she rammed it up the far bank, she could see the lights of the snowmobile that was pursuing her. They were illuminating the naked tree tops ahead of her. Hoping that she was on the home stretch to Route 19, she increased her speed.

Her eyelids were heavy now, her fatigue and the glare from the snow in the pitch darkness seemed to be consuming her. She was frightened that she might again fall asleep, and even if she could find a hiding place from these people, she knew that she dared not stop here in the middle of nowhere. Pastor Kenzy had warned that the blizzard might return with a vengeance, and she had to find shelter for the children.

In spite of her good intentions, however, she found herself nodding off, and when she again awakened, she was gripped with a sense of horror that she was about to crash. She was nearly hallucinating and found herself toying with the idea of prying her eyelids open using toothpicks. She tried forcing her eyes as wide open as possible, but that only served to allow more of the glare to enter, and then they would begin to involuntarily close.

She imagined that she was alternately falling asleep, and then a few seconds later, her eyes would flutter open and she'd feel the hair rise on her neck, and she would try to slow the machine to regain control. She even had the illusion that someone was guiding the machine, keeping her out of trouble. Twice she slowed, reached down for a handful of snow, lifted the helmet, and rubbed it on her face. It was shocking for an instant, but as soon as the blood flowed back to her face, she felt unaccountably warm and started to doze again.

It was after one of these horrific awakenings that she heard Michael scream a warning.

"Mommy, they're right behind us."

And they were. The glare of their headlights momentarily blinded her as she looked into the mirror device above her heads-up display.

She immediately accelerated in an effort to keep them from passing her and cutting her off.

Then Michael shouted another warning, and her heart sank.

"Mom, we're sliding!"

The pastor's warning came rushing back. *"Keep an eye on the GPS and watch for the narrow lines that indicate changes in elevation.*

I forgot, she thought in desperation. *What else did he say? Oh, God, help me to remember. Yes! Thank you!* "When the lines on the GPS are close together, you'll be entering the narrow gap between the mountain and the ravine."

But it was too late. Above the whistling of the wind, Chris imagined that she could hear water crashing over the rocks far below. She turned her head to the left, and saw nothing but a black void.

What had the pastor told her? *Why is my mind so clear now?* she wondered. *Why not before I got into this mess. What did he tell me?*

"Keep to the right... maintain adequate speed to avoid sliding."

She pulled the handlebars to the right, but the machine continued sliding straight ahead, and it was obvious that she was skidding on ice that lay just beneath a thin layer of snow. Even if she could have steered to the right, she no longer dared try because her pursuers were pulling up just behind her, working their way around on her right side.

Somehow I've got to get ahead of them. Somehow I've got to get over to the right! Please, Lord? For the kids?

There was no time to think. She gunned the engine, but it seemed to hesitate. Then, after an instant, it backfired loudly, and her snowmobile surged forward. Chris should have felt relief, but instead her heart sank.

An instant after the backfire, there was an answering thunderous crack from high up the mountainside.

"Oh, dear God!" she exclaimed. She remembered the pastor's warning: *Avalanche!*

She'd been a skier and fully understood the danger. In fact, she'd memorized the words from *The Skier's Guide to Safety.* "Avalanches are among the most serious natural hazards to life and property because of their potential to carry enormous masses of snow at dizzying speeds."

Too late, the pastor's warning came back to her. *"Don't rev the engine too much because the racket could trigger an avalanche."* She remembered how he'd told of the three teens who had perished here just a couple of years before.

Suddenly she heard the sound of a rushing wind sweeping down the mountain from her right — a huge volume of air being pushed rapidly down the mountain by an enormous mass of snow — and she imagined that she could feel the ground vibrating beneath her snowmobile. She could see nothing, but she could envision a mountain of snow sweeping toward her.

"Mommy, the snow is sliding," Michael cried. They both heard the roaring of the avalanche far up the mountain.

Well, she thought, "In for a penny, in for a pound," and when she opened the throttle wide, there was another backfire, and her machine leapt forward.

But the two men racing beside her on the right had heard that sound too and hadn't misunderstood the significance of the awesome noise that followed. The thousands of tons of snow that had begun rushing down the mountainside sounded like the roaring a hundred freight trains coming straight at them.

She looked to the right to see whether she had enough of a lead to move in front of her pursuers. It was too late. They were between her and the mountain slope. She recognized the man on the rear of the other machine. He'd been one of her husband's captors. Regardless of the danger to himself, he was obviously dedicated to his assignment. He was trying to stand, precariously straddling the seat, his body twisted so that he could aim his rifle at her. It would be impossible to miss. The weapon's muzzle was only a few yards from her face.

The driver, however, had ideas of his own. He was terrified by the mass of snow sweeping down the mountainside toward him, and far more concerned with his own survival than that of his passenger. Just as the man was squeezing the trigger, the driver jerked the handlebars to the right, tumbling his rider onto the snow-covered roadway beside Chris, and causing his shot to go wild. And, with that rifle report, a second answering *boom* resounded from farther up the mountainside.

With the load on her pursuer's snowmobile reduced by half, the machine shot ahead of Chris. The driver was obviously no longer interested in her, but only intent on reaching safety before the avalanche swept him away.

Chris finally remembered that she should check the heads-up display, and when she did her heart almost stopped. She had slid to the left edge of the road, a full twenty feet from the right side of the road, and was driving along the very edge of the cliff, perilously close to sliding over the edge.

There is no way, she realized, *that I can reach the uphill side of the road; and, even if I do, I'll just position myself for the avalanche to roll us up inside a giant snowball and sweep us down into the ravine.*

Grafton Mountain

Ten Miles Northeast of the Kenzy Farm
Vermont's Mystery Mountains
Early Christmas Morning

Jack Kenzy had not been driving the horses hard because he was trying to conserve the team's strength. Nor did he want to exhaust the precious cow that was being led behind the sleigh. Most importantly, he was trying not to cause his wife any unnecessary additional discomfort.

The old country road that he was following up the side of Grafton Mountain had been little more than a cow path when it finally received its first coat of asphalt nearly a century before. *Whoever named this a mountain was stretching the truth a bit,* Kenzy mused. *It's much more than a hill, but something less than a mountain.*

The trail Kenzy was following meandered up the mountain as though its designer had no special destination in mind and was in no particular hurry to reach it. And that in fact was how the trail had been laid out over a hundred years before, because it had started as an actual cow path.

Kenzy had heard the story many times, but he wasn't sure how much was truth and how much was fable. During the late 1800s, a young couple had purchased a worn-out hillside farm about two miles up the slope from the base of the mountain. In the beginning they were dirt poor, scarcely able to pay the dollar an acre for the hard-scrabble quarter-section from which they could harvest little more than rocks. They owned a couple of work horses, a cow, a small flock of chickens and a shack that they called home. Yet they were full of hope, as is the nature of most young pioneering couples.

As the story went, the zigs and zags in the trail that the Kenzys were following had been surveyed by that farmer's single milk cow, a homely old bovine named *Blossom*. Local gossip even described her appearance. She was a brindle with warm brown eyes, bony hips and a clunky old brass bell hanging from a chain around her neck. She gave just sufficient milk to meet the needs of the growing family and a gallon or so extra that they were able to sell to a neighbor. Blossom's milk and the eggs from his wife's chickens represented the farmer's only cash income.

Every morning after milking, old Blossom was freed to wander up the mountainside. She would move from one patch of grass to the next, cropping a little here and a little there, in no particular hurry to reach her pasture. She experienced little in the way of adventure, and then only on one occasion. One spring day, when the streams were heavy with the melt-off from the heavy winter snows, and the red clover and wild flowers were in bloom, Blossom did not come back down the hill for her evening milking. The farmer had never experienced any problems with Blossom, so he immediately set out to search for her. What he discovered was so extraordinary that even one-hundred and fifty years later, people still spoke of it.

He followed her muddy trail up through the open fields that lay steep on his side of the mountain. As he drew within a half mile of the top of the mountain, he reached the long, low cliff that rose like a pewter crown above the spring grass. He was familiar with the escarpment and knew that it ran for a long way around the mountain to his right. As he expected, Blossom's muddy trail went toward the rock wall. He turned to follow her, making his way alongside the base of the cliff. The farmer paid little attention to the cliff itself, for it was lost in the shadow of the setting sun.

But then he thought he heard Blossom's bell, and he turned toward the cliff. He was amazed to discover a cave in the side of the cliff, and got his feet wet in the small stream that flowed out its mouth. *I suppose she went in here to get out of the sun or to get a drink,* he thought. Whatever her motives, he found Blossom standing nearly up to her neck in a pool of water just inside the mountain. The bank was steep, and she'd been unable to get herself back out after sliding in. He bent down, took her leather collar in hand and pulled with all his strength while she kicked her way up the bank.

The instant she was back on dry ground, she began moving toward the cave's entrance, swinging her bony rump and moving with what little dignity she could muster. The farmer, however, found himself gazing up the tunnel. He was amazed to discover that he could actually see the setting sun at its far end, and realized that the tunnel cut straight through the massive spur of rock that formed the crown around most of the mountain's crest. The cow had discovered a shortcut that would save her nearly a mile on her trek to the pasture, but had been she had been stopped from marching clear through the mountain when she almost drowned in the deep pool.

It would be decades before geologists would explain that this tunnel had been carved by a stream that flowed down from the other side of the escarpment and through a fault in the rock. In flood season, the low point in the cavernous tunnel filled almost to the ceiling with water. During dry seasons, however, his neighbors actually drove buggies through. It became a popular local attraction where people stopped to picnic on their shopping trips to the nearest village. It came to be known as "Blossom's Folly."

The farmer wanted no part of it. He refused to take any chances with his precious cow and went to the expense of putting gates at both ends of the tunnel to keep Blossom out, but to allow local curiosity seekers to pass.

Through the years, the farmer became modestly prosperous, and his herd grew. Each morning after the milking was finished, he released the cows to find their way to pasture. And each evening one of his sons would go out to meet them as they started down the hill for the milking. Year after year they followed that same easy path, and the trail was widened as they alternately churned the earth to mud during the spring rains and packed it down under the August sun.

Many years after Blossom took her last stroll up the mountain, that old cowpath became a wagon road. And several decades later, the automobile supplanted the wagon. The path that the cows had safely navigated became a perilous country road where several people lost their lives on its wet and icy curves. The public outcry resulted in a new road being built on the far side of the mountain, and after being blocked off and forgotten the old road slowly disintegrated.

I haven't thought much about this old abandoned road since I was a kid, Kenzy thought, *but things have changed. For anyone trying to get away, this forgotten byway is the ideal route into the mountains.*

He turned toward his wife and experienced a wave of emotion. She wasn't doing well. He too felt slightly feverish, but his was the fever of a man whose mind was filled with concerns.

What a night! he thought. *In just a matter of hours I encouraged a conscripted serving girl to help a man escape from the Chinese, I sent another woman and her two children on their way to what may be their deaths, and we've abandoned our home. Those ideas all seemed good at the time, but when you put the life of an-*

*other human being at risk, particularly the love of your life, your
perspective changes. And now I've taken this dangerous route because I couldn't think of any other way we might avoid our pursuers.
And if God doesn't help us, I doubt that Abigail will survive this
journey.*

He remembered the Old Grafton Road from his childhood, but
now he realized that his memory was faulty. He had assumed that,
because the road always seemed to remain relatively clear of snow, it
would be unobstructed now. But he had given no thought to the reason why it had remained clear of snow. Now, too late for him to do
anything about it, his memory was returning.

Fifty years earlier the county highway department had erected
snow fences along the right-of-way where the contours of the land
and the vagrancies of the wind caused snow to accumulate in deep
drifts over the road. The fences — tall barriers made up of wire and
thin lathe slats — slowed the wind to the point that it was unable to
carry the snow along. The flakes then dropped to the ground and
piled up in drifts between the fences and the edge of the road.

Not anymore, he realized with regret. *I haven't seen a snow
fence since I was a kid. Society thought it had discovered a better
way — snowplows and salt trucks.* He shook his head. *Well, plows
and salt are no more. Ironic,* he thought. *They were expensive to buy
and operate, the salt caused car bodies to rust through, and all in all,
it was very costly. But costly or not, there are no longer any snow
fences, let alone trucks to plow or salt to spread.*

He flicked the reins to keep the horses moving. He knew that
as long as he kept to reasonably level terrain and didn't let the horses
get into deep snow, he had a wonderful vehicle for traveling cross-
country through the snow. His greatest concern now was that he
might lose his way in the darkness and bury the sleigh in a drift, but
so far he had done all right. He had taped a flashlight to the front end
of the sleigh's wagon tongue, right where it ran between the horses,
and it had proved a very effective headlight.

In one way the pristine snow was a help because it spread the paltry light. He turned to stare at the dully yellow beam the flashlight was now casting in front of them and realized that he would need to change the batteries soon. He only had a half-dozen left, and in this brave new world batteries were both rare and costly, but he desperately needed that light to continue on his way. He needed to get his wife to shelter as soon as possible, and he wanted to get out of sight before any pursuer might spot the glow from down the mountain.

He had been forced to stop the sleigh about two-thirds of the way up the mountain to rest the horses. They'd pushed their way through several deep drifts and were tiring. Steam was rising from their nostrils, and he used a towel to wipe away the mucus and icy crust that had begun to build up on their muzzles. Then he rubbed down their flanks. One at a time, he raised each foot and used the point of his pocket knife to scrape the ice from their hooves.

That done, he retrieved their nose bags from the back of the sleigh, checked that they contained a sufficient quantity of corn, and pushed his way through the drift to hang one of them over each of the animal's heads. Then, while they chomped hungrily on the grain, he returned to the back of the sled, stamping his freezing feet to restore circulation. Again, using his pocket knife, he cut the sisal cord from a three-string hay bale, ripped off a quarter of the hay away, pulled it apart and dropped it in front of the cow.

"Okay, Bessie, eat up," he told her, and she eagerly bent her neck to snatch a mouthful from the snow. While her jaws worked from side to side grinding the hay, he made himself busy wiping her down. Then he readjusted the horse blanket he'd fastened over her back and checked her hoofs. When he was satisfied that he'd done all he could for the three animals, he moved toward the sleigh to check on his wife's condition.

He had considered his priorities. *Horses first. Without the horses we'd be on foot, and we'd both surely die. Abigail wouldn't make it a hundred yards up this mountain, and I wouldn't make it much further.* He frowned. *I must not, I dare not entertain failure!*

"Oh, Lord," he prayed, *"please don't let anything happen to my beloved wife."*

He climbed up into the sleigh, knelt down on the seat next to her and put his arm around her. She opened her eyes and gave him a wan smile.

He forced a smile and asked, "How are you doing, my darling?"

"I'm okay, Jack. Don't worry about me."

"Don't be silly," he said. "I know that you're as strong as a horse."

She ignored this patent falsehood and instead replied, "You know that I don't like to be compared with an animal, particularly not with a horse."

He laughed hollowly, troubled that she had expended the energy for that response.

She peered over the front of the sled where the flashlight dimly illuminated the exhausted horses heads, both now almost touching the snow as they sought the last grains of corn in their feed bags.

"Well," she said, "if I'm only as strong as those horses, then I'm in bigger trouble than I thought."

He laughed.

"As soon as I get some hot tea in you, you'll be as good as new."

She smiled, then dismissed him as she shrugged back down into her blankets and closed her eyes.

In the next few minutes, he lowered a shelf that was hinged to the side of the sleigh. Then he set up a propane gas stove, scooped up a teapot full of snow and set it over one of the burners. After that, he set a pan of beef stew alongside it. And five minutes later he was offering a steaming cup of tea to his wife. She tried to insist that he should eat all of the stew, but he would hear none of it and began to feed it to her a half spoonful at a time.

After the first bite, she pushed his hand away, and said, "I love you with all my heart."

"And I, you!" he replied. "Now eat your stew."

Her tone became less bantering. In a whisper, she said, "I don't know whether I can make it, Jack."

"Yes, you can!" he said emphatically, trying not to choke on his words. "It's not much further. You've got to try!"

"Of course, I will," she said, more to comfort him than to commit herself, and they both knew that her words lacked conviction. She removed her gloved hand from beneath the blanket and reached up to lightly cup his chin. It was an infinitely tender gesture. Then he bent forward and kissed her forehead, trying to hide the tears that slipped unbidden from his eyes.

The snow stopped falling, and when they reached the crest of the old road, the pastor drew up to let the horses blow. While they rested, he sat staring at what the locals called *The King's Crown.* The cliff was actually tilted outward and was wrapped around most of the top of the mountain. It rose high above the old mountain road, curving down and around until it disappeared from sight. Its tilt gave it a jaunty look, and the rounded crest of the mountain appeared to protrude up through it, so that it really did look like a crown on a king's head.

To the right of the road, the hillside fell away sharply, leaving Kenzy no choice but to follow the old road. If he could safely traverse that road beneath the looming cliff, he'd come out on the far side of the mountain where the Blossom of Blossom's Folly had grazed over a century before.

A gibbous moon, alternately masked by passing clouds, bathed the snow-blanketed countryside in dim and ghostly shadows of purple and mauve. He turned to look at Abigail and was relieved to see that she was sleeping, her breathing shallow, but at least steady. He whispered, "Thank you, God," then stepped down to remove the feed bags from the horses heads.

For a moment, the snow reflected the light from the moon so well that it was almost like driving in twilight. In fact, he could distinguish the shapes of the evergreens far down the mountain. He climbed back on the driver's seat, slapped the reins over the horses' rumps, and said "Giddy-up." As weary as they were, the two horses pressed their shoulders into their Coblentz collars and jerked the frozen runners free from the snow's grip.

The sudden movement had barely roused his wife, but when he suddenly yanked on the reins and shouted "whoa," the confused horses almost became tangled in the harness. The rig came to a sudden stop, and she came fully awake.

"My stars!" she exclaimed. "What in the world are you trying to do to those poor animals, Jack?"

"Ssh!" he said, his eyes staring out into the distance.

"Don't you shush me, Jack Kenzy."

"Be quiet, please," he hissed, and pointed down the steep, snow-covered road that lay before them."

"What? I don't see anything," she whispered.

"Not on the road," he whispered. "Look up above the cliff." He pointed. "At the very top. Do you see that fissure in the snow?"

She gasped, immediately understanding. "Oh, Jack! What can we do? We've got to get off this mountain, but we dare not go on. We'll have to turn around and go back."

Their conversation was interrupted by the muted sound of a snowmobile engine. As he turned his head to track the noise, he saw what looked like a dark speck sweep up over the summit of a hill about a half mile behind them.

He turned to look at Abigail, his eyes dark with resignation, but his face still held the merest hint of a smile.

"Well, we can't go back now! And if we continue down this trail, and that snowpack breaks loose, we may very well be swept into eternity." He laughed. "Still, my darling, it's not the first time we've found ourselves between a rock and a hard place, is it?"

Her face lightened, as though reconciled to the inevitable, and oddly her face looked younger, smoother, the lines gone, and she no longer looked strained.

"Well," she smiled, "we've enjoyed rich, full lives, and as you've so often assured me, those lives are still in the hands of the King."

"And?" he asked.

"And I think it's all downhill from here," she laughed, unable to restrain a bit of dark humor.

He shook his head in understanding, and a look of abandon appeared on his face. Then he twisted to his left, found the slip knot that held the end of the rope to which the cow was tied, and yanked it loose. The rope end dropped to the snow, and he frowned sadly. Bessie was on her own now, and the chances of her survival were slim to none. But she wouldn't have even that much chance tied to the back of a racing sleigh. Without another word, he raised the reins and slapped the lines down hard. "Giddy up!" he shouted again at the startled animals. "It's time to run."

And they did!

"Should you be shouting, Jack?" she asked above the sizzling sound of the runners.

"No," he answered with a reckless laugh, "but I wonder if it matters."

"Do you think we can make it?"

"Not through the avalanche area, but as I recall, the uphill end of Blossom's Folly is about half way down the length of this cliff. If neither we nor it are buried in snow, I'll try to get in, but if it's flooded, or if the other end is blocked with snow...." He left the rest of the statement unspoken.

And then the sleigh was racing down the steep slope beneath the shadow of the huge mass of snow that hung precariously above them.

Kenzy held the reins loosely, almost indifferently, and let the horses run free. His other hand was gripped tightly in Abigail's. Above the sound of the panting horses and the wind, he imagined he heard the racing snowmobile drawing nearer, and wondered if the driver understood the danger to which he was exposing himself, but he never bothered to look back.

As the wind whistled about them, and they raced into the darkness, he overheard Abigail's prayer: "...yea, though I sleigh through the valley of the shadow of death, I will fear no evil, for thou art with me...."

Avalanche Country
Old Butter Creek Road
South of Butter Creek, Vermont
Early Christmas Morning

As involved as Chris was with trying to keep her snowmobile from sliding off the slippery road into the ravine on her left, it was easy enough to keep an eye on the pursuer's machine. Painted a bright red — and racing a few yards ahead of her on her right — it made a sharp contrast with the snow as it flashed past her in the dull moonlight, competing with her to outrun the onrushing avalanche. The driver edged toward her, evidently trying to force her toward the ravine without actually risking the danger of a collision.

Well, whatever happens to them, they brought it on themselves, she thought, even while regretting that the driver was almost certainly racing into a godless eternity. Then, busy with her own problems, she dismissed them from her thinking.

It seemed strange. She was no longer sleepy. On the contrary, every nerve in her body was alive with the prospect of death roaring down the mountainside toward them. Then, as she checked her heads-up display, she realized that they were inexorably sliding toward the abyss on their left, and the avalanche suddenly dropped to second place among her concerns. It no longer seemed relevant because she was about to plummet onto the rocks that lay in the roaring stream far below, so the worst the avalanche might do would be to render the coupe de grace, burying them beneath a mountain of snow.

She thought it odd that, even though events were moving incredibly fast, her mind seemed to be able to process her thoughts at an even faster rate. She suddenly accepted the fact that they were either going to slide off the edge of the road into the ravine or be swept over the edge by the avalanche.

Well, she decided, *I don't intend to be swept over that cliff,* and she felt herself slammed back against the seat as she twisted the accelerator and the snowmobile leapt forward. The increased speed, however, did not enable her to move away from the abyss. In fact, she knew that she was still losing ground.

Something was nagging at her memory. *What was it that the pastor and I were kidding about? Or were we kidding? Oh, yes, a paraphrase of the scriptures, "Walk by faith and not by sight." What was it? "Walk by the instruments and not by sight," he'd told her. That was it! But she'd remembered it a little late.* And then she wondered, *is it too late?*

She kept the skis turned slightly to the right, hoping they'd grip what little snow lay upon the ice and provide the traction she needed to stay on the road, but they continued to slip inexorably toward the gorge. She took a quick look at the heads-up display and realized that she had several hundred yards to go before she could hope to find herself out of the path of the avalanche, but she knew there was no hope of that. The roar of the avalanche was already deafening.

It's almost here, she thought. *There's no way I can make it in time.*

"Lord, save me," she shouted aloud, not realizing that she was echoing the words that Peter had cried as he sank beneath the waves. Then she added, "Save my babies!"

The avalanche was moving as fast as an express train, raising a shower of snow that blew across the road from the mountain side. Then a little wave of snow actually swept across the road's surface. It didn't amount to much, just some light snow drifting around the snowmobile's skis, like the first light wave of a changing tide racing up the sand and wrapping itself around a person's toes before disappearing into the sand. But a mountain of racing snow couldn't be far behind. There were only seconds left to take any action. But what?

The growing weight of that initial wave began to build up and push the snowmobile toward the cliff. The machine was slowing and in a moment it would probably stall as the snow deepened. Then they would be buried – rolled up, and spun over the edge of the precipice. But the heads-up display indicated that she was still moving at a high speed, perhaps forty miles an hour, and she had a crazy idea.

If we're going to die, she thought, *then let it be where our bodies may be found someday.*

Without conscious volition, she found herself turning the snowmobile to the left, actually racing toward the edge of the cliff and away from the avalanche, the engine screaming as she sought to squeeze out all the speed she could get. Her headlights flooded the ground ahead, and she aimed for what appeared to be a slightly rising overhang on her left, a narrow point of land that extended out over the ravine.

This is not the first time I've been faced with almost certain death, she thought, *and it would not be the first time that the Lord has delivered me, though I can't see any way of escape. Still, the Lord knows the desire of my heart, so let him do what he thinks best.*

A strange parallel between her situation and that of the three Hebrews at the fiery furnace occurred to her, and she was amazed that her mind could drift in such a manner at a time as this.

They were threatened with death because of their faith, she thought, but they did not acquiesce. Instead they testified of God's saving power. And from what I understand, I am being pursued because of my faith in Jesus Christ.

What was it the three Jews had told Nebuchadnezzar? What did they say that set him in such a rage? Something like, "If we are thrown into the blazing furnace, the God whom we serve is able to save us. He will rescue us from your power."

In other words, she thought, *whether God keeps the kids and me alive in this world or takes us home to live in heaven, we will escape from our pursuers. We will either escape to heaven or escape to fight another day.*

The snowmobile had reached the edge of the cliff, and she accelerated across it, taking off into space like some crazy daredevil. Out of the corner of her eye, she thought she noticed the other snowmobile on the road suddenly engulfed beneath a huge wave of snow, but she had no leisure to ponder that. They were airborne, and Chris imagined them dropping like a rock.

She suddenly realized that the brain could operate on more than one level at a time, because she found herself quoting a familiar passage.

"Yeah, though I walk through the valley of the shadow of death...." Then she corrected herself. *But I'm not walking through the valley, at least not yet. Right now I'm flying over it. Or maybe into it."*

She wondered how far their momentum might carry them. Would they drown in the torrent that had carved this chasm or would they crash into the opposite cliff face? She pictured the three of them buried deep beneath tons of ice and snow, perhaps never to be found, and her heart almost gave way; but she gritted her teeth and resolved, *I will trust in the Lord!*

It would have been a fairytale ride, flying through a snow-filled sky, but without a load on the snowmobile's drive belt, the scream of its engine intruded on her thoughts, almost drowning out the deafening roar of the avalanche which had burst over the cliff microseconds behind them. Chris could see a flurry of snow trailing them, as though its claws were reaching out for them, a living thing determined to take them to its breast and sweep them to their deaths. Was it her imagination, or could she hear Michael and Mary screaming?

She steeled her heart, trying to ignore them, knowing that any infinitesimal chance that might remain rested only on her control of the snowmobile.

What am I thinking? What chance can we have? But she nevertheless kept a death grip on the handlebars, fearing that it might tip to the right or the left, dumping one of them off, and separating her family. So she fought to remain balanced on her seat.

Her eyes continued to follow the path that the headlights carved through the snowstorm. She looked up to try to see the top of the far cliff, to orient herself, to anticipate the crash, wondering when her heavier-than-air machine would finally run into the proverbial rock-filled cloud. The heads-up display somehow captured her attention. She was focused on those squiggly lines that indicated her elevation. She was trying to make sense out of them. The little symbol that represented her snowmobile appeared to be crossing over one of those lines, over the top of the far cliff, and she found herself involuntarily bracing for the inevitable impact.

But there was no impact. *That can't be!* she thought in disbelief. Her eyes were drawn back to the real world, to the path through the falling snow that her headlights were illuminating, and she saw a snowy landscape suddenly unveiled in front of and below her.

"Hold on! she screamed instinctively, trying to warn the children, though she was sure they were all about to be killed. It was a good thing she had warned them, for when the machine struck, it landed on its skis, then bounced high in the air, and when it came down the second time, it seemed to be skidding downhill at an angle, almost ready to flip over on its side. She wrenched the handlebars to make a correction, and then her hands were almost jarred loose by the shock of the snowmobile slamming down again, and she had all she could do to keep the it from swiveling one way or the other.

She prayed that the children hadn't been thrown off, but then she heard them laughing and shouting to one another, and her heart almost burst with the wonder of it. But the snowmobile continued racing down the steep hill at a dizzying speed, perhaps faster than when it had leapt the cliff. A tree seemed to race by, just inches from her left knee.

Is it possible, she wondered, *that we cleared the top of the chasm, and are racing down the slope on the opposite side?*

There was really no time to reason it out, only to try to stop the machine before they crashed into something.

The engine was no longer screaming, but instead was adding its incredible power to the speed of their descent on what seemed like a very steep ski slope. She retarded the throttle and felt the machine slow slightly in the deep snow.

Oh, Lord, don't let us start another avalanche!

The machine raced on, and she began leaning toward her right, steering slightly in that direction, pulling back on the brake lever. The hillside was less steep here, and she reduced the incline more by running diagonally across it. The machine slowed even more, and after what seemed like a long time, finally came to a stop.

Chris sat there, her heart pounding, and it took her a moment to grasp the fact that they hadn't crashed, that they must have somehow fortuitously cleared the chasm and landed on the steep incline on the far side of the cliff.

Fortuitously nothing! she thought. *That was the hand of God!* She began to giggle hysterically. Then she found herself quoting, *"...for he shall give his angels charge over thee..."* She would have held a praise and prayer meeting right on the spot, but she had too much else demanding her attention. The adrenalin was still flowing, and she felt awake, alive! But then she came to herself.

She checked the GPS, and it was still functioning. There was no question that they had actually leapt across the deep ravine through which Butter Creek passed and had come to rest in a narrow east-west valley that lay parallel and several hundred yards to the south of it.

We have to get out of here, she thought. *They will be after us.* Then a voice within seemed to say, *"Peace, be still."* She tried to recall what had happened back there. There was no question in her mind that the man with the rifle who'd fallen from the other snow-mobile had been buried by the avalanche, and if the man driving the snowmobile had managed to escape, which she doubted, he would probably assume that they too, being behind him, would have perished.

When she got off the snowmobile, she found herself shaking so hard that she almost collapsed. She alternately laughed and wept, and realized she was in shock. *I've got to get myself under control,* she realized. She knelt down beside the children to check on them, and Michael asked, "Mommy, are you okay?"

Tears welled in her eyes, and it took her a moment to regain control, but she smiled at the two of them, and replied, "Yes, honey, praise God! I'm doing just fine."

"Oh, good!" Mary shouted, her eyes shining. "Can we do it again?"

"Yeah, Mom," Michael laughed. "Can we do that again? It was awesome!"

"No, Honey. I think we'll just bow our heads right now and thank the Lord that we are all safe."

Chris drove the snowmobile slowly down the remainder of the steep hill until she reached a narrow, frozen-over creek at the bottom. There was a smile fixed on her face. *I would call that unbelievable, but it happened. So instead, I'll call it what it really was...a miracle.*

She was startled when she heard a disembodied voice say, "Re-calculating," and laughed aloud when she realized that it was the GPS trying to determine the route she was to follow to reach the Christian camp. *Maybe,* she thought, *just maybe we'll make it after all.*

New Found Friends
Mountainside Hideaway
About 25 miles northeast of Kenzy Farm
Early Christmas Morning

The two strangers who had aided the captives at Butter Creek were Pastor Jack Kenzy and Sheriff John Thomas. After they helped the woman and her two children on their way, they climbed on their own snowmobiles and accompanied one another to the Green Mountain Feed and Grains Store.

The store owner topped off their gas tanks while they had something to eat, then they headed for their respective homes, Kenzy to his nearby farm, and Thomas to his mountain home about twenty miles to the northeast. The last thing that Thomas told Kenzy was that he expected Kenzy and his wife to join them at his family's well-disguised hideaway as soon as possible.

Thomas shared his home his best friend's family, Michael Webb. Upon arriving home, Webb told him that he had received a report from someone at the inn that the Chinese were on the way to the Kenzy farm. Thomas, the former sheriff of Black River Junction, immediately contacted the Kenzys by walkie-talkie. His warning to Abigail Kenzy took less than fifteen seconds.

"That was short enough, Mike. There's no way anyone will triangulate on that walkie-talkie wavelength in that short a time."

"Let's hope not," the chief agreed, then immediately changed direction.

"Look John, I know that Jack may be in trouble, but we've got problems of our own. I don't think we should leave our wives and children alone while the Chinese are scouring the countryside looking for escaped prisoners."

"As long as JoLynn and your wife keep the kids inside, they will be safe here," the sheriff countered. "You ought to know. You designed this place, and the camouflage is second-to-none."

"I'll admit that we did a pretty good job of making our little duplex look like a part of the cliff face, but I'd still rather be at home in case some undesirables show up."

"Look Chief Webb, we've been friends for most of our lives, and I rarely argue with you, but this time you're dead wrong."

Whenever John used his professional title, Michael knew that he was angry, but even before he had an opportunity to reply, his wife Patricia joined the conversation.

"He's right, Michael," she joined in. "Abigail is ill, and we can't just leave the two of them out there by themselves, maybe freezing to death.

"Oh, man," Michael laughed, covering his head with his forearms as though to protect himself. "Now you've even set my wife against me."

But it was his wife, not his friend, who responded to that jibe.

"Michael Webb. If you want to sleep on the floor for the rest of the week, you'll apologize to me right now! You know that I have a mind of my own."

"Ain't that the truth?" he whispered under his breath.

"What's that?"

"Nothing, honey." He turned back to his friend. "Can't we compromise? One of us stays here, and one of us goes out and tries to find them?"

"No. It may need both of us. Come on, Michael, Jack's no youngster, and Abigail has been ill for quite a while."

Michael knew he was right, but he wasn't quite ready to surrender. My wife is siding with you, and turn about is fair play. I'll appeal to your wife's sense of fair play. "What do you think, JoLynn?"

"If you're looking for any sympathy from this quarter, you're barking up the wrong tree, Michael. I've prayed about this, and I think my husband is absolutely right."

"But he just got back from Butter Creek. He needs to rest up."

"Don't make excuses for me, Michael. I'll be okay. I can rest after we're dead."

"Yeah, that's what I'm afraid of."

JoLynn, ignoring their barbs, was all business. "You never mind that kind of faithless talk! You two get suited up. We'll pack some food and a couple of thermoses of hot coffee. You need to get on your way right now."

Michael shook his head in surrender and started pulling on his warm clothes.

"Both snowmobiles?" he asked John.

"Yeah, we might need them. If one breaks down, we'll have a spare. And if the Kenzys are on foot, we'll be able to carry both of them."

"Yeah, right. You're the king of being prepared, aren't you?"

But the sarcasm rolled right off the sheriff's back. "Somebody has to be. Remember that time we were camping...," he began to reminisce, and Michael cut him off.

"We all remember, John. We've heard the story a thousand times."

"Then maybe it's time to learn something from our experiences, don't you think?" he shot back. Then, to relieve the tension, he put a big smile on his face and said, "Okay, you grab the first-aid kit and we'll get this show on the road."

Downhill Racer
Early Christmas Morning
Grafton Mountain, Vermont

When Kim Ling's snowmobile reached the summit of Grafton Mountain, he spotted Jack Kenzy's horse-drawn sled racing down the mountain a quarter-mile ahead of him. It was obvious that Kenzy's horses were struggling to fight their way through the knee-deep snow that covered the old abandoned road.

Kim Ling studied the sheer granite cliffs that rose thirty feet above Kenzy's sled and his breath caught. Above the cliffs, the mountain rose for several hundred feet, and was capped with a deep layer of snow.

It surprised Kim to see Kenzy taking such an enormous risk by steering beneath the cliffs. Watching him risk his life by moving deeper into what was obviously an avalanche zone made Kim aware that the pastor must believe he was being pursued by an enemy. He was suddenly sick at heart to realize that Kenzy might very well be racing to his death in an effort to evade him.

He stood, straddling the snowmobile, almost paralyzed with fear, indecision gripping him. He cupped his mittened hands around his mouth, preparing to shout.

Shout what? A warning? It's futile. Kenzy knows what he faces. And even if he could hear me and he recognized my voice, which is highly unlikely, what good would it do? He can't turn around and come back up the mountain, and he doesn't dare stop. Worse, if I shout, I might start an avalanche.

Although he was peering through the half-light in order to keep Kenzy's sleigh in view, he suddenly imagined that he saw something quiver on his periphery. Now thoroughly frightened, he turned and stared directly at the summit, but everything seemed okay. He didn't notice anything unusual.

It must have been my imagination, he thought. He started to breathe a sigh of relief, only to gasp as he watched the top of the mountain seem to tremble before his eyes. The snowpack was abruptly rent in two, and a massive area appeared to be slipping very slowly downhill. Then the sound reached him, like a bolt of lightning striking nearby, and Kim watched helplessly as the massive wave of snow began to sweep rapidly down the mountainside toward the horse-drawn sleigh far below.

He watched in fascinated horror as Kenzy raced the horses through the shallower snow toward what appeared to be a rent in the cliff wall. About twenty feet above the sled, Kim noticed a tree which had somehow rooted itself in the almost-vertical cliffside. When the first wave of tumbling snow flew out over the cliff and crashed to the road behind the sleigh, it sprayed up into the sky, obscuring Kim's view. He continued to stare into the semi-darkness until his eyes ached, but the horses and sled had disappeared. It seemed like a long time to Kim before the roar of the snow crashing down the mountainside finally subsided.

He sat on the idling snowmobile, stunned by the turn of events. With the watery light of the sun just breaking over a far-off peak, he could see no sign of Kenzy's sleigh. All he could see was snow piled so deep that only the tip of the tree up on the cliff still protruded through. He tried to calculate how high the snow rose above the level of the old road and was staggered by his conclusion.

No one is going to dig that sleigh out from under that mass of packed powder! He wondered what he should do. *All my plans about escaping the Chinese and joining the militia hung on my talking with Kenzy,* he thought. *Now what?*

The roadbed beneath the cliffs was now buried under twenty to thirty feet of snow. He listened to the low rumblings as the mass of snow beneath the cliff settled into place. Then he examined the top of the mountain and decided that most of the snow had already slid down over the cliff. With a feeling of helpless dread nearly overwhelming him, Kim drove his snowmobile very slowly down the mountain toward the spot where Kenzy had disappeared.

Unexpected Survivors

East side, Grafton Mountain
Vermont's Mystery Mountains
Christmas at Sunrise

Kim Ling drove his snowmobile slowly over the rough snow piled deep beneath the cliff by the avalanche. He didn't know much about snow slides, nor whether the snow was well-packed, and he was afraid he might drop through the surface into an air pocket and be buried alive like Pastor Kenzy.

He stopped his snowmobile next to the tall cedar tree beneath which he'd seen the sled disappear. Now, however, only the top few feet of the tree protruded through the deep snow that had been deposited by the avalanche. Kim leapt off his snowmobile and began digging furiously, hoping to reach Kenzy before he smothered.

After a couple of minutes of frenzied effort he found himself unable to go on. He was gasping for air and soaked with sweat and, if he had realized it, was red faced from the exertion. Standing waist-deep in the hole he'd dug, he scooped up one last armful with his mittened hands. The words of his prayers came as wheezes, and he knew that he'd lost the battle when he could feel his heart pounding

No one, he finally acknowledged, *could survive being buried beneath this hard-packed snow for this long.*

So intent was he on his labors that the sound of the approaching snowmobiles didn't register on his consciousness. All he had been listening to was the water dripping from the rocks above, the scraping of his hands in the snow, and the heaving of his own lungs. He was involved in a lost cause, but he was determined not to quit until he dropped.

"Who are you," someone shouted, "and what are you digging for?"

Kim was lifting out another armful of snow when the voice intruded on his dark thoughts. Turning in surprise, he dropped most of the snow back into the hole. As he looked toward the speaker, defeat was registered on his face and in the slump of his shoulders. He pulled himself erect as he took time to try to catch his breath and frame an answer. After a long moment, he replied.

"I was up the hill when the avalanche started," jerking his head to indicate the direction from which he'd come, "and I saw a sleigh here. If you help me, maybe we can reach the driver in time."

The man's voice was oddly cold. "What do you suppose started the slide?"

Kim just stared at him.

"Chinese, aren't you?" the man asked, accusation inherent in the question.

"My family has lived in America for four generations," Kim answered coldly, no longer tolerant of the suspicion in which he was held by Americans, nor the contempt he received from the Chinese.

"Really? Where?"

"Please! We're wasting time. Won't you help me dig?"

"Where?"

"Burlington."

He glanced toward another man who had moved his snowmobile around behind Kim. The second man was aiming a shotgun at him.

"Burlington is the headquarters of the Chinese army," the man said, his voice heavy with menace.

"Can't we wait to talk until after we dig?" Ling begged.

"Why are you so concerned about some stranger?"

"He's not some stranger," he snapped back. "He's my friend!"

"Another Chinaman?"

"No, an American."

"Name?"

Kim didn't want to reveal that hid friend was a Christian. That too could prove fatal. So he simply answered, "Jack Kenzy."

"You were chasing Pastor Kenzy?"

Kim just looked at him, realizing that he had been stupid to imagine that everyone in this rural area wasn't familiar with the pastor. He simply nodded his head in acknowledgement.

"What did you want with Kenzy?"

"I was trying to catch up with him."

"Why?"

To answer that question would expose Kim's service as a spy on behalf of the resistance, and depending on the loyalties of these two men, might result in his own summary execution.

And even if they are patriots, if they learn of my secret relationship to the freedom fighters, it might well result in gossip that would get back to the Chinese. They simply don't have the need to know. On the other hand, he thought, *failing to be forthcoming might be equally as fatal. And every minute wasted leaves Pastor Kenzy in greater peril of suffocation.* He decided to tell his story as quickly as possible.

"My name is Kim Ling. I am ... that is, I was a newsman for a Burlington TV station. I was conscripted by the Chinese to fly one of the copters they stole from my station."

"And you eagerly joined their cause, eh," the man said, making it a statement.

"No, of course not!"

"Of course not?"

"Absolutely not! They had my wife and kids."

"So you worked for them."

"Yes. Before my family was killed by the Chinese, Pastor Kenzy came to me and asked me to continue flying for the Chinese so that I might be able to pass information back and forth."

Suddenly the demeanor of his interrogator didn't seem so menacing. Then man with the shotgun spoke up.

"I saw this guy on the news several times. He might be okay."

The first man gnawed his lip; finally nodding in agreement.

"Why were you chasing Kenzy?"

"I was sent to Butter Creek to serve as an interpreter for a couple of hard-nosed Chinese officers who were to pick up a man named Rhodes."

"Ah, now things are beginning to make sense."

Kim Ling's confusion showed on his face.

"Okay. So, somehow you got away from the Chinese, chased after Jack, and he thought you were the enemy. Does that pretty much sum it up?"

"I'm not sure. About Pastor Kenzy, I mean. Maybe."

"Which brings us to this place. Why are you digging here?"

Kim pointed up at the tip of a cedar tree still exposed above the snow. "I know it only looks like a shrub, but before it was buried by the avalanche, that was a tall tree. The pastor was driving his horses toward that tree when the avalanche started."

"And did he get pretty close to the cliff?"

"It looked to me like the horses were going to run right into the rock wall, but the blowing snow obscured my vision."

"Now there's a word for you, *obscured,* the man with the shotgun laughed." But when Kim looked at him, he saw that he was smiling.

"Don't you care?" he asked.

"Yes, I care very much. But unless he got out of the path of the avalanche, it's too late."

"Can't we dig a little more?"

"If he made it this far, he might have gotten into the tunnel."

"Tunnel?"

"Somewhere around here, there's a cave. The story goes that it was formed by a stream cutting through this spur of the mountain for a few thousand years. Everyone in the area knows about it."

"Blossom's Folly," the other man offered.

"Yes," the first man agreed, "Blossom's Folly. Anyway, Kenzy would have known about it. He's lived around here all his life, and it's one of the first stories I heard when I began spending summers up here. If the floor of the cave is reasonably dry right now, it would be fairly safe. It's big enough to take a pickup truck or a sleigh. So if he got inside, and that's a big if, then he might be okay."

"But won't he die for lack of air?"

"More than likely he will make his way through the mountain and come out the other side."

"You mean that he might be safe?"

"I think that if we drive around the mountain, we just may find him coming out the far side."

Kim's relief was evident, and a smile lit his face. But it was obvious that the other two men weren't entirely satisfied with his story. The older of the two turned to Kim.

"Mount up and follow me."

Kim nodded.

"Stay close, because my friend will be following right behind you."

Assault at Liberty Christian

East Shore, Allison Lake
West of Butter Creek, Vermont
Christmas Morning, 3 a.m.

Chris spotted the sign for Liberty Christian Camp and turned off Route 19 onto a narrow, snow-covered, tree-bordered lane. Her nerves were nearly shot. The only thing that was keeping her awake was a renewed and inexplicable sense of fear. She was so exhausted that she felt she was dreaming. She wanted to stop right where she was and sleep, but she knew that with this cold, she and her children would never wake up. They had to reach the cabin that Pastor Kenzy had told them about.

The glare of the headlights on the snow had given her an intense headache, and she wondered whether it was possible to become snow-blind at night. She would have lost hope were it not for the anticipation of moving the children into the promised cabin, building a fire, and getting a few hours of much-needed sleep.

The snowmobile's engine was just ticking along, and she was struck by the beauty and silence of the forest around her. The snow was soaking up the sound of her engine, and she realized that no one

was likely to hear it at any distance. She was just consoling herself
with this fact when she saw that the lane suddenly took a sharp turn
to the right, and she managed to steer the machine around it without
ramming into the stonewall that lay along the side of the road.

Her eyes were slow to follow the sweep of her headlight's, and
when she finally looked down the lane, she thought she saw movement. Her heart seemed to stop, and she brought the machine to a
halt. Then she heard a shout.

"Hey, Mike. Get out here quick. I think we got us a snowmobile."

Her mind was clouded with fatigue and confusion, but she had
no difficulty in interpreting those words as threatening. She moved
slowly forward, swinging the handlebars from side to side, sweeping
the headlights back and forth through the trees ahead. The man who
had shouted was running toward her when the door of a cabin
opened, and someone was framed in the light from within. He came
running out carrying what looked like a rifle.

Well, my dream of a nice warm cabin is out, she realized without humor. *And now we've got to get out of here, and fast.*

Off to her right was a row of little cabins. To the left was a flat
area with a few picnic tables set beneath tall, well-spaced trees. Beyond the picnic ground was what looked like a huge flat field, devoid
of buildings or trees.

The lake! she remembered. *I have to make it across the lake.*
She shook her head in a futile effort to clear the cobwebs. Swinging
the handlebars toward the cabin again, she saw that the two men
were making their way toward her, both lifting their feet high, struggling through the deep snow.

"Just hold on there," one of the men shouted. "No one's going
to hurt you."

"Now what would have given me any such concern?" she muttered.

She grasped the throttle and twisted it hard. The machine leapt
toward the two men, and in a panic she leaned hard to her left, yank-

ing the handlebars around, skewing away from the men who were now not more than twenty feet away. One of them leapt toward her and slid on his side to land just a yard or two away, but she was already off across the picnic area, turning as far from the men as she dared. Chris realized she was driving much too fast and overcompensated by decelerating too quickly. She felt her daughter slam up against the back of her seat, and the engine actually stalled.

"Oh, Lord, she cried aloud, "please help us!"

The audible response to her prayer was a laugh filled with contempt, and she knew that the men who were again drawing near had absolutely no respect for God.

She tried restarting the engine and it just spun over, but failed to fire. She realized that she might have flooded it. Chris knew that it needed time for the excess gasoline to evaporate, but she didn't have time to wait. In desperation, she tried again, all the time praying. Then she wondered, *Why doesn't the guy with the gun shoot,* and her question was immediately answered.

One of them was shouting, "Shoot them, Mack! Don't let them get away." But the other guy gasped, "I can't. I might hurt the snowmobile."

Then she heard their feet crunching in the snow and looked back over her shoulder.

"Hurry, Mommy," Michael shouted. "They're going to catch us!"

One of them was only a few yards away, and she knew that she and her children were mere seconds from a far worse fate than they had experienced under the Chinese invaders. In desperation, she twisted the key one final time. The engine coughed. Then it caught. *No time to warm it up!* she knew, and she prayed, "*Please don't let it stall!*"

She twisted the handgrip as far as it would go, and the acceleration threw her back against the seat. Her eyes were on her rearview mirror as the snowmobile leapt forward, and she saw the nearest guy drop his rifle and leap for the back of her machine. He just managed to get his fingers around the tail light assembly, and she felt the machine slow. In another instant the other man would pile on, and then they would be lost. But the snowmobile was still accelerating, and suddenly she saw his fingers slip loose, and then he was sliding face-first through the snow behind them.

She took a quick look through her face mask toward the lake, and it appeared that the ground in between was free of obstacles. When she peered at the rear view mirror again, she saw that Mack's buddy had picked up the rifle and was aiming it point blank at them. There was an explosion, and she cringed, but didn't feel the impact of the bullet.

But her would-be assassin did. When Mike had dropped the rifle in order to dive for the snowmobile, the muzzle of his weapon rammed into the ground, and its muzzle was clogged with snow and mud. When his buddy picked it up and fired it, the weapon exploded in his hands, ripping his check open to the bone and blinding him in one eye.

Unaware of this, Chris drove several hundred yards out onto the ice, then turned in a tight circle to see whether they were still pursuing her. Surprised that she and the children were alone on the ice, she checked the readout on her face plate. She located Tower Rock about a mile away, but she was suddenly afraid to cross the broad lake in the dark.

When she was convinced that she was well out of reach of the men at the camp, so she shut off her headlights and turned south, paralleling the eastern shore. She was forced to move very slowly because clouds kept passing beneath the watery moon, and she could barely see. She traveled about a half-mile south of the Christian camp. The snow-covered ice reflected back what little light there was, and she noticed that at one point there appeared to be an opening in the shoreline. Assuming it was some sort of inlet, she slowed her speed to a crawl and found herself entering a small protected cove. Among the trees, she thought she saw the roofline of a cabin.

Moving as slowly as possible, her engine merely puttering, she reached the shore line, but did not enter the cove. She turned the headlights on for just a moment and confirmed that she had indeed seen a cabin. She was about a hundred feet away and could see that the snow covering the ground around the cabin appeared undisturbed. It didn't matter. She knew that she couldn't go any further without rest. She had to take a chance, and she had to get the children under cover before they all froze to death. Accelerating slightly, she ran the snowmobile up off the ice until she drew near the front door, then turned the snowmobile around in a tight circle so that it was pointing toward the lake.

When she reached the front door, she knocked gently. Receiving no response, she knocked a little harder. Then she tried the door. It opened a crack and hoping there would be no more rude surprises, she leaned in. Meeting only silence, she pushed the door open the remainder of the way and took a step inside.

Turning on the flashlight that Abigail Kenzy had given her, she looked over the one-room cabin. There were two bunks on the far wall, with blankets neatly folded and stacked. There was a table and four bentwood chairs in the middle of the room, and a wood-fired kitchen range and counter with a sink on her left. Shelves along the back wall appeared to be well-stocked with food. Alongside the range was a stack of kindling and some old newspapers.

Flashlight in hand, Chris ran out to carry in the sleepy children. She laid them on the lower bunk, and covered them with one of the blankets. Then she carefully closed the thick plank door and laid the bar across the brackets that were there to secure it. Checking the windows to make certain that the heavy curtains were fully closed, she moved to the kerosene lantern that sat on the table in the middle of the room. Pressing the little lever that raised the globe, she opened the carton of matches that sat next to it, struck one against the abrasive strip on the side of the box, waited until the flame took hold and lit the wick. When she had it adjusted so that it didn't smoke, she lowered the glass shade.

She sighed, but it was almost a sob. They had shelter, heat, light, and food, but she was physically and mentally exhausted, and she didn't feel in the least bit secure.

She moved across the room to the big wood stove. It obviously served both for cooking and heating. She opened the cast-iron door on the firebox and happily discovered that some far-sighted individual had carefully left crumbled newspaper and kindling ready for lighting. Reaching for another match, she lit the newspaper. Then, as the flames began snapping and curling around the kindling, she experienced a momentary sense of well-being. As she felt the heat radiate on her face, she raised her hands and said, "Thank you, Lord Jesus."

With the kindling burning fiercely, she dropped several pieces of firewood on top, then closed the door. She opened the air inlet wide and made certain the flu on the chimney was wide open and drawing well. Once the room began warming, she would dampen it down.

Turning from the stove, she took the oil lamp from the center of the table and examined the packages of freeze-dried foods on the shelves. It wasn't Kenzys' cabin, but it was a godsend, maybe even better, and she was very grateful. At least the three of them were alone here. She experienced a fleeting temptation to remain here for several days, but the pastor's instructions had proven accurate so far, and his advice couldn't be ignored. As soon as they'd eaten and slept a few hours, she would cross the lake to Tower's Point.

The top of the iron stove was soon glowing a dull orange, and the cabin was almost uncomfortably warm. She shut the damper slightly, and the roar of the fire settled into a comfortable murmur. There was a little hand pump next to the sink and a bucket of water setting beside it. She lifted the bucket and poured water into the top of the pump to prime it. Then she pumped furiously until it began hiccuping brown water out of the spout. After a moment, the flow steadied and the water cleared of its rusty color. She filled a coffee pot from the pump and set it on the stove to boil. She'd take no chance on drinking contaminated water.

When her hands had warmed a little, Chris was able to tear open a couple of the aluminum packets containing chicken stew. She emptied the contents into a pot, stirred in the prescribed amount of water and set the pot on the stove. The children awoke grumbling, but they were like little birds, and after she'd forced a few bites into their mouths, they eagerly fed themselves. After she wiped their faces and hands, she put them back to bed and they immediately fell into an exhausted sleep. Then she crumbled onto the other bed only to discover that she could not relax. She lay there reviewing the events of the past twenty-four hours when sleep finally overtook her.

She didn't know what awakened her, but she was suddenly very frightened. Perhaps it was because the fire had gone out and the cabin was cold, but she had a strange premonition of disaster. Without hesitation, she roused her son and got him on his feet, then she picked up Mary and carried her to the door. She didn't hear any sound outside, so she settled her daughter against one shoulder, then gingerly lifted the bar and slowly opened the door.

As his mother went out the cabin door, Michael noticed that she'd left the snowmobile helmet on the table. He caught it up and pulled it over his head in order to keep his hands free. The helmet fit loosely and wobbled around, but he knew he'd be giving it back to his mother in a moment.

The waning moon was just adequate to light the surface of the lake, and Chris saw the silhouette of a man pushing his way through the snow toward them. He appeared to be following the snowmobile tracks that she had left a few hours earlier, and he was now only a few hundred yards away from the cabin.

How could I have been so stupid? she berated herself. *I forgot that there was no snow falling to cover our tracks.*

"Michael," she hissed. "Quick. Get on the snowmobile." With his sharp eyes, he had already seen the man, and he was already in motion. As he moved toward the back seat, a gunshot broke the morning calm.

He heard his mother gasp, and as he turned to learn the cause, he saw her leg fold under her and watched as she collapsed to the snow. Mary had fallen from her arms, but was evidently unhurt because she crawled to her mother's side and put her arms about her.

Michael stood staring at his mother and sister for a moment, then turned to discover that the man was drawing dangerously near. The guy was now cradling the shotgun in his arms and was laughing almost hysterically.

Michael's father had begun teaching him to handle firearms when he was just eight years old. The boy immediately guessed that his mother had been struck by buckshot because another of the pellets had embedded itself in the sole of his leather boot, and his toe felt as though it had been stung by a hornet. His father had been very safety conscious, and Michael had been taught that.00 buckshot could be lethal at up to one-hundred yards. Since this guy was still nearly two hundred yards away, he had hit them by blind luck, and the shot couldn't have had the impact it might have had if he were closer. Since his mom was down, however, it was obviously bad enough.

Michael turned to look at his mother one more time, choked back a sob, and leapt onto driver's seat of the snowmobile. He was only average height for an eleven-year old, so he had to straddle the seat far forward and stretch his arms wide in order to reach the grips on the handlebars. Even as leaned far forward to reach for the key, he realized that his mother might still have it in her pocket. But she didn't. She had left the key in the ignition! Michael didn't even try to reason why his mother might have forgotten to remove it the night before.

As he turned the key, he heard the man shout, "Don't you move that snowmobile!" Michael ignored him, and surprisingly, the engine stuttered to life. For a moment it ran quietly, as though on just one cylinder. Then the choke adjusted itself, and the engine roared. Michael stared out across the snow-covered lake at the on-coming man. With the engine running smoothly he grabbed the shift lever and accelerated across the snow-covered ground toward the lake. At first he thought to distract the man, to somehow frighten him away.

I don't want to hurt anybody, he thought. *I just want him to go away and leave us alone.* Then he realized, *But this man is bad, and he hurt my Mom.*

He had only driven a snowmobile once, a couple of years before, and that was with his father sitting behind him as he had steered the machine in figure-eights around the center of a huge field. Yet he wasn't frightened of the machine, nor of the danger represented by the man he was rapidly approaching. Nor was it was not a matter of childish pride or bravado.

Michael was slightly distracted by the movement of shadows that seemed to sweep in great arcs across the surface of the lake, but he didn't give them much thought. They were probably produced by the limbs of trees swaying in the wind or by clouds sweeping by overhead, but it pleased him to imagine that they were the shadows of giant eagles flying between him and the moon, or even of angels sent to protect them. Those shadows circling about on the snow-covered lake gave him a sense of immense security, though he had no idea why they should, and had less time to consider the reasons.

He was, after all, little more than a child, and if he hadn't come to know the Lord, he'd have had absolutely no concept of security or of the power required to provide it. His mother had explained how the misuse of power by America's leaders had failed the people, and stripped them of their security, but he had little understanding of abstract concepts.

Yet he had no difficulty understanding that it had been wrong of that man to shoot his mother. And though he didn't think of himself as a young David facing a giant Goliath, he did possess the starry-eyed innocence of a boy who believed that right makes might and that he was attacking somebody evil in the name of the Lord.

Somehow, he thought, *I must stop this man!*

When the man saw the snowmobile coming across the ice toward him, he laughed with delight. He had been filled with rage when he'd watched his friend bleed to death as a result of the wounds he suffered when his rifle exploded. Now he would get even.

The woman's bringing her snowmobile to me, he exulted. *Come on, baby; come to papa!*

But a moment later he wasn't so certain, and began sidestepping cautiously, trying to stay out of the path of the slow-moving snowmobile, wondering what the woman driving it had in mind. And when the machine turned slightly so that the headlights were blinding him, he became momentarily frightened. Deciding not to take a chance, he raised the shotgun, pulled back the hammer on the remaining unfired barrel, and aimed it toward the headlights.

Michael had the advantage. He had their attacker framed in the beams of his headlights, and could see him trying to shade his eyes from the glare. It was at that moment that one of the shadows seemed to lift from the ice and swoop between the snowmobile and the man with the rifle, momentarily blacking out the light. Then, as the shadow moved on, the man was again illuminated. He raised his gun to aim at the oncoming snowmobile, and Michael immediately squatted down in order to offer the smallest possible target.

As he moved, the helmet tipped forward over his eyes. He heard the weapon discharge and the sound of the buckshot punching holes above his head in his windscreen. It was seconds before he had completed a mental inventory and determined that he was unhurt.

Then he imagined that he heard an imperious voice shout, "Turn!" When he failed to do so, something seemed to slap his left hand, causing him to momentarily lose his grip on the handlebar and resulting in the snowmobile swinging sharp right.

With the headlights no longer in his eyes, the man was momentarily dazzled. Then the lights reappeared just a few yards away, coming straight for him. He dropped the gun, and stepped to the side, planning to leap on the driver as the machine went by. But something was wrong. The sled abruptly turned toward him, and the bullet nose of the snowmobile struck him in the hip, throwing him up and over the windshield. When he struck the snow covered ice, he was in agony, convinced that his leg was broken. Raising his arm in a feeble effort to ward off the inevitable, he watched in horror as the snowmobile circled and raced back toward him.

Michael saw the man raise his hands, but he was unable to turn the snowmobile. It was as if it had a mind of its own. There was a loud thump, and the machine rose slightly in the air, then settled back down and raced on.

I'm sorry, Michael cried over his shoulder. *I didn't want to hurt you, but you shouldn't have hurt my Mom.* Then, as the boy brushed the tears from his eyes, the shadows that had been swooping around him seemed to sweep away across the lake before fading from view.

Michael now had no difficulty turning the machine and steering it back to where his little sister sat crying by their mother's side. He pulled the machine up to within a few feet of them and left it idling while he climbed off and went to his mother's side.

Michael put his arm around his little sister as he knelt beside them. She was awake, but she looked very pale. He felt something sticky on his hand, and when he held it up to examine it in the snowmobile lights, he saw blood. He looked down and saw that it had saturated her snow pants around her upper leg.

He remembered his first-aid training from the church scouting program. The first thing they'd taught him was to offer a brief prayer for the patient, and to remain calm, so he took his sister's hand and they prayed together. Mary was sobbing quietly, obviously too exhausted to carry on more.

Michael slipped off his belt, and ran it around his mother's leg above the blood-soaked hole in her ski pants. He was slim, so the holes in the belt pretty much lined up with the thickness of his mother's thigh. He pulled as tight as he could, buckled the belt, and prayed silently that the bleeding would stop.

Then he tugged on his mothers jacket. "Mom, you've got to get up!" Her eyes moved slowly to focus on his.

"Michael, you're alive?"

"Sure, Mom."

"But the man."

"The man's lying out there somewhere," and his little hand swept the lake, "but I don't think that he'll bother us anymore."

"He won't bother us because Michael ran him down with the snowmobile, Mom," Mary told her.

"Is that true, Michael?"

"Not exactly," he answered truthfully, and he wondered whether his mother would believe his amazing story. He knew that his mother might be angry, and was determined to tell the truth.

"I tried not to, but the snowmobile ran him down."

She looked at him, just a little boy, and realized that he would have had difficulty steering the machine. *It might have been an accident,* she thought.

"What is this war doing to us?" she whispered aloud, and he knew that she didn't expect an answer. His response surprised her.

"Hurry, Mom. You've got to get up. We've got to get out of here in case he is okay, and we can't carry you."

"No, of course you can't, honey."

Although she was past exhaustion, Chris still had the capacity to recognize their peril, and in spite of her exhaustion and the gnawing pain in her leg, her concern for her children was a stimulus to action. With her crawling, and Michael and little Mary trying to steady her, Chris managed to get to the back seat of the snowmobile and pull herself aboard. Then Mary took her customary seat, this time propped between her Mommy's knees rather than those of her older brother.

"Can you really drive this thing, Michael?"

"It's a little hard to reach things, Mom, but I just did."

"Yes, I guess you did, didn't you?" she mumbled.

Clouds were passing over the moon, and when Michael could no longer see the cabin behind them in the darkness, he turned right and headed across the lake toward what looked like a rocky pinnacle. He remembered Pastor Kenzy telling his mother that she was to head for the pinnacle.

The sun was still behind the mountains to the east, and its thin watery glow was just able to penetrate the darkness and bring hope that this would be a milder day.

Michael knew that he needed to concentrate on his driving because the ice was rough, and there had been boulders protruding through the surface just offshore at Camp Liberty. He was afraid that he might face similar hazards on the west side of the lake. He was no longer concerned with his pursuers now. Last night one of them had a gun explode in his face, and the this morning the other was probably laying on the ice, suffering from broken bones. Neither one of them was apt to follow them across the lake.

And, if there really were people named Tower on the west side of the lake, they might finally find safety and get help for his mother.

In the meantime, his mother was propped on the back of the snowmobile fighting to maintain consciousness. She was frightened. But it wasn't of her own safety she was thinking. She was concerned for her two children. What would happen to them if she succumbed to this wound? Nor could she get her mind off her husband. *Was his escape successful? Is he alive and safe? And, if so, where is he?*

Ironically, she and her husband were separated by less than a mile, but while she was running for her life, he was safely ensconced in a cavern beneath the mountain that loomed just over her shoulder to the east. Like her, however, he had to deal with his own terrible fatigue as well as with two interlopers who also, coincidentally, threatened his life.

The Towers' Homestead

Southwest Corner, Allison Lake
Pre-dawn Christmas Morning

While young Michael Rhodes was driving the snowmobile across the lake in the darkness, Don Tower and his wife were at work in the small barn that served as the hangar for their old airplane. It was nestled beneath a cliff, a vast stone overhang — sort of like a natural band shell — not more than two hundred yards back in the woods from the edge of Allison Lake. A narrow tree-shaded lane led north from the barn to the end of what had once been a Department of Defense airfield. A quarter-mile to the south of the barn, the gray mass of Tower Rock pierced the forest canopy.

Don Tower was leaning over his workbench, trying with near-frozen fingers to compress a very small spring that held a tiny ball bearing in a shallow orifice in the body of the plane's carburetor. His wife struggled with both hands to keep the slippery carburetor body from moving while he worked. The spring had already shot out of the cavity once while he'd been trying to screw down it's retainer clip, and they'd had an awful time finding the ball bearing on the dirt floor.

This time the screw took hold and he was able to take a full turn. They both sighed with relief. He met her eyes across the workbench and she smiled. Even after all these years, they never tired of one another. She said one word, "Praise," he responded with "the," and she finished with "Lord!" and they both laughed. The three word phrase was a praise offering that they often made together.

"I had one of these on order, you know," he said, nodding at the carburetor.

"Would it have worked?"

"I really don't know. I specified a rebuilt carb for the original 1941 Continental F140 engine, but unless it somehow finds its way here, and I get an opportunity to install it, we'll never know."

"You couldn't be sure it was the right part before you ordered it?"

"No. There have been so many changes to the original L3 since this plane was built in 1941, including changes in design and model numbers, that I just don't know. And that doesn't take into consideration the shortcuts that a lot of mechanics took through the years, cobbling things together with whatever parts they could find that they hoped might work. Most of these old airplanes are gone now, either in scrap piles or at best unfit to fly. Even when the Web was still up, it was almost impossible to find replacement parts."

"But you think you might have succeeded in ordering the right carb?"

"Yes. It might even be sitting on a shelf at the Butter Creek Post Office right now, covered with dust."

"And our plane won't fly again unless we get it?"

"No, it'll fly as soon as we get this reinstalled. It's just that this one has a small pit in the housing."

Her eyes held a question, and he responded quickly.

"The tiny imperfection isn't in a place that makes it dangerous. He lifted the carburetor up and held it in the light of the gasoline lantern. "I bought this one about 5 years ago, and I've rebuilt it once. It will be fine when we get it reassembled."

"Then, why...."

"I'd like to have a spare on hand, that's all. Just in case."

He pointed toward the L3B. "That's why I love this little airplane. She's so uncomplicated that it's easy to keep her flying. It's just canvas skin over a wooden frame and a 65 horsepower gasoline engine. It's lightweight, and flier-friendly."

"Honey, I've heard this so many times."

"Turns out it's perfect for this location."

"How so?" she asked.

"First, as you know, the old DOD airfield here is all but shot. But this little plane will land on very short fields of dirt, grass, even snow-covered. Second, if we have an opportunity to help the resistance groups, we can use it for spotting as well as ferrying officers or communicating between their headquarters and the forward locations near the front. We could even rig up litters to carry wounded."

"Don, do you have any idea how many times you've told me this?"

"Sorry. You are the only one I have to talk to, and you also know how much I love this plane."

"More than me?"

"I'd have to be a real fool to admit that," he laughed. Then he grew serious. "You know that this was used as a spotter plane during World War II, and it's going to be a spotter plane again."

"I don't understand."

"It would be almost impossible for the Chinese to pick it up on radar because there is so little metal in the rig. That is, if they have radar, which I doubt. And because there aren't any computers or microchips anywhere in the plane, her electronics weren't damaged by the nuclear radiation at the beginning of the war."

"And other planes were?"

"Undoubtedly. Before the war, most experts were estimating that pretty much every plane and automobile in the United States would be disabled because their electronics would be fried by the nukes our enemies might fire at us."

"But you don't sound as though you subscribe to that view."

"I do to a large degree."

"Large degree?"

"Older motor vehicles might be okay, but virtually every car built since 2007 has had a bunch of computerized devices built into them. Those computers controlled everything from fuel injectors to cooling systems – not to speak of steering, brakes, radios, even rearview video. With that sort of sophistication came all sorts of opportunities for failure and abuse."

"Abuse?"

"Yes. If an owner signed up with the manufacturer for certain services, he could sit behind the wheel and speak with someone a thousand miles away about mechanical problems, or even have them call a cop for assistance."

"Yes, I knew that."

"But what you might not have realized, Jenn, is that whether the owner signed up or not, the manufacturers and police also had the ability to turn on that equipment and listen to conversations in any car so equipped, and to continually track their movements and exact location."

"Wow!"

"And, worse, those with access could shut off an engines or lock the ignitions on a variety of cars from a remote location, even millions at a time, while the vehicles were in motion — even if they were operating at high speeds.

"The really bad news was that, since everything was computer-controlled, it was not a great challenge for the Chinese or the Russians to hack into an automaker's computer system and shut down the cars they manufactured just prior to the opening of hostilities. It wasn't the first time they'd hacked major American corporate and financial institutions."

Jenn went to the little pot belly stove and held out a pot. "You want some?"

"No, I'm coffee'd out."

As she poured a cup for herself, she said, "I remember that those massive hacker attacks were regularly reported on the news."

"Yeah, but they were evidently just dress rehearsals in their preparations for war. Over a period of years skilled computer hackers working for various governments successfully shut down networks serving our banks, manufacturers, the military, and even our federal intelligence agencies. And when they were ready to go to war, they shut down pretty much everything at once."

"Cyber warfare, right?"

"Exactly," he agreed.

She stared across the barn into the shadows. "You know what bothered me?" He didn't answer, and she went on. "When those early cyber attacks occurred most Americans didn't seem to get overly concerned about them or see them as a danger to their freedom, let alone as a prelude to war."

"No, nor did Americans seem concerned that more and more of their personal information was exposed to strangers or that their freedoms were being whittled away."

"Do you suppose that they felt they could trust our politicians with the knowledge?"

"Oh, sure!"

She tried to stifle her own disgust. "The truth is that most Americans were too busy pursuing their own interests and shoveling down the carefully prepared propaganda that they got on the evening news."

"Well, events proved otherwise."

"So," she asked, "what about those planes, trains and automobiles you were referring to?"

"To get into that, you have to understand something about nuclear explosions."

She laughed. "I have found occasion to study a little about that since the war began."

"I'm sure," he agreed.

"I know that the energy released when a nuclear weapon is detonated is about half blast and half thermal energy."

"Thermal energy?"

"As in millions of degrees Fahrenheit for maybe less than a second," she replied.

"You really did your homework, didn't you?" he laughed.

"Well, a million degrees for a fraction of a second would have represented a big challenge to Shadrach, Meshach, and Abednego."

Not to be side-tracked by a husband who delighted in changing the subject, she snapped a quick reply. "It wouldn't have mattered how hot Nebuchadnezzar made that furnace," she replied. "The Lord would have handled it for those faithful Jews." He nodded in agreement and she went on. "Depending on how a bomb is designed and where it's detonated — in the sky, under the ocean, or next to several skyscrapers — the amount of ionizing and residual radiation vary."

"Whoa! You're getting over my head now."

"I told you!" she said with what might have been interpreted as a smirk. "I studied it."

"All we were concerned with here in Vermont were two things."

"Only two?" she asked with sarcasm.

"Sure. Vermont was small potatoes, not worth a direct hit."

"So?"

"So," he replied, "we were a long way from the nearest explosion, and we probably wouldn't have to worry about either blast or heat. The first thing we had to be concerned with was staying underground long enough for the radioactive half-lives of any fallout to dwindle enough so that we wouldn't suffer from radiation poisoning."

"Okay, we both know that that we needed to get underground for about two weeks," she said, "and since Vermont has more than its share of caves, a lot of people survived. What was your second concern?"

"When the bombs were detonated high above the earth, they emitted Gamma rays."

"I was getting to that," she said. And your point is?"

"Those rays interacted with the earth's magnetic field to produce something called electromagnetic pulse, or EMP."

"Okay. Sounds like we both read the same book."

"Maybe," he laughed. "Anyway, the pulse caused metal objects —such as the high-tension cables that carry power from city-to-city— to act as antennas."

"I don't understand."

"The *antennas* generated high voltages by interacting with the EMP. Those huge voltages radiated out to destroy unshielded electronics, such as the scores of small computers under the hood of most cars."

"Is that why you took all of our computers and radios into the shelter when you thought war was imminent?"

"Exactly. And why I taxied this plane into the underground hangar...." he began, but she ended it for him.

"...As well as the snowmobile, ATV, and outboard motor, right?"

"Right. And it's the same reason that wise people used to wrap their credit cards in aluminum, before putting them in their wallets."

"Yes, so that identity thieves couldn't stand next to them with their little gadget in a paper bag and scan their credit cards."

"Bingo! Give that lady a kewpie doll."

"And after all that reading, I don't get it," she admitted.

"The aluminum foil around the credit cards created what's called a *Faraday Cage.*"

"I didn't pick up on that in my reading," she said.

"A Faraday Cage is an enclosure formed by material that conducts electricity, such as copper or aluminum. It can be a solid enclosure or a mesh., and its used to block electric fields. The English scientist, Michael Faraday, who invented it in 1836.

"But not all of our electronics still work."

"No, that's true. I didn't think to shield our alarm clock, and it has at least one ruined microchip. And if we hadn't been able to park the vehicles underground, I doubt that I could have wrapped them in aluminum foil to protect them. It's a complicated thing."

"Still, you did pretty good, not knowing for sure that a war was coming." She smiled. "We must be about the only survivors in Vermont who still have a working laptop." She walked over and gave him a hug. "You're not such a dummy, Mr. Tower."

"Well, thank you very much, Mrs. Tower. You do all right yourself."

"So it was the EMPs that damaged America's cars?"

"For the most part, yes. They generated extremely high voltage that fried the integrated circuits and the computer chips."

"What about the old two-way radio you have in this plane?"

He smiled. "It uses old-fashioned vacuum tubes. They are far more resistant to voltage shifts, and I've already tested it."

"And it works?"

"Oh, yeah," he smiled.

"Well," his wife observed with her characteristic optimism, "look on the bright side. We have one of the few airplanes in America that will still fly."

"And an old Jeep that still runs," he added.

"And a snowmobile."

"Yes," he laughed, "so we must be very careful how we employ them, particularly since we only have about 500 gallons of gasoline."

"But I don't understand why it's so important to you that we keep the plane in operating condition."

"Simple. First, we might be able to help fight back. But if we can't, and we find ourselves threatened by anyone here, we grab our weapons and those emergency packs that we made up," and he pointed to two backpacks hanging on the wall by the big rolling doors, "and we take off for distant places." He turned to look at her, and she knew that he was dead serious. "I don't intend to let happen to you what happened to Tommy's mom."

"I was just thinking about her," she mused. "We haven't seen her lately."

"Even though she's an R.N., she has to be careful because Tommy suffers with Down syndrome, and with all the stress they are experiencing, he could become a real problem."

"Yes," she agreed, "not to speak of the fact that the poor kid is susceptible to every little illness that comes along."

"Yeah, and she no longer has access to any of the drugs he might need," he mused.

She nodded, then changed the subject.

"So, there's still a chance that the replacement carburetor might be at the post office?"

"Yes, if the people that the Chinese put in charge haven't confiscated it."

"The Bentons?" she asked

"Yes, the Bentons. They are the most dangerous people in Butter Creek right now, and they were given charge of the post office, though I'm sure there is precious little mail moving from town to town these days."

"We always knew they were unscrupulous," she said, "but I never thought they'd stoop so low as to betray their own country."

"I guess they'd do about anything to feather their own nest," he answered.

"It's a wonder they haven't sent someone here looking for us," she agreed, and shook her head to signal her disgust.

"They probably don't think we have anything worth hiking through miles of forest to steal," he said. He looked out the window toward the mountain that stood on the opposite side of the lake.

She noticed him looking east and immediately linked her thoughts with his. "I wonder how the Sennetts are doing."

It never ceased to amaze him as to how their two minds seemed to mesh. He knew well enough that the two of them thought alike. *No, that's not it. She knows how I think. I'm not sure I really understand how her mind works at all.*

"I had hoped to get the plane airborne before this blizzard hit. I wanted to see if I could spot Joe from the air. The last few times I flew over the valley, I didn't see anyone."

"I wonder who burned their beautiful little house," she mused, her sorrow evident.

"And why they instead left the barn standing," he added.

"Well, it could be a while before you're able to fly over and take a look," she said.

"I'd really be worried about them if I didn't know about that hideaway they have in the caverns."

"That's true," she replied. "I really think they took all those precautions because of their little granddaughter. At their ages, and with all they've been through, I don't think they would much care one way or the other if it weren't for little Sarah."

He nodded. "Well, they should be fine. Even if someone found their hideaway, Joe knows those caverns like the back of his hand. They'd never find them."

"Still," she thought aloud, "I'd like to know how they are doing. And I'd love to spend some time with them."

"Yes," he agreed "Whenever I've been discouraged, they've always had the faith to help me get my face back off the floor."

"Likewise," she smiled.

"You never have your face on the floor," he laughed.

Kim Ling — Double Agent
North Side of Grafton Mountain
Christmas Morning

The man that Kim Ling had been instructed to follow suddenly spun his snowmobile around the mountains' eastern spur, and decelerated as he rode down into a wide bowl-shaped hollow that lay on the north side of the mountain. Ling pulled up alongside him, and the other snowmobile stopped behind Ling. Kim turned his head and found the African American's eyes on him, his gun resting across his knees. *He's taking no chances,* he thought, *but at least he no longer looked angry.*

The wind began whipping around them, and Kim noticed the two men taking anxious looks at the sky. It had clouded over again and it seemed obvious that they were in for more snow. Kim was pretty much indifferent to what these two men would do to him if the pastor didn't show, and so began examining his strange surroundings. On the far edge of the hollow he saw an opening in the cliff wall, its dark maw accentuated by the pristine snow that lay beneath the opening.

"No prints in the snow!" the man behind him observed in an almost fatalistic tone, and the other man nodded.

"Looks like they didn't make it in time."

Instead of replying, the older man gunned his engine slightly and drove slowly toward the cave. He was a stone's throw away from the cave when a pair of horses appeared in the portal, and a second later the sleigh they were pulling came into view, two people hunched on the seat. Kim let out a sigh of relief, and when he turned toward the man behind him, he saw a smile splitting his face.

When the sleigh had cleared the cave and pulled up alongside the nearest snowmobile, the driver shaded his eyes against the snow's glare. Raising one eyebrow, he fixed his gaze on the older of Ling's two captors and said, "Well, John, I didn't expect to see you here."

"Pastor," he replied dryly, "we were beginning to wonder whether we were going to have to go back and dig you out of a snow bank with our bare hands."

"Well I'm relieved that you didn't have to go to such extremes."

"What took you so long?"

"The iron runners on this old sleigh were made for sliding over snow, not stone. The horses had a hard time dragging us through the cavern."

The man named John turned his attention to the other passenger and with obvious concern asked, "How's Abigail?"

The pastor's flippant reply belied the look of concern on his face. "She needs some rest and something decent to eat, but she'll be all right. She's a tough old bird."

With that, the woman whom they assumed to be asleep opened her eyes against the glare and elbowed her husband. "Old bird, is it? You'd better watch yourself, Jack Kenzy!"

The men laughed, and the pastor looked out across the snow to see who else had been awaiting them.

"Hello, Kim!" he said, a smile on his face. "This is a propitious meeting." And with those words, the two other men seemed to relax.

Then the pastor saw the man behind Kim. "Michael! It's grand to see you again. Old friends, well met."

"Jack, it's good to see you and Abigail!" the second man replied. "Our families are waiting for the two of you back at our hideaway."

"As tired as we are, I need to speak with Kim as soon as possible."

"That had better wait another half hour," the man named John replied. It sounds like this blizzard is whipping itself up again."

"No, I must return soon," Kim said, "or my usefulness will be at an end. It may already be too late."

"Back where?" Kenzy asked.

"To your farm, first. That's where the Chinese left me to wait when they went in pursuit of the escaped woman and her two children."

"You aren't going to make it back in this storm," John warned.

"If I don't, then I might as well not return. As fouled up as things are, if they caught me, they'd just shoot me."

His words weighed on them, and they gathered around the sleigh for a quick conference. Kim filled them in with what the General had told him during his drunken confessional, and the men were jubilant with the news.

"Do you really believe what he told you?" the pastor asked.

"Yes, I do," Kim replied. "But apart from relying on my judgment, we can always fall back on – *in vino veritas.*"

"Why, yes, I guess we might."

"What's that mean?" John asked.

The pastor smiled. "It's Latin for, *In wine there is truth.*"

They all laughed.

"Why don't you come with us, Kim?" the pastor urged. "You have no reason to go back there. They probably realize that they have no hold over you any longer."

"Two reasons, pastor. First, I'm living out the Apostle Paul's exhortation, presenting myself a living sacrifice."

When they heard that, the two men who had threatened him exchanged pained expressions.

"Second," Kim went on, "I can't think of anyone else who might provide you with solid intelligence."

It was Abigail Kenzy who broke the silence. "You're a great man of God, Kim Ling."

"No ma'am. Just world-weary."

"Don't argue with an *old bird*," she replied, and they all laughed.

"Are you sure this is what you want to do, Kim?" John asked.

"No, I don't want to do it. I just know it's what I should do."

"In that case, let me give you this," and he rummaged through his saddlebag and removed a book. When he opened the cover, Kim saw that it was hollowed out. It contained a miniature telegrapher's key and a set of ear buds. "Any chance you know Morse code?"

"As a matter of fact, I do."

"Well this book has a built-in radio that will enable you to keep in touch with us. There are instructions and a tiny code book packed with it, which includes the varying times and days to make your calls. It goes without saying that you must not lose the code book."

John slipped the book back into a small vinyl case and handed it to Kim. They all knew that if Kim were found with it, it would be a death sentence.

"I had another thought," Kim said. "If I learn anything vital while airborne, and I have the opportunity, I'll write it out, wrap it around a rock, tie a strip of bright-colored cloth to it and drop it from my copter."

"If you give us your helicopter's identification numbers," Michael suggested, "we'll get the word out that our people shouldn't shoot at you."

"And if it got back to the Chinese that I wasn't being shot at, they'd shoot me."

"Not if our people appear to be shooting at you," Michael replied. "The operative phrase there is *appear to be shooting at you.*"

"Good thought," Kenzy agreed. "Have your people shoot toward the helicopter, but make certain they miss."

"Yes," Kim replied in a sober voice, "but please make sure they miss." And everyone laughed. "I really don't want people to shoot me out of the air. It won't be the fall," he added. "It will be the sudden stop when I hit the ground." He went on quickly before anyone else could comment. "According to General Eng, you've taken down at least one of his copters already, and there are only two of us left."

"Really?" the pastor remarked. "We knew we hit one, but it disappeared trailing smoke, and we didn't know we'd brought it down. That's good news."

John had been studying the sky. Clouds were racing toward the horizon, and his frown reminded them all that they needed to get moving.

He looked at Kim Ling. "One more question," he said. "Do you have any idea how many drones they have?"

"I haven't been able to find that out," Kim replied, "but I got the impression that they don't have any that carry weapons, and only two or three that are quipped with surveillance cameras."

"How can that be?"

"They were counting on receiving hundreds of them when their ship came in."

"When will that be?" the younger man asked.

"Never," Kim smiled. "That's the ship that was sunk."

"No second ship?" Kenzy asked in amazement. "They don't anticipate any additional support?"

"No," Kim replied. "Everything they were counting on lies in mud at the bottom of the Panama Canal." Then he added, "And from what the general told me, all the efforts of their leaders in China are directed at repelling attacks by the Russians in the north and Japanese in the east."

"What are you saying?" John asked, almost too overwhelmed by the good news to accept it.

"I'm saying that the war that the Chinese helped start is not going well for them in Asia, and that they have no spare resources to send here. I'm saying," Kim Ling finished, "that the Chinese invading America are on their own."

Kenzy was simply beaming. "All right," he said, "let's pray," and he called upon the Lord to send his angels to give their cause favor, to watch over Kim Ling, and to heal Abigail. They were shaking hands all around when Kim cocked his head to the side, as though trying to hear something above the rising wind.

"I don't believe it! He muttered.

"Believe what?" Kenzy asked, but Kim was already shouting, "Everyone into the cave!"

"What's going on?" the sheriff demanded.

"Helicopter!" Kim shouted as he raced his snowmobile toward the cave entrance.

Kenzy, still seated next to his wife on the sled, whipped up the horses and turned them back to the cave entrance. The other two men were slower starting, but their machines got them underground while the pastor's sleigh, towed by the two weary horses, was still exposed.

The rear of the sled was just passing into the cave when the beating of the copter's blades became almost deafening, and the aircraft swept over the crown of the mountain. The unarmed aircraft hovered outside the cave for a moment, but when the rising winds almost drove him against the cliff face, the pilot turned and headed toward the northwest.

The interior of the natural tunnel was probably as bright as it had ever been as a result of the light shed by the headlights of the three snowmobiles. The three men pulled up close beside Kenzy's sleigh.

"Do you think he saw us?" the pastor asked.

"I don't have a doubt in the world that he saw you," John replied, but I think we all got inside in time."

"Then why didn't he land and come after me?" Kenzy demanded.

"Because," Kim told him, "It's too windy. Those gusts are getting violent. And since he couldn't tie his machine down, it might actually have flipped over. It wasn't worth the risk. And he's probably low on fuel. I think he's on the way home."

"Then we'll be okay?" Kenzy persisted.

"I think he's already radioed Burlington with these coordinates, but there's no way in the world that anyone can get here before we are long gone."

"I think Kim has summed it up nicely," John told them. And as much as I'd like to stay in the shelter of this cave, I'd much rather get on home, so I think we'd better say our goodbyes and get out of here."

"Amen," Kenzy agreed, but our horses are tired.

"We will lead the way for you, driving very slowly and side by side. That way, we'll break a trail for the horses, and if you get into trouble, we'll abandon the sleigh and take you two with us."

"I really don't want to do that," Kenzy replied, "but we'll trust the Lord and do the best we can."

"Well said, Pastor. And now we'll say goodbye to you, Kim. God go with you."

"And with you as well," Kim replied, as he accelerated out of the cave and drove off into the rising storm. Just before he exited the tunnel0 they heard him shout, "A Merry Christmas to all, and to all a good night."

Mary Rhodes Survives

The east side of Tower Rock
Allison Lake
Christmas Morning, about 7 a.m.

Apart from those who were riding on the snowmobile, four others heard the crash.

Two of them, a nurse and her Down Syndrome teenage son, both wearing fishermen's rubber waders, had been slowly working their way across a patch of shallow water that lay between the shoreline and the vast surface of ice that extended as far as the eye could see across Allison Lake.

When the blizzard died in the early hours, they had immediately left their little shelter for Allison Lake. Wearing snowshoes, they made their way through the forest, skirting the deep drifts as they covered the three miles between their remote cabin and Tower Point.

As she and her son neared the lake, they spotted the sheer gray surface of Tower Rock. It was a natural phenomena that deceived the viewer because it appeared to be a solid limestone mass. It rose high above the treetops and was nearly a hundred yards wide at its base. It stood like a sentinel, marking the southwest corner of the lake, but few people had ever approached it. It was far from any roads, and its remoteness discouraged visitors. Then, during the 1960s, a large area had been fenced by the Air Force.

Although Tower Rock appeared inhospitable and extremely difficult to climb, the woman led her son directly toward it. As they drew near, they could occasionally glimpse its peak through the tree tops. The wind had almost swept the ground clear of snow near the base of the pinnacle, and they bent to remove their snow shoes before moving closer.

With her son following closely, the woman pushed her way through a thick copse of evergreens that grew at its base. The trees hid a cave in the rock wall. The tunnel was just wide enough for the two of them to walk shoulder-to-shoulder through its short length. Then the passage turned into a narrow cleft, its vertical sides sheer, so that they could tip their heads back and see the sky above.

After another dozen yards they found themselves in an open area about forty feet in diameter, the ground covered with a thick layer of moss, and the sky almost a perfect circle high above. It was a strange place — perhaps the caldera of an ancient volcano — and though open to the sky, a very dark place because the walls were obsidian. It was difficult to see in the gloom, but there were several small natural caves opening into the walls at ground level. They were all low-roofed, and the woman would have to bend over in order to enter any of them. Nor would she think of doing so for fear that they might be the winter resting places for hibernating bears or other dangerous animals.

Nor was there a need to enter those forbidding caves in order to find shelter. On the far side of the clearing stood a small one-room cabin that had been built of native stone brought in from the outside. The building was startling because its white marble facade stood in vivid contrast to the black walls of the caldera. The carefully cut marble stones had been laid up with mortar, and the building was tight and snug. Little snow or rain seemed to fall into the cleft, and the roof of the cabin — made of stout, hand-hewn beams and covered with thick, moss-covered, cedar shingles — kept the interior dry.

It was a comfortable stopping place, but as far as she was concerned, it was a little too close to the Towers' cabin to make it her home. Apart from the Towers, she wasn't concerned about anyone else finding them. Only a few of the older residents in this part of the valley had been aware that this place existed, and most of them had perished as a result of the war. The Sennetts knew about it, but they were elderly, and since they lived beyond the mountain on the east side of the lake, they were unlikely to hike this far.

The woman lifted the latch and opened the door, and the boy followed her inside. He was largely oblivious to his surrounding, and took no note of the floor that had been made of precisely fitted marble slabs. He followed his mother to a wooden bench where they set their heavy packs. Then she crossed to a fireplace where, during her last visit, she had left dry wood for a fire. She unscrewed the lid from a metal can and poured about an ounce of kerosene over the kindling, then carefully struck a match and lit it. Her son was so eager to watch that he was pressing against her shoulder.

As the flames took hold, his eyes widened in delight, and he uttered a long "Wow!" "Over here, Tommy," she told him, and made him sit on the bench. With a wide smile on his face, he sat transfixed, his eyes on the dancing flames. Within a matter of minutes a roaring fire was heating the chill stone walls, and Tommy sat patiently on the bench, holding a golden oak leaf and humming contentedly to himself.

His mother picked up a pair of tongs from beside the fireplace, and reached up inside the flu to adjust the damper. The chimney reached only a few feet above the roof, but she had come to realize that the sixty or seventy-foot-tall cleft in the rock itself exerted a powerful chimney effect.

Whoever had built this place had been a fine stone mason, but that wasn't unusual in Vermont's quarry areas. Years before, Don Tower had told her that his great-grandfather had used this very cabin to hide runaway slaves while they made their long and perilous journeys along the underground railroad from the southern states to Canada.

She turned to her son. "Tommy, honey, please bring in some firewood." She had to repeat herself before her son turned to her with a vacant look on his face. *The third time's the charm,* she thought, and patiently repeated her request. At this, he went outside and came back with one small stick of firewood. His mother knew that he was letting almost as much heat out the open door as the wood he was bringing in would produce, but she was patient with him and made allowances for his affliction.

She thanked him effusively at the end of each of his slow circuits, and the smiles he returned were radiant. The split logs he brought her had the clear smooth grain of ash, and she knew they would burn down to a substantial bed of coals without generating any smoke. If anybody happened to be in the area, the fire would not betray their presence. She stacked more wood on the fire because she wanted to warm the place well before leaving for the lake, and she wanted a nice bed of coals when they returned because she hoped to broil their fresh-caught fish.

When her son next returned to the cabin, he was carrying two pieces of firewood in his arms, and he looked at his mother with an immense sense of accomplishment. She smiled at him and said, "I am very proud of you, Tommy."

In a voice that seemed oddly coarse for a child, he said, "I love you, momma." And she replied, "I love you too, honey."

As soon as the room began to warm, she made tea. Then they dressed to go fishing. She helped him pull on his rubber waders, then struggled into her own boots, and retrieved their small fish net from one of the packs. When their preparations were complete, they left the cabin. Using a flashlight, they found their way back through the natural tunnel and down through the woods toward the southwest corner of the lake.

The sandy shoreline was covered with worn boulders, some as small as a coin, some so large that they obstructed their view. He followed close behind as she made her way toward the water's edge. Gazing at their surroundings under the gibbous moon, she realized that the boulders created a confusion of light and shadows. Even in daylight, no one would spot their tracks unless they almost stumbled over them.

I don't want to meet up with anyone, she thought. The last time she had met strangers, her husband had been murdered trying to protect them, she had been violated, their home ransacked, and her son beaten and left for dead. She was unable to deal with the fact that her own sanity had been threatened.

They reached the edge of the stream where it entered the lake, and waded out into the shallow water. The water temperature was right at thirty-two degrees, but they were warm enough in their stout winter clothes, and their boots would keep them dry up to their waists. They waded out from the shoreline until they were standing in nearly two feet of water. They spread a small net, and dragging it between them they began walking parallel to the shoreline. Their eyes probed the shallow water, hoping to trap any fish that might have been attracted with the flashlight.

So intent were they on their task that it was a moment or two before the alien sound of a gasoline engine penetrated their senses. When the woman identified the roar of a snowmobile coming toward them across the south end of the lake, she raised her eyes to search the surface, but her head was little more than three feet above the water and, the dim light that precedes sunrise was being reflected off the snow-covered ice, making it difficult to see. Worse, though the sun could not yet be seen in the east, its heat was beginning to warm the snowy surface, creating a low-lying cloud of fog that muffled the sound, making it impossible to judge how far away the machine was, let alone whether it was heading in their direction.

She couldn't imagine that it would be coming their way, as the few survivors who had lived around this end of the lake knew well enough to avoid the thin ice that lay in this corner, not to speak of the boulders that protruded above the ice here and there. So her first impulse was to remain where they were and continue fishing. But then the roar grew louder, and she yelled at her son to make for the shore.

When she shouted at him, he turned to her slowly, a look of intense confusion on his face. He frowned uncertainly, trying to understand what she required of him. She tried to hide her sorrow when, not for the thousandth time, she took in his round head, slightly mongoloid features, large eyes and protruding tongue. It saddened her that his almost ever-present cheerfulness had momentarily deserted him.

"Tommy," she shouted again, "we must run to the shore!"

He looked at the net in his hands, and at the large bass that had become entrapped in its folds, and his eyes seemed to ask, *What do I do with this?*"

Sensing his hesitation, she spoke calmly. "Drop the net, honey, and run to the shore."

Confused by this sudden change of plans, he looked down at the mittens with which he held the net, then back at his mother.

"Drop...?" he asked, confused and disturbed.

"Yes, honey. Drop the net, quickly!"

He looked down at his hands again, then back toward her, and when he saw her bite her lip and nod, he very slowly and carefully laid the small cork floats that bordered the upper edge of the net down on the surface of the water, and stood watching in apparent fascination as the fish extricated itself and swam away.

Then he turned back to the woman. "The fish went away, Mommy."

The noise of the racing engine had reached a crescendo, and her son turned to look out across the ice just as the approaching snowmobile slammed across the top of an unseen boulder, rose in the air, and seemed to lunge right for them.

She watched as two people were thrown clear of the machine to land on the snow-covered ice, then saw the snowmobile flip on its side and slide off the ice into the lake. They were standing just a few feet away when the racing engine submerged and abruptly shut down. But she scarcely noticed the fate of the two who lay inert on the ice because her attention had been captured by the sight of a small child that was straddling the back seat when the snowmobile disappeared beneath the surface.

The woman began lifting her knees high, fighting her way through the deepening water toward the place where the machine had disappeared. In the beam of her flashlight, she could see the snowmobile clearly as she drew within a couple of yards. It had righted itself as it floated to the bottom and now rested in about three feet of water, its handlebars almost breaking the surface. The child's appeared to be caught on the back seat, and she was futilely beating her arms in an effort to free herself. The woman could see the child's silent scream of terror as the last of the air in her lungs bubbled out of her mouth.

The water began overflowing the top of the woman's boots. She could feel them filling with the freezing liquid and knew she couldn't stand much of this exposure herself. It felt as though her legs were burning and that someone had smashed her toes with a hammer. But she knew that she couldn't leave the child there.

Looking down through the clear water, she realized that the child had probably been protected from serious injury because she'd been nestled between the high seat backs, but she was now in immediate danger of drowning because her clothes were entangled in the bent and damaged frame of the machine.

She reached down into the water, grabbed the child's coat, and jerked on it until something gave and she was able to yank the drowning child loose. Then she lifted her out of the water and flipped her upside down over her head so that the child's stomach and solar plexus were pressing down hard against her shoulder. Then, as she made her way toward shore, she began pressing up and down on the child's back, squeezing her stomach and chest until she saw fluid gush out of the child's mouth to run down her coat, and the child began a spate of violent coughing.

With an enormous feeling of relief, she immediately began moving back toward Tower Rock on the far side of the stream's mouth. By that time, her son was at her side, and being a big boy for his age, he took the child from her as they fought their way toward shallower water.

"What about the people?" he asked.

"We're too wet and cold," she answered. "We need to get home."

"But they will be cold, mommy."

"Doesn't matter. We have to go home."

"But what about the people?"

Her teeth were chattering now, and she saw that the little girl was actually turning blue.

She turned to her son. Even when she was unable to make him understand her, she always avoided talking down to him. As a rule, she spoke softly, with a smile and with much love. "We may save this little girl," she tried to explain, "but if we try to help them, we will all freeze." She knew that she had only a very few minutes before the heart of the child in those soaking wet clothes would stop forever.

"Why don't we go to Mr. Tower's?" he persisted. "Mr Tower is a nice man, and we haven't seen him in a long time." He seemed to be looking far away and a little smile curled his lips. "He gives me candy."

"No!" she shouted, shocking the boy into silence. She was usually so gentle with him, but her recent antipathy toward the male of the species again manifested itself. She trusted no man since the attack. Her son could never know about her feelings, would never understand. He followed dumbly as she made her way across the mouth of the stream that flowed into the lake, the child in his arms, the icy water that seeped through his clothing seemingly unnoticed.

His mother didn't venture to the actual shore until they were well away from the scene of the crash. She shrewdly reasoned that no one would ever suspect that anyone else had been in the area at the time of the accident, and had no intention of leaving footprints in the sand. She believed that it was unlikely that the bodies laying on the ice would be discovered until the ice melted in late spring, if ever. She regretted her seemingly crass attitude, but she knew she was un-equal to the challenge of saving the others.

Reaching the boulder-strewn shore, she moved carefully among the rocks, making certain that their tracks would be hidden from anyone who might, by the slimmest chance, happen on the accident and look casually in this direction. With the likelihood of more snow, there was a good chance that the bodies and the tracks would be buried by the end of the day.

The boy looked back with tears in his eyes. The remains of the two other victims looked so sad to him, like dark sacks laying on the snow-covered ice.

His mother led him around to the back side of Tower Rock, then through the cleft to the abandoned cabin. As soon as they were inside, she began stripping the clothing off the little girl.

"Stir up the coals and put more wood on the fire," she ordered her son. After a moment, he moved to obey her. She watched him for a moment to make certain that he wouldn't forget something, or hurt himself. She smiled. He was doing fine.

Opening her backpack, she pulled out her own change of clothes. Then she stripped down the child and began toweling her dry with a coarse towel. She ignored the child's cries of protests as her blood rushed to the surface and her skin lost its blue tinge and began turning a bright red. The woman wrapped her in a spare shirt. It hung below the child's knees, like a nightgown. Then she unrolled her sleeping bag and zipped the little girl up so that only her face was exposed.

Having regained consciousness, the child began to whimper, crying for her mother. The woman ignored her, instead brewing some tea and forcing the girl to sip the hot liquid.

Finally, she looked to her own needs. She removed the boots, pulled off her soaking wet slacks, and toweled herself down. Shaking violently, she pulled on dry slacks, then drank the remaining hot tea, sharing it with her son.

She could hear the wind rising and knew it would be suicide to go back out with the possibility that they'd be caught in a blizzard. She began stacking the food from their backpacks on a shelf. She thought there would be enough to keep the three of them alive if the storm should last a few days. She hoped so.

"We'll bring in the rest of the wood," she told her son. "That way we won't have to go out if it gets too cold."

Return to Kenzy's Farm
Grafton Mountain
Christmas Morning

Kim Ling reached the crest of Grafton Mountain just as the storm wrapped itself around him in mindless fury. He'd made it through the rising storm by keeping the looming shadow of the stony crown on his right. It suddenly seemed as though he was driving his snowmobile into the teeth of the wind, and if it weren't for his compass, he would have driven in circles. All he could see were radiant snowflakes that seemed to race toward his headlights. He was lost, cold, hungry, and realized that he had very little fuel left.

What good did it do me to try to turn back for Butter Creek if I'm just going to freeze to death on the way? he wondered. Then his lips twisted momentarily in what might be taken as a self-deprecatory smile, and he remembered God's promise. *"Commit your way to the LORD, Trust also in Him, and He will do it."*

Once again he found a joyous sense of abandon as he surrendered himself to head into the unknown. The world might call it an existential leap of faith, but Kim Ling knew from experience that God was with him.

Doesn't matter what happens, he thought, *nor where I find myself; I'm with the Lord. More importantly, he's with me!*

He'd fought a battle with himself, and now he realized that by God's grace he had achieved a hard-won victory. With the loss of his family, he'd become almost suicidal. Now he not only accepted the loss, but realized that the Lord had some special work for him. He was determined to fulfill whatever role that God might have for him in helping to drive out the invaders and provide other survivors with the opportunities that his family could never enjoy.

He was giving the challenge a lot of thought. His outer life must appear as it always had, even though his inner life was tremendously changed. He might never become a truly happy man, he reasoned, nor shake those phantoms that had been his despair and madness, but it wouldn't be God's fault. He still hadn't completely come to terms with the deaths of his wife and two children.

Kim was now content to take on a task that would challenge him to the limit. It would refocus his attention away from the loss of his family. Just as importantly, he might prevent the enemy from doing to others what they had done to his loved ones. He was no longer concerned about his own life. Death? He would almost welcome it. In a real sense, he was free. Not reckless, like many young men who go to war with an irresponsible bravado that endangers the lives of others, but a freedom that enabled him to venture without fear of personal consequences. What was it the Apostle Paul had written? "For to me, to live is Christ and to die is gain."

And though he could never bring his family back, he was confident that one day he would see them again in heaven. For many Christians, he knew, that concept was comforting, but merely theoretical. For him it had become a conviction, an absolute certainty, and he had the accompanying sense of assurance that could only come from the Holy Spirit.

The air was dry and icy cold, and Kim had wrapped a scarf around his face to preheat the air he breathed. Even then, he could appreciate how pure and delicious it seemed. And then it wasn't. Suddenly he could smell smoke.

And where there's smoke, there's fire, he reasoned, and he turned upwind to follow the acrid fumes to their source. The air was so polluted now that he was beginning to cough, and he swung off to the side to get out of the cloud. He topped a ridge and pulled to a stop, surprised to see the last of the Kenzys' farmhouse collapsing in flame.

Wait, he reasoned. *Their house was ready to collapse when I left here hours ago. It has to be completely burned away by now. If this is the Kenzy farm, then that's a different building.* As he drew closer, he realized that it had to be the carriage house that was enveloped in flame, and the person standing in the wavering light cast by the flames had to be the Benton woman. He raced toward her at full speed, and at the last moment decelerated and skidded in a circle around her.

"It's about time you returned," she screamed. "I've been freezing here. Where have you been?"

"Well," Kim shot back, "I can see you've made yourself a dandy campfire. Have you been toasting marshmallows?"

"I'll be toasting more than marshmallows before I'm through with you," she promised. "Now take me back to town!"

"Why did you burn down the only building you had left to stay warm in?"

"It was an accident. I started a little fire in the middle of the floor and it got out of hand."

He shook his head in disgust, and asked, "Why didn't you go back with the lieutenant when he returned?"

"He hasn't returned," she snarled.

"He what?"

"He hasn't come back," she shouted, and there was a rare ring of truth in her words. Then she ordered, "I want you to drive me to town."

"I have orders to wait here for the lieutenant."

"If he's not back by now, he's not coming back."

That's probably true, Kim realized. *Whether he found the woman he was chasing or not, he might have become lost, or he might have decided to return directly to the village.*

"Well, one of us needs to wait here in case the Lieutenant comes back," he told her.

"And if he doesn't return, that person will freeze, and I don't plan to be that person," she declared. "So either take me back to

Butter Creek or get off that snowmobile so that I can drive myself into town."

As far as I'm concerned, Kim thought, *you can stay right here and keep on waiting. But I'm not a murderer, and I can't leave you out here in a blizzard.*

"Do you think you can help me find our way back to town?" he asked her.

"You'll take me?" she asked, her surprise evident.

"Get on the back," he ordered.

They completed the three-mile journey in less than twenty minutes, but not because she was of any help. He used his compass to travel due west and, because the snowfall was so heavy, almost ran into the side of a house on the edge of town.

Winding his way through the village, Kim finally pulled the snowmobile around the back of the inn and parked it in the lean-to. Then he followed the Benton woman into the building.

The inn was never a pleasant place, but in her absence, conditions had become deplorable. The serving girl, who'd been treated little better than a slave, had escaped. And with her absence, and the innkeeper laid up in bed with a concussion, nothing had been cleaned. The sink was carelessly stacked with dirty dishes, while pots and pans coated with congealed food lay about everywhere. Unidentifiable scraps were scattered about on tables and floors, and empty bottles and pieces of paper lay underfoot.

It was clear that the men who had been called in to pursue the escapees had made themselves free with her property, and she was so angry that Kim thought she might have a stroke. Even the cash register appeared to have been rifled. Not one scrap of the Chinese scrip that was used as legal tender remained, let alone the secret cache of silver coins she'd hidden behind the cash tray.

She began screaming hysterically, looking for something or someone on whom she might vent her wrath, but in spite of her profane ranting, Kim burst out in laughter. A raccoon that had evidently smelled the food and crept in through an open door was running from one corner of the inn to another looking for a way of escape. When the shrieking woman attempted to block his path, he reared up on his hind feet, bared his teeth and claws, and snarled threateningly at her. She screamed shrilly and tried to leap atop the bar as the coon raced between her feet. Then the animal raced toward the kitchen door which Ling, doubled over with laughter, was holding open to accommodate the animal.

With this immediate threat to her life removed, she turned on the two remaining men in the bar, hitting them over their heads and shoulders with an old worn broom. Kim continued laughing as she cursed the drunks who had made free with her liquor. With broom in hand, she tried to drive them out into the snow, but they simply laughed at her, and when she began blustering threats, one of them drew a gun and she instantly subsided. But vitriol continued to flow from her mouth. While she was living up to her reputation as the "Wicked Witch of Butter Creek," Kim used her phone to try to call Burlington.

He was surprised how quickly someone came on the line. "Communications! Sergeant Wong speaking."

When Kim identified himself to the commo sergeant, he was told to hold and was left waiting for several minutes. He was surprised when General Eng himself came on the line.

"What's going on there, Ling? Where's Captain Wei?"

"I don't know, General."

"What do you mean, you don't know?"

"Should I start from the beginning; that is, did the Captain contact you after we arrived here?"

"No, he didn't. So I guess you had better start at the beginning," the general replied.

"We arrived here only to learn that there had been a double escape."

"A what? How could one man escape twice?"

"Yes, sir. I mean, no sir. Two different parties escaped."

"Two parties?"

"It's complicated."

"Well, un-complicate it," the general ordered.

"Your people here had locked the man in a woodshed out behind the inn, and the girl who worked here helped him escape."

The general swore, then demanded, "Explain what you meant by two escapes."

"Yes, sir. One of your men, a corporal, was transporting a woman and her two children to Burlington, but because the roads were becoming impassable, he stopped here at the inn. She and her children disappeared a couple of hours after the man escaped."

"And she just walked off into the snow?"

"No, sir. It appears that they stole a snowmobile belonging to the innkeeper."

"And what was the innkeeper doing while all this was going on?"

"He'd been knocked unconscious by the serving girl."

"And no one went to his assistance?"

"It seems that he assaulted her while she was making up the bed in the guest room upstairs."

The general was silent for a moment. He had the picture.

"And the other men there?"

"Drunk, sir, except for the American who was in charge of them."

"Where is he? Let me talk to him."

"My understanding is that he was knocked unconscious when he went to check on the prisoner and left to freeze in the snow."

"Tell me this. What about the captain?"

"He sent the lieutenant and me, along with one other man and the innkeeper's wife, to a farm east of town to see if the woman had stopped there with her children. While we were heading in that direction, Captain Wei took the driver of the SUV with him in the snow cat to pursue the escaped man."

"Stupid!" the general snarled. "The woman was nothing. You all should have followed the man." The line went silent for a moment, and Kim wondered whether the general had disconnected. Just as he was about to hang up, the general asked, "What did you find at the farm?"

"The woman and her two children had stopped there and were evidently helped to escape by the farmer. The lieutenant and one man pursued her, but never returned."

Then the dread question came.

"And you?"

Kim didn't hesitate. "I found another set of tracks, those of a horse-drawn sleigh, that had gone out the back of the carriage house."

"And?"

"I left the innkeeper's wife at the farm to tell the lieutenant where I'd gone, and I pursued the sled."

"And did you catch up with it?"

"In a manner of speaking."

"In a manner of speaking?" The general swore in Chinese. "Ling, can you be more specific?"

"Yes, sir. Sorry, sir. I got within about a quarter of a mile of them, but there was an avalanche, and they disappeared. After it was over, I rode down to where I had seen them, but the snow was very deep, and there was no trace of them."

And that's the truth, as far as I care to tell it.

"So then, what did you do?"

"I returned to the farm and found that Mrs. Benton, that's the innkeeper's wife, had burned down the carriage house. So I brought her back here and immediately called you."

The general was silent, and Kim heard a roaring sound outside the inn.

"Wait, general. I think I hear the snow cat pulling up now."

"Good! Put the captain on as soon as he comes in."

"I'll get him, sir."

When the captain took the phone, he said very little beyond, "Yes, sir" and "I'm sorry, sir."

He remained thoughtful and quiet after the call. The innkeeper's, frightened by what had transpired, quietly prepared them something to eat. They waited through the night, and when the lieutenant failed to return, the two of them headed back to Burlington in the snow cat.

Upon their arrival, Kim was questioned briefly by the general, but the onus for the failure was laid on the captain and the missing lieutenant. Kim was on his very best behavior for the several days and, when there were no repercussions, concluded that his story had been accepted at face value.

The Towers to the Rescue
Tower Point, Allison Lake
Christmas Morning

Don and Jenn Tower continued their banter as he torqued down the last bolt that secured the carburetor to the engine block, then began reattaching the fuel line.

When she failed to answer a question, he looked at her and realized that she was no longer paying attention to him. She had tipped her head to the side, as though listening for something, and he wondered what might have caught her attention.

"Do you hear that?" she asked, and then he did. With the leaves off the trees, sound traveled further through the woods, or they might not have heard anything at all. In fact, with the snow soaking up a lot of those vibrations, whatever was causing that racket had to be nearby.

"Sounds like a snowmobile," he replied.

She nodded. "As we were just remarking, there aren't many of those around any more. At least, not that still run."

Now they could clearly hear the snowmobile approaching, and they ran for their coats, not daring to risk the possibility that an enemy was about to catch them unprepared.

The little structure that they used as an airplane hanger had finally warmed enough for them to have discarded their overcoats, and now they pulled them on and headed for the door.

"Wait a minute!" he said, bringing her up short. He grabbed the rifle which he had left leaning against the door frame. "If we get separated," he told her, "try to get back to the silo. This could mean serious trouble."

As they were running out the door, they heard a crash, followed by the rending of metal, the sound of something scraping over ice, and finally a loud splash.

Her thoughts followed his, and they ran back into the building. While he grabbed a hank of bright yellow rope and a wide plank, she ran to the plane, reached behind the seat, and lifted out a plastic bag containing a tarpaulin. Then she unhooked the first-aid kit from beside the cockpit door.

"If he's in the water," he rasped, "there's not much time! Have you got something to start a fire?"

She snapped her fingers and ran to the workbench. Grabbing a quart can of kerosene, she smiled and said, "This and a match ought to take care of the problem."

He laughed with her as they headed out the door with their arms full. Then his face sobered. They'd already wasted at least a minute, and it would take several more to fight their way through the snow to the lake.

When they reached the shoreline, Don realized that they faced an almost impossible challenge. He couldn't see a snowmobile or any other kind of machinery, but he saw what looked like two bodies lying in the snow atop the ice. What was worse, the wind was rising, and clouds were hiding the moon. He turned back to his wife. "If they're still alive, we've got to get them off that ice and into shelter soon or they'll never make it."

"Right!" She dropped the load she had been carrying and said, "I'll go back and get the snowmobile," and turned to fight her way back through the snow toward the hangar.

He shouted after her, "Put what's left of the hot coffee in a thermos and bring that along. And" he added unnecessarily, "you'll have to take the wood road to the lake. Don't try to get through the trees and make sure you stay well away from the open water."

She didn't bother turning her head to shout a reply, but her tolerant "Yes, dear," was tinged with sarcasm.

"Oops," he muttered, acknowledging to himself that she was often better organized than he was. Then he turned back for the lake. He made his way north along the shoreline, actually moving away from where the bodies lay. When he was well away from the open water, he stepped gingerly onto the thin ice and began working his way southeast, toward the mountain that loomed on the far corner of the lake. When he was well out on the thicker ice, he turned so that he was walking parallel to the shoreline, moving south in the general direction of Tower Point and the spot where he thought the two bodies lay.

The open water that lay between the edge of the ice and the shore seemed to soak up the available light, and appeared as a narrow, black and impenetrable strip along the shoreline. As he cautiously approached the edge of the ice, he could only guess that the snowmobile lay immersed somewhere nearby.

It's only the grace of God that both riders were dumped onto the ice, he thought. *Otherwise, we'd have a drowning on our hands.*

At that moment the wind took on a shrill whine, biting through his clothes, and spurring him to push more rapidly through the snow. He was hurrying now to complete his mission, even as his concern grew for his wife's and his own safety. Long experience with the local weather had taught him that it was going to snow again.

He reached the first of the victims — an adult. He opened the plastic bag containing the tarp, unfolded it on the snow, and dragged its edge up against the body. He flashed his light over the face and realized it was a woman. Although he couldn't take time to check either of the victims for broken bones, he did pull off his glove and pressed his fingers to her neck. He was relieved to discover a weak pulse, but she was cold to his touch. He was fighting against time and hypothermia. He had to get them off the ice and into a warm shelter as quickly as possible. If too much time passed, the drop in their temperature would be irreversible.

She wasn't a big woman, but he knew he couldn't lift her. He pulled the hood of her coat tightly about her head to protect her face, then gently rolled her onto the canvas so that she wound up lying on her back.

There, he thought with some satisfaction. *At least she's not lying in the snow.* Then he moved quickly to the other victim. *It's a boy*, he realized, *maybe ten or eleven years old.*

This time he took a bit more care because he was going to have to lift and carry the boy several yards across the ice. The lad groaned when he moved him, but he had no alternative. He felt his own back spasm as he started to lift the boy. *Problem is, I'm no spring chicken*, he admitted to himself. *And I must not collapse here. Jenn could never lift either of us, and somehow she and I have to get both of them onto the snowmobile.*

Bent beneath the boy's weight, he grimaced with the pain as he struggled to carry him through the snow. When he reached the tarp, he knew he would be unable to kneel again. He tried to think of a way to set the boy down without dropping him, and finally let go of his legs while retaining a hold on his upper body. The boy's feet struck the tarp, and then he lowered him a little at a time. When he had the boy's shoulders at the height of his knees, the lad slipped out of his grasp, and his head dropped onto the canvas. He realized that the snow beneath the tarp had cushioned the impact, perhaps saving the boy from a concussion. *If he doesn't already have a bad concussion,* he thought. He somehow managed to drag the unconscious boy alongside his mother, then took the loose edge of the tarp and pulled it over them in an attempt to cut the icy wind that was draining the heat from their bodies.

He heard the quiet purr of their own snowmobile and turned to see his wife pulling out onto the ice about fifty yards further north than where he'd risked stepping onto the frozen surface. She drove quite a distance out onto the lake before turning back toward him. At no time did she accelerate above walking speed.

The wind was still rising, and the sky had darkened until it was again night. He saw that the snowflakes blowing in the beams of the snowmobile's headlights were growing thicker.

Time's running out, he thought.

When Jenn reached him, she was shocked by her husband's haggard appearance and realized that something was wrong.

"Your back?"

"Yes, I'm afraid so."

He was glad to see that she'd had the foresight to hitch their sled to the back of the snowmobile. It looked like one of those lightweight plastic tubs that masons use to mix mortar, and they might just be able to get both bodies on one load. While he stood shivering, she carefully pulled the machine up along the edge of the tarp.

"I'm going to need you to help me with the woman," he said, gritting his teeth against the pain. Without a word, she put the transmission in neutral, climbed off the machine, and dropped to her knees. Then she lifted the woman's shoulders so that the two of them were able to reach under her arms and drag her over the edge of the sleigh. After they had her lying along one edge, they went back for the boy. With two of them lifting, it proved to be a lot easier to move him. Nonetheless, Don was groaning with pain.

She stared at him. "Pretty bad?"

"Yeah. I'm not sure I can even get on the machine."

She offered her shoulder as support while he managed to get a leg over the snowmobile, so that he was straddling the back of the seat. Then, driving very slowly so as not to bounce them off the sled, she turned in a wide circle and headed for the shore.

As they moved toward the shoreline, he asked, "Do you hear the ice cracking under us?"

She laughed. "I thought that was your back."

"It might be," he admitted ruefully.

"Yes," she confessed. I've been listening to the ice, and I've been praying."

"Me too. We're concentrating a lot of weight on one spot."

"That's why I keep moving," she laughed.

It seemed like it took forever to get off the ice, and they both breathed a prayer of thanksgiving as she started up the grade toward the airplane hanger.

"I think we should go straight to the cabin," he suggested. "Right," she agreed, saving her usual facetious remark for another time. She passed the hanger and moved further back into the woods until they reached a log cabin that stood against a natural rock wall. Between the two of them they somehow managed to get the victims into the cabin.

While Jenn stripped the clothes off the woman and began wrapping her in warm blankets, he looked after the boy.

"Check her nose, fingers and toes," he ordered, and looked up to see that she was way ahead of him. She turned to smile at him, and he heard another, "Yes, dear."

She was the expert in first-aid, and he realized he was a little foolish offering her advice. "Just talking to myself, honey," he replied, and her laugh had just the right touch to remove any sting.

Then she looked at his haggard face. "But first I want you to take a couple of pain relievers."

"Can't waste time on that."

"It's not a waste of time. You'll only be a burden if you're crippled up."

"Well, thanks a lot!" he replied. "I'm so glad that you care." And they both laughed. He swallowed a couple of tablets and was turning back to the boy when his wife commented, "Praise the Lord, I think she will be okay, but she is mighty cold."

How cold?"

"Her temperature is 97."

"Let me have the thermometer." He placed the nozzle in the boy's ear and pressed the button. After a few seconds, he removed it and checked the readout.

"His temperature is down to 96.8."

"I started running a warm tub. We'd better get him into it."

"Be careful; we don't want to stop his heart."

"It's up to the Lord now."

But before they could get him into the tub, he awoke enough to swallow a little hot tea. Then, as weary as they were, Jenn kept watch over their patients while Don tried to sleep.

The boy, obviously exhausted, slept through the night, but with the amazing resilience of the young, seemed to be fine in the morning. The woman was obviously troubled. She kept mumbling a man's name, *David*, perhaps her son, and at other times she cried aloud for someone named Mary.

When Jenn heard the woman pleading with God to save her little boy and girl, she realized that they had a serious problem. She awoke Don to discuss it.

"There's really nothing we can do," they finally agreed. He summed it up. "There was no sign of a little girl on the ice when we found them, so if she had her daughter with her at the time of the crash she must have slid into the water...." His voice trailed off.

It was late morning when the woman finally regained consciousness and scrambled from the bed. The bruise on her forehead was of concern to her hosts, but concussion or not, she was not to be denied. She was obviously thrilled to see her son asleep on a mattress at the foot of her own bed. She smiled, and they saw her lips form the name, Michael. But when her eyes swept the room, and she realized that there was no one else there, she walked past them without a word, and stopped in the middle of the room that comprised the Tower's living room, kitchen and dining area. They watched her as she slowly walked around the room. The bathroom door was open, and it was immediately obvious that there was no one else in the house beside herself, her son and these two strangers.

She had a difficult time forcing herself to make eye contact with either of them — passing right over Don as though he weren't even in the room — and finally meeting Jenn's eyes. The plea in her own was met with tears of sympathy in Jenn's, and when the woman realized that there was no encouragement to be had in that quarter, she began to shake with sobs.

Jenn moved quickly to her side and put her arms around her. There was nothing she could say, nothing she could do. She held the woman until her sobs subsided into whimpers, then finally asked, "What's your name?"

The woman seemed not to hear her, so she repeated the question. This time her eyes began to move about in frenzy, as though desperately searching for something or someone. "I ... I don't know," she finally stammered, a trace of fear in her voice.

Jenn forced herself to reply lightly, "Oh, that's okay. You are probably concussed and have a little short-term memory loss. It will all come back soon," she promised, and was surprised to learn that she believed what she'd said.

Then the little boy was standing there, hugging his mother about her waist, and she looked down at him, a vacant smile on her face.

"You know your name, Mommy," he told her. "It's Chris."

"Chris," she said, as though trying to shape her lips around an unfamiliar word.

"And what's your last name, young man," Don asked.

"The boy turned to face him, and though Don was smiling, the lad seemed to draw back into himself, his suspicion obvious.

"My mommy told us not to tell anyone our last name," he responded firmly, his lip quivering, and just a hint of trepidation in his response.

"Good advice," the man answered. "We need to be careful who we share information with in this day and age. Sadly, even our names." He smiled. "I'll tell you what. We'll just go by first names, okay?"

The boy nodded. Then he slid around so that his mother served as something of a barrier between himself and their host.

"My name is Michael. My little sister's name is Mary." He looked up at his mother and whispered, "Mom, where is Mary?"

Instead of replying to her son's query, her eyes sought those of the other woman, her son's question hanging in the air. After a moment, Jenn Tower held her hands out, palms up. It was a gesture of helplessness. Then she raised her shoulders to communicate an unmistakable, "I'm sorry; I don't know."

Chris knelt and took her son in her arms, her sobs providing the most eloquent answer he would receive.

Nearly a half-mile to the south, a woman was asking a child for her name.

"My name is Mary," she cried, "and I want my Mommy."

The child sobbed while the woman held her on her lap, but her own thoughts were elsewhere and she didn't reply. The cabin hidden within the hollow at Tower Rock did not have sufficient food or firewood to last out another blizzard, and she had decided that they would leave for home as soon as the wind dropped. She wrapped the two children as warmly as possible, and they set out for their own home.

The teen took the little girl's hand and they set off following his mother along the narrow trail. They covered the two miles to their cabin just as the sky again turned from a watery gray to a threatening black and the wind again picked up.

McCord Disappears
Hidden Valley, Vermont
Christmas Afternoon

CC stood in the shelter of the woods and stared toward the Sennett farm which lay unseen beneath the cliffs on the southwest corner of the valley. Hidden behind an impenetrable wall of evergreens, the vacant farm was where he had found the precocious seven-year old Sarah, nearly a year before. His thoughts, however, were not on the farm nor on Sarah.

Jim McCord had disappeared! Without a word of warning, the new guy had left the caverns and set out through the snow for the far side of the valley. It was easy enough to determine the direction he'd taken. His footprints stood out like dark expletives against the pristine snow that covered the valley floor.

CC knew that he had to take action, but he was unable to put his random thoughts in any kind of order. He was instead rebuking himself for more bad judgment. His thoughts rambled. His state of mind was such that he was actually talking out loud, arguing with himself. First he was concerned with the fact that he had endangered the two youngsters, Jonathan and Sarah, by letting McCord remain with them as long as he had.

Yes, he thought, *I had little choice. It was either set him free to divulge our whereabouts or kill him, and I was not able to take that step. But I realize now that there must have been something else I could have done.*

He stopped punishing himself long enough to feel remorse over the losses they were apt to suffer.

We have enjoyed a wonderful life here in this valley. In the midst of the horrors that have overtaken most of America — and while most other survivors have been homeless, cold, sick and starving — we have an unimaginably comfortable home within the caverns and an abundance of food. We even have clean electric power to heat and light our secret underground home.

So what did I do? I lived in the midst of a garden of Eden and still became discontented. So, on Christmas Eve, of all times, I left two children whom I loved as though they were my own, and I went off in search of adult companionship.

He shook his head at his own stupidity.

Oh, my motives were fine as far as they went. I simply wanted to hear the voice of another adult. But instead I got myself arrested by the turncoats who serve the Chinese, and it's only because of young Jonathan's grit, and by the grace of almighty God, that I escaped.

He sighed. *Escaped to what? Bringing back Rachel with us has turned out to be a blessing, but look what we returned to! This guy, Jim McCord, turned out to be a real bad number. He never lent a hand, he refused to become part of our little community, he continually challenged my authority and frequently made implied threats.*

And Elizabeth, who arrived here with him, but disclaims any close relationship, seems somehow to be in league with him. As a result, none of us has any genuine confidence in her, even though she appears to be the more charactered, and even though she pitches in voluntarily to assist in every way possible.

Somehow CC missed the point that McCord and Ross would have shown up on Christmas Eve whether he'd gone to Butter Creek or not. It was Jonathan who finally reminded him that he should stop blaming himself, forget the cause of the problem, and just deal with the present.

Jonathan's right. What's past is past, and now I have to deal with the moment. That's what he tried to tell himself, but he was still in the process of excoriating himself.

Everyone had been forbidden to leave the immediate vicinity of the caverns because of the danger of attracting the enemy's attention, and particularly not while there was snow on the ground to show interlopers the way. So when McCord took off without a word, he proved to them that Jonathan had been right about him. "He's just no good!"

It's isn't difficult to imagine Jim's motives. He has revealed himself to be incredibly self-centered. Either he has gone to the enemy to divulge our whereabouts, or he has gone back to the cave that he and Ross shared before discovering our cavern. But why go back there? Elizabeth said it was small, cold, damp and dirty, and McCord loves the unearned comforts that we provide him far too much to wander far from here. So if he has returned to their cave — and that's where his trail in the snow indicates he was headed — then he must have gone to get something. But what could be of such value to him that he'd take a chance at being captured, let alone exposing himself to my anger. It couldn't be money. Money has virtually no value in this world.

CC gnawed on his lip. *It could be another gun. A gun would give him power. If he is able to ambush me, then he will be the King of the cave so to speak. And if there's one thing he's made clear since his arrival, it's that he wants to be king of something.*

While CC dwelt on his own sins of omission and commission, Elizabeth Ross was doing her own brooding. She was sitting at the dinette table in the motor home that CC had parked inside the cave, beginning to appreciate the good life she suddenly realized that they were all about to lose.

McCord is the wild card in the deck, she realized. *When he told me that he planned to slip away to get something from the cave, I was a fool to tell him where I had hidden my portfolio, much less to ask him to bring it back for me. In fact, he's almost certain to examine the contents, and if he does he will to try to sell them to the highest bidder. He might even try to open the containers, and that will irreparably damage them. And now he's gone, and I doubt very much that he will keep his promise to return.*

Worse, if he doesn't return, there is no telling what CC will do to me. Yet how much more do I dare tell CC? He's already hinted at his willingness to kill me. Or was he bluffing?

She bit her lip, shaking her head slightly as though trying to negate the possibility. She couldn't settle that matter in her mind, for he seemed to be a confusion of contradictions. Even though he was obviously an amnesiac, she had discovered him to be kind and generous. And if he weren't a true Christian, he certainly acted the part of a very godly man. She couldn't imagine him taking a human life except in self-defense, and then only under the most dire circumstances.

She heard CC dropping his insulated boots in the wooden box outside the door and realized that she was about to face the music. Earlier in the morning, right after he'd learned of McCord's absence, he had asked her a few questions which she had failed to respond. Now he would be demanding answers.

She was sitting there, trying to come up with something plausible, when CC returned to the motorhome. He ignored her and smiled in gratitude at Rachel as she handed him a steaming cup of coffee.

Her mind was racing. *Time has run out,* she thought. *I'm going to have to answer him. Although McCord originally helped me escape from that group of outlaws, I really haven't seen him do a single decent thing since. In fact, he's proven himself to be a pretty nasty character.*

Ross wasn't conscious that she was staring at her hands, but everyone else noticed as she held up her left, looked at it, then made a fist. Then she held up the right, opened it and smiled. She had thought alternately of the sneaky and tight-fisted behavior of Jim McCord, and compared it with the open honesty and kindness of CC.

I'll take my chances with CC, she decided, and wondered why it had taken her so long to reach that conclusion. *And, under the circumstances, I need to be honest with him,* she realized. She shrugged. *How's the saying go? When in doubt, tell the truth. Still, there is some information that I dare not trust to anyone, and that includes the secret of what McCord promised to bring back from the cave. It doesn't look like it will cost me anything to keep some of my secrets, and it might cost a great deal if I divulge them, so I'll tell the truth, but not necessarily the whole truth.*

"Well?" he said, as he sat down and turned to her.

"Okay," she said. "I'll tell you what I know."

But CC had not missed the earlier byplay — her body language and the decision-making process they'd all seen her going through — and he had another warning for her.

"Right now!" he insisted in a voice that seemed all the more menacing because it was so controlled. "Let me suggest," he added, biting off his words, "that it's pretty late in the game for you to do any more dissembling."

What is he doing, reading my mind? "I understand," she replied, and looked like she meant it. She began worrying her lower lip, seemingly on the verge of tears, concentrating on framing her next words.

"All right," she surrendered. She looked down for a moment, as though gathering her thoughts. Then, her chin firmly set, she looked up into his eyes with her characteristic boldness. "I think Jim went back to his cave to get something he considers valuable. I think he knows some of the invaders, both the Chinese and the Islamic terrorists, but I don't think he trusts them any more than we do. That's why I'm hopeful that he'll come back here."

CC had tried to imagine anything that was more valuable in these times than anonymity, isolation, food and shelter. He stared at her, his anger palpable.

"How stupid!" he fumed. "Nothing that he or you might have left in that cave could be worth compromising the location of our hideaway. Not jewels or even gold! And, unless he's an addict, not drugs or alcohol. It just doesn't make sense!"

She was not forthcoming and he decided to push her.

"And just what might that valuable something be?" he pursued, bitterness in his voice.

Elizabeth was too slow in replying.

"I don't want to have to pull these answers out of you a question at a time," he warned her. CC had been trying to ignore the fact that McCord might, at that very moment, be divulging their whereabouts to the Chinese, and that would leave him very limited time to get his little family safely away with enough food and equipment to provide even the slimmest chance of survival. And, he admitted to himself, the odds against them surviving were enormous.

He had a fleeting thought that, if they survived this crisis, he and Jonathan ought to cache a considerable amount of preserved food and supplies somewhere outside the valley so that they wouldn't find themselves empty-handed if they were forced to abandon this home without warning. Even while he was filtering those thoughts, his attention was focused on Elizabeth's reply.

"I don't know what valuable thing he might be after," she answered honestly, and that was true.

McCord obviously has something of his own that he considers valuable that I don't know about, she thought. *CC didn't ask whether I might have something valuable, and I'm not volunteering any information. What I told him is the truth.*

Even as she continued to dissemble and offer only half-truths, she realized that she'd been a fool to trust McCord. She should have gone along with him to gather her own possessions instead of letting him talk her into trying to cover for him during his absence. Better yet, she should never have reminded him about the portfolio and just left the objects where they were.

Picking up on her hesitation, CC suspected the truth and decided to challenge her.

"What surprises me is that you would trust him enough to let him return alone to get your things."

He is he reading my mind! And he's right. I was too obtuse to consider of the likelihood that Jim would steal my possessions.

"I didn't say anything about him bringing back anything of mine."

"Oh, didn't you? I must have imagined it," and CC offered a bleak smile. "Well, whatever the case," he went on, "I intend to have you locked away by the time Mr. McCord returns, and unless he is able to hide the item or items before we see him, we will examine *everything* he brings back very carefully. I will not allow our home to be further endangered by permitting anything our enemies might consider valuable to be kept anywhere in this valley.

Elizabeth's eyes followed CC's hand as he unconsciously touched the handgun holstered on his belt. It was obvious that he no longer trusted her any more than he trusted McCord. She opened her mouth to say something, swallowed hard, then turned away.

"What?" CC demanded.

"There is something." She bit her lip and avoided his eyes.

His lips were compressed in a straight line. When he spoke, it was almost a whisper, and now the threat seemed palpable.

"Tell us about it. If there is anything of value, why would you wait until now to go after it?" Then he laughed at her. "And for the life of me," he repeated with sarcasm, "I can't understand why you'd trust McCord to get it for you."

She gulped. *He's right. I was a fool. Worse, he obviously considers me in partnership with McCord. And, in a sense, he's right.*

"Whatever it is, it was probably safer where you'd hidden it than it will be here. Valuable or not, all you and McCord have done is provide a clear path through the snow for any of our enemies to follow from there to here."

Elizabeth's lips curved down in defeat, and she nodded her head in grudging agreement.

"It was stupid," she acknowledged. "I realize that now."

CC shrugged her words away. He was surprised that she'd make such a confession, and concluded charitably that she probably didn't have any more control over McCord's thinking than he did.

In an attempt to deflect his anger from herself, she said, "I know he thinks the items that I brought along might be valuable, but he has no concept of what they really are. He probably thinks they are jewels or something." Then, in a transparent attempt to distract CC, she said, "Jim warned me that we need to guard everything from somebody named Joseph Sennett."

"Joseph Sennett?" CC's mind raced. "What does McCord know about Joseph Sennett?" When she didn't reply, he said, "It's true that Joseph Sennett once lived in this valley, but he's dead."

"Joseph Sennett lived here? And he's dead?" It was Rachel, and there was no questioning the shock in her voice.

"Well, a man named Joseph Sennett lived here, though I don't know whether it's the one you're referring to, but no matter what McCord has gone to retrieve, it isn't worth giving our location away."

"Some things are worth any risk," Elizabeth countered.

"Some things, perhaps, but not what you or he are likely to value."

She relented, deciding to tell the truth. "It's not a question of what you and I value. It's a question of its value to others...to America. And to what lengths I..." she hesitated, "correction... to what lengths we are justified in going to keep them safe from our enemies."

"Well, that's certainly a grandiose claim."

"Yes, I suppose it does sound far-fetched. But consider this. Jim says he has a list of the leaders of the invading forces who, independent of one another, are trying to take over our country, including radical Muslims, Chinese, and Soviets — and he assured me that his information is valid." She really doubted that McCord had anything of importance, but she knew that she did.

CC shook his head in angry repudiation.

"Then all he has is something that's useless to us, but so important to our enemies that they'd stop at nothing to get their hands on it, is that it?" His eyes opened wide, as though he'd just realized something. "Wait a moment! Are you suggesting that you both have something that is of interest to the bad guys and that neither of you knows what the other has?"

When she didn't respond, CC pressed on. "Okay, you said that he assured you that he has a list of names." CC looked at her, his anger and unbelief getting the better of him. Something had finally clicked.

"So you knew that he was going across the valley, and you didn't warn me?" His anger was palpable, but he got it under control as he went on. "And if McCord has such a list, why didn't he leave it with some trustworthy official somewhere along his route, say in Washington, Baltimore or even Plattsburgh? Or, for that matter, why did he come this way at all? And why in the world would that old man, Joseph Sennett, have been interested in such a list?"

"I don't know anything about any old man," she whispered, tears appearing at the corners of her eyes. "The Joseph Sennett that cut me loose in the outlaw's camp was a young man.

Rachel interrupted. "A young man?"

"Never mind Joseph Sennett!" CC exclaimed, cutting them off. I want to know about the items McCord went to get.

"Well, it isn't going to do any good to badger Elizabeth," Rachel said. Can't you see that she's confused and sorry?"

CC turned, planning to snap at Rachel, but reigned himself in, realizing that she might be right. He moderated his tone. "That may well be, but all of our lives are at stake," and he nodded toward Sarah.

Rachel's eyes widened in understanding, and she nodded her agreement. Sarah started to cry, and Rachel hugged her, giving CC a poisonous look. He lifted his hands, palm up, then shook his head in frustration. *Sarah's frightened, and Rachel's making me the bad guy.*

Nonetheless, he heeded Rachel's censure and for the moment ceased his interrogation.

"Well," he thought aloud, "we can't follow McCord or we'll just leave more tracks. We'll have to hope that it snows." The tone of his voice made it clear that he didn't expect snow any time soon.

His frustration was obvious. "If I'd known McCord felt that he had to leave, I could at least have shown him a much safer way to go."

In a soft voice, Rachel asked, "Would you have let him go?"

CC sighed. "No, probably not. But I might have been willing to accompany him."

He looked at his watch. "Time's short," he muttered. "McCord could be in the act of betraying us right now." He turned to Rachel. "Please take Sarah with you while you gather freeze-dried foods, sleeping bags, first-aid supplies and some cooking gear. We need enough food for at least three days. Sarah will help you find them."

Without waiting for a reply, he turned to Jonathan. "You gather rifles, ammunition, and anything else you think we might need if we have to run."

His words were enough to make them all realize that the situation might be far more serious than they'd imagined.

Rachel frowned, remembering that CC was the survival expert here.

Jonathan pointed at Elizabeth. "What about her?"

"She's going to wait here, perched on this swivel chair. Get some of those long plastic wire ties, and we'll bind her ankles and wrists."

Elizabeth was both furious and frightened, but she realized that it was pointless to resist the inevitable. "Okay," she said, "I'll stay here and I promise to be quiet, and maybe that will prove to you whose side I'm on."

CC stared at her for a moment. "It might help," he answered grudgingly. Then he relented. "If you'll promise me not to leave the motor home and not to warn McCord, we'll leave you untied."

"I promise," she told him, both surprised and touched, and then she thought with a sense of enormous relief, *This is the man who once threatened to kill me? Ha!*

The Portfolio

The Motor Home
Hidden Valley, Vermont
Christmas Day, about 6:00 p.m.

When CC returned from his search for McCord, he was in an even worse mood, but he felt better when he peered through the screen door and discovered that Elizabeth had kept her promise and remained in the motor home.

Then he noticed McCord sitting in the shadows on the swivel chair, his gaze intent on Elizabeth. She was unbuckling the straps on a backpack that CC hadn't seen before. It was a high-priced rig, and she was unfastening a portfolio that was strapped to the back of it. The portfolio was large, about two feet high and nearly three feet long, and over two inches thick. It didn't appear particularly heavy, however, because she lifted it with ease.

CC knew that the two of them didn't have that portfolio with them when he and Jonathan had found them asleep in the motorhome after finding their way into the caverns, so he concluded that it must have been among the items that McCord had carried back from their cave.

I wonder why he'd bothered carrying that back for Ross. And I wonder what he brought back of his own. CC's eyes widened when it came to him that she might have stolen a painting from the museum where she'd been employed.

She finished unbuckling the various straps that secured her portfolio to a backpack, then, with a grunt, lifted the backpack and handed it to him. McCord immediately opened one of the zippered pouches on the side of the backpack in order to check the contents.

Evidently the backpack belongs to McCord, CC concluded. *I wonder what he's got in there. It doesn't look like Ross knows or cares. Maybe she does know, but doesn't care.*

As she straightened up in her chair, the portfolio balanced across her knees, she noticed CC's reflection in a wall mirror, and she turned away so quickly that the portfolio slipped to the floor. Realizing that she couldn't hide it, she held it up in front of her like a shield, as though hiding behind it, the bottom edge resting on her lap.

CC opened the screen door and stepped up into the motor home. At the same time, McCord leaned forward from where he was seated on the chair and gave CC an arrogant smile. Then he leaned back against the cushions, a smug expression on his face, as though he was dismissing CC's presence as unimportant.

Jonathan stepped up into the motor home and stood behind CC.

"What's in the packs?" CC asked quietly.

"None of your business!" Ross snapped. Her response was out of character for someone who, just a half-hour before, had supposedly been concerned about her relationship with the group.

There was a metallic whirring noise from the chair, and CC turned to see McCord spinning the cylinder on a revolver.

"She wouldn't tell me either," he said, "but I have little doubt that she's walked off with a valuable painting from the art museum where she worked."

His tone was condescending, the voice of an opportunist who'd willingly switch loyalties and betray one acquaintance in order to gain advantage with someone who might have more to offer. His voice had the tone of someone who believed he held the upper hand.

As he leveled this accusation, he also leveled his revolver at CC saying, "Bang, bang, you're dead!" At the same time he used his heel to push his own knapsack into the shadows between the swivel chair and the wall of the motorhome.

"Where did you get the gun?" CC asked in a cold voice. *Stupid question,* he thought. *It's obvious that he picked it up at his cave, and now he intends to intimidate me with it. Or worse.*

His thoughts were interrupted by the sound of a cartridge being slammed into the chamber of a shotgun, and he couldn't help smiling as McCord jumped, then swiveled his head toward Jonathan.

He had been standing behind CC, but had moved off to the side and was pointing the 12-gauge at McCord's midriff.

Jonathan was staring fixedly at McCord. "Maybe you'd better drop your gun," he told him. McCord stared at him for a long moment, as though trying to appraise the teen's determination. Then he slowly and carefully set the revolver on the floor.

When McCord finally complied, CC stepped forward, hooked the gun with the toe of his shoe and slid it across the floor out of reach.

"I cannot believe you would do something as stupid as draw a weapon on us."

"I assure you," McCord said, "that you were not in danger."

"Really? What was that you said, 'Bang, bang, you're dead?'"

McCord shrugged his shoulders. "It was a joke."

"Sure it was," Elizabeth interjected, her sarcasm expressing the feelings of everyone else in the room.

"I'm sure you remember," CC went on, "that I forbade you to touch any weapon."

McCord didn't respond, but in an attempt to deflect their anger, he pointed at Ross and said, "She has more explaining to do than I have."

Elizabeth was glaring at McCord, bitter denial in her glance. "I didn't threaten anyone's life," she said. And then with what sounded like great sincerity, she said, "My fondest wish is to become part of this little group."

"Maybe they don't want someone who is a liar and a thief."

"I'm not a thief!"

"How do you explain the paintings in that portfolio?"

"I didn't steal any paintings," she said evenly, "but I am sorry that someone couldn't have rescued some of the magnificent works of art. They're probably all ruined by now."

"Ruined?" Rachel had just entered the motor home, slipping around CC to find a place out of the way at the table.

"Yes. Once the electricity in the Boston area failed, the pumps that kept the museum's underground vault dry would have stopped operating, and I have no doubt that everything down there is now immersed in thirty or forty feet of filthy water, probably forever."

CC wrapped his fingers around McCord's upper arm. Pointing at her portfolio, he asked, "What's in the portfolio?"

Jim yanked his arm free, his eyes fixed on Elizabeth.

"I don't know," he snarled.

"That doesn't make sense," CC countered. "You told us that you were a spy, and that you always checked out anything that interested you. And now you expect us to believe that you lacked the curiosity to look inside that portfolio? As a self-declared spy and an unscrupulous opportunist, your curiosity would have compelled you to look inside the case."

"All right! So I looked, but I didn't touch. All I could see were layers of foil and foam board sandwiched together and heat-sealed in a plastic wrap. I figured if Elizabeth packed it that way, she must have had good reason, and I might damage whatever it is if I broke the seal."

"Thank God!" Elizabeth whispered.

"Besides, it has no value to me. There's not much of a market for works of art right now, in case you haven't noticed. Besides, I didn't think there was any need. If she stole a painting, it is undoubtedly one of the finest. And if a market for rare paintings should develop, well, time will tell what happens to any artwork that she may have stolen."

Elizabeth's eyes widened. "Those words suggest that you mean to wind up with whatever's in here."

"I didn't say that," he retorted, but his sly smile made his intentions clear.

Jonathan leaned over and started to unzip the portfolio.

"Don't open that!" she shouted. Without rising from the chair, McCord leaned forward, grasped a handful of her hair and jerked her head back, providing Jonathan the opportunity to snatch the portfolio from her hands and move it to the table.

"Please," she pleaded, almost in tears. "You'll damage them." She turned quickly and slapped McCord in the face causing him to release her hair. Then she was across the small room in two steps, struggling to wrest the portfolio from Jonathan's grasp.

She looked at CC, tears in her eyes. "Don't let them open it," she begged.

CC turned to Jonathan. "You'd better leave it alone."

The teen immediately held the portfolio out to Elizabeth. With a smile of gratitude, she took it from him, and leaned it against her knees on the floor.

CC stared at her for a full minute, the pulse in his temple throbbing, his patience clearly razor-thin.

"All right," he asked, "what's in the case and why can't we open it?"

She hesitated a long moment before framing her reply.

"Okay, first the reason for not opening it." Her fingers drummed on the portfolio until she noticed that everyone was staring at her fingers, and she forced herself to sit still. "I had to wrap the contents so that they wouldn't be destroyed by exposure to air."

"I don't understand," CC said.

"I don't understand either," Rachel seconded. "Why all that special packaging?"

"They are very delicate," she explained.

"I bet I know," Jonathan interjected, but CC's frown silenced him.

Elizabeth's answer was succinct. "If they are exposed to air, they will probably crumble."

"Never mind that. I want to know what you've got there."

"I know, I know!" Jonathan shouted, holding up his hand like a school student eager for permission to speak.

Annoyed more with Elizabeth than with Jonathan, CC nodded tolerantly at the boy.

"I saw an article in a newspaper about a year ago and asked my father if we could go to Boston to see them."

"See what?" CC demanded, more irritated than ever, but now curious in spite of himself.

Elizabeth, realizing that Jonathan did in fact probably know what was in her portfolio and that there was no advantage in refusing to answer, opened her mouth to speak, but not before the boy blurted out his incredible revelation. "She has the *Declaration of Independence!*"

Not knowing how to react to Jonathan's words, Rachel's mouth dropped open in disbelief, and Jim, for some unknown reason, laughed aloud.

CC was staring down at Elizabeth. "That's not possible. The *Declaration* is in the National Archives in Washington. I've seen it. At least, it seems to me that I remember seeing it there."

But searching Elizabeth's face, CC realized that as incredible as it sounded, she might actually have the document in her possession. In a tone of unbelief, he asked, "You are telling us that you actually have the original signed copy of the *Declaration of Independence* in that case?"

"More than that," she replied. "I not only have the original autograph of the *Declaration of Independence,* but I also have all four pages of the *Constitution*."

"But, why? How?" he stammered.

"The documents were in the basement where I was working. They were scheduled to be displayed at the museum the day following the attack." She looked from one face to another. "For me as an individual, they had no special monetary value, but," and she leaned down to wrap her arms around the case, "for me as an American, they are now more valuable than all the masterpieces in the world."

"So," McCord challenged, "you stole them."

"Don't be absurd," she countered. "With the electricity off, they'd have been destroyed within a few days." She shook her head in anger at what she considered his willful stupidity. "I didn't steal them, idiot. I saved them!"

For a moment, everyone was too stunned to speak, but CC's exhalation turned into a low whistle.

Jim muttered something under his breath.

CC turned to him. "What did you say?"

"I just realized that everybody who is playing tug of war over the future of the United States would love to get their hands on those."

"Who do you mean," Rachel asked. "Why?"

"The Chinese and Russian communists, as well as the radical Muslims, would all love to get hold of those documents."

Jonathan showed his surprise. "What would they want with our Constitution?"

"It's in their interests to destroy anything and everything related to our political and historic traditions," McCord pointed out.

"Although I'm an atheist, I'm realistic enough to recognize that Christian traditions and the rule of law were vital to America's birth and her survival and would be a target of America's enemies. Apart from their efforts to crush Christianity, which they understand breeds a hunger for freedom in people's hearts, those documents would certainly top the list of things to destroy. It's more than lip service to say that those documents undergirded our way of life.

"But to destroy historic documents?" Rachel said in amazement.

"Of course," McCord responded. "Consider how ISIS destroyed vast ancient treasures throughout the mideast. And these are far more important than the relics of dead civilizations.

"I studied political science, but I guess I still don't understand," Rachel persisted.

"Consider the wording." McCord began reciting aloud.

"When in the course of human events it becomes necessary for one people to dissolve the political bands which have connected them with another and to assume among the powers of the earth, the separate and equal station to which the Laws of Nature and of Nature's God entitle them...."

He looked around the room. "Did you hear me? The founding fathers wrote 'Nature's God.' One thing most enlightened people of the world agree on is that there is no god. And they certainly won't want Americans holding up this old document and claiming that even George Washington believed. So, yeah, I've never been more serious."

"I see," enjoined CC. "In the eyes of a depraved world, that document melds God, country and freedom."

McCord seemed to have forgotten his anger and was getting into the moment. "One doesn't have to agree with the sentiments expressed in those documents to appreciate the power that those ideas have over little minds."

CC's look was incredulous. "Little minds? Those documents were the product of some of the greatest minds in history!"

McCord ignored him and went blithely on. "The Chinese are subtle," he observed. "As a people that prides itself on thousands of years of their own traditions, they recognize the importance of history and tradition in the life of any nation. As you know, over the past few decades, the debate in America over the constitutionality of every law we passed had become more and more heated, and it was even suggested by one president that we scrap the Constitution itself."

"Well," Jonathan offered, "they goofed. They managed to destroy America before they actually voted the Constitution out."

Part 2: Four Months Later

Chris and Michael
Near Tower Point
Allison Lake
April 28

Four months had passed since the night Michael had crashed the snowmobile and Mary had disappeared. They had been dismal months of snow, ice and vicious cold. It had been an unusually bitter winter even for central Vermont.

For Chris it had been a period of uncertainty and despair, and while spring was struggling to take hold in central Vermont, there was little sunlight in her heart, let alone the hearts of other Americans who had somehow managed to survive the long winter.

Chris sat perched on a large boulder on the shoreline of Allison Lake, her feet dangling above the water. She was staring out over an expanse of melting and rotting ice, her eyes probing the patches of open water, terrified to discover her little girl's remains but unable to terminate her search.

In order to reach the waterline of the shrinking lake, it was now necessary to walk down what had become a long, sloping gravel beach, an area that had been underwater for as long as the Towers could remember. When little Michael had asked why the lake's level was down several feet, Don Tower had been unable to offer an explanation. He told Michael that, for all the years his family had lived on the lake, they had never been able to find the place where the lake drained.

"There has to be some cavern beneath the surface that drains it. With the level down, we might be able to find it after the ice melts," he added, "if we take a boat around the shoreline, or I might even be able to spot it from the air."

The idea of searching for the stream that drained the lake, excited Michael, but Chris wasn't particularly impressed even after he explained that the portion of the lake she could see from Tower Point represented less than a quarter of the entire lake system. On that basis, the quantity of water that had disappeared from this lake and the unseen lake to the north was enormous.

The lake's problems were of little interest to Chris. She was absorbed with concerns for her missing husband and the loss of her daughter.

The Towers seemed to understand her mental confusion, and she knew that they had been praying for her continually. It took only a week from the time the Towers had taken them in for them to build up a mutual trust, and that's when Chris told them her true identity. They tried to help her understand that it was wrong of her to blame herself for her child's loss, but even if it weren't her fault, she was still crushed.

How will I explain her loss to David? she asked herself repeatedly. *How can I explain my failure to him?* And that brought her full circle to another series of questions with which she continually battered herself.

Will I ever see him again? Shouldn't I have tried to get out of that SUV on Christmas Eve and gone to him so that he would have known we were alive, so that he could know how we love him...loved him? She punished herself endlessly, as was evidenced by the dark smudges that lay beneath her eyes from too many sleepless nights.

As the sky brightened, her tired eyes picked out the familiar patch of khaki green that lay just offshore atop the decaying ice. It was the remains of the canvas tarpaulin that the Towers had left laying on the snow the night of the rescue. Her mind went off on a tangent, curious as to why the ice appeared thinner beneath the scrap of canvas, then realized that the canvas was undoubtedly absorbing heat from the sun, while the snow that covered the surrounding ice reflected the rays back.

The first day she had noticed the tarp, she had become very excited and raced to find the Towers. But Don had explained why it had been left laying there. They had been in too much of a hurry to get her and Michael indoors to bother retrieving it. This had launched her into another period of depression, and she hadn't returned to the shore for several days. But she soon found it impossible to stay away.

She had begun seeing the frozen-in-place tarp as a point of reference, sort of like a buoy anchored a hundred yards offshore in the southwest corner of the lake. She would focus on the scrap of canvas, then scan everything between it and the shoreline as far as the south shore. Next eyes would return to the canvas, and trace a path around the end of the lake toward the western shore where she sat, searching for any sign of the sunken snowmobile or, God forbid, her child's body.

She was so intent on searching the open water that she did not hear her son working his way through the woods from the Towers' cabin.

"Hey, Mom," he shouted, his excitement obvious. "You should see what Mr. Tower just showed me."

She slid to the edge of the boulder to make room for him to climb up and sit beside her.

I've got to do better for Michael, she resolved. *He's the only living soul I have left. To my shame, it took Abigail, in her loving way, to point out that I'm not being a very good mother to him.*

She put her arm around her son, and for the first time noticed that he had become little more than skin and bones. *It's not for a lack of good food,* she thought. She knew that the Towers were continually prodding him by preparing special things to eat. But he was rarely tempted. *Is it because he's worried about me or because he feels guilty about Mary? she wondered.*

When Michael snuggled up against her, she turned to look at him and forced a smile.

"And what did Mr. Tower show you, Michael?"

"You won't believe it, Mom!"

"Try me."

"Well, he took me back into the woods and showed me their airfield."

"He really does have an airfield?"

"Oh, yes! He said that it used to be a lot longer, but there was an earthquake, or a flood or something, and it washed about half of it away into the lake."

"Oh, that's too bad."

"No, Don says that it was good because the runway is still long enough to take off in his airplane, but that it looks so small from the air that anyone flying overhead will think it's useless."

There was a bit of censor in her response. "*Don* says...?"

"Oops! Sorry. I meant 'Mr. Tower.' But he did tell me to call him Don. He said that we are buddies."

"Well, if he told you to call him Don, I guess it's all right, but I want you to show him respect."

"Oh, I do respect him, Mom. He's a great man."

"Like your Dad?"

"Sure, like Dad."

She frowned. "You haven't forgotten what a great man your Daddy is, have you?"

She spoke in the present tense to encourage her son. With her daughter's death, darkness had settled over her soul, and now she had grave doubts about her husband's survival as well. Unfortunately her son had sensed those doubts.

"I couldn't forget Dad. Mr. Tower talks about him all the time. He says that he listens to some secret radio station, and that even now Dad is frequently mentioned. He's one of the people the resistance fighters look to as an example. Don hopes that they will find him one of these days so that Dad can take a position of leadership."

As unlikely as that seemed, his words lightened her morning. She squeezed Michael's shoulder.

"The Towers have been very good to us. Their foresight in storing food and other survival equipment and their Christian love and generosity have proven to be the only thing standing between us and starvation. And since we're all Christians, perhaps you should call him *Brother Don*."

"Mr Tower is a lot older than Daddy, isn't he, Mom?"

"Where did that come from?" she laughed. "You'd better not let Mr. Tower hear you say that!" Then she laughed again, and her son sensed her mocking him. "At any rate, he seems to get around quite well for an *older* man, doesn't he?"

"Oh, I didn't mean really old. Just older than Daddy."

He rattled on, the way boys do sometimes, seemingly unable to differentiate between the significance of one thought and the next.

"Don said he wants to take me up in his airplane." When he saw her frown, he quickly added, "If that's okay with you."

She forced a smile, but he sensed her displeasure.

"We'll have to talk about that."

"But we are talking about it, Mom." He looked down, disappointment in his eyes.

"Flying small planes was uncertain enough before the war," she told him. "Now, with all those bad people out there, it could be a lot more dangerous."

"Oh, Mom," he remonstrated.

"Michael..."

"Yes, ma'am," he replied, resignation in his voice.

"So, what else have you been doing?"

"He took me to see the silo."

She had heard it mentioned and assumed it was part of an old farm, perhaps all that remained after an adjoining barn collapsed or burned.

"What was the silo like?" she asked, in an effort to express her interest in whatever interested her son.

"It was incredible, Mom!"

"A silo? Incredible?"

"Yes! We went through a solid steel door about this thick," and he held his hands about three feet apart.

"You mean the opening was about that wide, don't you?"

"Oh, no. The opening was really, really wide. But the door itself was this thick."

"Michael, how many times have I scolded you for exaggerating?"

"I'm not lying Mom, honest! Anyway, Don, I mean, Mr. Tower, turned on a flashlight, and we went down a whole bunch of flights of stairs, and then we came to another huge door, like they have on a bank vault...."

"Michael," she interrupted, convinced he was spinning a tale, "a bank vault door that's several flights beneath the forest floor?"

"Sure, that's what I'm trying to tell you." He tugged on her sleeve. "Listen, Mom..."

"All right, I'm listening," she said, and she really was.

"It's why the government built the airfield."

This didn't make any more sense to her than the bank vault door, so she held her silence.

"This door was really big too, but it seemed to open easily after he worked the combination lock. Then we went into a room where he pushed a button, and a machine turned on and lights came on."

"A generator," she mused aloud.

"Right, that's what he called it!" happy that his mother seemed to be paying attention. "So we went down a couple of more flights of stairs to a big room. He said it had been the crew's quarters, where the men lived when they were guarding the missile."

Now it was becoming clear to her.

"There's a missile silo in the woods?"

"That's what I've been trying to tell you, Mom."

"Oh," was all she could think of to say, and she let him run on.

"Well," he added, "Don, I mean Brother Don, said that there is no missile in the silo. The silo is concrete and goes down in the ground 185 feet, but it's pretty well full of ground water now." He'd been talking so fast that he had to take a breath before going on.

"Don told me that he and Mrs Tower used the crew quarters as a bomb shelter and that's how they survived the war, and that's where they want us all to go if any bad people come here."

She nodded, suddenly understanding.

"And he said that it would be almost impossible for anyone to break in there, and it's really beautiful, Mom. All bright and modern, with really cool furniture and everything. I asked him why they didn't live there, instead of the cabin. Do you know what he said?"

"I'm going to guess that he said that they like the trees and the lake and the sunlight and the fresh air."

He looked at her in wonder. "That's right, Mom. How'd you know that?" Then he elbowed her. "Ah, you already knew all about it, didn't you?"

"No, Michael," she smiled, "I didn't."

"Then how did you know why they don't live there."

"Don't you remember how we came to hate staying in Grandpa's root cellar for those first two weeks after the war started?"

"Oh, yeah. Gramps called it a fallout shelter, but it was awful — so crowded and dirty and smelly."

"And how anxious we all were to get out into the sunlight?"

"Well, that was nothing like Don's silo, but I guess I understand."

"But remember this, Michael. Grandpa's presence of mind in equipping what you call that crowded and dirty and smelly root cellar saved us from dying of radiation poisoning."

"That's true, Mom. Grandpa's pretty smart, isn't he?"

And even as she nodded her head in agreement, she wondered whether her parents had been able to survive after their farm was confiscated by the Chinese.

Kim Ling Condemned
The Green Mountain Feed and Grain Store
Near Butter Creek, Vermont
1st of May

General Eng leaned against the porch railing that skirted the front of the Green Mountain Feed and Grain Store. The Chinese had stashed a large quantity of military goods in the store and warehouse, and Eng was watching intently as his heavily armed troops supervised the exhausted Americans as they loaded their trucks.

The general appeared to pay no attention when he heard Kim Ling's helicopter sweep in for a landing in the field adjacent to the store, but he was anticipating no little satisfaction in continuing to play this unwilling conscript like a cat plays a mouse. For the time being, however, he planned to conceal his true feelings and instead stood gazing over the crowded parking lot.

The gravel area that lay in front of the store and the adjacent warehouse was crowded with tractor-trailers and alive with activity. Eng was not satisfied with the work accomplished. Nor did he attempt to hide his indifference to the suffering of the Americans whom he'd ordered dragged from their homes to load his trucks. Most were near starvation, and none had been given anything at all to eat since they'd been brought there under guard the day before. Nor had they been given a rest break in the past four hours.

General Eng believed that appearances were important, and as he stood looking down on the unhappy laborers, he tried to give an impression of an invincible conqueror. To the men who occasionally glanced at him through angry bloodshot eyes, however, he was just a paunchy, near-sighted, middle-aged oriental — a comic caricature of a real soldier. But in spite of his almost laughable appearance, the Americans didn't sell him short. Like most bullies who derived their strength from others, he was notorious for inflicting pain on friend and foe alike, and at only the merest whim. Many of the Americans had seen evidence of his vicious behavior, and several had lost wives and children because of this hated enemy.

The three-dozen Americans laboring here were guarded by only half their number, and Eng was hiding his concern about the number of casualties he might suffer if the Americans should suddenly rise against his men. He sensed that it would take only a chance word to ignite their anger and provoke a bloodbath, so he was struggling to give an impression of invincibility. Although he was certain his men would ultimately annihilate all the Americans, he knew that they would in turn suffer casualties, and they could not afford even a few.

Eng wanted to complete this onerous task and take his loaded convoy of tractor-trailers to Black River Junction where he planned to rendezvous with the much larger body of Chinese troops that were reported to be moving up from Rhode Island.

A number of Americans had flocked to Eng's banner early in the war, but he knew he could only rely on them as long as they believed he would be victorious, and they would profit from his success. As a result, he knew that he could only rely on the dedication of his own well-trained troops.

Just yesterday he had divided the meager force that he had brought with him from Burlington to Butter Creek, sending more than half of them south to Black River Junction. Except for the Chinese non-commissioned officers who were in charge, most of the men that he had sent away were renegade Americans who had joined his army. For the most part, they were troublemakers and ne'er do wells, and he was happy to send them on what was probably a wild goose chase. What was sobering was that he had received a message that a half-dozen of those men had deserted last night.

The American turncoat, James McCord, had come to him just the night before with a story that the escaped Christian leader they had been hunting was hiding in a cavern at the west end of a valley just a few miles to the south. After threatening McCord with what would happen to him if he were discovered to be lying, Eng had his pilot fly McCord about a half mile from the end of the valley, so that he could quickly make his way back to the cave that he claimed was the man's hide away.

Even though he despised the American turncoats that served him, he still felt uneasy about sending them away. The fact was that Eng's forces were already severely depleted, and he dared not let these barbarians realize how tenuous his foothold had become in the northeastern United States. The American mercenaries – for that was all they really were – required an undue share of his dwindling resources and the general made sure they received just the minimum. He could no longer afford to waste precious food and medicine on anyone, not on his own sick and dying men and especially not on the American turncoats who grudgingly served him. For this reason he had sworn his most trusted doctors to secrecy and ordered them to *allow* the more seriously injured and ill among even his own men to expire. He had told the doctors, "We cannot afford useless mouths."

Eng stared sightless across the parking area as his thoughts wandered. *These Americans are proud, impulsive and often stupid brutes. But even dumb oxen and stubborn mules have to be handled with care.*

He held nothing but contempt for the captives that were now loading his trucks. They were near starvation, as were the families from whose bosoms they had been snatched. Many Americans had been able to flee when his troops had gone to their homes to demand their labor. Those loading the trucks, however, hadn't received any warning of the approaching Chinese and had been taken unawares during the night. They had been brought here and forced to work through the remainder of the night and into midday. Right now they were carrying heavy containers from the warehouse to the tractor-trailers that were parallel-parked, their front bumpers pointed toward the buildings.

Eng was suffering some disillusionment. His belief that the Chinese could consistently win by intimidation didn't seem to be working here. He had been keeping his eyes on the Americans and couldn't help but note a growing obstinacy. He had originally considered their superior attitude an element of their white supremacy syndrome, but he had trouble reconciling that argument with the fact that there were several races and ethnic groups represented among the conscripts, and that they were friendly with one another. *They are all barbarians,* he concluded.

When one of the Americans, a black man, stopped work because he was wracked with a fit of coughing, one of Eng's troops had slammed him in the kidneys with the butt of his rifle. As the man fell to the ground, the trooper kicked him in the side and left him writhing there. The Americans who were working near the stricken man emitted a strange growling sound, and even after one of the Chinese officers shouted a warning, the angry noise barely subsided. Eng was truly shocked and a bit frightened at the response of the workers when the white man who knelt to help the injured man was knocked unconscious by the same sentry. The workers began to surge toward the guard, and it was only when a couple of the Chinese fired their machine guns into the air that the angry crowd subsided.

Have none of these Americans any sense of their proper place in their own society? he wondered.

The Chinese were still pointing their weapons at the unarmed Americans who, in fact, surrounded them, and it seemed to Eng a near thing that the Americans didn't attack his men with their bare hands. After a moment, two more Americans stepped slowly forward, their hands held chest high with palms out, and they were permitted to help the two injured men to their feet. The guards appeared satisfied that they had quelled any possible resistance, but they had no real idea of the flame they had kindled.

These were China's elite, and since they considered guard duty beneath them, they were intent on completing this job as quickly as possible. Nor were any of them trained in logistics, let alone something as mundane as loading trucks efficiently. If there was an efficiency expert among them, he was keeping that fact to himself. They had no idea that these *stupid American brutes* were about to take advantage of their ignorance.

The general had assigned Captain Tao Li Wei to lead this insulting duty. Captain Wei had initially attempted to have all the Americans work together to load one truck at a time. It was Wei's thought that by keeping the Americans together and moving supplies from only one building at a time, his troops would be able to control them more effectively. The Americans, however, proved to be quite clumsy, crowding together, stumbling into one another and dropping and breaking their loads open. Their ineptness had stalled traffic because men had to kneel to repack the open cartons.

Their clumsiness infuriated General Eng, who never for a moment imagined that the witless Americans were doing it on purpose. And as much as he'd like to have one or two of them beaten senseless as an example to the others to be careful, it would be counterproductive and perhaps even dangerous. Time was of the essence, and since he needed all these men working, he didn't want to antagonize them further. As a result, the general did the unthinkable. He undercut his subordinate and took charge, ordering Wei to divide the Americans into three groups of a dozen men each. When each of the three groups were lined up along the front of the porch at something resembling parade rest, Eng looked down at Wei and spoke to him in English.

"You will assign each of these groups to separate tasks," he ordered, his voice making it clear to Wei's subordinates as well as to the American conscripts that the captain had fallen short of his expectations.

Oblivious to the fact that he had undercut Wei's authority and damaged morale — or perhaps indifferent to that fact — the general pointed to the group on his right. Then he spoke in Chinese, and Wei translated. "These," he said, pointing at the nearest group, will move everything from the cellar beneath the store to the first of the tractor-trailers. These," and the word seemed filled with contempt, as though he was speaking of oxen or mules, "These," he repeated, pointing at the second group of men, "will move everything from inside the store to the second truck."

"But, sir," Wei started to interrupt, "two men are...."

"Spare me your interruptions, Captain," he snarled. They will do the job exactly as I outline it or someone will suffer the consequences." He moved his eyes slowly down the row of faces. "You understand what I am threatening, do you not?" Perhaps the captain understood, but it was unclear to his listeners whether it was the Chinese or the Americans who would suffer any consequences.

Nevertheless, after Captain Wei had translated, a few of the Chinese soldiers nodded in agreement, while the Americans stood mute. Presuming that his listeners appreciated his threat, the general continued.

"The third group will move materials from the warehouse to the third truck. When a group finishes loading one truck, they will move to another until they have cleared the contents of the building to which they've been assigned. Is that clear?"

When there was no immediate response, the general shouted, spittle flying from his mouth. "Is that clear?" he repeated. The Chinese, to a man, didn't need an interpreter and shouted in their native language what the Americans presumed was an affirmative. Among the American conscripts, no one so much as nodded.

"When the groups that are to empty the store and the cellar complete their work, they will immediately go to the assistance of the group that is clearing the much larger warehouse. They will move in through one door, and out through the other, so that they won't stumble over one another." From his smile, it was clear that he was quite satisfied with his plan.

Wei did not interrupt, but was inwardly amused at the idea of men having to pick up heavy items at the front corner of the warehouse, then carry them all the way to the rear corner, then across the back, and finally back up the aisle on the far side to reach the other front door. The captain estimated that they would have to walk up to four times as far as they would if they simply turned around with their load and walked straight out the door they had entered.

"I want these trucks packed as quickly as possible," Eng shouted.

"But sir," Wei tried once more, "we won't know what items are on which truck."

The general's face seemed to freeze, and it made Wei's blood run cold. The captain realized that he should not have pointed out Eng's mistake.

"When we reach our destination, Captain, and we have joined our compatriots, you will be honored with the task of emptying the trucks and sorting their contents while other more competent officers plan the next step in our campaign. Do you have any other questions?" The general continued to stare at Wei until he finally answered in a choked voice. "No questions, sir."

"We were speaking of loading the trucks," the general went on, as though never interrupted. "By following my instructions, these groups," he explained, as though to a child, "won't be crowding and jostling one another."

And that was quite true. As a result of the general's instructions, one group was working in the cellar of the store, another worked above them on the main floor of the store, and a third was laboring in the large warehouse. And that's where, unknown to Eng, his problems would start.

The Chinese had only eighteen men, including Captain Wei and his two lieutenants, to oversee the Americans. The three officers, of course, were not about to perform menial guard duty, so they stood together on the loading dock in front of the warehouse, well away from the general who paced back and forth along the porch in front of the store. From where they stood, the officers could watch the movement of the heavily laden men as the came out the doors of the buildings, until they disappeared between the closely parked trailers. They realized one thing that the general, in his ego, had obviously overlooked.

Wei had only three lieutenants and fifteen enlisted soldiers to guard three groups of twelve Americans each. Eng had divided his fifteen troops into three groups of five men each, and assigned each of the three lieutenants to one of the groups of guards. Every time Wei gave an order, however, the lieutenants would turn to look at the general to see whether he might overturn the order. It was an impossible situation, and even as Wei finally began to work things out to the evident satisfaction of the general, he knew that they were in trouble.

Of each group of guards, one of the men was assigned to perimeter guard duty. Those three men were not actually monitoring the Americans, for they were to patrol the perimeter of the property, guarding against any possible escape attempt or a surprise attack from outside. Three men were not nearly enough to cover the quarter-mile perimeter around the four-acre clearing that was occupied by the feed and grain store.

Of the four remaining men in each of the three cadres of guards, one was required to remain inside his assigned building to keep an eye on things — whether the cellar, the store or the warehouse. The second of the four remaining men was required to remain in or near the back of the tractor-trailer while the Americans were loading the items. A third man was required to be at the doors where the Americans entered and exited their particular building. That left just one man to patrol the path along which the Americans carried their burdens from the buildings to the rear of the trailers before returning empty-handed to the buildings. That one man could not see around corners, and since the laborers were being forced to move out of the buildings, up or down stairs, across loading docks and down the gravel drive to the truck cabs, his job was impossible. And there were workers continually moving in both directions.

None of the Americans appeared to do anything overtly wrong, but it wasn't long before the twelve men in each group somehow found themselves strung out, with a few inside the buildings, more on the long walk to the trucks, and others lifting the goods on to the trucks and positioning them in the dark interiors. It was impossible for the Chinese to keep an eye on all of them at once.

Eng seemed oblivious to the inherent danger, but his men clearly were not. The only thing his troops feared more than being attacked while walking out of sight between the trucks was the likelihood of being verbally scourged by the general for pointing out his errors. So they quietly worked out their own solutions.

The guard in the warehouse, for example, was to watch the laborers as they picked up their burdens and headed toward an exit door that was eighty feet away. That meant that he couldn't see what the others were doing in the back of the building as they labored behind the stacks of goods.

Nor could the man outside the door assist him. He had to divide his attention between the men going in and out of the building and the men who were moving items from the loading dock toward the trucks.

And the guard on the parking lot had to shift his position frequently so that he could try to keep track of each man, from the time he exited the building until he disappeared between the trucks.

Finally, the guard at the rear of the truck was forced to move to the corner so that he could monitor movement between the long trailers. When he turned away, and tried to peer up over the high tailboard, he was unable to see what was going on in the dark interior. For example, one guard failed to see an American working far inside a trailer as he opened a carton labeled, *Rifle, Caliber 5.56 mm*.

With guards stationed in the buildings and around the parking lot, and the Americans obediently carrying cartons from the buildings to the trucks, the general had the impression that everything was running smoothly, but it was impossible to watch all the men at the same time. The Americans were orderly, so after they had each made a couple of trips carrying the cartons, the Chinese troops began to relax. Only when two men stopped to speak to one another was a guard's attention engaged, but the diversion made it impossible for him to see the activities of the bearers working behind him.

And although the Americans were truly exhausted, they had seen an opportunity, and the spark that glowed within them began to grow into an obsessive flame. It was a flame that wasn't to be quelled short of death. One man had slipped onto the back of a truck and now lay hidden behind a stack of cartons that contained assault weapons. When the guard moved away, someone whispered an all-clear, and he quickly opened a couple of cartons and began unpacking weapons and ammunition.

One guard was no longer able to keep track of the men passing him, so when several reappeared, he assumed they were all returning together after carrying their heavy cartons past him to the truck. He was unable to see the man who stood behind the trailers waiting for the perimeter guard to turn his back, whereupon he signaled another man who slipped into the woods undetected, carrying two assault rifles and a carton of ammunition in his arms. In a matter of ten minutes, several dozen weapons were stacked behind trees in the forest, along with several thousand rounds of ammunition.

Kim Ling's helicopter had landed minutes earlier, but the general pretended indifference while Kim Ling shut it down and made his way to the store. When Ling finally appeared on his periphery, Eng let him wait. The general had begun to worry about what information he might have shared with Ling. He realized that he had drunk too much during these discussions, and he was feverishly searching his memory, trying to determine whether he had provided Ling with any vital information.

In the past, it was Eng who had always been able to get people to provide the information he wanted, whether out of fear, greed or pride, and he tried to reassure himself that Ling had been thoroughly intimidated and would never dare repeat anything he had told him. But, for the first time in the general's life, he felt a strange uncertainty in his dealings with another human being. Kim Ling was somehow different.

A long record of success in getting his way, however, had given the general an unjustified pride in his own abilities. Yet he felt no such confidence when dealing with Kim Ling, perhaps because he didn't understand him. It was as though the younger man was on a higher plain, and that Kim was somehow, unimaginably, impervious to the general's influence and totally indifferent to his threats.

It wasn't that Ling didn't seem to care whether he lived or died. The general had brought many individuals to a point where they would prefer death, and he had either been able to manipulate them or he eliminated them. It all came back to the fact that he couldn't understand Ling, and he tended to distrust and even hate anything or anyone that he didn't understand. He suffered a niggling of doubt, an actual fear that Kim Ling could not be ruled by fear.

Is it possible that Ling has some purpose or loyalty unknown to me that keeps him focused, that makes any other consideration irrelevant?

Yet the general believed that there had to be more to it than that. Kim Ling seemed to have a goal, an agenda of his own, and this made no sense at all.

What could Ling possibly want? What could he hope to attain? Does he mean to oppose us in our efforts to rule America? Absurd! He is a nobody! More to the point, he would need to be willing to stake everything he possesses on such an ambition.

He believes that we are holding his wife and children and that their future survival hangs on his complete obedience. So he believes he has more at risk than merely his own life. He may be willing to die to achieve some nebulous goal, but he has exposed his concern for his family, and I know he wouldn't risk their lives. The important thing is that we must continue to persuade him that they still are under our control. If, however, he wishes to sacrifice his own life, I will be pleased to accommodate him.

Kim Ling had carefully hidden his belligerence from his captors, but he sometimes infuriated Eng by acting as though the general were no more significant than a fly buzzing noisily about him, just the merest annoyance, something to be brushed aside and forgotten. That was unforgivable, and if the general had not needed Kim Ling to pilot one of his two precious helicopters, and had he not been certain that Ling was held in check by the threat to his wife and children, he thought that he would have long since done away with him.

At the same time, Kim Ling held a strange fascination for him. Kim did not exhibit any anger or hatred. He seemed to have no feelings at all except, extraordinarily, a sense of pity for the general. And when the general realized that Ling sincerely pitied him, he became intensely angry. He neither wanted, nor needed any man's pity. Yet this pity somehow endeared Kim and made him appear almost transcendent and untouchable. The general was worse than perplexed. For though Kim Ling's occasional displays of pity made the general angry, he also felt strangely grateful.

Certainly, he thought, *I've had suffered enough to justify the pity of others. But I don't want anyone's pity. I don't need anyone's pity!*

He had always succeeded on his own, and he believed that when his life was over, he would take his rightful place among his venerable ancestors.

It was all very perverse. He thought he should hate Kim Ling, but he had an odd feeling of affection for him, even while sensing a need to destroy him. Eng had always been a man of iron, but there was something otherworldly about Kim, and this was eating at his effectiveness. He had once talked with Kim Ling for hours at a time until he realized that he might have been trying to explain his actions, even to justify himself. The general had received a strange relief from these shared moments, a sense of surcease. But in spite of that, he had felt it necessary to terminate the meetings. Exposing himself to another human being made him weak.

Worst of all, the general was dumbfounded when he realized that he was almost afraid to take action against Kim Ling. In the past, he would have immediately terminated a person. Hadn't he ended his own father's life without a moment's hesitation? But with Kim Ling, it was as though some unseen force was inhibiting him.

As a result, Eng found himself drinking more than he ever had before, taking refuge in the pleasant haze that these alcoholic bouts produced. And with drink clouding his capacity to reason, he yielded to his emotions, and more and more of his decisions were erupting out of frustration and anger. Suddenly all he wanted was to be free of restraints, to be able to lash out, and not to have to explain his decisions to anyone.

And, in fact, he had no one to answer to. With communications to China cut off indefinitely, he was out of touch with his superiors. He was now free of both the comfort of their commands and the possibility of their censure. He had become something of a god in his own mind and could do pretty much anything he wanted. And that brought his thoughts back to Kim Ling.

It was odd that he was now able to step back and look at himself with any objectivity. He had never been an introspective man. And now that self-examination was effecting his leadership. As, in the past, he was laying traps for others, but now it seemed that he was the one falling into those traps. And since there were now no rules — since he was making the rules — and since he no longer had to answer to anyone, he felt that he'd completely lost his perspective.

On the one hand, I may have made a mistake by placing too much confidence in Kim Ling. On the other, I can excuse myself for relying on him simply because I had no other choice. I needed a pilot, but he is, when all is said and done, merely an American conscript. Still, I am grateful that there is no possibility of my facing an inquiry in China for my handling of the matter. I trusted Ling, and I am coming to believe that he violated my trust. If this proves to be true, he will pay with his life.

While Kim Ling awaited the general's pleasure, two Americans were standing down on the gravel parking lot, not a dozen paces away, almost hidden from view by the railing of the wooden porch on which Kim Ling and the general stood. These weary men were struggling to carry a styrofoam carton whose molded slots contained four Russian RPG rocket launchers. The men had their heads down and were for all appearances completely focused on their work. But one was whispering, "Those two Chinamen don't look too happy with each other."

The other man glanced toward the porch above them and replied, "No, they sure don't."

"Well, it means nothing to me," the first commented. "One Chinese is pretty much like another. As far as I'm concerned, the only good Chink is a dead Chink."

"I haven't known many Chinese," the other responded, "but the few I have met were truly fine people. I don't think you should characterize them as *chinks.*"

"Politically incorrect, eh?"

"No, just common sense and common decency."

"Okay, I get it. Apart from that, they don't look like the best of friends."

"Agreed. Let's keep our ears tuned. Maybe we'll learn something."

While this whispered conversation was going on, the general continued to pretend to ignore Kim Ling. When several minutes had passed, he finally cast an imperious glance across the platform and pretended to notice him. His first question was intended to be disarming.

"Ah, Kim Ling. Did you have a quiet flight from Burlington?"

Kim could never get over how a man with this soft, singsongy, almost feminine voice could erupt at any moment into an incoherent and vicious killer. There was no question in his mind why those who knew the general sought every possible excuse to avoid him, and why, when they had no other choice, they invariably approached him with terror in their eyes.

Kim Ling knew that Eng's question was specious. The general was indifferent to the comfort and well-being of anyone but himself, and he was only concerned about the comfort of his subordinates when it impacted their willingness or ability to serve him. The general was only interested in things that ultimately advanced his own program. Kim's reply had been carefully rehearsed during his flight and was now respectfully delivered.

"During the course of the flight, I was fired on repeatedly by unseen individuals on the ground, but the damage does not seem serious."

"You mean they actually hit your machine?"

Kim Ling did not reply, but simply pointed toward the copter's windshield.

As the general strode toward the helicopter, he could see several bullet holes in the windscreen, plus several more in the fuselage.

He gnawed his lip. "This resistance from the Americans is growing more serious." Turning back toward the store, he asked, "Have you seen anything of our other machine? I expected Feng Jiang and you to arrive together."

Kim thought he detected a hint of slyness in the question, as though the general was trying to appear indifferent. *But why would he be indifferent about one of his two precious copters gone missing?*

Kim Ling turned to follow the general as he replied.

"No, sir. Feng took off about ten minutes before me, and I haven't seen him since."

Kim hated to lie, and wondered whether he could have come up with a better reply. He knew he was on shaky ground. He had already decided to desert his Chinese masters in order to locate and join up with the resistance. He'd planned to do so this morning, and he would not have come to this rendezvous at all if he weren't in desperate need of fuel. This need led him to offer his first unsolicited comment.

"I hope you have fuel on hand, General. My tanks are nearly dry."

"Yes, yes," the general replied, waving toward a tank trailer. "There's nearly five hundred gallons there.

"With full tanks, how many miles could you go?"

"That depends, sir."

"On what?"

"On how fast I fly, on whether I have to repeatedly land and take-off, on how much weight I'm carrying, and even on how much time I spend hovering or going in circles."

"Optimum number of miles?"

"Well, I can stay up about about three-and-a-half hours on a full tank, and my maximum range is about 250 miles."

"So you can easily go a hundred miles and return?"

"Yes, sir, if I'm not carrying too much weight, if I don't have severe head winds and if I can pretty much travel in a straight line."

"You seem to have a lot of *ifs* there, Ling."

"Yes, sir, I guess I do. There are a lot of variables, General."

The general didn't respond, but instead pointed across the lot. "Sergeant, set a detail to filling the gas tanks on that helicopter."

"Sir," Kim interrupted, "the fuel may be dirty. They have to run it through filters."

"I'm sure they are aware of that, Ling."

"Yes, sir."

Suddenly, his ambivalence toward Kim Ling struck the general as ludicrous. He liked the man in spite of himself, but even as he spoke of refueling Kim's helicopter, he was plotting to ultimately execute him. Kim Ling's life was a small thing, after all, and the general immediately dismissed him from his thoughts and went on to other matters.

Considering the evidence, he realized that his own situation was probably hopeless. His limited forces didn't appear to stand a chance of fulfilling their mission, but the Americans didn't know that, and he took comfort in the fact that throughout history many victories had been wrested out of the mouth of defeat. Still, serious doubts lingered.

The tide is beginning to turn against us, he thought, *and the likelihood of our receiving any reinforcements from Beijing are virtually nonexistent. I must soon look to my own interests.*

Kim Ling's thoughts paralleled those of the general, but while the general was thinking in terms of conserving his wealth and power, Kim was thinking on a far more basic level — his personal survival. He had bad news to share with the general, and he knew that Eng hated bad news and often punished its bearers.

I have to find the right words, Ling thought. *I have to concentrate. I can't allow myself to live in the past. If I don't concentrate on the present, I'll very likely die in it.*

He was careful, therefore, to phrase his remarks to include himself among the unfortunate beneficiaries of these circumstances. It wouldn't do to distance himself from those he was forced to serve. And in order to make the report more palatable, he planned to save the least-disturbing reports for first and last, sandwiching the worst news in the middle. If he had been aware of who was about to make an appearance, he wouldn't be at all confident; but he didn't and he went ignorantly ahead.

"I have got some bad news, General."

The general tipped a jaundiced eye toward him.

"As I was coming in for my landing, I noticed that the highway just south of here lies under several feet of water, obviously as a result of the recent rains. We won't be able to send the trucks south until the level drops."

"But we must go south!" the general expostulated, and he again inexplicably found himself expressing his concerns to this man for whom he felt both an incomprehensible affection and an abiding hatred. The general was so upset that he didn't realize that he was shouting.

The general pointed toward the highway. "There is a rumor that a group of armed Americans is gathering to the west of us, and that, like us, they plan to move south toward Black River Junction. If we don't get these supplies to our small outpost there, those upstarts might cause our troops trouble!"

Kim Ling was shocked at this admission. Everyone within the sound of the general's voice, friend and foe alike, had heard his words. Not that Kim cared. Such revelations were apt to discourage the Chinese while boosting the morale of the Americans. What shocked Kim was the knowledge that anyone else making such a remark would be summarily shot for defeatism. The fact that the general had made the statement in front of his own men, much less their prisoners, was clear evidence that he was losing control and that the Chinese invasion forces might be in serious trouble.

Kim stole a glance at the Americans to assess their responses. Guarded smiles on a dozen faces told the story. When they had heard the general comment about the possibility of a militia group attacking the Chinese invaders at Black River Junction, Kim knew that all of them were eager to add themselves to that group. All of the Americans present had suffered at the hands of the Chinese. Most had handled firearms since childhood. More than a few had become deadly shots during their teen years, and had been relied on by their families to supplement their food supplies by bringing home wild game.

Before the general could say more, Kim Ling continued. "I'm afraid there is other bad news." The general's head snapped around, his eyes searching Kim's face. *There's something more than a look of suspicion there,* he realized, but he realized that it was too late to change course, and he plunged on.

"The high water problem I mentioned is temporary, and might clear up overnight. But the highway is permanently cut off a few miles south of here, near the top of the mountain, and if you take the trucks up there, they won't be able to get over the crest."

The general looked at Kim in disbelief.

"What do you mean, the road is cut off? he demanded. How can that be?

He's really asking two things, Kim realized. *First, how can the road have been suddenly and permanently cut off? And second and more important, why do I have this information and what part did I have in contributing to this disaster? I don't know whether he's going to blame the impassable road on me, but it's clear that the his legendary anger is about to really explode.*

Yet the general's next statement, made in a calm and quiet voice, amazed him.

"Lieutenant, I cannot accept your report."

"Sir?" he replied incredulously.

"I repeat. I reject your report."

"But sir," he persisted, thinking that a pretense of helpfulness might improve his situation, "the water that blocks the road here is the least of your worries. This morning, I flew all the way to the top of the mountain. There is a valley to the west of the highway that has somehow been flooded and the overflow appears to have washed the highway out. If the drivers go up there, they will be stuck. They would have to back their trailers down the mountain for nearly a mile before they could find a place to turn around."

"I know the valley of which you speak. In fact, I sent two squads of our best troops there to search for an escaped prisoner, but I haven't heard from them since yesterday. Evidently their radio is out."

"Sir," Kim Ling again expostulated, "I flew the entire length of that valley this morning. The cliffs at the east end have collapsed the end of the valley. The fallen rock formed a huge earth dam and the entire floor of the valley is deep under water."

"Did you see any of our troops?"

Kim was tempted to say, *"Yes, I saw several bodies floating in the muddy water,"* but he was able to tell the truth without further endangering himself. "There was no sign of life. None at all."

"Perhaps my men have taken shelter in one of the caves they reported finding and are remaining there until the water level recedes."

"Yes, sir," he replied. He didn't want to dissemble and regretted any dishonesty. He wanted to stay alive in hope that his skills might play a role in the ultimate defeat of these invaders.

"Let me understand you, Ling. You are suggesting that a massive quantity of water somehow inundated the valley, then flowed out of the valley, washing out the rock ledge that supported the state highway. Is that correct?"

"I guess that is as good an explanation as any," Kim agreed. He again omitted the word, "Sir," and the general glared at him.

"Yes, sir," he added tardily. "That's what I believe happened."

"And you are reporting that the valley is still flooded."

"Yes, sir."

"I still don't understand what that has to do with the highway? How could the flooding of the valley affect the road? Are you suggesting that the road was somehow irreparably damaged? Are you a civil engineer?"

"No sir. I can't explain how it happened, but I saw the result. It's very clear that a lot of water must have poured out of the entrance to the valley...."

"And?" the general interrupted.

"... the water washed out nearly a quarter-mile stretch of the highway, and...."

"What are you saying?" the general shouted again. You're telling me that the surface has been washed away, that we can't patch up that road, or that these trucks can't get through a few muddy ruts?"

He looked back and forth as though searching for someone to override the pilot's report. "We must get these trucks over that mountain today!" he shouted.

Then his eyes took on a look that Kim Ling could only describe as cunning.

"Tell me, Ling, what were you doing flying over the highway to the south of us when you were supposed to be flying directly here from the northwest of us?"

All work had come to a complete stop and the eyes of everyone, soldiers and conscripts alike, were surreptitiously viewing the two men, and every ear was straining to take in their words. Some of the Americans who had been struggling to suppress their smiles now looked concerned.

"Sir...," Kim replied, "I saw a cloud of smoke up on the top of the mountain, and thought I should investigate."

"And what did you find?"

"It wasn't smoke. It was a massive cloud of dust, evidently thrown up when the cliffs collapsed into the valley. That's when I noticed that the highway was gone."

"Gone? You keep saying that. It's not gone!."

"Well, sir, the side of the mountain is almost sheer there where the valley ended at the highway. The highway's builders had blasted out a ledge along the side of the mountain over which they laid the highway. But now the side of the mountain − the ledge that supported the highway − appears to have collapsed into the valley below. As far as I can see, there is no longer a ledge or a highway."

The general's face was suffused with blood and he looked ready to explode, but Ling rushed on.

"In fact, I doubt that you can even reach the mouth of that valley, not by vehicle or on foot. It looked like there is a long gap where the highway used to be, and only a sheer cliff remains that extends from the valley entrance for a couple of hundred yards down what was the highway."

The general's silence was ominous.

Then Ling had an inspiration.

"General, I'm just trying to provide you with needed intelligence on which to base your plans. Perhaps you might consider having one of your men go up there to survey the scene. He can radio you back with his assessment. But in my opinion, State Highway 19 is, for all intents and purposes, irreparable."

The general continued to stare at him in utter disbelief. With contempt in his voice, he shouted, "You are lying! We will get over that mountain."

Kim was losing his own composure and for the moment he didn't care. "You will have to find another route to get the convoy to Black River, General" he snapped in return, then clamped his jaws closed.

"You fool," the general shouted hysterically, "the only alternative is for us to drive back toward Burlington on these county roads until we can find another route south. We would have to drive in a huge circle. It could add a day or more because we would be continually harassed by the American reactionaries who are hiding in the forests, shooting at anything that moves." The general was literally wringing his hands, and the conscripts were again exchanging smiles with one another.

Kim Ling heard the whoppa-whoppa of an approaching helicopter, and tried to hide his concern when General Eng turned his head to search the skies for its source. As the aircraft drew near, they could hear the engine skipping badly, and from Kim's point of view, it was only the work of the devil that was keeping the machine airborne at all.

Two of the Chinese troops pointed their machine guns in the direction of the approaching aircraft, but it was soon obvious that it was not some unexpected threat, but their own missing machine.

The general turned to stare at Kim Ling, and when Kim was unable to hide his consternation, the general's eyes took on a feral cast. Kim knew that the incoming helicopter had to be piloted by his enemy, Feng Jiang, and therefore the general, like a prowling leopard, was about to pounce on him.

The copter set down in the field next to Kim Ling's machine, and the general started towards it. Kim stayed where he was and stared fixedly at the copter until he saw the pilot, Feng Jiang, climb down from the aircraft. Feng shook hands with the general, then turned to search the faces of those standing around the front of the store until his eyes locked on those of Kim Ling.

With a very unpleasant smile on his face, he raised a hand to point at Kim Ling. Even before the general had reached the side of his personal pilot, Kim knew that he was living on borrowed time. Jiang would immediately inform the general that Kim Ling had disabled his engine and left him stranded deep in the forest to the north. That accusation would be more than enough to condemn Kim to death.

Kim grimaced. *I obviously miscalculated the damage I did to his copter. Worse, I misjudged his capacity to make repairs and get it in the air again. My weakness was that I didn't want to kill him,* Kim thought, *but this is war, and it appears I shouldn't have hesitated. One thing's certain. This isn't one of those occasions when I will have an opportunity to learn from my mistakes. I left him alive. He won't offer me the same courtesy.*

The two Chinese officers stood near the helicopters, heads together, deep in conversation. Kim Ling saw the general turn his head toward him when Jiang pointed his way. Then he led the general to his copter, raised the engine cowling and pointed inside. Finally the two men turned and walked toward the store. When they reached the porch, the pilot was staring at Kim, a malicious smile on his face, while the general gave no hint of any problem. The general gave Jiang a light pat on the back, an act that every one of the Chinese troops would recognize as an extraordinary gesture of affection from this otherwise cold and dangerous man. Jiang seemed to swell with pride, and with a wolfish grin for Kim Ling, he whispered something in the general's ear.

"Yes, of course, Feng," the general replied. "You must be famished. There is a variety of canned food inside, and my orderly will prepare whatever you want. With that, Jiang's demeanor became even more fawning.

Kim Ling was not surprised. *I wonder if he's going to get down on his knees and lick the general's boots.* The general seemed indifferent to Jiang's behavior and continued speaking to him as he turned to Kim Ling, a calculating smile on his face. "As soon as you've had something to eat, Feng, please rejoin me so that we can finish this nasty business."

Jiang drew himself to attention, snapped a smart salute, waited until the general answered it, smiled once more at Kim, did an about-face and disappeared through the store's front door.

The general's next words surprised and confused Kim. He turned to the captain whom he had accompanied to Butter Creek the previous winter.

"Captain Wei."

"General?" he replied, snapping to attention.

"Once the convoy has departed, you are to proceed as ordered."

"Yes, sir," Wei replied.

Kim wondered what that was all about, but the general wasn't going to leave him in the dark for long. He turned to him with a broad smile.

"You'll no doubt be interested in the captain's assignment, Ling, as it very much concerns you."

Kim's face had lost something of its color, but he had so far been successful in hiding his apprehension, striving to remember that the Lord was always there with him.

"The captain has been assigned the task of burning these buildings after the convoy has departed for Black River Junction."

Kim's face revealed his confusion, but instead of providing clarification, the general turned back to Captain Wei.

It was clear to all that Eng despised his second in command, and that the captain was terrified of the general, but Kim Ling had no idea why. The captain seemed to cringe in anticipation of an inevitable dressing down, only to have the general alter his personality as quickly as a chameleon his color.

"You are to proceed as ordered," he instructed him in an even and almost cordial voice. "Keep these barbarians under guard," he ordered, indicating the American conscripts with a wave of his hand. Lock them in an empty tractor trailer and take them with you so that you can use them to unload when you reach Black River."

That statement was met with another angry growl from the conscripts. They had been promised that they would be allowed to find their way home once they had finished here. Now they were learning that they would be taken more than forty miles south and had no idea what their fate would be after they reached there. There was some grumbling and moving about, but when a couple of the guards slapped the stocks of their weapons, the men subsided.

Wei looked uncomfortable, but felt compelled to ask. "Aren't you going with us, sir?"

"I will take the helicopter up the mountain to survey the damage that Ling here claims has occurred. If I think you can get the trucks over the mountain," and he gave Kim Ling a hard look, "I'll radio you. If you do not hear from me within an hour, you must assume that the road is impassable, and proceed northwest from here. Continue northwest toward Burlington until you find a road that will allow you to make the turn south toward Black River Junction." Then, almost as an afterthought, he asked, "Do you have a road map?"

"Yes, sir. I found an old map of Vermont here in the store, but I'm sure the general is aware that the belligerents have torn down most of the road signs in order to frustrate our efforts to find our way around. These maps are outdated because Americans have been relying on GPS units for years."

"I doubt that there has been a lot of road building in these mountains over the past ten years," the general observed wryly, "and I don't want any excuses. Just pay close attention to your map and to the readings on your odometer between turns, and you ought to be all right."

"I'm sure that the general hasn't overlooked the fact that the Americans who are reported to be heading for Black River Junction will very likely be traveling the same roads."

"You have fifteen well-armed troops here. I have no one else to send with you, and though there are troops in Burlington, I couldn't get them to rendezvous with you in time. You are elite soldiers dealing with civilians. Look to yourselves!"

The captain came to rigid attention and replied, "Yes, sir!"

Then Wei asked, "Will you be flying directly to Black River after you check the highway, sir?"

"No. We'll continue up the valley to see whether we can make contact with any of the members of our squad. Then we'll come back this way and follow the road until we locate you."

The captain dared one last question. "Will you be flying with your regular pilot, General?" He pointed at Kim Ling. "Or will your he be flying you?"

And now the general's face took on a crafty look. "Oh, no," he smiled. "My regular pilot, will take me. Mr. Ling has made his last flight."

The captain looked surprised, but it was to Kim Ling that the general had directed his words. Kim Ling was no longer having difficulty maintaining an impassive countenance. He had again silently consecrated his life to the service of the Lord and considered his future to be in God's hands.

The general beckoned to the lieutenant. "Have two men take Kim Ling down into the cellar beneath the store."

"Sir?"

"You heard me! Bind his wrists and ankles securely, and tie him to one of the supporting columns. When the building burns, Ling will help feed the blaze."

Captain Wei was surprised. "I don't understand."

"Perhaps my pilot can explain, Captain," as he saw Feng Jiang walking out of the store, wiping his lips on the sleeve of his blouse.

When he sensed that he had the attention of everyone within hearing distance, Jiang smiled broadly.

"Kim Ling and I were flying here together when he radioed that he was having engine problems, so we landed near one another in a clearing deep in the forest. As soon as I stepped down from my copter, he put a couple of bullets into my engine compartment. My engine died, and I thought I was next, but he foolishly abandoned me there, believing that I would not be able to hike out through the forests and arrive here before you had departed for Black River."

Kim Ling just stared at him, his own face a frozen mask, and the Chinese pilot went on. "After Ling took off in his copter, I removed the cowling on my machine and saw that the only damage done was a severed wire. I didn't have any tools with me, so I started walking downhill, figuring that sooner or later I would find a stream or a lake. Where there's a stream or a lake, one will sooner or later find people, isn't that right Kim?" He hurried on, not anticipating a reply. "And I was right," he added almost pompously. "Before long, I stumbled on a farm, and, after convincing the owner that he'd prefer to loan me some tools and a good riding horse rather than his wife, I was able to return to the meadow, make the repairs, and arrive here in time." He sneered at Ling. "The rest," he smiled, "is up to you, Sir."

"Quite right, Jiang," the general replied before directing his attention to Kim Ling. "So you see, Ling," the general said, "your treachery has been exposed."

"And your perfidy, General, your treachery," Kim replied evenly, "was exposed several months ago."

The general's eyes widened in surprise that Kim would dare respond.

"I really don't understand why you try to use words like perfidy, General. You'll never be able to live up to the Harvard degree you purchased."

It was clear to most of those listening that Kim was trying to make the general angry.

"You are hastening disaster, Ling!"

The general began fumbling with both hands in an attempt to unsnap his holster.

"Of course," Kim Ling replied calmly. "And I have no fear, for I know both my destiny and yours." *And I know that, if I have a choice, I prefer to be shot rather than being burned alive, and the time for bowing and kowtowing to you is over.*

The general had the holster unsnapped now, but seemed unable to draw his Type 77 pistol.

"What's the matter, General? You don't feel threatened, do you?" Kim badgered. "After all, you are surrounded by at least a dozen of your own men, and they are all carrying automatic weapons. There's no reason for you to exhibit cowardice. Bullies like you are always bold when supported by real men."

"How dare you speak to me in this manner! I'll show you what it is to feel threatened!"

"How dare I? You're going to make me feel threatened?" Kim Ling laughed, and was thrilled that the Lord gave him the grace to take the middle road between hysteria and weeping.

The general's face went white, his skin stretching tight over his cheek bones. Then, for no reason he could think of, he suddenly felt uncertain, and his eyes roved the area, trying to ascertain what danger he might be ignoring, for why else would Kim Ling display this attitude of arrogant impunity?

Ling's situation appeared hopeless to the Americans watching this outburst, yet he continued speaking in an even voice, loud enough to hold the attention of everyone on the parking lot. Heads had even begun to appear in the windows of the buildings. The Chinese guards were now standing carelessly alongside their American captives, and the eyes of men all over the parking area were turned toward the four men on the porch. Even the perimeter guards ceased their vigil and turned to watch what they were certain would be a violent outcome for the Chinese-American pilot. No one had ever seen the general confronted in such a manner, and regardless of nationality, most of the men appeared delighted with the possibility of some unusual entertainment.

"Let's consider how I dare," Kim Ling persisted. "First, you tore me away from my family and made me an involuntary conscript in your miserable army. That's the first *how dare I.*"

And before the general could respond, Ling hurried on.

"Apart from that, you murdered my wife and our two children. That's alone is ample reason for me to dare, don't you agree?"

The general looked shocked, not out of remorse, but because Kim Ling had somehow learned the truth, and he made a mental note to discover from whom Ling had garnered the information. That person would not go unpunished.

"And that's not to speak of the fact that I was born in the United States," Kim continued, "and have always been a proud American, whereas you are part of an army that launched a vile sneak attack against my homeland. How about that for another *How dare I?*"

With those words, the Americans within hearing distance understood that Kim Ling was one of their own, a man whose reckless heroism was about to cost him his life, but also a man for whom they suddenly felt a fierce respect and affection.

"You stand condemned out of your own mouth!" the general shouted.

"If I am condemned, I can only regret that I don't have more evidence of my guilt to present to you. I have done too little to halt your evil aggression. But wait! Let me add this. My great-grandparents arrived in the United States with very little in worldly possessions. By dint of hard work, simple living, and shrewd investments my ancestors built up a small chain of grocery stores specializing in Chinese foods. They came to America for the opportunities that they believed could only be available in a nation whose government is based on Judeo-Christian traditions. In fact, my grandfather frequently quoted the words of Jesus Christ: *You shall know the truth, and the truth shall set you free.*"

The general was almost stamping up and down with rage, but all he could find to say was, "Bah!"

Now every man in the parking lot had edged toward the porch where Kim and the general stood, and when one of the Chinese guards quietly threatened a man and ordered him back to work, a chorus of shouts went up from the Americans, and the guard subsided.

Kim Ling smiled. "I prophesy that you won't succeed in exporting your failed communism to America, General!"

"Failed? We have not failed. You have failed. You have not invaded our country; we have invaded your country."

"And the reasons should be obvious," Kim Ling shot back.

"Obvious?" the general stuttered.

"Of course! We had something worth stealing. And, unlike the Chinese, the USA is not imperialistic. Apart from that, I'd like to know why any sane person would ever dream of invading your country with its teeming billions living in spiritual and economic slavery and suffering the poverty which you as an individual have had a major part in promulgating. Sure, you invaded America. But this was still the greatest country in history, in spite of the fact that a godless government and a largely corrupt society had run amuck and was throttling free enterprise and freedom of religion."

"Keep talking, Kim Ling," the general spluttered. "You are digging your own grave."

"I think you already said that," Kim replied. "But why don't you end it? You know that you've shared too much with me, and that I am now therefore dangerous to you. And I've certainly listened to more than enough of your drivel. Go ahead! Draw that pistol and shoot me," he challenged.

"Have you told your men any of the things you shared with me?"

The general's face turned white, and his hand again seized the butt of his pistol.

"Did you know," Kim persisted, turning to his rapt audience, "that eighty percent of the Chinese troops who landed on Rhode Island have died as a result of hunger, disease and radiation poisoning? Ask him," and he pointed to the general. "He told me."

"That's enough Ling!" the general shouted.

"...and that the ship carrying the aircraft and heavy weapons the Chinese here had been promised was sunk months ago in the Panama Canal..."

"I've warned you for the last time...."

"Wait, now, general. You told these things to me. Why not share them with your own men?"

The general looked around and realized that his men's eyes were glued on him, eyes filled with fear, and maybe something more. Hatred?

"And, General Eng, you told me that you are wondering whether you can maintain your toehold in America." Kim looked out at the conscripts who were now smiling, and he smiled back. "Well, I'll tell you right now, go ahead and shoot me, and I think your toehold will completely disappear." He laughed. "Go ahead. I'll be honored to be America's next martyr." His words brought forth a spontaneous cheer from the Americans.

Furious, the general finally freed his stuck gun, pointed it toward Kim Ling, and fired a half-dozen rounds. The first bullet struck Kim in the side, spinning him around and knocking him to the ground. Another struck one of his own lieutenants who had been moving toward Kim to restrain him, mortally wounding him. The remaining bullets struck the corner of the warehouse, missing a Chinese guard by inches.

Now the Americans were milling about, trying to decide what to do, while Eng's troops struggled to restore order. Firing a few rounds into the air, they began striking the Americans with the butts of their weapons, then pushing them into a tight-packed group against the side of one of the trailers.

Out of sight of the Chinese, two men dropped to their knees and crawled beneath a tractor-trailer. When they saw that all eyes were directed elsewhere, they ran across the narrow gap that lay between the trucks and the front of the store. Reaching the porch, they threw themselves to the ground and crawled between a brick column and a section of decorative lattice that masked the area under the porch. In a moment, they had disappeared into the shadows beneath the deck.

Almost everyone else was watching the general as he walked to where Kim Ling lay. He raised his foot, and using his toe, tapped Ling's injured leg several times, and though Kim gasped with the pain, he managed to stifle his cries. Eng then turned to Captain Wei.

"Have this trash taken to the cellar, and make sure he is securely tied to one of the columns that support the main floor."

"Yes sir," Wei replied. "Sir, he's bleeding badly. Should we bind that up."

Eng thought that over for a moment. "Yes," he smiled. "We want him very much conscious when we set these buildings afire."

The captain nodded toward the Chinese officer that the general had shot. "What about the lieutenant, sir? His wound looks grievous."

Eng turned toward the man who was lying unconscious further down the porch. It was obvious to everyone watching that the general had given no thought to his injuries.

"See to it!" he ordered indifferently. "Right now, I need something to drink." He turned, and followed by his pilot, entered the store.

Another Kangaroo Court

Green Mountain Feed and Grain Store
Near Butter Creek, Vermont
1st of May

The two men who had scurried beneath the porch of the Green Mountain Feed and Grain Store had been friends for many years. Their families had camped together near Butter Creek several years before, so they were somewhat familiar with the area. Just the day before they had been resting in the shade of a tree on a country lane when a pickup truck came around a curve in the road taking them by surprise. Realizing it was too late to hide, they had just enough time to toss their weapons over the top of a stone wall just seconds before the truck pulled up alongside them.

Two Chinese soldiers jumped down and waved their weapons at them. There was no communication problem. The two men climbed into the back of the truck, then watched intently as one of the soldiers casually searched the area where they'd been sitting. They breathed a sigh of relief when he failed to take the trouble to climb the few feet up the embankment to look behind the stone wall.

The language problem turned out to be a blessing in disguise because the Chinese were unable to get the men's identities, or question them about what they were doing on that road or ask where they had been going. Had the Chinese seen their weapons or discovered that one of these men had once served as the sheriff of Black River County, they would have taken a far greater interest.

The two men were surprised and anything but pleased when the Chinese dropped them off only a half-mile down the road at the Green Mountain Feed and Grain Store. It had been their original destination, but they did not expect it to be crowded with Chinese troops and American civilian prisoners.

They learned too late that the Chinese had long since appropriated the facilities to store arms and equipment, and it was soon obvious that they were augment the unwilling laborers being forced to load precious supplies onto trucks.

Happily, they had not been identified and were treated no differently than any of the other Americans laboring under the watchful eyes of the Chinese guards. But the next day, after they'd picked up some vital information about the problems the Chinese faced, and when they saw the commanding general shoot one of his pilots, they considered it prudent to try to escape.

Now, kneeling among old candy bar wrappers and cigarette butts in the dirt beneath the porch, they could hear very clearly the conversation that continued above their heads. The general ordered his men to bring the owner of the feed and grain store to him, and they heard boots scraping above their heads as dust sifted down on them through the cracks. When the owner was brought before the general, it turned out to be a one-way conversation, and the eaves-droppers realized the general was taking out his frustrations on the old man who owned the place.

"I trusted you to remain here to protect our supplies," the general shouted at the old man. "You not only did not protect them, but it's reported to me that many of the cartons are missing, while others have been opened, their contents rifled, and that there are numerous items missing. It appears that you actually distributed weapons and supplies to dissidents."

When the owner failed to respond, the general made an attempt to sound conciliatory.

"We thought you were on our side."

The owner remained silent, but managed, unseen, to wink at the Americans in the parking lot.

"Well," the general demanded, "what do you have to say for yourself?"

When the owner finally replied, his words were pronounced precisely, and he spoke in a very dignified voice. There could be no misunderstanding his words.

"Well, Mr. Eng," he began, and the men under the porch heard his words cut off with the distinct sound of someone being slapped hard.

"Perhaps you will do me the courtesy of using my proper title the next time you address me."

"If you want me to reply," the man said, "you won't strike me again."

There was what sounded like a punch, followed by the sound of a body crashing to the porch floor above their heads. It was obvious the old man was lying just above them, for his body blocked the sunlight that penetrated between the boards.

Then the harsh bark of Eng's voice was again heard.

"Don't tell me what I can or cannot do, old fool!"

They heard the old man's rasping voice, little more than a whisper, but filled with defiance.

"I'll paraphrase the answer I heard your American pilot give just before you shot him. It certainly applies to me as well.

You have invaded my country, murdered my wife, robbed me of my property, destroyed my means of income, and physically abused me."

They could hear him take a deep breath before continuing in a rasping voice. "You accuse me of giving your equipment away. The truth is that it happened without my knowledge or participation."

His breathing was pronounced as he evidently tried to struggle to his feet, and there was still a hint of the audacity in the old man's voice. "Now that I've learned of your losses, I'm ashamed that I didn't assist in an effort to clean these warehouses out and put their contents into the hands of those who would use them to oppose you."

They heard Eng laugh. "Well, since you share so much in common with my earlier victim, it seems only appropriate that you also share his fate." His voice rose. "Captain Wei, take this man to the cellar and tie him next to the other traitor."

The men hiding beneath the porch were shocked. They had heard stories about the owner of the Green Mountain Feed and Grain Store. He had always been generous to a fault. He supplied his neighbors with seed and farm equipment when no bank would consider giving them loans. He had traveled out into storms to help people through sickness and childbirth. He had given money to widows and taken orphans into his home. He was the epitome of godliness. If the general carried through on his threat, he would certainly make a martyr of the man. Many people who had been merely struggling to survive would suddenly take up arms against the Chinese. The two men peered at one another in the half-light beneath the porch and agreed that they had to find some way to help the two condemned men.

They looked both directions before crawling beneath the porch toward the back of the building. They were able to remain out of sight until they reached the back of the store. Making certain that there was no one in sight, then ran the short distance from the rear of the store to the edge of the forest.

They hadn't walked a hundred feet into the trees before they realized that they were being stalked by several heavily armed men. Surrounded and unarmed — certain the Chinese had followed them and that they were about to die — they raised their hands in surrender.

Two New Recruits

Near Green Mountain Feed & Grain Store
Butter Creek, Vermont
1st of May

The two unarmed men were crossing a small, moss-carpeted clearing when they heard the slide of a weapon slam home. They immediately froze in place and raised their hands above their heads, moving only their eyes to try to determine the source of the threat. They could see the muzzles of several weapons pointing at them through the thick foliage on the far side of the clearing, but could not make out any faces because they were obscured by the leaves and the camo paint their assailants were wearing.

They heard leaves crackle beneath someone's feet as he moved up behind them. Then the sheriff felt something pressing down on his shoulder, and looked down to see the barrel of a rifle. Having no other option, he dropped to his knees. Without a word, his friend knelt beside him. As their assailant moved to one side, the sheriff could see that he was dressed in Chinese military fatigues.

Well, the sheriff thought, *out of the frying pan and into the fire.* He frowned. *Except now we have a much shorter life-expectancy than when we were just part of a group of prisoners loading trucks.*

His attention was captured when several men stepped into the small clearing. They heard a laugh, and the sheriff dared to turn his head to look for the source.

"Well, look what the cat dragged in," the man said. The sheriff looked at him in disbelief. It was one of his former deputies, dressed up like a Chinese soldier, and he dared an angry response.

"I can't believe that you've become a Chinese mercenary, Carlson," he responded.

"What, Chinese?" he laughed. "No way! Ed Bower, the owner of the feed and grain, got these weapons and uniforms for us from the stock the Chinese stored in his warehouse. We pulled off the Chinese insignias and plan to dye them a different shade as soon as we can."

The sheriff's next words struck the smile from Carlson's face. "Well, you might be interested to learn that the Chinese plan to burn Ed Bower alive later today for that very reason."

"We'll see about that!" Carlson responded, his anger infusing the words.

Turning to the others, Carlson introduced the two men as friends. Then, wasting no time, and leaving several men behind to watch the feed and grain store from the forest's edge, Carlson led them through the woods to a larger clearing where several dozen armed men were gathered.

They were led to Jack Kenzy, the elected leader of the group, who immediately revealed that he was well-acquainted with them. In what had been a closely guarded secret, they had all been members of a select group that had exchanged encrypted emails for several years prior to the outbreak of war. More recently they had comprised the core of the local underground. Now they were looking one another over with smiles. After a long wait, they were finally determined to undertake aggressive action against the enemy.

The group listened avidly as the two men gave a brief account of what had been going on at the feed and grain store. As additional men gathered about them, they related the news that the Chinese invaders were evidently in trouble, and a sense of excitement pervaded the atmosphere. Their excitement turned to rage, however, when they learned that the Chinese general planned to execute Ed Bower by burning him alive.

Pastor Kenzy introduced the younger of the two men as Michael Webb, the former fire chief of Black River Junction. Then he introduced John Thomas as the sheriff of Black River County. The possible addition of an experienced law officer to their ranks brought smiles to the faces of the men present.

Webb stepped forward and repeated what the two of them had overheard at the co-op. He told them of the general's plan to burn the place down around the owner's ears, and the sheriff interrupted to tell them that that they also planned to murder a Chinese-American along with their friend.

When Kenzy asked the name of the man, the sheriff said, "They're going to kill Kim Ling, Jack. We need to go get them both out of there."

"Who's this Kim Ling?" someone demanded, "and what do we care about another Chinaman?"

"Yeah," someone else agreed. "It's Ed Bower we care about. He's been nothing but a blessing to the people of Butter Creek. What do we care about some Chink?"

"There's no question that we must save Ed Bower," Kenzy replied, "but this *Chink*, as you call him, is as American as any of us, and has, at the risk of his own life, been providing us with most of the meaningful intelligence that we've received. Ling has already lost his wife and children, and if he doesn't top the list of people that should matter to us, he's mighty close." He paused for effect, then went on. "Even if we didn't have an obligation to him as fellow Christians, Kim Ling undoubtedly possesses information vital to our cause."

The sheriff held up his hand for attention. When the group grew silent, he added, "We can also use his skills as a helicopter pilot."

"He's that Kim Ling?" someone in the back of the crowd asked. "I used to love his politically incorrect news reports on Burlington TV."

The group's respect for Kenzy couldn't be greater, and the combined remarks of Ling's three supporters stilled any further criticism. They all pushed forward to greet these two new members of the group, and while some were discussing their concern about the Chinese plan to murder their friend and benefactor, Kenzy's mind was taking a different turn.

He carefully examined the sheriff's face. The man was perhaps forty years old, an inch over six feet, well-built, with a square jaw, blue-gray eyes and dark hair graying at the temples. The laugh wrinkles around his eyes spoke of a healthy personality, while the lines etched about his mouth revealed the cares he'd been bearing. In uniform he'd be the poster boy for law enforcement officers.

The fire chief was physically more imposing, but lacked the sheriff's force of personality and keen intelligence. As the pastor studied the two men, it occurred to him that the chief was a Watson to the sheriff's Holmes. Then his thoughts turned another corner.

Up until now, he thought, *we've limited ourselves to guerrilla warfare — sniping at the enemy, attacking his aircraft, and limiting ourselves to assaulting inferior forces with overwhelming superiority. But with his experience as county sheriff, and his knowledge of Black River County and its people, he is especially welcome at this time, particularly if we are going to fight our first real battle there. In fact,* Kenzy reasoned with humility, *he's definitely more qualified to lead our little group than I am.*

While the pastor was musing over the sheriff's qualifications as a leader, a general discussion had begun concerning what might be done to rescue the two condemned men at the feed and grain store. As the sheriff sought to quiet them down and bring order to the discussion, a young man, a former lieutenant in the national guard, made his way through the woods toward the group. He had been scouting the Chinese positions around the store.

I wish we had a lot more men with his experience, Kenzy thought, as he watched him make his way toward him through the crowd. As he drew near, he shouted, "Pastor, I think we can take those guys."

"Ah," Kenzy smiled, "our prodigal scout returneth unscathed." That brought a laugh from a few of the men. Then he turned to the sheriff and the fire chief. Pointing toward the approaching man, he told them, "Karl Nielsen is our most experienced man. He served tours in both Iraq and Afghanistan."

The fire chief turned and saw a man of medium height, well-muscled, with a definite military bearing, approaching.

"Nielsen had been looking at the pastor, but then he noticed the standing next to him. In an almost Pavlovian reflex, he stopped, snapped to attention, and saluted smartly. The others were startled at this unusual behavior, but then realized that he was not saluting the pastor; he was saluting the sheriff. The sheriff appeared both surprised and embarrassed, but responded by waving his hand toward his forehead in what might charitably have been called a salute.

Neither of the men was in uniform, but there was no question in anyone's mind that they had both served in the military.

"Karl, how are you?" the sheriff asked, a warm smile lighting his face.

"I'm just fine, sir," Nielsen replied. Then he gushed, "Carol had another baby."

"What's that make now, two boys and two girls?"

"Nope," he laughed. It's three of each now."

Everyone laughed when the sheriff commented, "You've spending too much time at home."

But the group went silent when they noticed that Nielsen had been staring at the sheriff with something between hero-worship and awe.

"General," he said, "you have no idea how glad I am to see you alive."

"General?" Kenzy asked. He had no idea that the sheriff had also served in the military.

"Just a Brigadier," the sheriff replied.

Nielsen wouldn't let it rest at that. Turning to the group, he said, "General Thomas was my commanding officer in the National Guard before the federal government shut the Guard down and disarmed us for refusing to take up arms against our own citizens. Before that, I served under his command during a tour in Afghanistan." Then he added, "He's got The Medal."

"The medal?" Kenzy repeated.

"Yes, the *Medal of Honor*, what some mistakenly call the *Congressional Medal of Honor*."

The sheriff, obviously embarrassed, broke the ensuing silence. "Captain Nielsen was one of my battalion commanders before I made him my personal aide."

"General," Nielsen remonstrated, "you know that all I ever wanted to do was command a battalion. I didn't want to be your dog robber!"

"Yes, and I had to constantly remind you that junior officers do not argue with their superiors and that you lacked the wisdom to see that the pathway to promotion required you to serve as my aide for a while. But that's neither here nor there. This is a different war, and all of us are going to have to fit in wherever we can do the most good."

"What's a dog robber?" Kenzy asked absently.

"Dog robbers," the sheriff replied, "are aides-de-camp who are shameless, fearless, and desperate enough to snatch food from the mouths of snarling dogs or starving babies in order to keep meat on their general's tables."

Most of the people around the circle laughed appreciatively, but Kenzy's thoughts were elsewhere.

"Is that so?" he asked absently. "Why would a general run for sheriff?"

The sheriff's voice became flat. "Because I was no longer a general. I wasn't nearly old enough to retire, but because I wouldn't align myself with the politicians, they got rid of me."

Kenzy nodded his understanding, then changed the subject, leaving everyone confused. They looked at him as if he were somehow disconnected, and in truth he was. Turning to the sheriff, he asked, "Correct me if I'm wrong, but did I just understand you to say that we are all going to have to fit in wherever each of us can do the most good?"

"That about sums it up, yes," replied the sheriff, as confused as everyone else by the direction the conversation was taking.

Then Kenzy surprised everyone by clapping his hands together, slowly at first, but more rapidly as a number of the others joined him. The retired general and the fire chief looked totally adrift, and simply stared at him as though he might have come unglued.

When the pastor stopped clapping, the others followed suit, but again his listeners found it impossible to follow his thoughts, for he seemed to go off on an entirely different tack.

"Recognizing valor is very important," Kenzy commented. "The American people have a great debt to these two men, and he pointed toward the just-identified general and his former adjutant. And that's not to speak of the fire chief, as well as any other first responders that may be here among us. It's a debt that we can never repay."

"Reverend,...." the embarrassed sheriff tried to interrupt, but Kenzy waved him to silence and went on.

"The way our veterans were treated after Vietnam is a grave blot on our country's history, but in a way, what happened to the brave men who fought to preserve world-freedom in Somalia, Iraq, Afghanistan, and throughout the world was worse."

A few faces revealed their confusion, but the preacher pressed on.

"The number of suicides among the men who returned from Afghanistan and Iraq was unprecedented in the history of war and can be traced directly to the leadership failures in Washington.

"Too many of our heroes returned home in flag-draped coffins. Others suffered terrible injuries that would leave them mentally and physically crippled for the remainder of their lives. But virtually everyone who came home from those wars were wounded in some way. And when the dead came home, some were refused honor guards, military salutes and Christian prayer. So their wounds might not have been visible flesh-and-blood wounds, but they were nevertheless wounded to the depths of their being.

"And we all know what they came home to," he said, his voice rising in indignation. "They came home to a government that was apologizing for our nation, asking forgiveness from the very perpetrators of evil that were murdering our people, especially the misguided religious fanatics who sought to destroy America."

"Hey, Pastor," someone shouted, "you're preaching to the choir."

"I suppose so," he agreed, "but it's a good time for this reminder because some of us are about to put our lives on the line, and we'd better know why."

"All of us, Jack!" someone else declared. "We're all going to put our lives on the line. No more pussy-footing around!"

And there was a chorus of amens.

"So get to the point," someone else shouted. "You're acting like one of them long-winded preachers."

"Okay," Kenzy laughed with the others. "One more observation, and then I'll make my point. We Americans became so full of ourselves, so hungry to satisfy our own lusts and desires, that we couldn't see that we were trading off our liberties for an illusion of security and short-term pleasures. And because we took this fire to our bosom, people from around the world who were sworn to destroy us wound up running our country. We were not defeated from outside. We rotted out from within, and millions of Americans have perished as a result of our collective failures.

"And that's why we are here today, you and me. We are engaged in a war to restore a nation where peaceful and industrious people will be safe from those who would slaughter others in the name of their perverted religion and destructive philosophies."

The preacher took a deep breath and got his voice under control. Then he shouted, "And now it's time to take our country back!"

"We're with you, Pastor," someone shouted, "so let's get this show on the road!"

This put an end to the speechmaking, but the general was thinking something else. *If we ever do restore our electoral process, Jack Kenzy should be our next U.S. Senator.*

And Kenzy was thinking something entirely different. *If we are going to have an army here, it's General John Thomas, not I, who ought to lead it.*

And he said so.

CC Abandons Hidden Valley
Caverns at West End of Hidden Valley
Vermont
May 2nd, 7:35 a.m.

CC stared up through the limbs of the enormous hemlock which rose high above the beach on which he lay, and tried to comprehend the enormity of the disaster that had overtaken his tiny fellowship.

Yes, he was grateful that he had not perished with General Eng and his pilot when their helicopter crashed and exploded. And, of course he was grateful that he had somehow been ejected through the cargo bay door prior to the crash. And he was still trying to understand how he could have fallen sixty or seventy feet, buffeted from branch to branch through the enormous evergreen above him, only to splash down relatively uninjured in the shallow water of the lake.

Talk about having Him give his angels charge over me! he thought. *This was a miracle.*

But in spite of the fact that he had survived the crash, he couldn't dismiss the pain. Nor could he decide which injury hurt more – the massive bruise on his thigh or the blow he'd received to his head when he'd hit the bottom of the lake. He was having difficulty focusing his eyes, and with his blurred vision he didn't need a doctor to tell him that he was probably suffering from a severe concussion.

As CC looked up through the evergreen's fuzzy growth, his muddled thoughts wandered back to the Impressionists, and he was amused by the possibility that those 19th Century painters owed their success more to poor eyesight than to artistic insight.

Then his thoughts turned from famous painters to his own little groups' dismal prospects. Yet, as his eyes focused on the undersides of the spreading branches that had broken his fall, he found himself ashamed that he was once again, and so soon, questioning God's loving care.

Just thirty minutes earlier they had all survived an attack made on them from a helicopter. That assault, coming from the air, had been a shocking surprise, and they owed their unexpected survival to the courage and uncanny marksmanship of their new-found friend, Joseph Sennett.

CC couldn't deny the fact, however, that although the five of them had survived, they now faced tremendous obstacles. They had fled the well-stocked cave that had served as their home for over a year and traveled west through a labyrinth of tunnels to reach the far side of the mountain that enclosed Hidden Valley. They were running for their lives, trying to escape from the pursuing Chinese.

Yet, something else was occupying CC's thoughts that made all these other events pale by comparison. It was for him at once both shocking and frightening. He was recovering his memory. Perhaps the blow to the head explained it, but he was experiencing a strange kaleidoscope of revived memories. It was both fascinating and terrifying. He suddenly *knew* that the woman he'd seen the night he escaped from the Butter Creek Inn was his wife, but he still could not remember his own name. And just as suddenly he realized that he had once been a radio talk show host, but beyond that, little else.

He was at war within himself. He realized that he was badly hurt and should not try to move about. At the same time, he knew that they all had to get away from this place before more of their enemy caught up with them.

He was convinced that it was the hand of God that had saved the five of them from almost certain death, and it would be the hand of God that would assure their escape.

His mind flashed back to that morning's attack. It had come just as the five of them left the security of those dark caverns and gathered on the ledge that extended over the lake below.

While they had been looking in different directions — one staring upward at the soaring cliffs, another out across the ledge to the breathless beauty of the lake and the forest beyond — Sarah had slipped away. It was Jonathan who first noticed her as she leaned out over the edge of the cliff, exclaiming at the lakeshore far below.

"Sarah, get away from there before you fall," Jonathan had shouted, but it was a moment before she turned and obediently backed away. It was at that moment that they heard the strange whop-whop of an approaching helicopter.

"Back to the cave!" CC had shouted, but it was already too late.

The sound became almost deafening as the helicopter crossed the top of the mountain and hovered high above them for a moment, then suddenly dropped toward them. The dust and grit that were whipped up by the revolving blades nearly blinded them, and the crashing sound of machine gun bullets smashing into the ledge and chipping rock from the cliffside brought terror to their hearts. Those who found themselves too far from the cave entrance ducked behind the large boulders that lay scattered along the ledge, but Sarah was caught in the open. Her screams were drowned out by the roar of the copter's engine and the clatter of a machine gun, and she stood there shaking like a reed in the wind, her eyes tightly closed, her little hands covering her ears.

It was CC, almost mad with terror for the little one, who had run out from shelter of the cave and dared to wave the copter off. Oddly, the gunfire did stop, but then the helicopter swept down to hover just above the edge of the cliff. Then a uniformed Chinese officer leaned out of the door and waved an automatic weapon at CC, beckoning imperiously for him to climb into the cargo compartment. CC stared at him, then ran to Sarah, hugged her to him, shouted something in her ear, and when she began to calm down, turned her around, physically pointed her at the cave, and yelled at her to run to Jonathan. Only after the teen had run out to gather her in his arms, and they had reached the safety of the cave, did CC turn and obediently move toward the copter. It was then that he had recognized the face of General Eng.

The last time I saw him was at the radio studio in Chicago, the day before the war. He was being handed a briefcase full of money by a guy I thought was a squeaky-clean politician.

CC reeled with the shock of his awakening memory, almost losing his grip on the aircraft's frame as he climbed up into the cargo bay.

It was clear that the general cared nothing for CC's motley little band. His actions indicated that he was more than satisfied to have captured CC, and as the helicopter had lifted abruptly away from the dangerous cliffside. To those watching from the mouth of the cavern, the general seemed to be playing games with him inside the copter. CC was made to sit on the deck in the small cargo hold behind the general's seat, while the general waved some article of clothing at him.

It was while the general was trying to terrorize his captive that his pilot noticed a man standing on the pinnacle of the cliff. When the pilot pointed him out, the general seemed to recognize him, and immediately ordered the airman to climb to a position where he could bring the man under fire. Things didn't turn out quite the way the general planned.

The man at the top of the cliff was Joseph Sennett, Jr., and his unexpected arrival probably changed the course of the war. Balanced on a spire of rock at the top of the cliff, he fired his rifle repeatedly at the perspex windshield of the copter, fatally wounding the pilot. Out of control, the helicopter had spun down the cliffside until one of its blades had hit the ledge and snapped off, catapulting the helicopter up and over.

CC had been kneeling in the cargo area, and the violent motion had catapulted him out the cargo door as the helicopter with its two occupants crashed into the lake, exploded in flame, and slowly settled to the bottom. At the same time, CC sailed through the air, struck the top of a tall evergreen and tumbled down through its thick branches to the water below. Breaking the surface, he remained conscious and was able to struggle to shallow water in spite of a blow to his head and severe bruising to his right thigh.

Injuries to the other four members of his group were limited to cuts and bruises caused by the rock chips that were sent flying by the machine gun bullets. Their injuries, however, were relatively minor, the greatest damage being the shock from the terror they'd experienced.

The others had made their way down a narrow ledge, and gathered on the lakeshore to join CC. They treated their wounds and began making final preparations for their long journey through the forest. There ultimate goal was the cave that Sennett had told them about.

They could see water riffling around a single twisted propellor blade that extended up out of the water, and seemed to point accusingly toward the top of the cliff where Sennett stood surveying the scene.

As they checked the contents of their backpacks, they were again reminded of how dangerously short they were of food and other necessities. CC divided his three magnetic compasses among them. One was to be shared by the two women, Rachel and Elizabeth; the second went to the teenager, Jonathan; and CC kept the third for himself.

"Where's mine?" little Sarah had asked, disappointment evident in her voice.

"I'm sorry, Sarah," CC told her. As always, he addressed her with respect, as he would an adult. "We are blessed to have even three compasses, and we wouldn't have these if that man we met in the cave hadn't given us one of his."

"But why don't I have one?" the 8-year old asked.

"Well, they are pretty complicated things to master, and we don't have time to teach you right now. Okay?"

"Okay," she replied unconvincingly. Her lower lip quivering, she tried to sound cheerful as she asked, "Maybe later?"

"You bet, Honey."

Compass or no compass, when CC pulled out the map that Joseph Sennett had given him a few hours earlier and pointed out their destination far to the northwest, Sarah paid close attention. Everyone else thought that the child's interest was cute, but not

Jonathan. Only a few days earlier he had been explaining to her how the scale on a map corresponded to various distances over the earth's surface, and how the various symbols represented mountains, rivers, and highways, and Jonathan was amazed at how quickly his precocious "little sister" had caught on to the concept of relative distances.

He remembered flattening the map out before her, then spreading his thumb and forefinger over the length of Hidden Valley. "In this case," he had told her, "one inch on the map equals about one mile on the ground." He didn't think she understood any of it until she took her little fingers and laid them across the scale of miles at the bottom of the map, then placed them above the highway between Hidden Valley and the Green Mountain Feed and Grain Store.

"So," she declared without fear of contradiction, "it's about three-and-a-half miles from where we live to where CC found the motorhome."

Jonathan had been stunned by the ability of an 8-year old to so quickly comprehend a relatively abstract concept and had checked her understanding by watching her scaling inches to miles all over the map. He hadn't had an opportunity to share the discovery of her amazing ability with the others, and didn't think that now was the time to bring it up.

While they were getting a quick tutorial on how to use the compasses, Sarah put her mouth up against Jonathan's ear. He tipped his head away quickly because it tickled when she whispered.

"It looks to me like it's thirty miles from here to that cave," she said, "but don't you think we will have to zigzag all over the place to get there?"

"I'm afraid so," he whispered back, "and in that rugged terrain it could take a week or two."

Rugged terrain? That's an understatement, he thought. *These are virgin forests with deadfalls everywhere. The trunks of trees lie hidden beneath moss and undergrowth. It's difficult to even see them, much less climb over them. And in some cases it will be impossible for Sarah.*

Jonathan looked at CC, his beloved mentor and friend, and wondered, *What can you be thinking?* Then he felt ashamed. It doesn't matter how difficult the journey might prove to be. We have no choice.

Sarah interrupted his gloomy musings. "If it will take a week or more, what will we eat? We only have enough food for a couple of days, don't we?"

How is it that the child among us has put her finger squarely on our problem, he wondered. *And that's not to speak of the fact that we're apt to have a bunch of well-fed soldiers chasing us while we're looking for nuts and berries to keep from starving.*

He didn't share these further discouraging thoughts with Sarah, but instead whispered back, "We're going to have to do our best to conserve our food, Honey."

And then she surprised him again, hissing into his ear. "If we stay near the water, we can fish." And he wondered whether anyone else had thought of that. Receiving an annoyed look from CC, he put his finger to his lips to forestall further questions, but she wasn't to be dismissed so easily. She put her mouth up to his ear again, and in an exaggerated whisper said, "Yes, and we need to trust Jesus."

Everyone heard that and turned to smile at her, and there wasn't a supercilious expression among them. The general consensus was, *"We could all learn something about faith from Sarah."*

Jonathan stared at her. *She's aware that our destination is a remote cavern far to the northwest and, to her credit, she harbors few illusions about the difficulty we will experience in reaching it. She understands that we will require days of difficult hiking through rugged forests, but I honestly doubt that her little legs will get her through. Yet she's stubborn and full of faith and might make it on sheer grit.*

As was so often the case, his relationship with this redoubtable little girl left him feeling oddly confident that she would survive even if she were once again cast alone on her own resources.

Turning his thoughts away from Sarah, Jonathan realized that he was still filled with anxiety. He was, as a rule, a very positive teenager, but today he suffered nagging doubts, doubts that he was unable to shake.

What's wrong with me? he wondered. *Less than an hour ago we were almost killed by a madman in a helicopter. After surviving that, why should I be nervous?* He stared out across the lake, and it came to him. Apart from all the challenges they had faced an hour earlier, things were now worse. Much worse! CC was hurt. *What else is going to happen?* he wondered, and his shoulders tensed as he began a mental inventory of potential problems.

The answer was obvious. There was the matter of their having left Jim McCord alive back in the caverns. Elizabeth had wanted to shoot him, but Jonathan wondered whether she would really have done so. He'd never heard the story of how she'd fought off an attacker in the sub-basement of the art museum.

Jonathan thought about the danger that McCord represented to them. CC had insisted that he and Elizabeth leave him bound and gagged in a location where someone would find him before he died of starvation. Jonathan had no doubt that CC's merciful act would ultimately boomerang on them, resulting in even more misery for the group. And Elizabeth agreed with him that, if the Chinese or their henchmen found McCord, he would happily lead them through the caverns in pursuit of CC.

Again Jonathan tried to shake himself free of his fears. He noticed that Sarah was watching keenly as Elizabeth smoothed out a map of central Vermont. She then laid tracing paper over that portion of the map from Allison Lake, where they were now resting, northwest to the area containing the cave that Joseph Sennett had marked as their goal. Then Elizabeth began to carefully trace the outline of the lake, and marking the major landmarks such as roads, streams, and mountains.

When Elizabeth noticed that Sarah was looking over her shoulder, trying to produce her own copy, she smiled at the child's clumsy efforts.

"I'm making one of these for each person carrying a compass, and if you would like one, Sarah, I'll copy it for you too."

The child's radiant smile was sufficient response, and Elizabeth worked quickly to trace the last of the maps they would need to reach the remote cavern.

It had taken them nearly an hour to pull themselves together and begin moving away from the mountain that stood between them and the beautiful valley where they had lived for the past year. In spite of the fact that they would probably never return, CC felt as though there was a magnet drawing him back. It was a battle simply to lift one foot up and put it down in front of the other. And when he studied the faces of his four friends, he realized that they too were probably feeling the same awful regrets. It was a paradise lost!

In spite of the fact that Joe Sennett had given them directions to his own well-stocked hideaway, none of them wanted to leave their relatively luxurious home with its large stock of food and supplies, its working farm, and its countless comforts.

Each of them had different feelings concerning Sennett. CC knew that Sennett had been defamed, and thought most of the notoriety was false. Sennett had left Rachel standing at the altar. She was no longer in love with him, and acknowledged that perhaps she never had been, but she still liked and respected him. Elizabeth, on the other hand, would desert the group in a moment to go with him wherever he asked. After watching Sennett shoot down the helicopter, and take a bullet for his pains, Jonathan thought almost as much of Sennett as he did of CC. And Sarah? Almost every night of her life, she had sat on her grandmother's bed for Bible reading and prayer. One of the people she had prayed for was a man whose picture sat on an end table by the bed – Joseph Sennett, Jr. Sarah had a deep love for this man in spite of the fact that she'd never been told that he was actually her father.

None of them was absolutely sure that Sennett's account about his cavern wasn't exaggerated, but since they were grasping at straws, and since the man had been wounded while saving their lives, they were inclined to trust his claims. The sad truth was that they had nowhere else to go. The frightening truth was that they would have to hike thirty or forty miles through almost impossible terrain to find his well-hidden cavern, and if it didn't prove to be as promised, they would probably starve to death during the coming winter. Finally, even if Sennett's cave existed, and it were everything he promised, locating it would be a bit like finding the proverbial needle in a haystack.

Worse, they knew that their enemies were likely to follow them through the caverns that they had just vacated, winding their way through the natural and manmade tunnels that riddled the mountain at the west end of Hidden Valley. Those same caverns had once offered them security, but now their enemies were likely to come streaming out of the caves, like ants crawling out of their mound, ready to sting and kill them. For the moment, however, the group could only hope that they might have a little breathing space before they were followed. Jonathan considered that possibility highly unlikely.

A couple of them had suffered cuts and bruises from rock fragments that had struck them when they'd been strafed from the helicopter, but CC's severely bruised hip and concussion comprised the worst injuries. Even without the necessity of carrying a weapon and a heavy pack, Jonathan knew that CC was going to slow the group down.

After everyone had been checked, their minor injuries treated, and the contents of their packs redistributed according to their needs and their ability to carry them, the five entered the forest where it grew almost to the waterline along the south end of the lake.

Before leaving the beach and following the others into the woods, Jonathan glanced across the lake toward Tower Rock. It stood almost a mile to the west, on the south end of the lake, and was the place where he and CC had hidden a cache of food, clothing, and weapons.

Then Jonathan took one last look up the length of the lake. He wished they had a boat. He couldn't imagine struggling through the trees and underbrush that ran along its perimeter. One could scarcely fight his way through the thick undergrowth, much less climb over the fallen and decaying trees. He thought of little Sarah and realized that she would have to be carried much of the time for she would often be up to her neck in the undergrowth.

As he turned to follow the others, he thought it ironic that they were going south when their destination lay to the northwest. But geographic boundaries – in this case, the lake – dictated their movements. They had to hike around its south end, then move off to the northwest.

A Morning Ritual

Near Tower Point
Allison Lake
1st of May, Sunrise

It had become almost a ritual for Chris. Each morning, she would leave the Towers' snug little cabin and make her way to the southwest corner of Allison Lake for her daily devotions. She invariably took the same seat on the same rock, and with an insulated container of precious coffee in hand, she would watch the sun rise.

This morning was no different. She checked to make certain that the binoculars the Towers had loaned her were hung securely from the leather strap about her neck, then set her insulated coffee container down on the cold rock next to the Bible they'd given her.

In the false dawn that preceded the sun's actual appearance, she put the binoculars to her eyes and peered at the far shoreline, carefully rotating the adjustment wheel to bring them into focus, trying to make certain that there was no human activity.

Then she turned her attention to the southeast shore, being careful not to focus on the top of the cliffs. Experience had taught her that she would be momentarily blinded when the sun crept over the mountaintop. It never ceased to amaze her how, when the sun began to clear the peak, the lake would take on a new dimension as it was suddenly shot with light.

Then, concerned that she might see the men who had assaulted them months earlier, she would sweep the entire length of the far shore with the field glasses, starting at the southeast corner of the lake.

She had long since concluded that the two men who had attacked her at Liberty Christian Camp had ultimately been responsible for the death of her daughter. Yet, searching the far shore for any hint of their presence was becoming less of a compulsion, for she had begun to believe that they had not survived their attacks on her and her children.

The one man who had shot at them when they were escaping from the Christian camp had evidently had his rifle explode in his face. He would be at least temporarily blinded and deafened, and without medicines and proper treatment, his wounds might well have infected and ultimately proven fatal.

And the second man, the one who had followed them down the lake and shot her, had been run over by Michael on their snowmobile. Then Michael had turned and run over him. If the man had suffered broken bones or severe bruising, and had been unable to drag himself off the lake and find shelter before the blizzard had resumed, his remains might still be laying on the ice on the far side of the lake.

She shook her head to rid herself of these visions. She had no regrets about any suffering that might have been suffered by those evil men.

They laid their traps, and they fell into them! Her mind couldn't set the business aside. *If we could have stayed in that cottage at the Christian camp until morning, as Pastor Kenzy had planned for us, and if those men hadn't chased us, and if we weren't forced to race across the lake in the dark, Michael would never have crashed into that rock and my little girl would be alive right now. If, if...IF!*

A tear rolled down her cheek, but before she could succumb to her sorrows, her attention was captured by a strange noise from across the lake. She heard a *whoppa, whoppa, whoppa,* and focused her glasses on the far side just in time to see a helicopter sweep across the face of the cliff. It hovered for a moment high above the lake, then slowly dropped down until it seemed to hang just above a ledge. She laughed. Helicopter! Her husband had told her that the proper name was "rotary-winged aircraft."

Funny, she thought as she studied the face of the cliff. *I never noticed that cave opening before.* Then she remembered that Don Tower had told her that his good friends, Nick and Mary Sennett lived in a little valley on the far side of that mountain, and that the mountain itself was riddled with natural and manmade caves.

As she continued sweeping the cliff with the powerful glasses, she saw several figures dashing across the ledge. Their images were so small that she had to hold the binoculars firmly in order to keep them in view. She was shocked when she heard a sharp staccato sound override the racket made by the helicopter, and she realized that it must be the sound of an automatic weapon.

The events that followed occurred so quickly that she found it difficult to grasp their significance. The helicopter hovered just above the ledge, and it looked like it was going to set down atop a little child. She caught her breath. *Could it be?* She wondered. Being careful not to swing the binoculars away, she very carefully adjusted the range. *No,* she thought with bitter disappointment. *It's not Mary.* As she continued to watch, someone ran out to guide the child back toward the cave, and she soon disappeared from view. Then the child's rescuer moved toward the aircraft, his hands in the air. She couldn't believe her eyes. *It's David,* she exulted. *It's my husband.*

But after a moment, he disappeared inside the fuselage, and reality set in.

She tipped the binoculars slightly in order to keep the helicopter in view as it suddenly rose rapidly up the face of the cliff. Then she heard the machine gun again, and scanned the cliff to see what they were shooting at. High up on the top of the cliff stood a big man wearing a camouflage outfit and carrying a long gun. She caught sight of him just as, in one fluid motion, he snapped the stock to his shoulder, aimed, and fired. A couple of seconds later she heard the unmistakable crack of the high-powered rifle. It was very confusing because the sounds that echoed across the lake were arriving a second or more behind what she was witnessing with her eyes, so about the time she heard the rifle shot, the helicopter began spinning around as though out of control.

Then the helicopter seemed to be falling down the face of the cliff. As it neared the ledge, the tip of one of its propeller blades struck the ledge on which the people had been standing a minute or two earlier. The blade snapped off, the helicopter seemed to spring back into the sky, and flipped upside down as it was catapulted out over the lake.

Someone was cast out of the cargo door, and she knew it had to be her husband. Even if a restraining belt had been available, he would not have had time to struggle into it. Chris was not aware that she was holding her breath as she watched his body spin through the air, finally landing in the top of a huge evergreen. Then she watched as he seemed to flop from branch to branch until he landed in the lake below.

She didn't see what happened to him because her senses were suddenly overwhelmed when the helicopter struck a massive boulder that rose up out of the lake, and exploded in flame and smoke. The

the concussion struck her, and even a mile away, she swayed for a moment, fighting to keep her footing on the rock. Then she stared in horror as the burning wreckage tumbled from the rock and disappeared beneath the waters of the lake, leaving only a pool of burning oil to mark its burial place. Her fevered mind, however, was no longer properly interpreting what she was seeing.

She was no longer seeing the helicopter, nor even her husband falling to his almost certain death. Instead she imagined a snowmobile racing across the ice, crashing into a boulder, bouncing into the air and smashing back down. She felt the shock and pain as she thrown from the vehicle and slammed onto the ice, and to feel darkness close in, but not before she watched helplessly as the snowmobile struck the ice and she watched helplessly as the snowmobile, with her little girl's body caught on the rear seat, slid across the ice, slipped over the edge, and disappeared beneath open water. Then there was only blackness. The dream was horrible. She blinked her eyes to try to rid them of the vision. She didn't realize that she was crying aloud, "Oh, God! Oh, God!"

Then the strangest thing happened. The vision wasn't over. A dour looking woman appeared walking waist deep in the water. The woman bent down, tugged on something, and drew the unconscious child from the freezing water. Chris again screamed in anguish and confusion. And then the vision evaporated.

It was almost more than she could bear. She hadn't even realized that she had risen to her feet, tears in her eyes, until she heard Don Tower called to her.

"You need to come down from there," he said. He had to repeat himself, and when she finally turned to look at him, he realized that she was in shock and he suspected what was going through her mind.

She wanted to shout that her daughter might not be dead. She wanted to shout that her husband was just over there, and needed her help, and her shaking finger actually reached in that direction, but it was as though her throat was paralyzed.

"We've got to get out of here," he shouted.

She stared at him for a moment, as though trying to comprehend his words.

"Where there is a helicopter," he said, "enemy troops can't be far away."

She raised her eyebrows in surprise. "But aren't we going to try to help them?"

"Help them? Help who?"

"Why the people that the helicopter was shooting at. My husband," she croaked. "They may be hurt. And if the Chinese were shooting at them, then they must all be good people."

"Look Chris, we don't know anything about what's going on over there. The Chinese might have been attacking a group of trouble makers, people who are as great a danger to us as to them. Or they might be fighting the Russians or ISIS. We would only put ourselves at risk by getting involved."

"But I think I saw my husband," she jabbered. "I saw a little girl...."

"We have got to get out of here," he insisted.

She stared at him dumbly, as though trying to comprehend his words.

She turned and pointed across the lake. Her mouth worked, but no words came out. Finally she found her voice, her eyes wide with shock and disappointment.

"Aren't we going to try to help them?"

"Help them? Help who?" he asked.

"Why, the people that the helicopter was shooting at. They may be hurt. And if the Chinese were shooting at them, then they must be good people. "*Maybe even my husband, she thought.* Then she had a strange thought, and clung fiercely to it. "I saw my husband up there!" and she pointed vaguely toward the ledge.

He forced himself to be calm and tolerant.

"That may well be," he said, making allowance for her excitement and the stress she'd been under for months. "although I can't understand how you could make out anyone's identity from this distance," and Chris was forced to admit to herself that he was right. Maybe it wasn't David.

Don Tower went on reasonably. "I can't offer any explanation for that, but I will observe that you've been under a lot of stress. People under stress sometimes see things differently."

"Are you saying that I'm delusional, Don? Crazy? Out of my mind?"

"No, no. Of course not," he answered hurriedly. Regardless of the truth, I know that we can't get around the end of the lake in time to make any difference anyway. And even if we reached that place, we would be apt to run into a patrol of Chinese troops looking for their missing helicopter. We might even be attacked by the very people you want to help."

"Well, what can we do?" she asked in desperation.

"If there are troops, they might come this way. We need to lock ourselves in the missile silo in case they show up."

When she didn't respond, he persisted. "You need to take care of your son." Chris. You are all that Michael has left."

"I care about my son more than you'll ever know," she rasped, "but there might be someone over there in desperate need of our help. I can't help wondering, What if my husband is over there?"

"There's one more thing, but I hate to offer false hope."

"What's that?" she asked, eager for any encouragement.

"If the man you saw is leaving the caverns, there are only two ways he can go."

She stopped, and since he was following her through the thick brush along the shoreline, he was forced to stop too. Looking into his eyes, she waited.

"We're in a valley here. He might try to push his way toward the west, but there are sheer cliffs a couple of miles out, so west is unlikely."

She nodded her understanding, wondering where he was going with this.

"He could go south, which seems the most logical course, except that the Chinese occupied Black River Junction months ago, and that's pretty common knowledge."

"I still don't understand," she shrugged impatiently, indicating that he should get to the point.

"Unless he has a boat, he can't go north up the other side of the lake because the cliffs come right down to the water in place."

Her eyes seemed to open in understanding.

"So," she said, "he might come around this side of the lake? We might see him?"

"It's probably a long shot, and I hate to hold out false hope, but yes," he said.

And she took his statement for what it might be worth, not holding out undue hope, but still determined to be watchful for any strangers coming their way. Then she had another inspiration, and looked back toward the woods that hid his little airplane hangar.

"Couldn't you take your plane and see what's going on?" she pleaded.

He frowned, then shook his head.

"No. I'm sorry. Right now nobody knows that we have an operable aircraft. If there are Chinese over there, and they saw me take off in it, they would be here waiting when I landed. We'd lose the plane and probably our lives."

Her chin dropped to her chest. She was defeated.

"But your son is here, and alive!" he persisted, and she stared at him for a moment before grudgingly nodding her understanding. After a moment, with tears again filling her eyes, she bent to pick up her Bible.

As she made her way down off the rocky shelf, she turned to him. "What about your cottage?" she asked. "What about your airplane?"

"We'll have to pray that they will remain undiscovered," he replied. "What's important is that we survive." He had a thought. "If we survive, maybe we will still be able to look for your husband."

They were just entering the cover of the trees when she stopped to look back, and he turned to follow her gaze. The smoke from the burning helicopter had dissipated, and without the aid of the binoculars, she saw no sign of life at all.

"You're right," she said. "I can't be tramping off to help a couple of strangers. My family has to come first."

The Broken Fellowship
Allison Lake, Vermont
May 2nd, 8:55 a.m.

The huge old trees at the south end of Allison lake were spaced far apart and the land beneath was relatively clear of undergrowth, almost like a park. CC led the others up the gradual slope away from the lake shore, and after about a half mile they found themselves on the edge of a large meadow.

They stopped to admire a half-dozen white-tail deer that were grazing on the far edge. They were all captivated by the scene, but CC became concerned when their tails, like little flags, suddenly fluttered and the herd began to race away from the shelter of the far trees and come directly toward them. But when they had almost reached them, they changed their minds and swung around to race toward the trees to the south.

"I guess we frightened them," Rachel suggested, but CC wasn't so sure.

He shook his head. "No, I don't think so. They were frightened by something or someone on the west side of the meadow.. If they'd known that we were here, they wouldn't have run toward us? Deer have poor eyesight," he added, "and it was only after they were almost on top of us that they noticed our presence and turned toward the south."

CC was concerned. It seemed more logical to him that they were spooked by something on the west edge of the meadow where they had been feeding. But he let the thought go, his persistent headache claiming most of his attention.

The early morning sun, low in the sky, was now at their backs. Their goal was to reach Tower Point at the southwest corner of the lake, so they moved toward the west side of the meadow where the herd had been feeding. Rachel and Elizabeth were now leading the way, speaking quietly to one another, while CC had dropped back and was limping along about a hundred feet behind them. Jonathan had stopped at the north edge of the meadow to adjust his pack, and Sarah remained faithfully by his side.

For some unaccountable reason, Jonathan felt dangerously exposed. He found himself repeatedly turning his head to look back through the trees toward the ledge where they'd exited the caverns. His tension had communicated itself to Sarah, and she too frequently turned her keen young eyes toward the mountain behind them. They'd been walking steadily uphill from the beach, but because the undergrowth was unusually sparse, the mouth of the cave was sometimes visible, even at well over a quarter of a mile.

His thoughts carried him back. *Was it only an hour ago that we were being strafed by that Chinese general in his helicopter? It was terrifying!* he thought. *We had just walked out on that ledge when the copter appeared and the man in the co-pilot's seat began firing his Uzi at us.* It was as if Jonathan could still hear the sound of the bullets smashing into the rocks around them, and smelling the rock dust that had been sprayed into the air by their impact.

Now the only evidence that remained of their life-and-death struggle were the broken tree branches that had been scarred by the blades of the crashing helicopter.

Their lives had been saved by a near-stranger. He had stood calmly near the top of the cliff, bullets from the Uzi striking the cliff face beneath him. He pulled his rifle into his shoulder, and shooting freehand, somehow mortally wounded the pilot and causing the helicopter to crash. Jonathan's eyes scanned the cliff as though he might again see Joseph Sennett standing on the crest, rifle in hand, a dark stain on his pant leg where his blood had soaked through. Jonathan knew that all the bullets from the helicopter had not missed their target.

His daydreaming was interrupted by a tugging on his own pant leg, and he looked down to see Sarah trying to get his attention. She pointed toward the meadow, and he realized that Rachel and Elizabeth were already more than halfway across, while he and Sarah were still standing among the saplings that bordered the near edge. She was right. They were trailing too far behind.

Jonathan was not only burdened with his own heavy pack and rifle, but he was already regretting his impulsive offer to carry Elizabeth's portfolio for her. The rugged case that contained the precious documents was not only bulky, but it added at least ten pounds to his load. With his own pack at over thirty-five pounds, and his rifle and ammunition totaling another fifteen, he had a man's load on his teenage shoulders.

And Sarah presented an additional challenge. In spite of how slowly he had been walking, Sarah's little legs had been hard put to keep up with him. Yet the group had to get at least a couple of miles into the forest before dark in order to reduce the likelihood of anyone successfully trailing them.

Jonathan wondered whether CC would let them take a break in the next mile or so. He was already sweating in the unseasonable temperature, but he noticed that the breeze seemed cooler, and when he looked to the east, he realized that the sky was clouding over and the sun had disappeared.

That's just great! he thought. *On top of everything else, a rainstorm is just what we need.*

Jonathan had started to urge Sarah on, but she was tugging on his pant leg again, and he inexplicably felt the hair rise on the back of his neck.

"Look," she said, pointing back at the cliff.

Instead of looking back, he trusted his instincts and shouted a warning to the others. Then he pushed Sarah down into the foot-high grass, and only then did he turn to examine the ledge.

It was no longer vacant. He could see several men moving toward the narrow trail that led down to the lake. Sarah had already scrambled away from him, and was on her knees watching their progress.

"They are pointing rifles this way," she shouted, her sharp little eyes picking out the details that he had difficulty distinguishing.

Sarah started to push herself to her feet, but Jonathan immediately pushed her down and dropped on top of her to shield her body with his own. He twisted around in an attempt to check the ledge again, but from the ground the grass and trees hid it from view.

He again shouted across the meadow to his friends, warning them, "Hit the dirt!" The words had scarcely left his mouth before he heard a rifle's sharp report.

It was followed by a confusing exchange of fire. Some of it seemed to come from across the meadow to the west, and he assumed that Rachel, Elizabeth, and CC were returning the enemy's fire. At first Jonathan reasoned that their plight might not be particularly dangerous.

Before those guys on the ledge can get down that narrow trail to the beach, we ought to be able to lose ourselves in those woods on the far side of the meadow. Sarah and I just need to lie here until they start down the cliff trail. Once on the trail they won't be able to see our movements, and we'll be able to run across the meadow and catch up with the others.

He parted the branches of an evergreen to check the enemy's progress and realized that he'd guessed wrong. Two of the men had indeed started down the narrow trail, but the third had remained on the ledge, and was now being joined by several others who had just emerged from the cave. Those on the ledge began to lay down continual fire on CC and the two women who were kneeling in the tall grass near the center of the meadow.

It was too late for Jonathan to join them. Even if he could sprint across the meadow, and somehow avoid being shot, little Sarah could never keep up with him. What's more, CC, Rachel and Elizabeth were in a far more precarious position than he and Sarah.

He looked to see where CC had been heading, but could no longer see him at all. He wondered whether CC had sprinted toward the small wood that lay in the center of the meadow, leaving the women behind to cope, and what could have possessed them to stop right there where the enemy could continue to bring fire on them.

This is no time for a prayer meeting, he thought. *They should be running for cover.*

He raised his shoulders slightly to get a better look, and suffered another jolt. He could see someone lying in the grass between the two women, and that someone had to be CC. Jonathan's conclusion was immediately confirmed when he saw them trying to get him to his feet.

He already had numerous bruises, including that beauty on his hip, Jonathan thought. *Now what?*

With CC between them, his arms hanging limply over their shoulders, the two women began stumbling toward the small wood, and Jonathan realized the worst. CC had been shot.

He now understood that their small group was in very serious trouble. He started to unsling his rifle, intending to return the fire of the men near the cave mouth. Then he realized that the men who had come down from the path from the ledge would soon be upon them, and if he fired, he would simply reveal his position. Sarah might be seriously injured. Worse, he would lose the portfolio that contained the priceless documents that Elizabeth had brought from the museum in Boston.

Was it only a few hours ago that we agreed as a group that these documents are more important to the future of America than our lives are? It sure didn't take long for us to be tested on that decision.

Jonathan realized that he must get those documents away before they fell into the hands of America's enemies, whether the Chinese, Russians, or the Jihadists.

He turned to look back across the meadow. CC was down again, lying on his back. The women each grasped him under one of his arm. They lifted his torso, and were struggling to drag him head-first out of the line of fire and, and, traverse the last few yards to the copse of trees that lay at the center of the meadow.

He became aware that Sarah was pleading with him, tears in her eyes. "Can't we help them, Jonathan?"

Jonathan turned back and forth in confusion. The man who had saved their lives, who had given them a home, and who had been a father to them, had been shot. His life was in danger. There was nothing for it but to try. The teen rose to his feet, and dropped the portfolio and his heavy backpack. Gripping his rifle in both hands, he was just setting himself to sprint across the meadow when he saw CC, who was still facing his way, say something to the women. Marcie immediately turned, grasped Jonathan's intentions, and vehemently shook her head.

"No," she screamed. "Run and hide. H-i-d-e!" And as her voice trailed off, he thought he heard her say, "...and God bless you."

"As they disappeared into the woods, dragging CC between them, he shouted a reply.

"Keep going south! Sarah and I will try to catch up with you later."

There was no indication that any of them had heard his words, but Sarah had heard Rachel, and she understood their significance. She immediately choked back her tears, and braced herself for whatever might be coming.

Jonathan suddenly realized that his last words were irrelevant. Even if his three friends were able to evade the Chinese-led mercenaries who had wounded CC, there was no chance in the world that he and Sarah would dare to follow them south. If they were to attempt it, they were almost certain to be swept up in the same dragnet.

Jonathan turned back toward the cliff, trying to judge how long he and Sarah might have remaining before their pursuers reached the meadow. There was no sign of anyone on the cliffside trail, and it was obvious that he and Sarah had no time to tarry. They needed to find a hiding place immediately.

Later perhaps they could make it around the end of the lake to Tower Point. If they could make it there, they might be able to replenish their food from the cache that he and CC had set up earlier. And if they could remain there a few days, there was a chance that CC and the others might show up to replenish their own food supply.

But with CC injured, and the group split up, that possibility now seemed a forlorn hope. And that discouraging thought was quickly followed by the realization that he was merely a teenager, and if anything happened to him, eight-year old Sarah would be helpless. Between the danger to the child and the potential loss of the priceless documents he suddenly found himself burdened with, an overwhelming responsibility had been dumped on his shoulders.

He took one more look toward the trees where CC had disappeared. It was obvious that Sarah also understood their predicament. Without a word she jumped to her feet and ran back toward the lake. Taking one last look over his shoulder, Jonathan grunted as he shouldered his load. Then he turned and followed her into the forest.

Please visit us!

www.frankbecker.com

SPECIAL THANKS...

Thanks to those who came alongside with technical knowledge, editorial assistance, frequent encouragement and prayer, including:

Special thanks for editorial work and proofreading:
* Carol Kenzy *
* Patricia Pursely *
* Pastor Jeremy Stopford, M.A. *
And my wife, Joy Becker, M.A., plus our four children and our incomparable granddaughter, Rachel.

Technical guidance:
Jamieson Becker.
Dr. Edward (Ted), M.D. and Elizabeth Hughes.
Rev. Alexander W. Salay.
Dr. Michael Tower, PhD.

And much gratitude for the encouragement and prayers of loyal readers.

51076073R00221

Made in the USA
Charleston, SC
14 January 2016